PRIZE STORIES
1992
THE O. HENRY
AWARDS

PRIZE STORIES

1·9·9·2

·THE·
O. HENRY
AWARDS

◆

*Edited and with
an Introduction by*

William Abrahams

DOUBLEDAY

NEW YORK   LONDON   TORONTO   SYDNEY   AUCKLAND

92 05950

PUBLISHED BY DOUBLEDAY
a division of Bantam Doubleday Dell Publishing Group, Inc.
666 Fifth Avenue, New York, New York 10103

DOUBLEDAY and the portrayal of an anchor with a dolphin
are trademarks of Doubleday,
a division of Bantam Doubleday Dell Publishing Group, Inc.

Book Design by Patrice Fodero

Library of Congress Cataloging-in-Publication Data
Prize stories. 1947–
New York, etc. Doubleday
v. 22 cm.
Annual.
The O. Henry awards.
None published 1952–53.
Continues: O. Henry memorial award prize stories.
ISSN 0079-5453 = Prize stories
1. Short stories, American—Collected works.
PZ1.011   813'.01'08—dc19   21-9372
MARC-S
Library of Congress   [8804r83]rev4

ISBN 0-385-42191-5
ISBN 0-385-42192-3 (pbk)

April 1992
1 3 5 7 9 10 8 6 4 2
First Edition

CONTENTS

PUBLISHER'S NOTE

This volume is the seventy-second in the O. Henry Memorial Award series, and the twenty-sixth to be edited by William Abrahams.

*   *   *

In 1918, the Society of Arts and Sciences met to vote upon a monument to the master of the short story: O. Henry. They decided that this memorial should be in the form of two prizes for the best short stories published by American authors in American magazines during the year 1919. From this beginning, the memorial developed into an annual anthology of outstanding short stories by American authors, published, with the exception of the years 1952 and 1953, by Doubleday.

Blanche Colton Williams, one of the founders of the awards, was editor from 1919 to 1932; Harry Hansen from 1933 to 1940; Herschel Brickell from 1941 to 1951. The annual collection did not appear in 1952 and 1953, when the continuity of the series was interrupted by the death of Herschel Brickell. Paul Engle was editor from 1954 to 1959, with Hanson Martin coeditor in the years 1954 to 1960; Mary Stegner in 1960; Richard Poirier from 1961 to 1966, with assistance from and coeditorship with

William Abrahams from 1964 to 1966. William Abrahams became editor of the series in 1967.

In 1970, Doubleday published under Mr. Abraham's editorship *Fifty Years of the American Short Story*, and in 1981, *Prize Stories of the Seventies*. Both are collections of stories selected from this series.

The stories chosen for this volume were published in the period from the summer of 1990 to the summer of 1991. A list of the magazines consulted appears at the back of the book. The choice of stories and selection of prizewinners are exclusively the responsibility of the editor. Biographical material is based on information provided by the contributors and obtained from standard works of reference.

INTRODUCTION

Each year a "Publisher's Note," summarizing the history of the O. Henry Awards, appears at the beginning of this annual collection. I want to emphasize the sole condition (and restriction) laid upon the editor: the awards are to be made to American authors, writing in English—translations are not eligible—for stories published in magazines during the preceding twelve months from one midsummer to the next.

There are twenty-one stories in the collection this year. Taken together they represent the contrasting, often contradictory but certainly rewarding varieties of form and content characteristic of the contemporary American story. Definitions are elusive. In a collection as heterogeneous as this, whose stories have not been chosen to exemplify a predetermined theme or to discover a tendency or to promote a fashion—this year minimal, next year maximal—it seems proper to suggest that each story defines itself.

In Joyce Carol Oates's "Why Don't You Come Live With Me It's Time" the narrator, looking back to herself as an insomniac teenager, recalls: ". . . sometimes I'd switch on the radio close beside my bed, I was cautious of course to keep the volume low, low and secret and I'd listen fascinated to stations as far away as Pittsburgh, Toronto, Cleveland, there was a hillbilly station broadcasting out of Cleveland, country-and-western music I would never have listened to by day. One by one I got to know the announcer's voices along the continuum of the glowing dial, hard to believe those strangers didn't know *me*. But sometimes my room left me short of breath, it was fresh air I craved, hurriedly I'd dress pulling on clothes over my pajamas, and even in rainy or cold weather I went outside leaving the house by the kitchen door so quietly in such stealth no one ever heard, not once did one of them hear *I will do it: because I want to do it* sleeping their heavy sleep that was like the sleep of mullusks, eyeless. And outside: in the night: the surprise of the street transformed by the lateness of the hour, the emptiness, the silence: I'd walk to the end of our driveway staring, listening, my heart beating hard. *So this is—what it is!* The ordinary sights were made strange, the sidewalks, the streetlights, the neighboring houses. Yet the fact had no consciousness of itself except through *me*."

What a marvelous image this is, a moment evoked in all its particularity, and a metaphor also, I think, for the creative process: a story, a fact, coming to consciousness in the mind of the writer, who then translates it into words on the page. Whatever its "prehistory" may be, the story is only finally, fully alive in the text that we read. There too is context, in a kind of symbiotic relationship to it, nourishing the text. Places, voices, intimations, the climate of the culture, the ever-changing spirit of the age—all these in large or small degree provide the context of the story, that very private personal form, so distanced from the blurring, buzzing, homogenizing public assaults of the media.

Sometimes, as in "Puttermesser Paired" by Cynthia Ozick, context enters the story as a crucial, defining element. In the meticulous opening of this artful tragicomedy, the narrative-to-come is prefigured: "At the unsatisfying age of fifty-plus, Ruth Puttermesser, a lawyer, a rationalist, and an ex-public official, took a year off to live on her savings and think through her fate. In the second week of her freedom—no slavery of paper-work, no office to go to (she had bled out a wide tract of her life in the corridors of the Municipal Building)—it came to her that what she ought to do was marry."

We are in New York of the present, precisely and risibly caught in a wealth of realistic detail, where Puttermesser, "an elderly orphan," is to embark upon her quest for a suitable husband. It is the *fact* of New York that underlines and clarifies the irony of Puttermesser's *fiction*, and determines Ozick's pre-sentation of it. As a seeming realist she leads us forward, reas-sured by the presence of an actual New York, persuading us that Puttermesser and her quest are as real as the ordinary ev-eryday world in which they happen. Then, as the extraordinary reveals its fateful contours, we find ourselves accepting the so-lution Puttermesser produces for herself: that she will appro-priate George Eliot's biography and reproduce it in her own life, not as a novelist but as a woman, even down to marrying a facsimile George Henry Lewes of her own.

"Puttermesser Paired," for all its gliding backward progress into the Victorian age, is very much a story of New York in the present—hence indispensable to the irony at the heart of Ozick's art: that Ruth Puttermesser, an intelligent professional woman living in New York in the last decade of the twentieth century, should elect as her model to copy the life of a great nineteenth-century English novelist. Doing so, she can only ar-rive at the inevitable, foreordained ending, as indeed she does, comically, tragically, hauntingly, unforgettably.

"Puttermesser Paired" is this year's First Prize story, and as such leads off the Table of Contents. The other twenty stories, all O. Henry Awards winners, are placed only with a view to showing the variety of the collection—questions of precedence or rank don't apply.

My thanks to Heidi von Schreiner and Arabella Meyer at Doubleday/Anchor.

—William Abrahams

PRIZE STORIES

1992

THE O. HENRY

AWARDS

Cynthia Ozick

PUTTERMESSER PAIRED

I. AN AGE OF DIVORCE

At the unsatisfying age of fifty-plus, Ruth Puttermesser, a lawyer, a rationalist, and an ex-public official, took a year off to live
on her savings and think through her fate. In the second week
of her freedom—no slavery of paperwork, no office to go to
(she had bled out a wide tract of her life in the corridors of the
Municipal Building)—it came to her that what she ought to do
was marry. This was not a new idea: it had been her mother's
refrain as far back as three decades ago or more, ever since
Puttermesser's first year in law school.

Ruth, Ruth [her mother wrote from Miami], there's nothing wrong
with having a husband along with brains, it's not a contradiction. For
God's sake pull your head out of the clouds! If you don't get married
where will you be, what will happen? Alone is a stone as they say and
believe me Ruthie Daddy agrees with me on this issue not only double
but triple, we didn't come down here to live in the heat with Daddy's
bursitis only in order to break his heart from you and your brains.

This innocently anti-feminist letter was now brown at the edges, brittle; in the fresh tedium of her leisure Puttermesser was sorting out the boxes stored under her bed. She was throwing things out. Her mother was dead. Her father was dead. There would be no more reports of the Florida weather, and no grandchildren to inherit these interesting out-of-date postage stamps and wrinkled complaints. Puttermesser was an elderly orphan. For the first time it struck her that her mother was right: it was possible for brains to break the heart.

She bought a copy of the *New York Review of Books* and looked through the personals. Brains, brains everywhere.

Fit, handsome, ambitious writer/editor, militant nonsmoker, witty, imaginative, irreverent, seeks lasting relationship with nonsmoking female. Must be brilliant, unpretentious, passionate, creative. Prefer Ph.D. in Milton, Shakespeare, or Beowulf.

University professor, anthropologist, 50, gentle, intellectual, youthful, author of three volumes on Aleutian Islanders, cherishes the examined life, welcomes marriage or long-term attachment to loyal, accomplished professional woman; well-analyzed (Jung only, no Freud or Reich, please). Sense of humor and love of outdoors a must.

Among dozens of these condensed portraits Puttermesser could not recognize herself. She was hostile to the outdoors; the country air—the peril of so many uneasy encounters with unidentifiable rodents, loud birds, monstrous insects, mud after fearsome Sag Harbor storms—left her moody and squeamish. She was no good at getting the points of jokes. The persecution of smokers she regarded as a civil-liberties issue. As for the examined life—enough! She was sick of examining her own and hardly needed to hear an Eskimo expert examine his. It was all fiction anyhow—those columns and columns of ads. "Vibrant, appealing, attractive, likable"—that meant divorced. Leftovers and mistakes. "Unconventional, earthy, nurturing, fascinated by Zen, Sufism, music of the spheres"—a crackpot still in sandals. "Successful achiever longing for strong woman"—watch out, probably a porn nut. Every self-indulgent type in the book turned up in these ads. Literature was no better. The great novels, rife with weirdos and misalliance— Isabel Archer entangled with the sinister Gilbert Osmond, Gwendolen Harleth's troubles with Grandcourt. Anna Karenina. Worst of all, poor Dorothea Brooke and the deadly Mr. Casaubon. All these bad characters—the men in the case absolutely, and many of the women—were brainy. Think of Shaw, a logician, refusing to allow Professor Higgins to wed Eliza, in open dread of foreordained rotten consequences. And Jane Austen: with one hand she marries Elizabeth to Darcy, clever with clever, and with the other she goes and saddles Mr. Bennet with a silly wife. People get stuck. Brains are no guarantee. Hope is slim.

The truth was this: Puttermesser had entered a new zone of being. From the Women Attorneys Association she received a questionnaire: "Aging and the Female Counsellor." Aging! Puttermesser! How could this be, when she had yet to satisfy Miss Charlotte Kuntz, her piano teacher? At Puttermesser's last lesson, forty-five years ago, Miss Kuntz had warned her sharply that such-and-such a sonatina needed work. It was just before summer vacation. Puttermesser promised to toil over the Tempo di Minuetto section all during July and August (the Andante was easier), but she put it off and put it off. Instead, she wandered in a trance in and out of the children's room of the public library; the rule was you could take out only two books at a time. Frequently Puttermesser appeared at the library twice in one day, to return two and to borrow two more. She read far into the rosy shadows of the summer twilight. The lower half of the sky was daubed with a streak of blood. "A beautiful day tomorrow," Puttermesser's mild father said. "That's what a red sunset means."

But Puttermesser's mother scolded: "In the dark! Again reading in the dark! You'll burn out your eyes! And didn't you *swear* to Miss Kuntz you'll practice every day during vacation? You're not ashamed, she'll come back and you didn't learn it yet? Nose in the book without a light!"

In late August a letter arrived. Miss Kuntz was not coming back. She was moving upstate with her elderly father. "As I have often mentioned, Ruth," she wrote, "you are intelligent, but require more diligence. Always remember: Every Great Brain Delves Furiously!"

By now, Puttermesser had put off practicing for so long that her hair was showing signs of whitening. If alive, Miss Kuntz would be a hundred and four. Puttermesser had still not perfected the Tempo di Minuetto section, so how was it possible to consider a questionnaire on aging?

Do you encounter discrimination on the part of judges? Employers? Clients? Court personnel?

Has your mental acuity or judgment noticeably slackened? If yes, how does this manifest itself?

Have your earlier positions (political, moral, societal) eroded? Are you, in your opinion, capable of new ideas? Flexibility? An open mind?

Have your earnings diminished? Increased? Are you treated with less respect? More? If more, how does your mature appearance contribute to this?

Has the feminist movement eased your professional situation? Are you harried less? More? No difference? How many times per week do you encounter sexist or ageist remarks?

Do you dye your hair? Use henna? Surrender to Mother Nature? If the latter, does this appear to augment or lessen your dignity among male colleagues? Female colleagues? The public?

Miss Kuntz was no doubt under the ground in Pleasantville, New York, together with her father. In Puttermesser's cramped apartment in the East Seventies—a neighborhood of ophthalmologists and dermatologists—there was no room for a piano;

the space near her bed could barely accommodate a modest desk. At night she could hear the high-school math teacher on the other side of the wall plunge her red pencils into an electric sharpener. Sometimes the math teacher did exercises on a plastic mat—unfolding, it whacked against the baseboard. A divorcée in her middle thirties, who counted out loud with each leg stretch. She was working on her figure in the hope of attracting a lover. An announcement addressed to the math teacher had been thrust into Puttermesser's mailbox.

SINGLES EVENT!
ATTENTION! EDUCATED UNUSUAL SINGLES
TEACHERS' MIXER EVERY FRIDAY NIGHT
8:30 P.M.
MEET YOUR PEERS WITHOUT SNEERS OR TEARS
BRONX SCIENCE, HUNTER HIGH,
STUYVESANT,
OTHER TOP SCHOOLS WELL REPRESENTED
$3 DONATION TO COVER PUNCH AND CHEESE
NOTE TO MALE TEACHERS: MORE MEN WANTED!
BRING YOUR (PROFESSIONAL) FRIENDS
CALL GINNY (718) 555-3000 FOR DETAILS

Puttermesser contemplated calling Ginny—she, too, was an educated unusual single. Instead, she slid the sheet under the math teacher's door. The building, with its dedication to anonymity (each mysterious soul invisible in its own cubicle), was subject to jitters and multiple confusions. Mixups, mishaps, misdeliveries, misnamings. To the doorman she was Miss Perlmutter. If you asked the super to send the plumber you would get the exterminator. Without warning, the pipes dried up for the day; you could try to run the faucet and nothing would come out. Or the lights would fail; the refrigerator fluttered its grand lung and ceased. All the refrigerators up and down the whole row of apartments on a single corridor expired together, in one extended shudder. You could feel it under your soles, right through the carpeting. The building was a nervous organism; its familiar soughings ricocheted from cranny to cranny. Puttermesser could tell which floor the elevator was stopping on by the pitch of its motor. She knew by the thump in the hall, and by the slap of sneakers heading back to the elevator, and by the rattle of all her locks, the moment when the new telephone book landed on her doormat.

Thump, slap, rattle. Something had landed there now; the sneakers were in flight. The chain lock was still swinging and tinkling. Puttermesser laboriously fiddled with it, and then with the other two locks. Each required one turn followed by a quarter turn. She worked as fast as she could. What if there were a fire? Robbery and rape or get burned alive: the New York predicament. All her neighbors had just as many locks; the math teacher had installed a steel pole that dropped into a hole in the floor.

The locks were undone. Puttermesser stuck her head out in time to see the flash of a yellow shirt at the end of the corridor. At her feet a chimney of huge, flat cardboard boxes rose up. There was a smell of noisome cheese.

"Hey!" Puttermesser yelled. "Get back here! I didn't order this stuff."

"6-C, right?" the yellow shirt yelled back. "Pizza!"

"3-C. You want the sixth floor. I didn't order any pizza," Puttermesser yelled.

"You Morgenbluth?"

"You've got the wrong apartment."

"Listen," the yellow shirt called. "Bike's in the street. Boss's bike. They take my bike, I'm finished. Half-dozen veggie pizzas for Morgenbluth, O.K.?"

"I don't know any Morgenbluth!"

Like a piece of stage machinery, the elevator hummed the yellow shirt out of sight.

Fecal smell of the stable—that cheese; some unfathomable

sauce. Puttermesser kept her distance from ethnic foods. She had never tasted souvlaki; she had never tasted sushi. With the exception of chocolate fudge and Tootsie Rolls (her molars were ruined and crowned), gastronomy did not draw her. What she was concentrating on was marriage: the marriage of true minds. Reciprocal transcendence—she was not thinking of sinew, synapse, hormone-fired spasm. Those couples who saunter by with arms like serpents wrapped around each other, stopping in the middle of the sidewalk to plug mouth on mouth: biological robots, twitches powered by pitiless instinct. Puttermesser, despite everything, was not beyond idealism; she believed (admittedly the proposition wouldn't stand up under rigorous questioning) she had a soul. She dreamed—why not dream?—of a wedding of like souls.

Only the day before yesterday Puttermesser had taken out of the Society Library on East Seventy-ninth Street—an amiable walk from her apartment—a biography of George Eliot. A woman with a soul, born Mary Anne Evans, who had named herself George in sympathy with her sympathetic mate. George Eliot and George Lewes, penmen both, sat side by side every evening reading aloud to each other. They read science, philosophy, history, poetry. Once, they travelled up to Oxford to see a brain dissected. Another time, they invited Charles Dickens to lunch; he enthralled them with an eerie anecdote about Lincoln's death. They undertook feverishly cultural journeys to Spain and Italy and Germany, sightseeing with earnest thoroughness, visiting cathedrals and museums, going diligently night after night to the theatre and opera. On steamers, for relaxation, they read Walter Scott. They were strenuous naturalists, pursuing riverbanks and hillsides for shells and fungi. Their house was called the Priory; nothing not high-minded or morally or artistically serious ever happened there. The people who came on Sunday afternoons—George Eliot presided over a "salon"—were uniformly distinguished, the cream of English intellectual life: they were learned in Chaldaic, Aramaic, Amharic, Phoenician, or Sanskrit; or else they were orators, or else had invented the clinical thermometer; or were aristocrats, or Americans. The young Henry James made a pilgrimage to George Eliot's footstool, and so did Virginia Woolf's father. George Lewes was always present—small, thin, blond, quick— an impresario steering an awed room around the long-nosed sibyl in her chair. She depended on him; he protected her from slights, hurts, cruelty, shame, and from the critical doubts of John Blackwood, her publisher, who took her at first for a clergyman. It was a marriage of brain with brain, weightiness with weightiness. Dignity with dignity. And of course there was no marriage at all—not legally or officially. Lewes's wife, Agnes, was an adulteress who went on giving birth to another man's children; but it was an age of no divorce. George Lewes and George Eliot, husband and wife, a marriage of true minds admitting no impediment, were, perforce, a scandal.

All this Puttermesser knew inside out: it was her third or fourth, or perhaps fifth or sixth, George Eliot biography. She had, moreover, arrived at that season of life—its "autumn," in the language of one of these respectful old volumes—when rereading gratifies more than discovery, and there were certain familiar passages that she had assimilated word for word. "And yet brilliance conquered impropriety" gave her a shiver whenever she came on it; and also "Consider how a homely female intellectual, no longer young, falls into a happy fate." O happy fate! Somewhere on the East Side of New York, from, say, Fifty-third to Eighty-ninth, or possibly on West End Avenue between Sixty-sixth and Ninety-eighth, a latter-day George Lewes lurked: Puttermesser's own, sans scandal. It was now, after all, an age of divorce.

The shopping cart was squeezed between the refrigerator and the sink, folded up to fit into the little alley where the roaches frolicked. Wrestling it out, Puttermesser recalled her mother's phrase for a divorced man: "used goods." Yet what else was there for her in the world but used goods? Puttermesser was used goods herself, in her mother's manner of speaking: she had once had a lover. But lovers are transients: they have a way of moving on—they are subject to panicked reconsiderations, sudden depressions, cold feet. Lovers are notorious for cowardice, for returning to their wives.

Puttermesser wedged the cart against the doorjamb and bent to heave each big, flat box into it. When all the pizzas were piled up inside the wire frame, she double-locked her top lock and triple-locked her bottom lock and trundled the cart down the corridor to the elevator. It was like pushing a wheelbarrow filled with slag. The elevator smelled partly of urine and partly of pine-scented disinfectant; with the cart in it there was barely enough room to stand. She poked the button marked "6," but instead of grinding her upward, the thing headed for the lobby, now and then scraping against the shaft.

Two very tall young women were waiting down there. One of them was carrying a bottle of wine without a wrapper.

"You getting out?"

"I was on my way up," Puttermesser said. "You brought me down."

"Well, we can't all fit," said the tall young woman with the wine.

"Just *try*," said the other tall young woman. "If you could just move your laundry—"

The tall young woman with the wine looked into the cart. "That isn't laundry. Smells like throw-up."

Puttermesser's spine pressed against the back wall of the elevator. The buttons were beyond her reach. A large black plastic triangle—an earring—swung into her face; the bottle of wine drove into her side.

"What floor?"

"Six," Puttermesser said.

"How about that. Is this stuff for Harvey's party? You going where we're going, Harvey's party?"

"No," Puttermesser said.

"Harvey Morgenbluth? On the sixth floor?"

"That's where I'm going," Puttermesser said.

The door to 6-C was propped open; all its chains were dangling free. A row of spidery plants in tiger-striped pots lined the foyer—a tropical motif. It was the sort of party, Puttermesser saw, where children run through shrieking and no one complains. Ducks in police uniforms were shooting at evil-visaged porcupines in burglar's caps on a big color television in a corner of the living room, next to a white piano, but the children were paying no attention at all. A mob of them were chasing three little boys in overalls, two of whom seemed, as they sped by, to be identical twins. They raced through the living room and out into what Puttermesser knew had to be the kitchen (6-C's layout was the same as 3-C's) and back again. "No we don't, no we don't," all three were yowling. The two very tall young women from the elevator instantly made a place for themselves on the beige tweed carpet in front of the sofa, kneeling at the coffee table and pouring wine into paper cups, instantly hilarious; it was as if they had been dawdling there for hours. The sofa itself held a tangle of five or six human forms, each with its legs in one extraordinary position or another, and each devoted to a paper cup. Behind the children's screeches, a steady sea-noise burbled: the sound of a party that has been long under way, and has already secretly been defined, by the earliest arrivals, as a success or a failure.

This one was a failure; all ruined parties are alike. They pump themselves up, they are too boisterous, too frenetic, they pretend raucous pleasure. And this is true even of parties with cousins and young aunts; of families. The Morgenbluth apartment looked to be all family—husbands, wives, untamed offspring. Sisters-in-law, like the pair from the elevator. A birthday—one of the little boys', probably—but there was too much wine, and no balloons; besides, the children were being ignored. Puttermesser wheeled the cart straight toward the white piano and began lifting the boxes out onto the top of it. Cracker crumbs were scattered over the keys; a cigarette, with its snout still burning, lay directly on middle C. The boxes climbed upward in precarious steps.

"Leaning tower of pizza," someone quipped, and, from the tight little tone she caught in the voice, Puttermesser was certain that she was mistaken after all, that the noise all around was anything but domestic, that except for the children no one here belonged to anybody: no husbands, wives, cousins, aunts. It was the usual collection of the unattached. Roomful of the divorced on a Sunday afternoon in mild middle November. A "singles event": the math teacher, puffing on her mat three floors below, strained her torso in ignorance of the paradise of opportunity just overhead.

"It's about time we got some real food in here. You can't feed kids indefinitely on peanuts. Pretzels, maybe. Takes a grownup woman to remember nutrition. Any of these little sons of bitches yours?"

"I'd have to be their grandmother," Puttermesser said. It was the kind of remark she despised, and this stranger—a bearded man in his fifties, with a squashed nose and oversized, naïve eyes, gray and on guard, more suitable to a kitten—had forced her to it.

He was pecking at the peanuts in his palm. "Well, you don't look it—they say it's all in the chin line. Twins are mine, but only on alternate weekends. With me it's always a double felony. Not to mention a couple of breakups. Marital. The way you spell that is m-a-r-t-i-a-l." He put out his hand, greasy from the peanuts. "Freddy Kaplow. How long've you known Harvey?"

The New York patter. Mechanical spew of the middle-aged flirt; he was practiced enough. And too stale for such young sons. Already finished with the second wife, the mother of the twins. No doubt a grown daughter from the first marriage. The daughter and the second wife were, as usual, nearly the same age.

"Tell Mr. Morgenbluth his pizza was delivered to the wrong apartment," Puttermesser said. "Tell him 3-C corrected the error."

"3-C corrected the error. No kidding, that's how come you got here? Cute, I like that. Boy-meets-girl cute."

Puttermesser took hold of her cart and began to wheel it away.

"There goes Mother Courage," Freddy Kaplow called after her. "Hey! No guts!"

The two young women from the elevator, still curled on the carpet, were being even more hilarious than before; on the sofa the row of tangled legs had become attentive. Three pairs of trousers (two corduroy, one blue denim), two of panty hose. One of the men on the sofa—not the one in jeans—wore his hair in a ponytail, but was mainly bald in front.

Puttermesser tugged cautiously on the cart handle. "Excuse me. If you wouldn't mind, if I could just slide through here—"

"Hello there, pizza person, when do we eat?"

The balding man with the ponytail said, "I saw a bag lady the other day with one of those. She had it filled up to the top with piles of old shoes. All mixed up, no pairs."

"What'd she think she was going to do with them?"

"God only knows. Sell 'em."

"Eat 'em."

"Boil 'em in the bowels of Grand Central Station, *then* eat 'em."

"That's not funny," said a woman on the sofa. "I *work* with the homeless."

Puttermesser stopped. Pity for the ravaged municipality— reverberations from her days in officialdom—could still beat in her.

"In our program—it's a volunteer thing—what we try to do is get them to keep diaries. We read poetry, we do E. E. Cummings. They feel it when you're spiritually *with* them."

Another version of the New York patter. The wisecrack version and the earnest version, and all of it ego and self-regard. All of it conceit. Where was virtue, where was knowledge? Puttermesser was conscious of inward heavings and longings. She thought of mutuality, of meaning. So many indolent strutters, so much babble battering at the ceiling. That white piano with the crumbs. In no more than a quarter of an hour the windows behind the piano had begun to darken to blue dusk. Harvey Morgenbluth's beige tweed carpet, his paper cups, the hysteria of those hungry half-orphaned children running loose. Oh, for a time machine! London in the grave twilight of a hundred years ago, Sunday evenings at the Priory. Cornices, massive draperies in heavy folds, ponderous tables and cupboards with carved gryphons' claws or lions' feet, old enamelled landscapes hanging on tasselled cords from high roseate ceilings. A keyboard left open for the sublime and resolute hands. And in a great stuffed armchair in a shadowed corner, away from the lamp, the noble sibyl, receiving. Lives of courtliness, distinction; clarified lives, without tumble or blur. In George Eliot's parlor, a manner, or an idea, was purely itself. Ah, to leave careless New York behind, to be restored to glad, golden Victoria, when the electric light was new and poetry unashamed!

In the foyer several of the tiger-striped pots had been overturned into puddles of wine; Puttermesser drew her cart through a patch of country mud. The spidery plants sprawled. A child's shoe lay flattened under one of the pots. A child's sock had become a glove for the doorknob.

And there, at the littered entrance of 6-C, stood a Victorian gentleman. He was not very tall; his cheeks and wrists looked thin. He was distractingly young, with a blond mustache, and he was actually wearing a hat—a formal hat, not exactly a fedora, but something more stately than a mere cap. He had on a capelike raincoat—partially unfurled at each shoulder, cola brown, and grandly punctuated by big, varnished metal buttons as shockingly bright as cymbals. Sherlock Holmes? Oscar Wilde? A dandy, in any case, self-consciously on display. One arm was held high, the other low, and in between rode a large, flat rectangle wrapped in pale-yellow paper and tied with a white string.

Puttermesser humbly backed her cart into mud to let the dandy pass. He slipped by without taking any notice of her. She saw how she was invisible to him, of less moment than the tiger-striped pots displaced in his path. *She* had given way; the pots demanded his circumspection, and obliged him to go around them. It was worse than the Women Attorneys could imagine: the humiliating equation of a counsellor of mature appearance with the walls and ceiling of 6-C's desolated vestibule. A doorknob is more engaging than a woman of fifty-plus. The man's face hurt Puttermesser; its youth hurt her. For an instant his head was perilously near hers—picking through the uprooted greenery, he tilted so close that she caught sight of the separate tender hairs of his mustache. His eyes were small and serious. Puttermesser thought with a pang how such a head, with such a dignified hat, and such snubbing colorless irises, and such an unfamiliar gravity of intent, would be out of place in Harvey Morgenbluth's living room, among the New York flirts. And that big flat package: a map? A map of the city, the world? An astronomical map. Andromeda. Ursa Major and Minor. Or a graph. A business graph. He was only a salesman, so never mind. Anyhow, it was an illicit hurt: youth is for youth. An aesthetic error, a thin-skinned moral grotesquerie, to yearn after such a head, hat, cape; that nose, that mouth, those intimate hairs.

In her own apartment Puttermesser collapsed the cart and shoved it back into the alleyway between the refrigerator and the sink. There had been, she observed, a hatching: a crowd of baby roaches milled under the ray of her flashlight, then fled with purposeful intelligence. In God's littlest, the urge toward being and enduring; a soulless mite wills its continuity with all the force and fury of our own mammoth human longing. O life, O philosophy!

All the same, Puttermesser sprayed.

In the morning she heard the brush of something in flight under her door:

Dear 3-C:

Just a note of thanx for yesterday's delivery—Freddy Kaplow (your pal and mine) gave me the dope on this. Sorry for the trouble and sorry I missed you! I'd love to return the favor, so if you ever need a passport photo in a hurry (no charge) or anything else in that line call on me. (I'm in the photography business, by the way.) I specialize in commercial reducing and enlarging but also in children's portraits. If you're interested in having a portrait done of the kids I can offer you a 25% studio discount in honor of your Good Deed!

Yours hastily (scribbling this right in
   front of your door on my way to work)
HARVEY MORGENBLUTH
                              6-C

P.S. Hate to mention it, but your insecticide smells all the way out here in the hall! This means the little visitors get to climb the riser pipe up to yours truly! Thanx a lot, neighbor!

A page out of the *National Geographic:* a pair of civilizations adverse in temperament can live juxtaposed in identical environments. Archeologists report, for instance, that Israelites and Canaanites inhabited the same kinds of dwellings furnished with the same kinds of artifacts, and yet history testifies to intensely disparate cultures. 6-C's floor plan, Puttermesser reflected, was no different from 3-C's—she had seen that with her own eyes—but Harvey Morgenbluth had room for a piano and she did not. Harvey Morgenbluth gave parties and she did not. 6-C, the palace of exuberance. Harvey Morgenbluth had a business and Puttermesser currently had nothing.

Or, to reformulate it: despite exactly congruent apartment layouts, Harvey Morgenbluth belonged to the present decade and Puttermesser belonged to selected phantom literary flashbacks.

The day was secretly bright behind a gray fisherman's net about to dissolve into a full autumn rain. The coursing sidewalks, still dry, had the spotted look of rapid, dark rivers clogged with fish: all those young women in sneakers, clutching Channel 13 totes containing their office pumps and speeding toward desks, corridors, switchboards, computers, bosses, underlings. New York—Harvey Morgenbluth included—was going to work. And Puttermesser was idle. She was not idle: it was, instead, a meditative hiatus. She had stopped in her tracks to listen, to detect; to learn something; to study. She was holding still, waiting for life to begin to happen—why not? Venturing out for air, she was compelled to invent daily destinations. Most often it was the supermarket over on Third, if only for an extra package of potato chips; she hated to run out. Or she fell in with the aerobic walkers among the more populated paths of Central Park, close to the protective rim of Fifth Avenue. Or she went mooning through the Morgan Library, the Cooper-Hewitt, the Guggenheim, the Frick; or kept up with the special exhibits at the Jewish Museum—the pitiable history of poor, hollow Captain Dreyfus (hair-raising posters, Europe convulsed), shadowy old chronicles of the Prague Golem. New York, crazed by mental plenitude. The brain could not take in so much as a morsel of it, even at the rate of a museum a day. Paintings, jars, ornaments, armor, manuscripts, tapestries, pillars, flutes, violas, harps; the rare, the sublime, the celestial! Forms and illuminations, how was it possible to swallow it all down?

Hand in hand. The parallel gaze. No one knows lonely sorrow who has not arrived at fifty-plus without George Lewes.

From the express line in the supermarket (salty chips, cheese-flavored) Puttermesser headed for the Society Library, where she picked up the Yale "Selections from George Eliot's Letters" (pleasantly thick but portable, as against the nine-volume complete), then gravitated—why not?—to the Metropolitan Museum: the rain had started, anyhow. Among the Roman portrait busts on the main floor Puttermesser ate a clandestine potato chip. A female sculpture in a niche—hallowed serenity wearing a head shawl—who certainly ought to have been the Virgin Mary turned out to be nothing more than a regular first-century woman, non-theological; she was what the Romans had instead of Kodak. Puttermesser resisted this pleasing notion. She was unwilling, just now, to marvel at the objects and hangings and statuary glimmering all around—the rare, the sublime, the celestial—in this exalted castle of masterworks. Her mind was on the "Letters." George Eliot's own voice against Puttermesser's heart. She was tired of 3-C, of reading in bed or at the kitchen table. What she wanted was a public bench; why not?

From Rome she passed through Egypt (the little sphinx of Sesostris III; the granary official Nykairu with his tiny wife—no higher than his knee—and his tiny daughter; King Sahura in his headdress and beard; Queen Hatshepsut in *her* headdress and beard; and the great god Amun; and powerful horses, and perfect gazelles), and through polished Africa (Nigeria, Gabon, Mali), and through Southern Europe, and through Flanders and Holland, and straight through the Impressionists. Immensity opened into immensity; there were benches in all those grand halls, and streams of worshipful, pale tourists ascending and descending the high marble stair, but she did not come to the recognizable right bench until Socrates beckoned.

At least his forefinger was up in the air. The ceiling lights of that place—it was French Neoclassical Painting of the Eighteenth Century—seemed wan and overused. The room was unpopular and mostly empty—who cares about French Neoclassical? Puttermesser's bench faced Socrates on his deathbed. Even from a distance away she could see him reaching for the bowl of hemlock with a bare, muscular right arm. Socrates was stocky, healthy, in his prime. Part of a toga was slung over the other arm—and there was the forefinger sticking up. He was exhorting his disciples—a whole lamenting crowd of disciples, of all ages, in various grief-stricken poses, like draped Greek statues. A curly-haired boy, an anguished graybeard, a bowed figure in a clerical cap, a man in a red cloak gripping Socrates' leg, a man weeping against a wall. Socrates himself was naked right down to below his navel. He had little red nipples and a ruddy face and a round, blunt nose and a strawberry-blond beard. He looked a lot like Santa Claus, if you could imagine Santa Claus with armpit hair.

Puttermesser settled in. It was a good bench, exactly right. There were not too many passersby, and the guard at the other end of the long hall was as indifferent as a cardboard cutout. Now and then she foraged for a potato chip; the cellophane bag rattled and the guard did not stir.

Assuredly [Puttermesser read in the "Letters"] if there be any one subject on which I feel no levity it is that of marriage and the relation of the sexes—if there is any one action or relation of my life which is and always has been profoundly serious, it is my relation to Mr. Lewes.

* * *

I do not wish to take the ground of ignoring what is unconventional in my position. I have counted the cost of the step I have taken and am prepared to bear, without irritation or bitterness, renunciation by all my friends. I am not mistaken in the person to whom I have attached myself. He is worthy of the sacrifice I have incurred, and my only anxiety is that he should be rightly judged.

* * *

We work hard in the mornings till our heads are hot, then walk out, dine at three and, if we don't go out, read diligently aloud in the evening. I think it is impossible for two human beings to be more happy in each other.

Impossible for two human beings to be more happy in each other!

A rush of movement along the far wall: a knot of starers had assembled just at "The Death of Socrates." They stared up, and then away, then up again. They were fixed on the lifted finger. Inexplicably, it was directing them to look somewhere else. The knot grew into a little, circling pack. Something was being surrounded over there, under Socrates' feet. The chips, the salt, the love adventures of the famous dead. Out of the blue, Puttermesser fell into a wild thirst—George Eliot and George Lewes were travelling on the Continent, illicitly declaring themselves husband and wife. At home in England they were scorned and condemned, but in the enlightened Europe of the eighteen-fifties the best salons welcomed them without criticism; they were introduced to poets, artists, celebrated intellectuals; Franz Liszt played for them at breakfast, smiling in rapture with his head thrown back.

That fuss around Socrates. Puttermesser got up to see—anyhow, she was in need of a water fountain. Some fellow had set up an easel. She inched her way into the starers and stared. The canvas on the easel was almost entirely covered: here were the mourning disciples; here was that prison staircase through a darkened archway; here were the visitors departing; here on the stone floor under Socrates' couch were the chain and manacle. That suffering youth hiding his eyes as he proffers the hemlock. All of it minutely identical to the painting on the wall, except that on the easel Socrates still had no face—the fellow in front of the easel was stippling out the strawberry-blond beard where it starts to curl over Socrates' clavicle. Puttermesser stared up at the painting and back down at the copy. One was the same as the other. You could not tell the difference. She stood at the rim of the crowd and through a kind of porthole watched the shadow of the lower lip gradually bloom into being; she had a better view of the easel than of the copyist. A bit of shoulder, a sleeve pushed up, a narrow hand manipulating the brush—that was all. The hand was horrifically meticulous; patient; slow; horrifically precise. It worked like some unearthly twinning machine. A machine for uncanny displacement. The brush licked and drew back, licked and drew back. The ancient strokes reappeared purely. Puttermesser took in the legend on the plaque—1787, Jacques-Louis David—and saw how, after two centuries, Socrates' nose was freshly forming, lick by lick, all over again. She licked her lip; she had never been thirstier.

The drinking fountain was on another floor. She was gone ten minutes and came back to disappointment: the show was over. The room was nearly deserted. The fellow with the easel was dropping things into a satchel—he had already loaded his canvas onto some sort of dolly. He stopped to wipe a brush with a rag; then he rolled down his shirtsleeves and buttoned them. His shoes were beautifully polished.

Puttermesser's old, neglected worldliness woke. She had not always been a loafer. Until only a little while ago she had moved among power brokers, deputies, opportunists, spoliators, the puffed up. Commissioners and chiefs. She had not always felt so meek. It is enervating to contemplate your fate too steadily, over too protracted a time: the uses of inquisitiveness begin to be forgotten. She thought of what she would ask the copyist—something about the mysteries of replication: what the point of it was. Plainly it wasn't a student exercise—not only because, though he was fairly young, he could hardly have been a student. He was well into his thirties, unless that modest, orderly mustache was designed to deceive. And, anyhow, the will to repetition—Puttermesser theorized that she had glimpsed absolute will—was too big, too indecently ambitious, for a simple exercise. It looked to be a kind of passion. The drive to reproduce what was already there, what did it hint, what could hang from it?

She asked, instead, "Did you get to finish the face?"

The young man held up an index finger in the direction of "The Death of Socrates." On the wall Socrates mimicked him. "It's finished, see for yourself."

"I mean in your version."

"What I do isn't a version. It's a different thing altogether."
An elbow poke of enchantment—aha, metaphysics! "I saw
you *do* it. It comes out exactly the same. It's the same thing
exactly. It's amazingly the same," Puttermesser said.
"It only looks the same."
"But you're copying!"
"I don't copy. That's not what I do."
Now he was being too metaphysical; she was confused. She
was confused by delight. He stood there folding things up—
first the rag, then the easel. Above the mustache his nostrils
gaped in a doubling victory of their own. George Eliot's observation of Liszt—when the music was triumphant the nostrils
dilated. "If you don't want to call it copying," Puttermesser
almost began—it was going to be an argument—but instantly
quit. The syllables stopped in her mouth. Thin cheeks. Those
bright hairs under such a tidy nose. Without his hat it was hard
to be sure. Nevertheless, she was sure. She had studied him,
she had absorbed the veins of his right hand. She had observed
him and not known him. The deceptions of dislocation, the
misleadings! Uprooting dispels recognition; what is unexpected
cannot be seen. The Victorian gentleman in the vestibule of 6-C.
The dandy who had snubbed her because a young man is inca-
pable of noticing a woman of fifty-plus. She knew him now. He
was noticing her now. She had coerced it. She had made him
look right at her.
"Aren't you a friend of Harvey Morgenbluth's? We met at his
door," Puttermesser said. "In the middle of that party."
"I don't go to Harvey's parties. I go on business."
"Well, I live right under him. Three floors down." Fraudu-
lent. It would be right to admit that she had never set eyes on
Harvey Morgenbluth. "Was that a painting you had with you?
In that big package?"
Clearly he did not remember her at all.
"Harvey photographs my things," he said.
"He copies your copies."

"They're not copies. I've explained that."

"But the result is just the same," Puttermesser insisted.

"I can't help the result. It's the act I care about. I don't copy, I reënact. And I do it my own way. I start from scratch and *do* it. How do I know if Socrates' face got finished first or last? You think I care about that? You think I care about what some dead painter feels? Or what anyone with a brush in his hand thought about a couple of hundred years ago? I do it my way."

Puttermesser's terrible thirst all at once rushed back; she believed it might be the wizening of her actual heart. Her organs were drinking her up and leaving her dry. She had abandoned all her acquaintance for the sake of the arrival of intellectual surprise. Mama, she called back to her mother through the dried-up marshes of so many lost decades, look, Mama, the brain is the seat of the emotions, I always told you so!

In her mother's voice, Puttermesser said, "It's used goods, isn't it? Shouldn't you begin with a new idea? With your own idea?"

"This *is* my idea. It's always my own idea. Nobody tells me what to do."

"But you don't make anything *up*—some new combination, something that never existed before," she urged.

"Whatever I do is original. Until I've done them my things don't exist."

"You can't say it's original to duplicate somebody else!"

"I don't duplicate." He was hitching his satchel onto his shoulder by its strap. "I reproduce. Can't you understand that? Babies get born all the time, don't they? And every baby's new and never existed before."

"No baby looks like any other," she protested.

"Unless they're twins." The canvas went onto the dolly. "And then they lead separate lives from the first breath."

"A painting isn't alive," she nearly shouted.

"Well, *I* am—that's the point. Whatever I do is happening for the first time. Anything I make was never made before." He

gave her a suddenly speculative look; she was startled to catch
a shade of jubilation in it. Did he talk like this every day of his
life? She saw straight into the black zeros of his pupils, bright
islands washed round by faint ink. He poked one end of the
folded easel toward her—it was all contraption, with wing nuts
everywhere. "What would you think," he said, "of helping me
with some of this stuff?"

They walked with the contraption between them. The "Letters" were squeezed under Puttermesser's arm. Again, immensity opened into immensity, hall into hall. They passed through
majesties of civilizations, maneuvering around columns like a
pair of workmen, drilling aisles through clusters of mooners
and gapers. Precariously they wobbled down the great staircase. It was evident he could have managed all that equipment
on his own; he was used to it. She was an attachment trailing
along—an impediment—but it seemed to Puttermesser that
there was another purpose in this clumsy caravan. A kind of
mental heat ran through the rod that linked them. He had decided to clip the two of them together for a little time. She
understood that she had happened on an original. A mimic
with a philosophy! A philosophy that denied mimicry! And he
wasn't mistaken, he wasn't a lunatic. He was, just as he said,
someone with a new idea. He had a claim on legitimacy. He
was guilty with an explanation; or he wasn't guilty at all. The
thing jerking and bobbing between them, with its sticks and
screws, was an excitement—it made her keep her distance, but
it led her. It was a sort of leash. She followed him, like an aging
dog, sidelong.

Puddles on the sidewalk; she had missed the rain altogether.
The street was silted with afternoon light. Puttermesser surren-
dered her end of the easel—she hated to give it up. Found!
George Lewes, George Lewes in New York! He had a kind of
thesis, a life's argument. He had nerve. "I'll come by," he said.
"I'll drop in. The next time I have to be at Harvey's place. Here,
take one of these. It tells all."

He set easel, satchel, dolly down on the pavement. Then he pulled out a little red case and drew from it a white card. There was a telephone number accompanied by two lines of red type:

> RUPERT RABEENO
> REENACTMENTS OF THE MASTERS

Puttermesser, who had not laughed in a month, laughed: she was ready to be happy. "Do people know what this means when you hand it out?"

"It's self-explanatory."

She was still laughing; it made her as bold as an old politician. "Why would you drop in?"

"To explain the card." He bent to pick up easel, satchel, dolly. "Don't you want me to? Would you rather I didn't?"

"Come right now," she said. "I'm dying of thirst. I'll make some tea."

II. THE NIGHT READERS

Puttermesser's favorite tea was Celestial Seasonings Swiss Mint —each tea bag had an instructive or uplifting quotation attached to it. Henry Ward Beecher: "Compassion will cure more sins than condemnation." Victor Hugo: "Laughter is the sun that drives winter from the human face." Ralph Waldo Emerson: "Make the most of yourself, for that is all there is of you."

The box, too, was imprinted with wisdom. Rupert Rabeeno read aloud, " 'I have always thought the actions of men the best interpreters of their thoughts'—John Locke," and twisted the box around. "This next one's Nietzsche. 'He who has a why to live can bear with almost any how.' "

Reading from the tea bag tags was only a joke, a diversion. What they were really reading from was "Middlemarch." This was the beginning of a project: they were going to do all of George Eliot's novels—out loud, taking turns. The early chapters galloped, but after a while talk seemed to intervene; they forgot what had happened at the start of a chapter, and had to repeat it. Sometimes they skipped the reading altogether. Rupert Rabeeno was not one of those people who allow their lives to be obscured by the vapor of the merely inferential. He was amazingly explicit: he made Puttermesser *see* things. In a month or so she had been led through all the particulars of his childhood. She knew the contents of his mother's dusty jewelry tray—her high-school class ring, four pairs of screw-on celluloid earrings, one necklace of five-and-dime pearls, one broken watch in the shape of a violin—and exactly where his father used to keep the key to the store safe (in the toe of an out-of-style Buster Brown Mary Jane). His father had run a shoe store in a town outside of Atlanta. Rupert's two married sisters, much older, grandmothers several times over, were settled in Tampa and Dallas. He claimed, besides, two mothers. The first had died when he was only nine: it became his habit to dream over the sad remnants of her few poor trinkets. He thought he could catch a reminiscent sniff of her dress fuming out of the tray in her old chifforobe. His father had put it down in the cellar of the shoe store. His father's second wife—strong and rosy—worked in the shoe store just as Rupert's mother had, and to woo his affection rushed home to give him milk and chocolate graham crackers after school, just as his mother had. But he threw over his milk glass on purpose, and his stepmother watched him drag a spiteful finger through the spill, pulling the wet lines of it into a marvel of a cat with a lifted tail. After that he was sent for "art lessons" on Thursday afternoons to a little local academy, where his classmates were mostly girls. Tap dancing was in progress just across the corridor, accompanied by a quaking piano; it was a humiliating place altogether. He didn't *sound* very Southern, Puttermesser noticed: he had left the South a long time ago, and had travelled everywhere. Some years back, he said, he had fallen into a "subject," his first, at the Louvre: it was the "Officier de Chasseurs à Cheval de la Garde Impériale Chargeant," by Théodore Géricault. And before that he had done some translating from the Catalan; and a stint, before that, in "The Changeling," on the London fringe, playing De Flores.

Puttermesser heard all this with a formidable sharpness—he was charging her with the will to take hold of him. It was as if he had given her a razor to cut him out with: the whole figuration of his history. He wanted her to know precisely what he added up to. He discharged everything he had done—he had done a lot—in a shower of color and anecdote; he was against elusiveness. Stories, worn through retelling, shot out from him: she felt the knots and burrs of reused thread. And portraits: his curly-haired sisters, their husbands (a couple of doctors, one a gastroenterologist, the other a pediatrician), their children, the strangers their children had married; but he was lost to all of them now. He had left his family behind. He spoke of the curiously perfected reflections of the bridges over the Seine, of how when you looked at them you couldn't tell which was the true world, the one in the air or the one in the river; and of the part-time job he had held at eighteen, in a grimy record-pressing plant, listening over and over again for flaws in the grooves; and of how he had once been hired to teach English in a loft on West Fifteenth Street to fearful, pathetic newcomers up from the Caribbean, under a half-mad "principal" who required every pupil to trace over the principal's model sentences in green ink; and of how the shoe store, always dark and unpopulated, like an empty movie theatre, with its double row of chairs back to back, had all at once surprisingly begun to flourish and bustle, fevered, it seemed, by his stepmother's quick run over the old brown carpeting—so that the two of them, his nearsighted father and his rubicund second mother, could dare to open a second store in the next town, called, like the first, The Pair Fair.

It was almost too much. Puttermesser would not have minded a bit more mystery, the trail of something shielded, a secret stowed in a crevice. A spot, here and there, of opacity. He told her, with a compulsive comic vividness that shook her, of his clandestine night wedding, at twenty-three, to Cecilia Almendra, a little Argentine cabaret singer who turned out to be a runaway. Señor and Señora Almendra found them out and took the bride back to Buenos Aires—"before the consummation," he said. Señor Almendra (born Mandel, a refugee from the European cataclysm) raged; Señora Almendra sobbed. The girl had been registered at N.Y.U. and was supposed to be studying psychology; she never went to classes and wrote lying letters home. Her hours in the "cabaret"—a filthy bar on Avenue A—lasted until five in the morning. A bedroom farce with an unrumpled bed.

In the decade or so since, Rupert had lived without romance —not that kind, anyhow. Paris, and then London, and then Pittsburgh. He was sick of being a seedy wanderer bartering the baubles of trick and knack. In granite Pittsburgh he worked for a provincial satrap, the monarch of an intrastate railroad, and for half a dozen years threw himself into designing billboards. His grand, noisy posters, in riotous orange and purple and drumming red, jumped out at every station like oversized postage stamps connecting town with town. All the commuter lines that led to Pittsburgh were stitched together by Rupert's posters—he thought of them as brilliant beads strung on wire tracks. And he thought of himself as a polychromatic jack-in-the-box, ambushing the public. After the billboards, he switched to decorating cereal boxes. It pleased him that the selfsame jug, yellow and two-handled, overflowing with banana flakes, cropped up on tables from Tokyo to Tel Aviv; repetition wasn't far from continuity, and continuity not far from eternity. But in the end he didn't care for assignments and projects and campaigns. He disliked art directors and company bosses. Granite Pittsburgh crumbled for him; it was no better than a heap of sand draining through an hourglass. He missed being sovereign over himself.

Rupert Rabeeno was glutted with his own life—who isn't,

and why not? He liked to tell it over and over, as if in the telling he could keep it from shrinking away into the smallness of the nearly forgotten. He let go of nothing he had ever known or seen or felt. Or not felt. Whatever had happened once he meant to make happen again. Reprise invigorated him. And Puttermesser was the same. It came to her in a rush of deliverance as wild as cognition, wilder than consternation—she was the same, the very same, no different! Whatever had happened once, she conspired, through a density of purposefulness, to redraw, redo, replay; to translate into the language of her own respiration. A resurrection of sorts. Wasn't her dream of having George Lewes again—a simulacrum of George Lewes—exactly the same as Rupert Rabeeno's wanting to make things happen again? Wasn't she, all on her own, a mistress of reënactment?

On a snowy afternoon in early January—Rupert Rabeeno was just back from delivering one of his great flat parcels upstairs at 6-C—Puttermesser decided to tell her idea about George Lewes. It was less an idea than an instinct; it was a burning; it made her shy. She suffered—he might mock her; she would be humiliated. And the awful discrepancy, the moat of age. The first George Lewes (would Rupert Rabeeno consent to be the second?) was born in 1817. George Eliot was born in 1819. A match altogether on the mark, generationally intelligent, so to speak; two years between them, she nearly thirty-five, he thirty-seven, as decently appropriate as could be. Puttermesser's shame stung. A hag. A crone. Estrogen dwindling in her cells. Rupert Rabeeno was too young—he was two decades too young—to be a candidate for a simulacrum of George Lewes. A gap like that is a foolishness in whatever century.

She watched him rummage in her clogged inch of pantry. He plucked up a can of tomato-and-vegetable soup and emptied it into a pot. Then he poured in some water from Puttermesser's blue teakettle and began to stir. She was used to this: he loved soup. He brought two or three cans every time he turned up.

She had calculated just how to get it said. An announcement.

"October 23, 1854," she started off. And read: " 'I have been long enough with Mr. Lewes to judge of his character on adequate grounds, and there is therefore no absurdity in offering my opinion as evidence that he is worthy of high respect.' " The moist smell of onions heating in the soup curled around them. "Written," she explained, "right after George Eliot and George Lewes went off to Weimar together."

The soup splashed into two of Puttermesser's china bowls. "Why Weimar?"

"Goethe's city. Lewes was working on a book about Goethe. He was always working on *some*thing."

"Sit down and eat your veggies," Rupert Rabeeno commanded. "That woman's a prig. Too damn solemn."

Puttermesser said, "It's Lewes I'm thinking of." George Lewes, lighthearted, airy, a talker!

"He's on your mind a whole lot. So is she."

A clot of embarrassment coarsened her throat. "It's only a feeling," Puttermesser said. "A sort of . . . you know, a conceit. A literary conceit." She put her head down. It was unseemly. She was too old, by twenty years. "It's about ideal friendship."

He said, "I still don't see the point of Weimar. Going off somewhere. There's no point to it. We can stay right here."

So he understood her to the marrow. He was all quicksilver; he was ready. She saw how, once she had yielded up her little burning, he could better it, he could complicate it, he could shake the ash of theory from it and fire it into life. They drove through the rest of "Middlemarch" without interruption; or almost. Often she followed him out into the wintry town—after "The Death of Socrates" he had moved over to the Frick. In his own place, on West Fifty-ninth, a studio with a Castro Convertible, he boiled up a can of mushroom-and-barley. It seemed to Puttermesser that all the singles who had ever lived in this solitary room before him were roiling like phantoms in the steam. His suitcase was tidy and waiting—fresh shirts and turtlenecks, his shoe polish and his own toothpaste. His clothes were orderly, well brushed. She asked him where he kept his valet. He laughed; he was exhilarated. "No room for Jeeves! I hide him in my sleeves!" He showed her his favorite lamp—indispensable, he said, for snugness. He carried the lamp and the suitcase, she carried the shade. Laughing, they left shoe holes in the snow; at the curb the new snow was folding itself over last week's old black humps.

Rupert Rabeeno's lampshade was as wide as a bat's wing and cast phosphorescent reflections on the walls. At night under that greenish, fishy light—3-C was now spookily undersea —they finished "The Mill on the Floss." Rupert asked what next.

Puttermesser considered. "Not 'Romola.' George Eliot said that book was what made her into an old woman."

"Let's do the life," Rupert said.

They tramped in the New York slush to the Society Library and took out all the George Eliot biographies there were, including the one Puttermesser had returned not long before. Rupert wanted to see how they matched up, whether someone writing about George Eliot in, say, the nineteen-eighties was going to turn up the same George Eliot as someone writing in the nineteen-forties, or in the eighteen-nineties. It was like reënacting a landscape a hundred years later, he said. The same grove of trees under the same sky, but different. What altered it was whoever was looking at it. Puttermesser almost followed the argument but was indifferent to it anyhow. Copyist's talk. She didn't care about any of that. She rejoiced, she was anointed. The germ of her secret seeing had breathed itself alive. Here they were, side by side, reading aloud, an indoor January pastoral; she had passed through the sacred gate, she had entered ideal friendship. Rupert's reading voice was dark, with now and then a sharp scratchy click in it, the call of some imaginary bird—it was a chirp she could not hear in ordinary conversation. It meant he was seized. Snared. Sometimes a tic convulsed his eyelid; he was agitated, he was engulfed. He surpassed her in her little burning, he urged her on.

In her cube of a kitchen she told him her convoluted work history, and admitted to sour Rappoport, a Canadian with a wife at home in Toronto, who had once been her lover. Rupert, concentrating, beat at the soup—it was lumpy—and shook the eggs in their pan. After supper he cut her hair. The wisps fell from her nape and forehead, all over her shoulders and the floor. She watched in the mirror as he snipped, evening out the sides: it struck her that she was not yet a hag. Tiny hyphens of hair-cuttings fuzzed her neck; he blew them down inside her blouse and over her back. Her mouth in the mirror was content. Her tongue slipped out like a shining lizard. He never thought of her as unnatural; he never thought of her as too old. Nothing grotesque lay between them. She believed that now. They were friends, ideal friends. She saw how he had become more zealous than she.

When he went upstairs to Harvey Morgenbluth's she stayed behind. It was all business up there. She didn't care for Rupert's business; it opened into discord and combat. His business was postcards. He copied the masters. Harvey Morgenbluth photographed Rupert's doubles, in full color and full size, and reduced the photos before they went off first to the printer and then to a jobber for distribution. This was Rupert's living. "The Death of Socrates," for instance, with Socrates' face filled in, reappeared in packets of a hundred, sealed in transparent plastic. One hundred identically lifted Socratic fingers. One hundred identical youths bearing one hundred identical bowls of hemlock. There was a Rubens—"Venus and Adonis" —with a Cupid and a pair of dogs; there was van Gogh's "Irises" and Manet's "Woman with a Parrot." There was Turner's "Grand Canal, Venice," all ship and sky and water and misty distance. She thought him a genius—a genius ventriloquist; he could penetrate any style and any form, from a petal to an earlobe. He was at home in minuteness or in vista. The name of both painting and painter were printed on the back of each card—and, also, in minuscule letters: "Rupert Rabeeno, Reenactments of the Masters."

This was the subject of their small war. "If all it comes down to is postcards," Puttermesser said, "you might just as well send Harvey Morgenbluth into the Met with a camera."

"In the first place, he wouldn't be allowed. Which," Rupert said, "is beside the point anyhow."

"No, it's not. Every museum in the world sells postcards of its paintings."

"Exactly," Rupert said. "These are postcards of *my* paintings."

"It's a fraud."

This made him jolly. "Counsellor!"

"I didn't say it's illegal. I'm not talking about copyright laws. There aren't any copyright laws for French Neoclassicals. That leaves you with your conscience."

"My conscience!" He reared back as if she had smacked him, and let out a scratchy laugh. It reminded her of the snap, as of an unearthly pod bursting, of his reading voice.

"People are going to look at *your* Grand Canal and think it's Turner's."

"I made it," he said, with so much clarity that Puttermesser felt she could stare right through the unpainted circles of his eyes into whatever murmured behind them.

This murmur swept her. She brought his whole head into her arms. "Rupert, Rupert," she said. A fabricator of doubles, but he had no duplicity. She nearly believed in his case: that these weren't doubles he fabricated. It wasn't a manner or mannerisms he took from his prototypes. It was—could it be true?—their power.

She recited: " 'To see Kean act was like reading Shakespeare by flashes of lightning.' "

"What's that?"

"Coleridge said it about some famous actor."

And so their skirmish ended. She could not keep it up. If he didn't invent the work of his hands, he had, anyhow, invented himself. He wasn't a swindler, he wasn't an impostor. The postcards were his very own. She came on them in bookshops, and realized she had often seen them there before. A rack of his cards stood near the door when she went into a stationer's for a typewriter ribbon. There on the top tier was Picasso's "Gertrude Stein"—that autonomous skull, tile forehead, mouse's chin. But Rupert had made it.

III. THE UNSPEAKABLE JOY

Their night reading under the sea-green lamp: the names of the long, long dead. Brabant, Bray, Chapman, Rufa, Cara, Sara, Barbara Bodichon, Edith Simcox, Johnny Cross. Spectres. Of these, only Herbert Spencer survives recognizably on his own. George Eliot dared to beg him to marry her: she was infatuated. She had not yet met George Lewes. "I promise not to sin any more in the same way," she pleaded when Spencer turned her down; she could not imagine that he would end his days a bachelor. The philosopher of evolution could not evolve. "If you become attached to someone else, then I must die, but until then I could gather courage to work and make life valuable, if only I had you near me. I do not ask you to sacrifice anything—I would be very good and cheerful and never annoy you."

Rupert was reading this from the "Letters." Puttermesser slammed down her eyelids. She had those pitiful phrases by heart. The abjectness, the yearning. Dry Herbert Spencer, a man shut off; no feeling could invade him. But one day he brought George Lewes with him to the *Westminster Review*, where George Eliot—she was still plain Miss Evans—was working as editor. Lewes was playful, impudent, jokey; his face was pitted, he had a little, neat nose with big nostrils. He was an apt mimic and told clever stories without a speck of meanness. George Eliot at first thought him ugly; she was ugly enough herself. People said he resembled a monkey; they said she resembled a horse. He had free tickets to the theatre and invited her along.

He reviewed plays, books, art, music. His mind was all worldly versatility. He wrote on French and German literature, he wrote plays, he made a study of insanity, he wrote on history and science and philosophy, on anemones and Comte and Charlotte Brontë. She translated Strauss, Feuerbach, Spinoza; she wrote on Matthew Arnold, Tennyson, Browning, Thoreau, Ruskin. She read Homer, Plato, Aristophanes, Theocritus; she read Drayton and a history of Sanskrit.

"What a pair, what a pair," Puttermesser said.

She had discovered something disconcerting: Rupert confessed that until now George Eliot had been no more than a rumor for him. In high school in the town near Atlanta they had read "Silas Marner" in sophomore year. That was all of George Eliot he was acquainted with. The rest was new. He had never before looked into a biography of George Eliot. He had never heard of George Lewes or Johnny Cross or all those others.

"Why didn't you say so when we began? When we started the reading?"

"I thought you could tell." He put his hand on her hand. How dependable he was; how eager to satisfy. "Anyhow, I'm catching up. In fact I'm *caught* up. What do you know that I don't?"

She could not contradict him. It was as if he had swum into her brain and swallowed up its spiny fish, great and small, as they flickered by. Puttermesser was ravished: it was true, there was no difference between them. Under the sea-green lamp he was caught, he knew what she knew.

It was Lewes she wanted him to know.

They read until they were dried up. They read until their eyes skittered and swelled. The strangeness in it did not elude them: where George Eliot and George Lewes in their nighttime coziness had taken up Scott, Trollope, Balzac, Turgenev, Daudet, Sainte-Beuve, Madame D'Agoult (Lewes recorded all this in his diary), she and Rupert read only the two Georges. Puttermesser discussed what this might mean. It wasn't for "inspiration," she pointed out—she certainly wasn't mixing herself up with a famous dead Victorian. She was conscious of her Lilliputian measure: a worn-out city lawyer, stunted as to real experience, a woman lately secluded, eaten up with loneliness, melancholia ground into the striations of her face. The object was not inspiration but something sterner. The object was just what it had been for the two Georges—study. What Puttermesser and Rupert were studying was a pair of heroic boon companions. Boon companions! It was fellowship they were studying, it was nearness.

"George and George," Rupert said. "Practically a couple of twins."

"They were *lovers*," Puttermesser corrected.

In the mornings he snatched up his satchel and dolly and clattering easel and headed for the Frick. Puttermesser marvelled at the soaked threads of the canvas, glistening with bright, heavy oil. In the evenings, after supper, they pushed on with the two Georges. A history of money and family. The money went to Agnes, Lewes's easygoing, adulterous wife, and her brood of children by another man. Agnes in old age, unrepentant and very fat, with small, fat fingers twiddling in her lap, supported until her death by George Eliot's earnings: they mooned over her photo in one of those bricklike volumes that littered the kitchen chairs. But to Lewes's sons George Eliot was "Mutter." One died young—she nursed and mourned him as if he were her own. Another was attached to her all her life. Lewes, meanwhile, was coaxing her to try her hand at writing stories, though privately he doubted whether she could master drama. Overnight she bloomed into greatness. And was a pariah all the same. Her brother Isaac, still in the Midlands of their childhood, would have nothing to do with her. She wrote him and he refused to answer. His sister was living with a man who had a wife. His sister could not be received in respectable drawing rooms. In the end the world came to her. A daughter of Queen Victoria contrived to be presented to George Eliot.

Rupert read: " 'Our unspeakable joy in each other has no

other alloy than the sense that it must one day end in part-ing.' " For twenty-five years George Eliot and George Lewes had their unspeakable joy—each other, and fame, and homage, and Europe, and a carriage of their own, and comforts, and the admiration of the best minds, and the hoverings and adorations of the young, among them Johnny Cross. Johnny Cross helped Lewes find a house in the country—he was good at all sorts of practical things. George Eliot called him nephew. "My dear Nephew," her letters to him began; and ended, "Your affection-ate Aunt." He was a tall, comely young man of twenty-nine, introduced to her by his mother on a holiday in Rome. After Rugby, he went to New York to work in a branch of the family bank, and returned to London to do the same. George Eliot met Nephew Johnny Cross on George Lewes's fifty-second birth-day.

IV. THE AWFUL DISCREPANCY

The death scenes and their aftermath fell to Puttermesser. They were familiar to her, and unimportant. It was the living Lewes she cared for, the salvational Lewes, the merry Lewes of trans-formation. George Lewes died at sixty-one, in a dank Novem-ber. He had always been sickly. During his final hours the doc-tors bustled in and out. In front of the Priory their coachmen cracked noisy jokes. George Eliot did not go to the funeral. Day after day she shut herself up in her bedroom with Lewes's books and microscope; she howled and howled. Only the ser-vants heard.

Here Puttermesser stopped. It was over.

Rupert said, "We ought to do it."

"Do what?"

"Get married."

"*They* didn't marry," Puttermesser said, and closed the book.

"Hey, don't quit—there's more."

"No more Lewes."

"There's all the rest."

"You don't like her on her own. You called her a prig."

"That was before I knew her. Do the rest," he persisted.

So she went on with it. Two months after Lewes's death, George Eliot wrote to Johnny Cross, "Dearest Nephew, I do need your affection. Every sign of care for me from the beings I respect and love is a help to me. . . . In a week or two I think I shall want to see you. Sometimes even now I have a longing. . . . Your affectionate Aunt." And on a brilliant May day, at St. George's Church in Hanover Square, eighteen months after she had howled over the parting from Lewes, George Eliot married Johnny Cross. The new wife was sixty. Johnny's mother had died within days of Lewes. He was an orphan of forty.

Rupert danced around Puttermesser's tiny bedroom, where they had set up the sea-green lamp on Puttermesser's teak desk. "Look at that, look at that!"

"She needed someone to lean on," Puttermesser said. "It was her temperament."

"The body was hardly cold!"

"You can't lean on a dead man."

"Aha." Now he took her by the wrists. "Didn't I tell you that from the start? That first day in the Met? I told you—I'm the one who's alive!"

Puttermesser wondered at this. "Well, there's the honeymoon."

"I'll do the honeymoon!" Rupert said.

She watched him reconstruct Johnny Cross. Johnny Cross was, anyhow, a puzzlement. No one knew him, really. He was expected to be "deep," and he wasn't. He was handsome and genial and athletic and rich. He was no intellectual, though he worked at it gamely, in the same plucky way he chopped down a clump of trees or devoutly smacked at a tennis ball. He was a tremendous swimmer. He wasn't even remotely a writer, but he did turn out one astonishing book—astonishing chiefly because Johnny Cross had written it: "George Eliot's Life." The title was as obvious and direct as he was. He plugged away at it after she died: it was a genuflection.

Rupert saw quickly that the heap of biographies they had been reciting from—including Johnny Cross's—were useless. Johnny Cross appeared in all of them, to be sure—which didn't signify he was *there*. You might find him but you couldn't get hold of him. Rupert did what he could to conjure up the true Johnny. In a way, he remade him—Puttermesser thought it was a kind of plunder. Rupert was being preposterous and unfair, but she had to acknowledge that he was ingenious. He went after unheard-of combinations and juxtapositions: a letter, then a paragraph from one of the biographies, then again a letter. He threaded in and out of whatever was at hand. And what emerged from all that prestidigitation was Johnny Cross in love —but not with George Eliot.

"Good God," Puttermesser said. "The one thing everybody knows for sure about Johnny Cross is that he loved George Eliot. He adored her! There never *was* anybody else for him. When she died he never married again. You can't just contradict what everybody absolutely *knows*."

But Rupert pressed on with his evidence. It was, he said, right there in Johnny's unnatural behavior in the first weeks after Lewes's funeral. George Eliot had pleaded with him to come and help her with the business matters George Lewes had always taken care of: Johnny was good at money. He arrived carrying Dante's Inferno. George Eliot was in her sitting room rereading the Iliad—in Greek, of course—to take her mind off her sorrow. Johnny said he was hoping to get started on Dante to take his mind off *his* sorrow; he was mourning his mother. The trouble was, he had to read Dante in Carlyle's translation. The Italian he had picked up in Rome, with his mother, wasn't up to snuff. "Oh," George Eliot cried out to Nephew Johnny, "I must read that with you!"—she liked Dante better than accounting. They went at it word by word. She was massively patient. He was painfully attentive—this was his design.

Rupert held up "George Eliot's Life" under the sea-green

lamp and chanted: " 'The divine poet took us into a new world. It was a renovation of life.' There, that's Johnny confessing."

"Right! You see?" Puttermesser said. "A renovation of life! He's telling us how he adored her—"

"You're not getting it," Rupert said. "The fellow was infatuated. With Lewes."

"Rupert, that's ridiculous."

"I don't mean what you think. I mean incarnation. He was trying to jump right into Lewes's shoes—whatever Lewes was good at, Johnny was going to do. He was out for that. He was going to be Lewes for her. A reasonable facsimile. The idea was to impress on her that Lewes was still around. Accessible, in a manner of speaking. In another packet of flesh. The face was the face of Johnny, but the soul was the soul of Lewes. *That's* the point."

"Oh, I don't know," Puttermesser said, weakening. It was ridiculous, and it was not.

"And the night readings. He kept a record, just like Lewes. First Dante. Then she took him through Chaucer, Shakespeare, Wordsworth. The basics. He had to sweat it out. All of it right there in her sitting room in the Priory, right smack under a big blown-up photo of Lewes. For all I know he had his bottom in the same chair Lewes used to put *his* bottom in. And doesn't he ask her to play the piano for him? The same music she played for Lewes? Then she turns sixty, and Johnny kisses her hand."

"And then he marries her. George Lewes never did that! You keep ignoring that," Puttermesser said. "Marrying her isn't jumping into George Lewes's shoes!"

"You think she wouldn't have had a big church wedding with Lewes if she'd had a chance to? If the law had allowed it? Look, the minute such a thing gets to be possible—Johnny's definitely single—what does she do? She runs out to buy a trousseau."

Rupert plucked up a book from the stack on Puttermesser's teak desk and wet his thumb. "They're sending letters right

and left behind her back. Churning up the gossip. 'George Eliot
had been seen at all the fashionable milliners and dressmakers
in London. . . . Whatever money and taste could do to make
her look not too unsuitable a bride for a man of forty had been
done.' And after a quarter of a century of snubbing her for
living in sin with Lewes, brother Isaac writes to congratulate
her on her marriage to Johnny! And she's *grateful*. These are
conventional folks, Ruthie, believe me. It's Johnny you've got
to keep your eye on."

Puttermesser stared. "Why?"

"I'm telling you why. Watch him make himself into a second
Lewes."

"*You're* doing that. You're making him into Johnny Cross,
Reënactments." Puttermesser drew back. Her lungs felt fat
from too much air. "You're making him into a copyist!"

Rupert gave out a paradisal smile. "Isn't that what he had in
mind?"

"He was in love! And she was lonely, she was missing con-
nubial love. She'd been happy with Lewes, she wanted to be
happy again—" Puttermesser seized the "Letters" and shook
out the pages with a ferocity. "Damn it, Rupert, *listen!*

A great momentous change is taking place in my life—a sort of
miracle in which I could never have believed, and under which I still
sit amazed. If it alters your conception of me so thoroughly that you
must henceforth regard me as a new person, a stranger to you, I shall
not take it hardly, for I myself a little while ago should have said this
thing could not be.

I am going to be married to Mr. Cross. . . . He has been a devoted
friend for years, much loved and trusted by Mr. Lewes, and now that I
am alone, he sees his only longed-for happiness in dedicating his life
to me. . . . Explanations of these crises, which seem sudden though
they are slowly dimly prepared, are impossible. . . . We are going
away tomorrow and shall be abroad two or three months.

"And then they went off together. That's how it is," Puttermesser finished. "A pair of married lovers. You can't just go

and twist it into something else. You want to hear how she'd been feeling? *Here's* how she'd been feeling!" She was as piti- less as a conqueror. It was Rupert she wanted to conquer— Rupert's plan for Johnny Cross. She thumped a fist on the "Let- ters" and read out furiously, " 'Blessed are the dead who rest from their labors, and have not to dread a barren, useless sur- vival.' That's why she married Johnny Cross!"

Rupert looked meditative; he looked serious. Puttermesser took him in all over again—he was narrow, and blond, and burnished, and small. He was brushed and orderly. The clear, blank circles of his eyes were needled through by the fierce points of the pupils. They punctuated; they punctured.

"*We* ought to do that," Rupert said. "Not the going away part. The great momentous change—that part."

He *was* serious. It wasn't a snicker, it wasn't a crack tossed off. Puttermesser hated banter and flippancy; she had fled Har- vey Morgenbluth's party because of banter and flippancy. Ru- pert was a Southerner—he wasn't infected by the New York patter. "Like a few other people in the world, he is much better than he seems—a man of heart and conscience wearing a mask of flippancy." This was how George Eliot had once described George Lewes—though not right away. Her first impression was of a miniature fop, gyrating his arms, too talkative, shal- low. But Rupert was serious through and through.

"O.K.," Puttermesser said. "Let's do it."

She wasn't sure whether she had at just that moment agreed to marry Rupert Rabeeno.

"Let's not forget the honeymoon," he said.

"O.K.," she said. "The honeymoon. You do it."

She watched him do the honeymoon. He did it fastidiously, with a sort of military instinct for the organization of it—slips of paper to mark the pages, volumes set in consecutive order ready to hand, quotations culled on cards. It was curious how well he had prepared himself. Out of the jumble they drew from every night—maps, letters, journals, biographies, mem- oirs, pamphlets, books and more books!—he was fashioning something clever, something out of the ordinary. A destiny. Rupert went about doing the honeymoon with the same heat of immanence he had blown into "The Death of Socrates." He read, yelled, sang, beamed. It was all for Johnny Cross—for Rupert's theory of Johnny Cross, and Johnny Cross was only footnote and anticlimax. He wouldn't let her ride over his theory; she hadn't been able to deflect him. Puttermesser was jealous. Rupert had lavished nothing like this on George Lewes. Yet it really *was* happening again, a second round. Puttermesser was obliged to admit to herself the possibility that Rupert might be on the right track. The honeymoon of Johnny Cross and George Eliot was turning out to be purest mimicry of the honeymoon of George Lewes and George Eliot—the honeymoon that couldn't be called a honeymoon because there had never been a wedding.

Rupert did the wedding first. It was plausible to begin there, at the church at quarter past ten in the morning. Lewes's son, two years younger than Johnny, gave George Eliot away. All of Johnny's relatives came—his sisters, and their husbands, and his cousins, and his cousins' children. After the ceremony the bride and groom went back to the Priory with a pair of solicitors to sign their wills. Then they set out for Dover, to catch the next day's Channel steamer for Calais. In Dover they spent the night at the same hotel where George Eliot and George Lewes had once sojourned. ("When Johnny was still a schoolboy!" Rupert crowed. "The same hotel!") When they reached Calais Johnny noticed how much younger and healthier George Eliot was looking—it was as if she were being renewed by every familiar mile along the old route. ("It *was* the old route," Rupert pointed out.) They were heading for Venice. Johnny took them down to Milan through Grenoble and Mount Cenis, exactly the itinerary Lewes had designed for what George Eliot had called their "deep wedded happiness." A week in Milan, as before; and then Venice.

Venice! "What stillness! What beauty!" George Eliot whispered. (Rupert, reading from George Eliot's journal, was whispering, too.) "Looking out from the high window of our hotel on the Grand Canal, I felt that it was a pity to go to bed. Venice was more beautiful than romances had feigned. And that was the impression that remained and even deepened during our stay of eight days." But that was long ago, with Lewes. Their room was dizzily distant above the glistening water. In the afternoons, the two Georges meandered through the basilica of San Marco, thinking it resplendent but barbaric. In the Scuola di San Rocco they were transfixed by the homely Mary of Tintoretto's "Annunciation." They bought lace and glass and jewelry, and floated around the lagoon in a gondola decked out with colored lanterns. Under the Rialto bridge the gondoliers rested their poles and warbled their lungs out, to bring an echo out of the waves. (" 'O sole mio," Rupert sang. "Now watch-a John-nee," he sang.) Johnny Cross and George Eliot reached Venice a month after their wedding. It was fragrant early June. Sunlight and speckled cream palaces with ancient cracks running down their walls, and darkling shadows under the bridges—they intended to linger for an indefinite stretch of summer.

Instead, they quit Venice in the second week.

"Panic," said Rupert. "The honeymoon's secret shock. Its mystery, its enigma."

"All right," Puttermesser said. "Get it over with. You don't have to milk it."

V. THE HONEYMOON

They took a hotel directly on the Grand Canal, and had all their meals brought to their room. Much of George Eliot's new wardrobe had come with them in trunks. She was cunningly and handsomely dressed, the elderly erupting collarbone covered by the lightest of wraps, the youthful waist disclosed. Lewes's death had left her ailing and frail; now she was marvellously restored. She was robust, she was tireless. She marched Johnny out to churches and galleries, and lectured him on architecture, painting, sculpture, history. He followed her ardently. He was proud of her, he was proud of himself. It was achieved. It was all exactly as it had been with Lewes. They stood before the same ugly Tintoretto Madonna and circled the gaudy bowels of San Marco. The June heat thickened; it began to feel tropical, though inside the old stone churches it was cool enough.

But there was something amiss with the air; the air was strange, and bad; there was something amiss with the drains. The view (though not so high up) from the windows of the Hôtel de l'Europe was just what it had been for that earlier pair, the two Georges—the Grand Canal knife-bright in the morning, blood-streaked at sundown, glowering at dusk. The canal below was itself no better than a drain. The air that rose from it was a sick cloud, a pustule of spew, a fume. The open windows gulped it in, especially at night when there was a flicker of wind. At night, the stillness, the beauty: a pity to go to bed. Day after day the pair searched out gonging campaniles, out-of-the-way chapels, glazed portraits of holy babes and saints and bishops and doges, and when the heat ebbed slightly they rode round and round in gondolas, dazed by the blinding white cheeks of the palazzi. The beauty, the beauty!

In the evenings they settled in for supper at the snug oval table in their room. The napery was always blue, though the cloth, sweetened by some herbal soap, was changed daily, and a bowl of flowers, cut every afternoon, was set down on it to obscure the drifting smells of the canal. When the porter came to remove the trays—they ate simply, bread and fish and tea—Johnny and George Eliot were already sunk back into the Inferno. They had returned to Dante because it was clear that Johnny needed to brush up on his Italian now more than ever. Again, she was lavishly attentive, especially to the difficulties of the syntax. She saw a kind of phrenological sturdiness in the coronal arch as his head lowered to the discipline of the page, a dolichocephalic head belonging to a long-boned six-footer. She was glad that he was as different in appearance from Lewes as could be—nothing about him was a reminder. Lewes had been little and vivacious—occasionally too quick—and brilliant and versatile. Johnny wasn't quick, but he was worldly enough; he was a banker who could tell when a man was bluffing. "Thou dost not know," she teased him once, "anything of verbs in Hiphil and Hophal or the history of metaphysics or the position of Kepler in science, but thou knowest best things of another sort, such as belong to the manly heart—secrets of lovingness and rectitude."

His character was solid, well tried, he was steady and affectionate. It hurt her that she was so old, though *he* never thought of it. In Venice, despite all their happiness, she was consumed by it. Nothing could make her young again for Johnny; she knew it whenever she combed through the gray in her hair, or held the mirror to her eyes, with their bruised fleshiness run wild in the caverns beneath. Johnny was already well into balding, but the hair around his ears was dark and bunched with curls. His beard was frizzy. Behind it (his lovely mouth lost in the frizz) there perspired a striving boy with a nervous look. She noticed the look and understood. It was five weeks—almost six—since the wedding. They went to their beds every night as friends—he was her noble companion, her squire, her loyal pupil. How hard he tried! But he faltered over the Dante; she pointed with her finger, and he corrected himself. He was beginning to languish a little. The more she bloomed, the sounder she grew, the more he drooped. They had not yet lain as husband and wife.

It was exercise he was missing. He was, after all, a man of the outdoors, he played tennis and football, and rowed and swam. Venice, all that water, and no rowing—it was only the sunburned gondoliers and their indolent poles, it was only the dreamy floating, it was churches and galleries and pictures and history. Endless, endless history. Endless art. Endless beauty. He wanted some clean air, he wanted something strenuous.

("Pretty strenuous," Rupert intervened, "to keep on walking every minute in Lewes's shoes!")

Johnny said he needed a swim. The Grand Canal was a cesspool; it was right at their doorstep, just under their windows, but you couldn't swim in the canal. The Lido wasn't far. They ought to get over to the Lido, the other side of it, where there was a good sandy beach. On the other side of the Lido they sat sedately on a bench, among ladies and their parasols, and watched the line of tidal waves. Johnny said he longed for a sea bath. The bathhouses were nearby, and he had brought along his swimming costume. He would dash into the sea, have a decent splash, loosen up his limbs, and dash out again; it wouldn't occupy more than a quarter of an hour. She thought the weather wasn't suitable for such a venture: see, she said, raising the pedagogic finger that had so often guided him through the Inferno, you can feel the wind. I'm dying for a bathe, he said, it's the middle of June and hot as Hades. "Though the temperature is agreeable," she argued pleasantly, in that even, courteous contralto cherished by Lewes, and now cherished again by Johnny, "it has not the sort of heat that makes a plunge in cold water"—here she struggled to uncover a just simile—"as good as a drink to the thirsty."

They went back to their hotel. Johnny ordered an elaborate supper of lamb and tomatoes and pudding. The sommelier followed behind the porter with two small ruby bottles. She drank a glassful. Johnny drank several. He seemed roused, alert. She caught the thirst in his eye, and knew it was a shy celebration. The time had come. Over the last days she had observed his inwardness, his delicacy, his brooding. He had stood despondently before the very shapes and pictures that Lewes had looked on years before with so much brio and worshipful wit. Johnny was distracted. She was not surprised when, after the porter returned to clear the table, Johnny wiped his fingers with his blue napkin and declined to take up the Dante. She thought to tempt him with Comte—a diversion—but he turned away. She was discreet. The diffidence between them was natural. Until a month ago he had been a bachelor, doubtless no more celibate than any other handsome young fellow. But unlike herself—she had gone to bed with George Lewes for twenty-five years—he was new to the dignified rituals of conjugal intimacy. She made out some fresh tentativeness in him, a drawing away. It was restraint, it was mindfulness: he was whipping down animal nature until she was ready to give him a signal. She was a little frightened that he put the responsibility on her; but also excited. She, who was accustomed to leaning on a husband!

She retired into her dressing closet, a mirrored nook set apart, and chose a nightgown she had never worn before. She shut the door so that he would not see her too soon, and let down her hair. The nightgown feathered her bony shoulders with masses of concealing lace. It all at once struck her that, with her pleasant figure and loosened hair, she had, in the looking glass, the sweetness of a bride of twenty-two: she did not feel old at all.

When she came back to him she was disappointed that he was in his own bed. Nothing was different, it was like other nights. She had imagined he would be loitering at the window, say, listening for her, watching the black spirals the gondoliers' poles lanced into the water. She had imagined that he would wait until she hid herself—her little bride-self!—under her own coverlet, and then, hesitantly, tenderly, silently, he would set his limbs against her limbs at last. Instead, he was a stiff hunch in the other bed. His trousers were folded on a chair. The small wind sent the window curtains grazing over his head.

On second thought she was charmed by this backwardness. She reminded herself that the initiative was hers, and how could it be otherwise? He was reticent, he was a boy. Perhaps she had been mistaken—possibly he had no experience at all. Below, sliding along the Grand Canal, a convoy of gondolas was flinging up laughter and voices and loud singing in an Italian remote from Dante's. Some locals on a lark, or a party of gondoliers and their wild girls. The air, bad as it was, swelled every sound into a roar. Then the line of gondolas passed and she was alone with him in the quiet. *"Bester Mann,"* she murmured, and added some syllables from Goethe—Goethe, whom Lewes had so much loved.

She sat on the bed beside him and caressed the circle of his ear. "Dearest, dearest John," she said. He kept his back to her, and did not stir. She lifted the coverlet, and lay down close against him. He had not put on his nightdress; he was still in that morning's shirt. He had discarded his cravat—it was a thick serpent on the floor. She touched her naked toes to the naked bulge of his calf; with one bold arm she embraced his wide chest. His upper body was hot. The leg was cold. She was right to have discouraged a swim—was he ill? "Johnny, dear," she said. He did not answer. She was alarmed and faintly shamed; she removed her foot from his calf, and put her hand to the thigh of the other leg. It was cold, cold. Despite the trail of wind, the night was warm. It was growing warmer and warmer. The grooves flowing from her nose to the corners of her mouth, an old woman's creases, ran with sudden sweat; her armpits were sweated. She was not doing what he wished. She was too immodest, there was some direction he mutely intended which she could not interpret. "Johnny," she pleaded, "dear boy, are you unwell? Look at me, Johnny, dear, let me see your eyes."

He turned to her then, and showed her his eyes. They were unrecognizable—the rims of the lids as raw and bloody as meat, stretched apart like an animal's freshly slaughtered throat. Only the whites were there—the eyeballs had rolled off under the skin. An old secret shot through her like an intuition: a thing she had forgotten she knew. Johnny had a mad brother who was put away somewhere; Lewes had told her this long ago. Abruptly, the eyeballs fell back into place. He was not normal. He was unwell. The bitter, putrid wind, the drains, the polluted canal, the open window. He was breathing with an urgency; every inhalation seemed hard won. She could not get enough air for herself. They were entombed in a furnace. Down below, the fleet of gondolas was returning, the raucous party from before, or another just as noisy—she heard blasts of laughter, and common street voices, and singing, and this time a tremulous guitar. She was standing now; her brain was shuttling so rapidly that it shook her—there was a doctor in Venice, Dr. Ricchetti, whom English people consulted. She ran to the bellpull on the far wall, a little distance from the windows, to ring for the hall porter.

A tremendous swipe—the scream of a huge bullwhip or instant cyclone—cut through naked space. A projectile of some kind—she had seen the smudge of it fly past her own back. A stone—a ball, a bone—tossed up by some loutish member of the crew below. Straight through the window. But the bed was empty. Johnny was not in it. The curtain was ripped away. The projectile had flown not into but out of the window. The projectile was Johnny. She bent over the windowsill and shrieked. His elbows in their shirtsleeves dipped and rose, dipped and rose, like white fins. He was having his swim in the Grand Canal. The gondoliers mocked her cry: "Gianni, Gianni!" They leaped into the night water after him, but he would not be caught. For ten minutes they chased the white fins, and fished poor Johnny out by hooking his collar on one of their poles.

VI. THE MARRIAGE

Puttermesser had always hated that part. It was too ugly. She didn't like to think about it. Everything bright had ended with George Lewes's funeral. The rest was nothing. The rest didn't count. Johnny Cross, diagnosed as having been subject to "acute mental depression" on a single night of his life, came back to normal, never again had even a moment's worth of derangement, and died in 1924 at the age of eighty-four. But George Eliot weakened and failed. Six months after Johnny threw himself out of the window, she was dead.

Rupert remained cheerful. He didn't miss George Eliot; he had never admired her. Puttermesser, too, under Rupert's influence, had begun to withdraw a little. Possibly George Eliot *was* a prig. She shouldn't have kept Johnny from bathing at the Lido; it was preposterous. She knew he was no good at foreign languages—he couldn't master Hebrew, and mixed up *hiphil* and *hophal*. Then why did she terrorize him with Dante? But Rupert was still harping on his idea—Johnny impersonating Lewes. After Venice, Rupert persisted, in the little time left to their marriage, George Eliot and Johnny Cross went back to the *very same house* Johnny had once helped Lewes buy. "The identical four walls!" he said. "Proof! What more do you want?"

Puttermesser was impatient. She was getting sick of Rupert's idea.

"George Lewes didn't jump into the Grand Canal, did he?" She pushed away the last volume of Johnny Cross's biography. "Johnny just couldn't face sex," she accused.

She looked around her bedroom. A flood of disorder. Heaps of those biographies and maps and memoirs and diaries. An engulfing crust on desk and dresser and floor. Miniature skyscrapers on the windowsills. It was enough. She wanted all those books out. Out, out! Back to the Society Library! The only tidy corner was over near her bed, where Rupert had stored several stacks of his postcards, straight as dominoes.

Puttermesser felt routed. It was as if they had come through a riot. Something tumultuous had happened; she was exhausted, as after intoxication or trance. Rupert had made it happen: this shivering precariousness, this tumult. He had cast out George Lewes, bright-souled George Lewes, and hauled Johnny Cross in. Rupert's impersonation of Johnny Cross impersonating Lewes! It was too alive. It jarred, it aroused. All through his telling the honeymoon she fidgeted, she kindled, she smarted. Rupert was a wizard. He made the honeymoon happen under her fingernails, at the root of her spine. She suffered. It was Lewes she wanted, only Lewes. Didn't the two of them—herself and Rupert—put their heads together under the lamp? Didn't they ignite every passage between them? Yet Rupert took Lewes from her and gave her Cross. Done! The honeymoon was done. Ugly, ugly. She hated it. She had always hated the honeymoon. Rupert pressed it under her fingernails; it was a pole piercing her spine.

Rupert said, "I finished up that Frick thing. Vegetarian tomato, all right?"

Puttermesser said she wasn't hungry for soup.

"Finished up yesterday. A nice Dutch landscape. I have to see Harvey about it when it dries—I'll ask him then. What's wrong with vegetarian tomato?"

"Ask Harvey what?"

"Well, it takes two witnesses. I'll get Harvey next time I'm up there. You figure out who else."

Puttermesser concentrated. "Two witnesses?"

"That's how many you need to get married."

So he meant it. She saw that he meant it. He had been serious about it before. He was serious about it now. Lewes! Lewes, after all! Lewes had inspired him to it. Lewes had seduced him to it. Johnny Cross had got in the way, but the victory belonged to Lewes. Ideal friendship!

"I don't know anybody to ask," Puttermesser said.

"You know a lot of people."

"Not lately. Not this year."

"What about all those politicos in the Municipal Building?"

"I don't work there anymore and I'll never work there again. It was stupid to think I'd ever go back." She reflected on the webwork of her life. Her aunts and uncles were dead. The cousins, once a numerous and jolly gang, were scattered and aging. Half of them had been swallowed up by California—San Diego, Berkeley, Santa Monica, Lake Tahoe. By now most were senior citizens. And the receding gallery of all her old society: there they were, page after page in her little Woolworth address book, those ghosts of classrooms past and half-remembered offices, the detritus of her ascent to fifty-plus. Superannuated fellowship of gossip. Movie companions of yesteryear. They were all distant: either they were wrangling toward divorce, or they lived for their jobs, or they were tanning in the Caribbean, or they were absorbed in their children and their children's babies. Their children: the great genetic tide—the torrent—that separates those with offspring from those without. Three or four of Puttermesser's friends had already died in the lottery of early disease. In the roster of the living, there was not a soul she might want as witness to her wedding. Everyone was obsolete. She was clearing the way. A new life. Clean, pristine.

"But no, Rupert, you're the only one. It's only you. I don't have anybody else."

"I'm in lieu of the world," Rupert said.

She looked to see the mask of flippancy. But there was none.

"Oh, no," she protested, and let his tidy head come into her arms. "You're not in lieu of anything."

Late on a Monday afternoon they took the subway all the way downtown to the Brooklyn Bridge station and went up to the second floor of the Municipal Building. The familiar corridors were wide, battered, gritty; it was as if the walls repelled light. To Puttermesser's surprise, the Marriage License Bureau was no longer there. It had crossed the road to Chambers Street and settled in a former bank the color of an elderly cat's scarred hide. On their way out, Puttermesser surveyed her old territory; inside what had been her own office only months ago, motes hung languidly on smuggled beads of illicit sun. Somewhere a toilet was running. It was relieving that no one recognized her. She was now among the generations of the politically vanished. Estrangement narrowed her throat; her eyes stung in the dimness. She marvelled that she had once disgorged her lawyerly brain into this moribund organism, with its system of secretaries, clerks, assistants, its iron arteries shuffling with underlings.

On the trip back on the No. 6 line in the rush-hour crush, enveloped by the tunnel's grinding thunder, Puttermesser found herself smashed up against Rupert. The car swung like a cradle inside a concussion. Sunk into Rupert's warm shoulder, she felt herself without a past.

"A tomb," she told Rupert. "That place is a tomb."

"What?" he yelled out of the thunder.

"I'm thinking," Puttermesser shouted back, "that my savings are going down. I'll have to start again somewhere pretty soon. You, too, Rupert."

"I don't *have* any savings."

The car screeched around a turn. "You can't do postcards forever," Puttermesser yelled. "Your talent's too big."

"It's just the right size to fit on a postcard. You should see the nice job Harvey's doing on the Frick thing," he yelled back. "Harvey says O.K., did I tell you? About being a witness. And he knows two rabbis—one on the West Side who married him the first time, and one on the East Side who married him the second time. On Second Avenue, in fact," Rupert hollered.

"You should give up the postcards. You should give up Harvey."

The train, arriving at a station, came to a violent stop. Puttermesser was catapulted away. A river of bodies rushed for the door. A forest of bodies sprang up between herself and Rupert.

"All right," Rupert mouthed from across the car. "I'll give up Harvey."

The wedding day was Wednesday—the rabbi on Second Avenue was free that night—and by then they had found the second witness.

Puttermesser said, "There used to be a thumping sound, remember? No, it was before you got here."

"Thumping sound?"

"Well, it's gone. It's been gone for weeks. She's quit doing it. I bet she wouldn't refuse us. She's the one," Puttermesser said. "She's right next *door*."

The math teacher explained that she had folded up her exercise mat for good. It was hard work, and didn't do the job.

Anyhow, it was too lonely. She was enrolled nowadays in one of those new health clubs for singles over on Madison. Her name was Raya Lieberman; she wouldn't at all mind, she said, helping out at a wedding, as long as it was after school. It was true she had Math Club on Wednesdays, but she was perfectly happy to skip it for once. "I've got as good an extracurric supervisory attendance record as anybody, believe me," she assured Puttermesser. "The best, considering what comes down the pike these days."

The rabbi's study was on East Ninetieth, in his apartment. On the telephone he had inquired whether a modest ceremony at 9:30 P.M. in his study at home would be satisfactory, given that it was such a small wedding party and given also—he had a homiletic inflection—that the congregational sanctuary couldn't in any case be secured in the evening on such short notice; and Rupert had agreed. It was beginning to snow again, so the four of them went by taxi—the bride and groom, and the two witnesses. Puttermesser sat in the back seat between the math teacher and Harvey Morgenbluth. Rupert, straight-spined in his stately hat and capelike raincoat, was up front with the driver. Puttermesser had on her best black patent-leather high heels. Rupert and the two witnesses were all wearing their galoshes.

"You ever done a thing like this before?" Harvey Morgenbluth asked Raya Lieberman, leaning across Puttermesser.

"I've been a bride, but not a witness. You?"

"Never done anything like this. How many times?"

"How many times what?"

"How many times you been married?" Harvey Morgenbluth urged across Puttermesser's lap.

"Once."

"With me, it's twice. This is my second rabbi we're on the way to."

It surprised Puttermesser that Harvey Morgenbluth was a familiar apparition. She was habituated to his camel's walk and translucent, flushed ears and phlegmatic, oxlike forehead, well scored by parallel clef lines. It was not unusual for her to run into the math teacher on the way to the incinerator closet or the elevator, but now it dawned on Puttermesser that the flustered-seeming man whom she had often noticed weaving among the shabby old sofas in the lobby, hauling big, square cartons, was Harvey Morgenbluth. Occasionally he pushed them on a dolly. No doubt some of those cartons contained Rupert's postcards. A sourness rose in her. Four inches by six; that was their size. That Frick landscape, a spacious van Ruysdael—a bridge, the gnarled roots of a tree, dark clouds, strange light (dawn or dusk or afternoon before rain), a hunter, a fisherman, a long road, deep vista, two riders, one mounted, the other standing by, red cloak thrown over a shoulder (Rupert loved cloaks, capes, togas), black horse crosswise in the road, blocking it, blacking it, dotting it, swallowing up sky and earth—all that mastery shrunk to four inches by six. Rupert on the side of diminishment, how could it be? At the Met, that first time, hadn't she seen in him voluminous will, the will to be proxy for the punctilious windings and reverberations of huge precursors? Was Rupert with all his amplitude always to be reduced via the technologies of Harvey Morgenbluth? He had promised on the subway to give up Harvey Morgenbluth. Rupert had never explained why a reënactment had to be a dwindling. If it was a dwindling, how could you call it a reënactment?

Puttermesser reminded herself that it was normal to be jittery on the way to one's wedding. Who knew what unhappy divinations Rupert was hurling at her in the front seat, from under his cloak?

Harvey Morgenbluth, still heavy across Puttermesser's knees, was trying to find out from the math teacher if she was available for dinner and a movie next Sunday. "We could go over to the Baronet on Third, or the Beekman on Second. Or look, I've got 'Gone with the Wind' on tape, how about it?"

Puttermesser said briskly, "Don't you do those Sunday parties anymore?"

"Winding down, haven't had one in a bunch of weeks. The kids drove everybody crazy. And you couldn't get a type like Rupert—Rupert's a pretty open guy, but he wasn't interested. Nobody would open up."

Raya Lieberman said, "Nobody opens up nowadays. It's hard for people to be in touch. Everyone's a lonesome atom."

Harvey Morgenbluth whistled. "A lonesome atom, my God. You *said* it." He turned to Puttermesser. His flushed ears were all attention. "By the way, how's the roach problem? You really want to beat 'em, try sodium fluoride around the pipes."

The rabbi's name was Stewart Sonnenfeld. He introduced his wife, Jill, and his teen-age son, Seth, who was at that moment writing a report on Chaucer's "Prologue" for his English class. The four poles of the wedding canopy were held up by Harvey Morgenbluth, Raya Lieberman, Jill Sonnenfeld, and Seth Sonnenfeld. Puttermesser had retrieved her mother's wedding ring from an old felt wallet she kept inside an empty plastic margarine container at the back of the vegetable bin in the refrigerator to foil a burglar. The rabbi had cautioned Rupert to bring along his own wineglass for the ceremony, so that morning Puttermesser had hurried into Woolworth to buy one. Jill Sonnenfeld wrapped it in a paper napkin inside a paper bag, and Rupert stamped on it with his galosh. It exploded with a gratifying convulsion. In Puttermesser's apartment afterward Harvey Morgenbluth and Raya Lieberman each drank a Styrofoam cup of champagne (Harvey's present) and ate a piece of wedding cake—Puttermesser made do with an Entenmann's chocolate layer from the supermarket on Third—and then the two witnesses went off together.

"Into the night," Puttermesser said. "They've gone off into the night, imagine that. Maybe it'll take."

Rupert was poking in the corner closet where he kept his equipment; he was dragging out his satchel. "Maybe into the night," Rupert said. "More likely upstairs to 6-C."

"*We* took," Puttermesser said.

Her heart—her fleshly heart—was curled around itself, like a spiralled loaf of hot, new bread. Inside the cavity that rocked it, this good bread was swelling. Puttermesser waited for Rupert's head to come into her arms, against her heart's loaf. She waited for his voice, his dark reading voice, with its sharp click that could cut her with happiness, like a beak. The living, plain, painful flesh. Sometimes, for all the tumult of his history (he had handed over every winding of his life to her, he kept nothing back), he seemed new-made—as if she had ejected him from a secret spectral egg lodged in her frontal lobe, or under her tongue where the sour saliva gave birth to desire. He was her own shadow and fingerprint. She had painted him on her retina in her sleep. She felt him to be the smothered croak in her throat, a phlegm of chaos burst out of her lung. He had lived too long in her nerves, and her nerves were all wired to the transcendent. Desire, desire! She and Rupert—both of them—were too tentative.

He had pulled out his easel, and left it on the floor with the satchel. He crossed the living room to stand at the window. A hard wind hit the glass. There he was, mooning down at the snowy street below; she wondered if he was looking to see whether Harvey Morgenbluth and Raya Lieberman had really gone off into the night. The loaf in the middle of her chest ballooned; it grew and grew. Jealousy. Rupert's head struck her as still another loaf, all brightly honeyed against the snow-streaked panes. He had been born into the world two decades after her own birth. A long, long meadow, all grassy-green, stretched before him. Under his mustache the two points of his mouth were as elastic as a child's.

She saw that he was dusted over with gloom. He unbuckled one of his galoshes. He seemed indecisive about the other, but he shook it free. The race was behind them, the dream was dreamed. They had arrived at arrival. All wedding nights taste of letdown.

Puttermesser took off her black patent-leather high heels.

They had walked in the snow only a little—out of the taxi, into the lobby—but her feet were still damp. She shivered from the feet up. She went into the bedroom to fetch her furry winter slippers. The dresser mirror arrested, fleetingly, the figure of a woman. How quickly that woman fled!

When she came back into the living room, Rupert was wearing his galoshes again. He was wearing his capelike raincoat and his stately hat. He had his folded-up easel under one arm and his satchel in his hand.

There was something in his face she recognized. An indifference had seeped into the gloom. It was as if she had turned invisible. It was as if he did not recognize her: *that* was what she recognized. A snub—almost a snub. His face hurt her. His youth hurt her.

"Rupert," she said. "What are you doing, Rupert?"

"I can't stay."

"You have to."

"I can't. I can't, Ruth. I can't stay."

"Rupert, take off your coat. Please. Rupert, please."

"No," he said. It was not indifference. It was a burning. He was inside a furnace; he was speaking out of a furnace.

Puttermesser called after him, "Rupert! What are you *doing?*"

"I can't stay."

In the little vestibule he set down his satchel and aimed the easel directly in front of him, clutching it like a burning beam; like a spear. He raised it high and plummeted after it back into the living room. He was running for the window. Puttermesser feared he would fling his lance straight through the glass. But he stopped. He put down the easel and with both hands lifted the window wide. A shock of wind knocked over the stack of Styrofoam cups on the sill. The snow flew in, wet as a waterfall.

"Rupert, Rupert," Puttermesser pleaded. "Take off your coat. Shut the window. For God's sake, shut the window!"

He gave her his whole look then. She was falling into the tiny black holes at the center of his clean, powerful eyes. She was falling and falling, but instead of vertigo or delirium or disorder, there was only the candor of her own intelligence. She understood that he was altogether sane, altogether calculating, and as jubilant as a mathematician in the act of confirming an equation.

He picked up his things and walked out the door.

At the open window, hanging over the sill to catch sight of him dwindling in the street, Puttermesser squinted into the snow. It was pointless to call down to him as George Eliot had called down into the Grand Canal, but anyhow she called and called; the snow blew into her mouth. It was starting to stick to her hair. She leaned into the wetness until her hair was all white with snow.

A copyist, a copyist!

Lucy Honig

ENGLISH AS A SECOND LANGUAGE

Inside Room 824, Maria parked the vacuum cleaner, fastened all the locks and the safety chain and kicked off her shoes. Carefully she lay a stack of fluffy towels on the bathroom vanity. She turned the air conditioning up high and the lights down low. Then she hoisted up the skirt of her uniform and settled all the way back on the king-sized bed with her legs straight out in front of her. Her feet and ankles were swollen. She wriggled her toes. She threw her arms out in each direction and still her hands did not come near the edges of the bed. From here she could see, out the picture window, the puffs of green treetops in Central Park, the tiny people circling along the paths below. She tore open a small foil bag of cocktail peanuts and ate them very slowly, turning each one over separately with her tongue until the salt dissolved. She snapped on the TV with the remote control and flipped channels.

The big mouth game show host was kissing and hugging a woman playing on the left-hand team. Her husband and children were right there with her, and *still* he encircled her with

Copyright © 1990 by Lucy Honig. First published in *Witness*, vol. iv, No. 1, 1990. Reprinted by permission.

his arms. Then he sidled up to the daughter, a girl younger than her own Giuliette, and *hugged* her and kept *holding* her, asking questions. None of his business, if this girl had a boyfriend back in Saginaw!

"Mama, you just don't understand." That's what Jorge always said when she watched TV at home. He and his teenaged friends would sit around in their torn bluejeans dropping potato chips between the cushions of her couch and laughing, writhing with laughter while she sat like a stone.

Now the team on the right were hugging each other, squealing, jumping up and down. They'd just won a whole new kitchen—refrigerator, dishwasher, clothes washer, microwave, *everything!* Maria could win a whole new kitchen too, someday. You just spun a wheel, picked some words. She could do that.

She saw herself on TV with Carmen and Giuliette and Jorge. Her handsome children were so quick to press the buzzers the other team never had a chance to answer first. And they got every single answer right. Her children shrieked and clapped and jumped up and down each time the board lit up. They kissed and hugged that man whenever they won a prize. That man put his hands on her beautiful young daughters. That man pinched and kissed *her*, an old woman, in front of the whole world! Imagine seeing *this* back home! Maria frowned, chewing on the foil wrapper. There was nobody left at home in Guatemala, nobody to care if a strange man squeezed her wrinkled flesh on the TV.

"Forget it, Mama. They don't let poor people on these programs," Jorge said one day.

"But poor people need the money, they can win it here!"

Jorge sighed impatiently. "They don't give it away because you *need* it!"

It was true, she had never seen a woman with her kids say on a show: My husband's dead. Jorge knew. They made sure before they invited you that you were the right kind of people and you said the right things. Where would she put a new kitchen in her cramped apartment anyway? No hookups for a washer, no space for a two-door refrigerator . . .

She slid sideways off the bed, carefully smoothed out the quilted spread, and squeezed her feet into her shoes. Back out in the hall she counted the bath towels in her cart to see if there were enough for the next wing. Then she wheeled the cart down the long corridor, silent on the deep blue rug.

Maria pulled the new pink dress on over her head, eased her arms into the sleeves, then let the skirt slide into place. In the mirror she saw a small dark protrusion from a large pink flower. She struggled to zip up in back, then she fixed the neck, attaching the white collar she had crocheted. She pinned the rhinestone brooch on next. Shaking the pantyhose out of the package, she remembered the phrase: the cow before the horse, wasn't that it? She should have put these on first. Well, so what. She rolled down the left leg of the nylons, stuck her big toe in, and drew the sheer fabric around her foot, unrolling it up past her knee. Then she did the right foot, careful not to catch the hose on the small flap of scar.

The right foot bled badly when she ran over the broken glass, over what had been the only window of the house. It had shattered from gunshots across the dirt yard. The chickens dashed around frantically, squawking, trying to fly, spraying brown feathers into the air. When she had seen Pedro's head turn to blood and the two oldest boys dragged away, she swallowed every word, every cry, and ran with the two girls. The fragments of glass stayed in her foot for all the days of hiding. They ran and ran and ran and somehow Jorge caught up and they were found by their own side and smuggled out. And still she was silent, until the nurse at the border went after the glass and drained the mess inside her foot. Then she had sobbed and screamed, "Aaiiiee!"

* * *

"Mama, stop thinking and get ready," said Carmen.

"It is too short, your skirt," Maria said in Spanish. "What will they say?"

Carmen laughed. "It's what they all wear, except for you old ladies."

"Not to work! Not to school!"

"Yes, to work, to school! And Mama, you are going for an award for your English, for all you've learned, so please speak English!"

Maria squeezed into the pink high heels and held each foot out, one by one, so she could admire the beautiful slim arch of her own instep, like the feet of the American ladies on Fifth Avenue. Carmen laughed when she saw her mother take the first faltering steps, and Maria laughed too. How much she had already practiced in secret, and still it was so hard! She teetered on them back and forth from the kitchen to the bedroom, trying to feel steady, until Carmen finally sighed and said, "Mama, quick now or you'll be late!"

She didn't know if it was a good omen or a bad one, the two Indian women on the subway. They could have been sitting on the dusty ground at the market in San _____, selling corn or clay pots, with the bright-colored striped shawls and full skirts, the black hair pulled into two braids down each back, the deeply furrowed square faces set in those impassive expressions, seeing everything, seeing nothing. They were exactly as they must have been back home, but she was seeing them *here*, on the downtown IRT from the Bronx, surrounded by businessmen in suits, kids with big radio boxes, girls in skin-tight jeans and dark purple lipstick. Above them, advertisements for family planning and TWA. They were like stone-age men sitting on the train in loincloths made from animal skins, so out of place, out of time. Yet timeless. Maria thought, they are timeless guardian spirits, here to accompany me to my honors. Did anyone else see them? As strange as they were, nobody looked. Maria's heart pounded faster. The boys with the radios were standing right over them and never saw them. They were invisible to everyone but her: Maria was utterly convinced of it. The spirit world had come back to life, here on the number 4 train! It was a miracle!

"Mama, look, you see the grandmothers?" said Carmen.

"Of course I see them," Maria replied, trying to hide the disappointment in her voice. So Carmen saw them too. They were not invisible. Carmen rolled her eyes and smirked derisively as she nodded in their direction, but before she could put her derision into words, Maria became stern. "Have respect," she said. "They are the same as your father's people." Carmen's face sobered at once.

She panicked when they got to the big school by the river. "Like the United Nations," she said, seeing so much glass and brick, an endless esplanade of concrete.

"It's only a college, Mama. People learn English here, too. And more, like nursing, electronics. This is where Anna's brother came for computers."

"Las Naciones Unidas," Maria repeated, and when the guard stopped them to ask where they were going, she answered in Spanish: to the literacy award ceremony.

"*English*, Mama!" whispered Carmen.

But the guard also spoke in Spanish: take the escalator to the third floor.

"See, he knows," Maria retorted.

"That's not the point," murmured Carmen, taking her mother by the hand.

Every inch of the enormous room was packed with people. She clung to Carmen and stood by the door paralyzed until Cheryl, her teacher, pushed her way to them and greeted Maria with a kiss. Then she led Maria back through the press of people to the small group of award winners from other programs. Maria smiled shakily and nodded hello.

"They're all here now!" Cheryl called out. A photographer rushed over and began to move the students closer together for a picture.

"Hey Bernie, wait for the Mayor!" someone shouted to him. He spun around, called out some words Maria did not understand, and without even turning back to them, he disappeared. But they stayed there, huddled close, not knowing if they could move. The Chinese man kept smiling, the tall black man stayed slightly crouched, the Vietnamese woman squinted, confused, her glasses still hidden in her fist. Maria saw all the cameras along the sides of the crowd, and the lights, and the people from television with video machines, and more lights. Her stomach began to jump up and down. Would she be on television, in the newspapers? Still smiling, holding his pose, the Chinese man next to her asked, "Are you nervous?"

"Oh yes," she said. She tried to remember the expression Cheryl had taught them. "I have worms in my stomach," she said.

He was a much bigger man than she had imagined from seeing him on TV. His face was bright red as they ushered him into the room and quickly through the crowd, just as it was his turn to take the podium. He said hello to the other speakers and called them by their first names. The crowd drew closer to the little stage, the people standing farthest in the back pushed in. Maria tried hard to listen to the Mayor's words. "Great occasion . . . pride of our city . . . ever since I created the program . . . people who have worked so hard . . . overcoming hardship . . . come so far." Was that them? Was he talking about them already? Why were the people out there all starting to laugh? She strained to understand, but still caught only fragments of his words. "My mother used to say . . . and I said, Look, Mama . . ." He was talking about *his* mother now; he called her Mama, just like Maria's kids called *her*. But everyone laughed so hard. At his mother? She forced herself to smile; up front, near the podium, everyone could see her. She should seem to pay attention and understand. Looking out into the crowd she felt dizzy. She tried to find Carmen among all the pretty young women with big eyes and dark hair. There she was! Carmen's eyes met Maria's; Carmen waved. Maria beamed out at her. For a moment she felt like she belonged there, in this crowd. Everyone was smiling, everyone was so happy while the Mayor of New York stood at the podium telling jokes. How happy Maria felt too!

"Maria Perez grew up in the countryside of Guatemala, the oldest daughter in a family of 19 children," read the Mayor as Maria stood quaking by his side. She noticed he made a slight wheezing noise when he breathed between words. She saw the hairs in his nostrils, black and white and wiry. He paused. "Nineteen children!" he exclaimed, looking at the audience. A small gasp was passed along through the crowd. Then the Mayor looked back at the sheet of paper before him. "Maria never had a chance to learn to read and write, and she was already the mother of five children of her own when she fled Guatemala in 1980 and made her way to New York for a new start."

It was her own story, but Maria had a hard time following. She had to stand next to him while he read it, and her feet had started to hurt, crammed into the new shoes. She shifted her weight from one foot to the other.

"At the age of 45, while working as a chambermaid and sending her children through school, Maria herself started school for the first time. In night courses she learned to read and write in her native Spanish. Later, as she was pursuing her G.E.D. in Spanish, she began studying English as a Second Language. This meant Maria was going to school five nights a week! Still she worked as many as 60 hours cleaning rooms at the Plaza Hotel.

"Maria's ESL teacher, Cheryl Sands, says—and I quote—

'Maria works harder than any student I have ever had. She is an inspiration to her classmates. Not only has she learned to read and write in her new language, but she initiated an oral history project in which she taped and transcribed interviews with other students, who have told their stories from around the world.' Maria was also one of the first in New York to apply for amnesty under the 1986 Immigration Act. Meanwhile, she has passed her enthusiasm for education to her children: her son is now a junior in high school, her youngest daughter attends the State University, and her oldest daughter, who we are proud to have with us today, is in her second year of law school on a scholarship."

Two older sons were dragged through the dirt, chickens squawking in mad confusion, feathers flying. She heard more gunshots in the distance, screams, chickens squawking. She heard, she ran. Maria looked down at her bleeding feet. Wedged tightly into the pink high heels, they throbbed.

The Mayor turned toward her. "Maria, I think it's wonderful that you have taken the trouble to preserve the folklore of students from so many countries." He paused. Was she supposed to say something? Her heart stopped beating. What was folklore? What was preserved? She smiled up at him, hoping that was all she needed to do.

"Maria, tell us now, if you can, what was one of the stories you collected in your project?"

This was definitely a question, meant to be answered. Maria tried to smile again. She strained on tiptoes to reach the microphone, pinching her toes even more tightly in her shoes. "Okay," she said, setting off a high-pitched ringing from the microphone.

The Mayor said, "Stand back," and tugged at her collar. She quickly stepped away from the microphone.

"Okay," she said again, and this time there was no shrill

sound. "One of my stories, from Guatemala. You want to hear?"

The Mayor put his arm around her shoulder and squeezed hard. Her first impulse was to wriggle away, but he held tight. "Isn't she wonderful?" he asked the audience. There was a low ripple of applause. "Yes, we want to hear!"

She turned and looked up at his face. Perspiration was shining on his forehead and she could see by the bright red bulge of his neck that his collar was too tight. "In my village in Guatemala," she began, "the mayor did not go along—get along—with the government so good."

"Hey, Maria," said the Mayor, "I know exactly how he felt!" The people in the audience laughed. Maria waited until they were quiet again.

"One day our mayor met with the people in the village. Like you meet people here. A big crowd in the square."

"The people liked him, your mayor?"

"Oh, yes," said Maria. "Very much. He was very good. He tried for more roads, more doctors, new farms. He cared very much about his people."

The Mayor shook his head up and down. "Of course," he said, and again the audience laughed.

Maria said, "The next day after the meeting, the meeting in the square with all the people, soldiers come and shoot him dead."

For a second there was total silence. Maria realized she had not used the past tense and felt a deep, horrible stab of shame for herself, shame for her teacher. She was a disgrace! But she did not have more than a second of this horror before the whole audience began to laugh. What was happening? They couldn't be laughing at her bad verbs? They couldn't be laughing at her dead mayor! They laughed louder and louder and suddenly flashbulbs were going off around her, the TV cameras swung in close, too close, and the Mayor was grabbing her by the shoulders again, holding her tight, posing for one camera after another as the audience burst into wild applause. But she hadn't even finished! Why were they laughing?

"What timing, huh?" said the Mayor over the uproar. "What d'ya think, the Republicans put her here, or maybe the Board of Estimate?" Everyone laughed even louder and he still clung to her and cameras still moved in close, lights kept going off in her face and she could see nothing but the sharp white poof! of light over and over again. She looked for Carmen and Cheryl, but the white poof! poof! poof! blinded her. She closed her eyes and listened to the uproar, now beginning to subside, and in her mind's eye saw chickens trying to fly, chickens fluttering around the yard littered with broken glass.

He squeezed her shoulders again and leaned into the microphone. "There are ways to get rid of mayors, and ways to get rid of mayors, huh Maria?"

The surge of laughter rose once more, reached a crescendo, and then began to subside again. "But wait," said the Mayor. The cameramen stepped back a bit, poising themselves for something new.

"I want to know just one more thing, Maria," said the Mayor, turning to face her directly again. The crowd quieted. He waited a few seconds more, then asked his question. "It says here 19 children. What was it like growing up in a house with 19 children? How many *bathrooms* did you have?"

Her stomach dropped and twisted as the mayor put his hand firmly on the back of her neck and pushed her toward the microphone again. It was absolutely quiet now in the huge room. Everyone was waiting for her to speak. She cleared her throat and made the microphone do the shrill hum. Startled, she jumped back. Then there was silence. She took a big, trembling breath.

"We had no bathrooms there, Mister Mayor," she said. "Only the outdoors."

The clapping started immediately, then the flashbulbs burning up in her face. The Mayor turned to her, put a hand on each of her shoulders, bent lower and kissed her! Kissed her on the cheek!

"Isn't she terrific?" he asked the audience, his hand on the back of her neck again, drawing her closer to him. The audience clapped louder, faster. "Isn't she just the greatest?"

She tried to smile and open her eyes, but the lights were still going off—poof! poof!—and the noise was deafening.

"Mama, look, your eyes were closed *there*, too," chided Jorge, sitting on the floor in front of the television set.

Maria had watched the camera move from the announcer at the studio desk to her own stout form in bright pink, standing by the Mayor.

"In my village in Guatemala," she heard herself say, and the camera showed her wrinkled face close up, eyes open now but looking nowhere. Then the mayor's face filled the screen, his forehead glistening, and then suddenly all the people in the audience, looking ahead, enrapt, took his place. Then there was her wrinkled face again, talking without a smile. ". . . soldiers come and shoot him dead." Maria winced, hearing the wrong tense of her verbs. The camera shifted from her face to the Mayor. In the brief moment of shamed silence after she'd uttered those words, the Mayor drew his finger like a knife across his throat. And the audience began to laugh.

"Turn it off!" she yelled to Jorge. "Off! This minute!"

Late that night she sat alone in the unlighted room, soaking her feet in Epsom salts. The glow of the television threw shadows across the wall, but the sound was off. The man called Johnny was on the screen, talking. The people in the audience and the men in the band and the movie stars sitting on the couch all had their mouths wide open in what she knew were screams of laughter while Johnny wagged his tongue. Maria heard nothing except brakes squealing below on the street and the lonely clanging of garbage cans in the alley.

She thought about her English class and remembered the pretty woman, Ling, who often fell asleep in the middle of a lesson. The other Chinese students all teased her. Everyone knew that she sewed coats in a sweatshop all day. After the night class she took the subway to the Staten Island Ferry, and after the ferry crossing she had to take a bus home. Her parents were old and sick and she did all their cooking and cleaning late at night. She struggled to keep awake in class; it seemed to take all her energy simply to smile and listen. She said very little and the teacher never forced her, but she fell further and further behind. They called her the Quiet One.

One day just before the course came to an end the Quiet One asked to speak. There was no reason, no provocation—they'd been talking informally about their summer plans—but Ling spoke with a sudden urgency. Her English was very slow. Seeing what a terrible effort it was for her, the classmates all tried to help when she searched for words.

"In my China village there was a teacher," Ling began. "Man teacher." She paused. "All children love him. He teach mathematic. He very—" She stopped and looked up toward the ceiling. Then she gestured with her fingers around her face.

"Handsome!" said Charlene, the oldest of the three Haitian sisters in the class.

Ling smiled broadly. "Handsome! Yes, he very handsome. Family very rich before. He have sister go to Hong Kong who have many, many money."

"*Much* money," said Maria.

"Much, much money," repeated Ling thoughtfully. "Teacher live in big house."

"In China? Near you?"

"Yes. Big house with much old picture." She stopped and furrowed her forehead, as if to gather words inside of it.

"Art? Paint? Pictures like that?" asked Xavier.

Ling nodded eagerly. "Yes. In big house. Most big house in village."

"But big house, money, rich like that, bad in China," said Fu Wu. "Those year, Government bad to you. How they let him do?"

"In *my* country," said Carlos, "government bad to you if you got *small* house, *no* money."

"Me too," said Maria.

"Me too," said Charlene.

The Chinese students laughed.

Ling shrugged and shook her head. "Don't know. He have big house. Money gone, but keep big house. Then I am little girl." She held her hand low to the floor.

"I *was* a little girl," Charlene said gently.

"I *was*," said Ling. "Was, was." She giggled for a moment, then seemed to spend some time in thought. "We love him. All children love—all children did loved him. He giving tea in house. He was—was—so handsome!" She giggled. All the women in the class giggled. "He very nice. He learn music, he go . . . he went to school far away."

"America?"

Ling shook her head. "Oh no, no. You know, another . . . west."

"Europa!" exclaimed Maria proudly. "Espain!"

"No, no, another."

"France!" said Patricia, Charlene's sister. "He went to school in France?"

"Yes, France," said Ling. Then she stopped again, this time for a whole minute. The others waited patiently. No one said a word. Finally she continued. "But big boys in more old school not like him. He too handsome."

"Oooh!" sang out a chorus of women. "Too handsome!"

"The boys were jealous," said Carlos.

Ling seized the word. "Jealous! Jealous! They very jealous. He handsome, he study France, he very nice to children, he give tea and cake in big house, he show picture on wall." Her torrent of words came to an end and she began to think again, visibly, her brow furrowing. "Big school boys, they . . ." She stopped.

"Jealous!" sang out the others.

"Yes," she said, shaking her head "no." "But more. More bad. Hate. They hate him."

"That's bad," said Patricia.

"Yes, very bad." Ling paused, looking at the floor. "And they heat."

"Hate."

"No, they heat."

All the class looked puzzled. Heat? Heat? They turned to Cheryl.

The teacher spoke for the first time. "Hit? Ling, do you mean hit? They hit him?" Cheryl slapped the air with her hand.

Ling nodded, her face somehow serious and smiling at the same time. "Hit many time. And also so." She scooted her feet back and forth along the floor.

"Oooh," exclaimed Charlene, frowning. "They kicked him with the feet."

"Yes," said Ling. "They kicked him with the feet and hit him with the hands, many many time they hit, they kick."

"Where this happened?" asked Xavier.

"In the school. In classroom like . . ." She gestured to mean their room.

"In the school?" asked Xavier. "But other people were they there? They say stop, no?"

"No. Little children in room. They cry, they . . ." She covered her eyes with her hand, then uncovered them. "Big boys kick and hit. No one stop. No one help."

Everyone in class fell silent. Maria remembered: they could not look at one another then. They could not look at their teacher.

Ling continued. "They break him, very hurt much place." She stopped. They all fixed their stares on Ling, they could bear looking only at her. "Many place," she said. Her face had not changed, it was still half smiling. But now there were drops coming from her eyes, a single tear down each side of her nose. Maria would never forget it. Ling's face did not move or wrinkle or frown. Her body was absolutely still. Her shoulders did not quake. Nothing in the shape or motion of her eyes or mouth changed. None of the things that Maria had always known happen when you cry happened when Ling shed tears. Just two drops rolled slowly down her two pale cheeks as she smiled.

"He very hurt. He *was* very hurt. He blood many place. Boys go away. Children cry. Teacher break and hurt. Later he in hospital. I go there visit him." She stopped, looking thoughtful. "I went there." One continuous line of wetness glistened down each cheek. "My mother, my father say don't go, but I see him. I say, 'You be better?' But he hurt. Doctors no did helped. He alone. No doctor. No nurse. No medicine. No family." She stopped. They all stared in silence for several moments.

Finally Carlos said, "Did he went home?"

Ling shook her head. "He go home but no walk." She stopped. Maria could not help watching those single lines of tears moving down the pale round face. "A year, more, no walk. Then go."

"Go where?"

"End."

Again there was a deep silence. Ling looked down, away from them, her head bent low.

"Oh, no," murmured Charlene. "He died."

Maria felt the catch in her throat, the sudden wetness of tears on her own two cheeks, and when she looked up she saw that all the other students, men and women both, were crying too.

Maria wiped her eyes. Suddenly all her limbs ached, her bones felt stiff and old. She took her feet from the basin and dried them with a towel. Then she turned off the television and went to bed.

Tom McNeal

WHAT HAPPENED TO TULLY

Tully David Coates was a sleepy, smiley baby, "a child," said the Coateses' hired man a few years later, "who blinked open his eyes and believed at once in the good intentions of the world."

For Kansas, this was a pretty speech—Tully's folks needed a moment to respond. "A blessing," his mother decided, and his father, habitually unwilling to agree with her, said, "More likely a curse."

Their marriage was loud and wobbly, set loose in a farmhouse without close neighbors. Words were shouted, doors were slammed, locked, kicked open again. Tully brought out his coloring books. He hummed and colored, colored and hummed, waiting for his father to give up. Eventually his father would. He would withdraw to the barn, the tractor would pop and sputter, and once it had rumbled out of hearing, Tully's mother would suggest a horse ride into town or down to the creek, with Tully riding up front or, later on, hanging on to her belt loops from behind while his little brother, Marlen, rode forward. If the weather was bad, she might say, "Who's for cookies?" and they would bake a double batch with the radio on loud to oldies his mother would sometimes dance to, right there on the kitchen linoleum, twirling Tully along.

In Tully's fifth and sixth years the house grew quieter. His mother started getting headaches, not so bad during the day, but bad always at night. Tully's father began a course of peacemaking gestures. He took in his dishes from the table and on Sunday washed not just his but everyone else's, too. When he went to town, he consented to buy groceries, and would throw in the makings for sundaes, which Tully's mother loved. And he bought her the mare she'd seen for sale in Hutchinson, a big gray horse who turned out to be just as fast and trainable as Tully's mother had said she'd be.

Still, the headaches kept up, got worse, and one morning when Tully was seven, his father, sitting unshaven at the breakfast table, told him and Marlen that their mother had gone to a hospital during the night. He gave as the reason a growth in her head. A few days later he left the boys for an afternoon, and when he came back, he said, "I was up to Hutch. It's done for good. She's buried."

Tully nodded but didn't believe what he'd heard. He expected the next telephone call to explain some terrible mistake, the next car up the dirt drive to carry his mother, damaged in some minor way—winged, maybe, in some kind of shootout. But all the cars ever brought was long-faced neighbors with food in covered dishes. Nothing was the same around the place, not his father, not his brother, not his mother's horse or garden or kitchen—they all took on the dull look of things left behind. Tully decided that his mother had been called away on a secret mission by the government and couldn't get in touch with any of them even though she wanted to more than anything. He believed this was true even while telling himself that it was pretend.

In the spring Tully and Marlen stayed with a neighbor while their father drove through Wyoming and Nebraska, looking at land. Upon his return men began coming by the Coates place, writing checks and driving away with stock and equipment. Tully heard his father tell all these men the same thing. They were moving to an irrigated farm on the flats outside Goodnight, Nebraska.

Tully didn't know what flats were exactly, but he liked the sound of the town's name—it made him think of flannel sheets. He folded a note into a bread wrapper, went down to his mother's favorite sitting place by the creek, and tacked it to a tree. *If you can't find us we have gone to Goodnight Nebraska*, it said.

When they pulled away from that empty farmhouse outside Arlington, Kansas, the trunk and back seat and roof of the family Dodge were packed and strapped with all the Coateses' household goods. Three trucks fell in line behind them, each followed by a trailer, one of which carried the gray horse. Tully leaned far out the car window to look back and then held Marlen out for a view. "See?—it's like a circus moving!" he yelled, but Marlen pulled back and, hugging himself, began to whimper. Tully was glad when his father finally popped Marlen one and shut him up. There was no reason for whimpering. They were on an adventure, and at the end of it was going to be a new place to live. Tully poked his head out the window, stretched forward, began happily swallowing from the onrushing air. What he was feeling, though he didn't know yet what to call it, was the keen pleasure of leaving problems behind.

Time passed, months, years, and these lives took hold in the flats south of Goodnight. Tully's father farmed dutifully, cooked dutifully, accepted hail, drought, and flood without a word. Marlen grew plump and sullen, seemed always to expect the worst and believe he'd gotten it. But for Tully life was different. Things came easy to Tully. Pals came easy. School and sports came easy. Judging stock, fixing machinery, and bringing in crops came easy.

Girls also came easy.

"What's the big attraction?" April Reece asked him one night in The Spur, after watching him off and on for a couple of hours. Tully had come up beside her at the bar to order himself a beer between rounds of pool, and she'd started talking. April Reece was older than Tully and known for her flashy dressing and frankness. "No, really," she said, "it's beyond me," and Tully shrugged and turned up a palm as if to say that if it was true, it was beyond him, too. He was twenty-one, loose-limbed, hair the white-blond of cornsilk, pale green eyes in a smooth, unremarkable face. "Maybe it's that car you drive," April said, and drew a smile from Tully. He was interested in April—who wouldn't be?—but he made a point not to show it. He wandered off, played some cutthroat, gravitated back. She was wearing black—black sweater, black denims, black socks turned down over bright pink street shoes.

Tully covered the top of a dice cup, gave it a rattle, and with elaborate indifference said, "Wanna roll for a beer?" While they drank, she asked if he was still going out with the Smalley girl. "Ella and me're friends," he said agreeably, but it was less a statement of loyalty to Ella Smalley, though he had some of that, than it was a way of saying, Ask a question, get an answer. He thought of adding a truth, that Ella Smalley was *just* a friend, but he knew it would come out sounding puny. He signaled for two more beers. April liked a little tomato juice in hers. He himself couldn't stand red beer, but he liked pouring in the juice, which he did now, slowly, leaning forward to watch its color curl into the beer.

"Guess it doesn't take much to amuse you," April said, and Tully, letting his face open into a smile, said no, he guessed it didn't.

A month or so later, after sex with him on the warm, spacious hood of his old black Lincoln Continental, parked on a flat space overlooking the Niobrara, April pulled a blanket up around her and leaned on an elbow to regard him. "Well, I think the reason some girls go for you is that you've got this nice bland face, and in just the right light a girl can make it into anything she wants. It's a face that fits right into any of about six standard happy endings girls cook up for themselves."

Tully tugged the blanket back down, and she left them out there for observation, smooth floppy breasts with nipples the width of poker chips. Tully gave one breast a gentle lift with the back of his hand. "What six happy endings?"

April turned on her back, smiled, let her gaze float up into the night sky. "Can't remember."

Tully was amused that someone so reckless in public would be so careful with her secrets, but he didn't press. He rolled his pants into a pillow, set it between his back and the windshield, and sat up a little to bring into view the red beacon that topped a radio tower deep in the sandhills. He could also see it from his bedroom window at home; for years he had looked at it before going to sleep each night. It had been put up by the state patrol, but Tully always thought of it as something that belonged to him. It was a relay tower. By staring at it he could relay messages to anyone anywhere. To God or Abraham Lincoln or old Mr. Spence, the dog they left behind in Kansas. He told April how he used to really believe this.

A pleasant silence developed, and then April crooked a leg over his, gently took hold of his parts, and, after he'd come to life, said, "I love the way that works," which Tully figured for a lie, though a pleasing one just the same.

But April, her hand still at play, idly asked if his dating someone like Ella Smalley was a sign he meant to settle down.

Tully tried to think. "I don't know," he said finally, because he didn't. What threw him was the notion of what he *meant* to do. It suggested that planning out the next step was something people did, and the fact that he'd never given the line of his life any more thought than he might give to what crops to plant or where first to stalk his buck come fall made him feel suddenly deficient. So he was glad when April began kissing him again, sloppier even than before, but then, as things got interesting, April suddenly broke off a kiss and grabbed hold of his testicles so fiercely that Tully had to clench his teeth to keep from screaming. "Just one thing," she whispered into his ear, "and that is, if I hear of that Smalley girl or any other female for that matter winding up on this car hood with you, ever, I'm going to do something—don't ask me what—but something just to register my significant feelings about it, because this much of your life, Scout, is all mine." And Tully, in spite of his ferocious discomfort, mustered a laugh and said, "I'm paralyzed with fear," at which point April very slightly tightened her grip on him.

A month or so later, in June, Tully came in for supper and found the hood of his old Continental hanging from a cottonwood, where it had been rapped several hundred times with the ball peen hammer April still stood holding.

"Looks like it caught itself a meteor shower," Tully said. "Hoist it up there yourself?"

She nodded. "That was for Lori Hallick."

Tully worked up a smile. At least she wasn't mentioning Wendy Adams or Jill McIntyre. "Night has a thousand eyes," he said.

Ten days later April and her brother Ed drove the Continental, with its yellow replacement hood, into the open sandhills and used it for target practice. When she took Tully out to it that afternoon, she said, "Wendy Adams."

Tully circled the car, staring at the broken windows, taillights, and mirrors. April had let her temper take hold of her— something he believed he would never allow, a belief that produced in him now a kind of smugness he mistook for peace of mind. He grinned and said, well, the hood anyhow still looked usable. It was late afternoon, broad daylight, and April, glancing around, sliding out a grin, looked like someone who'd just caught the pleasant scent of mischief.

* * *

Ella Smalley was a different story. She was tall, skinny, and not especially attentive to her appearance. Her panty hose bagged and her eyebrows lay fuzzily against the grain, which made Tully want to lick a finger and smooth them down. Every now and then her wide, liquid brown eyes would take Tully by surprise, but by and large Ella was something Tully never gave much thought to. She was just there, was all, and always had been. She was quiet, she sneaked up on you like an orphan dog, always on the fringes of things, edging in with eyes down, looking up when it was safe. Ella Smalley saw a lot of things. She'd seen Mr. B. B. Holcomb, the town attorney, put a Sheaffer fountain pen, packet and all, into his inside coat pocket and leave Lloyd's Pharmacy, paying only for a Baby Ruth. She'd seen a fully dressed Indian man sitting below the crooked bridge alongside a woman wearing just a Human League T-shirt. One night through a cracked door she'd seen an aunt in horrible silent anger jab her uncle in the chest with her long hands, moving him backward across the bedroom until he sat down on the bed. Ella had wished her uncle would fight back, and then, when he didn't, decided he deserved it after all. She had been visiting. The next morning, when her aunt had served hot cakes and bacon in her usual manner, and her uncle had eaten hungrily and told a joke about hippopotamuses, Ella had gained a fuller view of adulthood. Usually she told Tully such things while they were cruising down the highway in the Continental. She liked riding along, to the Friday stock auction in Crawford, to the John Deere agency in Chadron, to Hollstein's Pack in Rushville—anywhere with a little distance to it. She would stare out the window and then, after a time, would turn to Tully and ask some little question. Did he think Mr. Shiff's wife was really his cousin? Did he know that Marlen, on a dare from the Heiting boys, had eaten six Mrs. Smith pies on the sidewalk in front of Frmka's IGA? Then a question that came sneaking closer, eyes down. Did his father ever laugh at *any*thing? Her mother said that not being unhappy is a kind of happiness, but she didn't believe it—did he? So what had his mother been like, exactly, or did he remember?

Reckless popped into Tully's head, but that didn't sound like the right word to use for your mother. He said "glamorous" instead.

"Glamorous," Ella said carefully, as if trying to fit this piece into whatever picture she already had of Tully's mother.

Tully stared down the highway. "Well, afternoons, for example, she'd read magazines and drink peppermint schnapps while taking bubble baths that went on forever. And outside the house she always wore bright-red shoes, candy-apple red, even in church." He shook his head. "And, like on her horse. She wore these chaps, like she was living in Marlboro country or something, and she'd come flying toward you, pull up short, and toss down a look that made you feel almost privileged, like it came from a movie star or someone."

Ella nodded. Her mother had told her that a son's slant toward the mother predicted his slant toward the wife, so she let a mile or two pass and said, "What else?"

"Not much. Except when my mother died, that mare actually grieved. Wouldn't eat or look anybody in the eye for days. It was the same horse we have now. Jackie, after Jackie Kennedy. My mom was always big on famous people. Named my brother after Marlon Brando, except she misspelled it." He let out a snicker. "Just like my old man to let her."

"Name your brother that or misspell it?"

Tully laughed. "Either one, I guess."

And then Ella would be staring out the window again, letting things settle, until something else occurred to her to ask.

Tully never talked to Ella about other girlfriends, and she never asked. The closest they had come to arguing was over the car he bought to replace the shot-up Continental. It was a broad-hooded Buick LeSabre. It had over 100,000 miles on it, she pointed out. It took oil and guzzled gas. She had in mind a Plymouth Horizon they'd seen with only 60,000 on it. "That was four hundred dollars more, you seem to forget," he said mildly.

But Ella, her face flushed, said, "That doesn't matter a fraction of one little bit."

Tully thought Ella believed she had a duty to make him more wholesome. He thought his job was to make her less. So, to keep her from uttering another word about, say, the notion of charity, he might lean over and nibble at the slow white curve of her neck.

Ella was slender, didn't have much of a figure, and wouldn't let a hand under her undermost clothes, but she knew how to kiss. She kissed like there was no tomorrow. In fact, she kissed better than Lori Hallick or Wendy Adams or even April Reece when you got right down to it, if only kissing was all there was to it.

Behind the Coates place, on a platform mounted at the lower end of the barn roof, there stood an apparatus that had caught April's attention: a steel drum fitted with water piping and a shower head. The stall below was floored with a wooden pallet and enclosed on three sides. By midafternoon on summer days the water in the drum would have grown pleasantly warm, and on one such afternoon Tully's father happened to lead old Jackie around the corner of the barn while Tully stood under the stream of water with April's arms locked around his neck and legs around his waist. His hands were stirruped under her hips, moving her slowly, but he stopped when his eyes met his father's.

"What?" April said.

"My old man," he said, and April followed his gaze. Tully's father was walking the old mare off toward her stable. April forced a laugh. "Guess he got an eyeful."

He had, but he hadn't. He'd averted his eyes. He'd glanced

at them, and then registered his chronic mournful look with Tully and kept walking. That was his way. He'd turned his eyes from every pretty girl Tully had ever brought around the place —every one, anyway, that Tully'd had doings with, which was something his father could always somehow detect.

As his father led the mare away, Tully out of stubbornness kept April around him, and they waddled as one into the barn, laughing, and finished up sitting on a saddle blanket still laughing and, toward the end, taking straw dust deep into their lungs. They had disengaged and stopped coughing and were listening to their own breathing when something chunked against the barn siding and then chunked again.

Tully crept over and peered through a window. His father was throwing rocks, *chunk*, pause, *chunk*, pause, *chunk*. "Work!" he yelled. "There is work to do, Tully David Coates!" He grubbed up more rocks over by the fence. "Work!" he yelled. "Work! Work! Work!" The word, repeated, seemed to slip free of its meaning—for a moment Tully thought he was listening to a foreign language.

"Jesus," April whispered, suddenly behind Tully, peeking out from behind him through the window. The rocks kept coming, and April, almost to herself, said, "Guess your dad's never going to like me now."

Tully looked past his father, stared out at the blank hills and white sky, and began to fill them in with greens, blues, an orange smiley sun.

His father kept shouting words and chucking rocks.

April said, "This is like a creepy movie."

"Just wait," Tully said. "Just wait."

He knew his father would eventually stop, and eventually his father did. He walked off, got into his pickup, and drove away, and the moment he was gone, Tully and April, as if by a spell, fell into their ease. April stood in a shaft of late sun. "Sure you got to get back to work?" she said, smiling at him there in the rich golden light.

Later in his life, if he stepped into the barn when the straw was dry and the angle of the sun just right, the feeling of this moment would come flooding back to Tully, and he would stand perfectly still so as not to lose the memory of those last simple kisses.

A few weeks later, while Tully's father and brother were off to a farm auction, a man came driving a late-model Chrysler up the long dirt drive of the Coates place. The plates said KANSAS. The man sat in the car with the windows rolled up, while his dust caught up with him and layered down over the car's shine. Then he got out and stood looking slowly around. Tully watched all this from the window of the Quonset shop where he was working on a pump shaft, honing down a new bushing for it from one too big. He switched off the grinder and walked out with a pipe wrench dangling from his hand.

"Over here!" he called out.

The man turned the wrong way. He was a big, wide-shouldered man with a stomach sloping evenly out from his chest. He looked maybe fifty. When, finally, he turned again, he seemed startled by Tully's appearance, and was looking at him in search of someone else, or so it seemed to Tully, who found himself doing the same thing with the man. Tully smiled but didn't offer his hand. "Do I know you?"

"Oh, I don't believe so," the man said. For a fat man he had delicate wrists and hands, and he had his white shirt sleeves rolled a couple of turns to show them off. From an interior pocket he withdrew a little brass case of business cards. *Mr. McC's Restaurant Supply*, they said. *Hays, Kansas. Mal McCreedy, Prop.* The man extended his hand. "McCreedy's my name."

"Tully Coates."

At these words the man's eyes laid back a little, seemed slightly less interested. He released Tully's hand and looked around.

Tully had seen this man somewhere, he was sure of it, but in some other form—in another getup, or maybe on the TV news. Tully was right-handed. The pipe wrench was in his left. He switched it and said, "Doubt if we'd have much need of restaurant supplies."

McCreedy turned and laughed drily. "Oh, no, I suppose not. Actually, I've been asked to look into the feasibility of a restaurant along Highway 20, either in Goodnight or Rushville. Using local-raised beef and chicken." He smiled. "Paying top dollar."

Tully nodded. He was no businessman, but the idea sounded half-baked.

McCreedy stared off toward the lambs and heifers. "You raise sheep and beef." He took a second look at the heifers.

"Charolais," Tully said. "We also raise some beefalo."

The man actually pressed his hands together. "Oh, perfect! Tourists would *love* ordering beefalo. How does it taste?"

"Above average," Tully said. He was wondering where these tourists would be coming from.

"*We?*" the man said, and when Tully looked confused, the man said, "I think you said, '*We* raise beefalo.' "

"Oh, yeah. My father, my brother, Marlen, and me. They're up to an auction looking for a truck to buy."

McCreedy took this in carefully. Then, nodding, already moving, he said, "How about showing me your operation?" Tully explained the cycle of backgrounding, summer pasture, and commercial feedlot, the average gain per day in each phase, but McCreedy didn't seem to be listening. He'd noticed the horse shed behind the barn. It was as if his whole mass tipped toward it. "You raise horses, too?"

"Just one," Tully said. Then, as they made for the shed, he said. "Thinking of serving horsemeat, too?"

The man didn't bother to laugh. He was walking faster. The mare was in her stall, poking her head out, curious. When McCreedy got to the fence, he slipped a hand into his pocket, brought it out cupped and empty, and made kissing noises. The mare ambled out, sniffed the empty hand, snorted into it. Then—and here a fat drop of sweat rolled coolly down Tully's ribs—the man cradled an arm around the mare's muzzle and let his fingers nibble at her nose and said in a crooning whisper, "Old Jackie, old Jackie, oh, old Jackie."

Tully became aware again of the pipe wrench in his hand. "Who are you?" he said, and the man, after just an instant, spun around wooden-faced. Tully had two shocks of recognition. One was that he *had* seen the man before, only he'd looked taller then, and not fat. Tully had been maybe five. The man had come to their place in Kansas and argued with his mother a long time out on the mud porch. The other thing Tully understood was that the eyes behind this man's wide, masklike face were Marlen's eyes.

"I'm—"

"I don't care who you are," Tully said, and moving forward, he tapped the mare's muzzle lightly with the pipe wrench, to move her back and the man away.

McCreedy threw his hands up in mock surrender. Tully followed him back to his sedan at arm's length, all the while staring at the spot on the man's head where his pink, big-pored scalp showed. But McCreedy evidently had no inkling, because when he got into his car and lowered the window by pushing a button, he said, "Your mother went with me to California, but I wasn't enough for her either," and then had the big car in reverse by the time Tully, dumbfounded, trotting close to the backing car, grasped what McCreedy was saying and, before he could think what to do, was swinging the pipe wrench into the driver's side of the windshield, shooting fine cracks everywhere through the glass and crazing the image of the man sitting behind it.

The next few days Tully slept fitfully, ate poorly, mentioned McCreedy to no one. On Saturday night, when he saw April, they drove out to Walgren Lake, where he discovered that he was a lot less interested in fooling around than she was. When she asked how come, he just shrugged. "Well, this is a scream," April said. This was a new word of hers. Everything was a scream. At first Tully had thought she might've picked it up from an old movie, but now he figured she was getting this kind of thing from her new waitressing job in Alliance, thirty miles south. She'd also begun calling everybody Slick. "Thanks, Slick," she said, for example, to Teddy Hill, whose name she knew, when they stopped off later at McCarter's Mini-Mart for snacks. They parked at the overlook and drank beer, and April tried again to get Tully's interest, but finally gave up. Tully said he guessed he just didn't feel like it. April, without hiding her annoyance, said she'd take a rain check, and Tully went home to sleep the sleep of the dead. He didn't, though. He woke up at three and lay in bed until dawn thinking up flamboyant ways of killing McCreedy, usually after looking him in the eye and saying, "It's been a scream, Slick."

It seemed to Tully that all his feelings—about his mother, his father, his own sunny life—had been pulled inside out, and the ideas released kept running around in all directions. He blamed everybody for his mother's leaving. He blamed McCreedy for being sleazy, his father for being first loud and then wimpish, his brother for being pink and obese. He blamed his mother for being bored, the farm for being boring. And he blamed himself for being pesky, for never leaving her alone, for whining outside that locked bathroom door the whole time she took her afternoon bath.

Facing things head on was not Tully's strong suit, but one day, while cultivating beans, he came across this hard little fact: What McCreedy had told him was not a revelation. It was a confirmation, a light turned on something he'd always sensed lurking off in the dark but never allowed himself to see. So this shifted things. He was not just his father's victim but his accomplice, too.

Tully began to work longer, harder; he was surprised how often barbs, thistles, and rusty metal tore at his arms. Sex, when resumed with April, was less frequent and took an angry turn. If she cried out, Tully would loosen his hold, but only just barely. At home he couldn't stop watching his father. He became resentfully aware of the way his father let Marlen or him make the lists of the day, the way he just read them and did what was written there. Tully began adding items. Ditch field three. Fence the river field. Weld the pipe trailer. His father did them all, and never said a word.

One day, at their noon meal, Tully's father was patiently cutting his pork chop into small neat pieces, cutting up his string beans, pouring a little milk on his potatoes, mashing them fine. So his wife left him, Tully thought. So what? So why didn't he just say she left and get on with it? Lots of people try to make a pissing post out of a person. That was bad. But it was worse when somebody swallowed it whole, made a life of it. Then it was pathetic.

Out of nowhere Marlen said, "Something gnawing on you?"

Tully started, turned. "Work," he thought to say. He made a grin. "More we do, more there is yet."

His father, still setting up his food, nodded without looking up. He was buttering bread now, making a project of evenness. Marlen, with exaggerated surprise, said, "Do I hear Tully moaning about work? Our very own work-hard, play-hard, sleep-hard Tully?"

"Caught me at a tired moment, is all," Tully said.

Marlen took a bite of fatty meat and said in a joking voice, "What's the matter, your pecker getting all the sleep lately?"

"Fuck you, Slick," Tully said before he could catch himself, and a change came over the table. His father set his fork down, the radio weatherman talked about highs and lows within the growing zone, and the smile on Marlen's face, when it broke, was like a dawning.

In the next few weeks Marlen seemed to feed on Tully's brooding, to come slowly to life. He worked with barbells in the basement and cut down on sweets. He walked jauntily out to his tractor, whistled while pulling ticks from the dog, sang in the shower.

It won't hurt
When I fall down off this barstool . . .

Tully knew that whether brother or half-brother, he should've been happy about this change in Marlen, but he wasn't, not at all. All he heard in Marlen's voice was a Mc-Creedylike cheeriness that just made him sourer.

"Your brother finally getting some?" April asked.

"Maybe in the ass," Tully said, and turned to April, who didn't laugh.

"You're really getting yourself an attitude," she said.

Ella put it another way. "For one full month now you've been like someone else," she said, and kept her arms folded against a little breeze. It was almost dusk. They stood near the last of her mother's garden, a few tomatoes, some soft squash. Tully sucked his molar and stared off toward a field of bleached-out vines.

"Your dad don't get those beans in soon, they'll be blowing all over the county."

After a silence Ella said, "It's like all the time I'm with somebody that looks like Tully but isn't Tully at all."

He narrowed his eyes and turned on her. "Or maybe vice versa. Maybe this is the real thing." He stared not into her eyes but just above them, at the fuzzy eyebrows. "You want to know what's got hold of me?" He wanted to tell her about McCreedy, and thought he was going to, but when he opened his mouth, he heard himself telling her instead about his father catching him and April showering together—"showering" was his one concession to her feelings. Ella turned away, and when her shoulders began to tremble, he knew she was crying. He would see later that making her cry might've been his intention, but now he said, "Ella, for chrissakes, c'mon." She turned away when he tried to face her. "Hey, you knew April and me were like that."

Ella made for the house. She stopped, though. She came

back. "I know what you do. I know what you and her do. I saw you once out by the river on top of your car, both of you thinking you were something unusually wonderful, even though it looked uncomfortable to me." She caught her breath. "So that's not it. But if what's been troubling you for a month is that your father caught you and her"—here Ella both lowered and tightened her voice—"*doing it*, then I don't want to hear about it, because you telling me something like this means you're thinking of me as your little friend, and the one thing I'm not, you . . . *birdbrain*, is your little *friend*." She must've sensed the unserious effect of "birdbrain," because for the first time her cheeks pinkened. She moved half-running toward the yard, and then her mother—what, Tully wondered, had she heard?—held open the back door, and Ella disappeared into the lighted opening of the house.

Tully saw April the next day, and again on Thursday. On Friday she was working a new shift, serving cocktails, in Alliance, and Tully was supposed to meet buddies at The Spur in Goodnight, but he didn't have the spirit for it. He tried phoning Ella, but Mrs. Smalley was screening the calls, which, he figured, was about what he deserved for going out with a girl still living at home.

Tully wandered out behind the barn, leaned against the fence, and listened to the crickets and the shush of the river on the bridge piles. He found his point of red light in the distance. He wanted to pass on his thoughts to somebody, but didn't know who. It was cool. From somewhere beyond the water came the smell of woodsmoke, and all at once the season seemed to have turned without his noticing. Tully, to his surprise, was about to start crying, when off in the dark the old mare began nickering and fidgeting.

Tully turned. There, moving along the pens toward the mare, was the outline of his father. "Dessert!" he sang out in a soft voice and rattled a paper bag. "Didja think I'd forget?"

Tully sat quiet and watched his father dip bits of squash in a small jar of molasses and feed them one by one to the old mare. When they were gone, he carefully folded the sack flat, stroked the mare's nose, and returned to the house.

What Tully did then was nothing planned out. He just walked in, went over to where his father was reading the paper, and said, "A fat, pink-faced man named McCreedy came by about a month ago."

His father's face looked as if a window shade had suddenly snapped up, showing a version of him Tully was never meant to see, a softer, younger, scareder version. After a second or so he got the shade back down. He blinked and stared evenly at Tully. "So?"

"This McCreedy said our mother didn't die in Kansas. He said she ran off with him to California."

His father's eyes slid away. In a reciting-style voice he said, "That is a lie. Your mother is dead." He laid the open newspaper across himself like a lap robe. "What did you tell Marlen?"

"Nothing. Not for me to tell."

"Nothing to tell," his father said, and closed his eyes.

It was a bad winter. It went on and on and on. Snow began in early October, and by November the downstairs windows were darkened by drifts. Blizzards came once in January and twice in March, when several calves were lost. The last blizzard was the worst. Pheasants turned into the wind and died where they stood. "Imports," said Coates, Sr.—worth noting, because in the course of the winter he all but gave up speech. He meant the pheasants weren't indigenous, had been brought in from China, couldn't cope.

He'd installed a double-drum woodstove in the Quonset, and he spent long days there repairing everything on the place that needed repair, from machinery to old chairs. The routine was slow and steady, returning something fixed and hauling off to the Quonset something broken. He never showed off his work, never looked at who was in a room. "He's like a ghost," April said one day. "Ever notice how a door doesn't make a sound when he passes through it?" Tully noticed plenty. He watched his father wearing his greasy down jacket even in the house, moving slowly from room to room, looking straight ahead with half-alive eyes. His father began to smell. Tully wished his father were one or the other, dead or alive, which he supposed was how it could get with people you were obliged to love but didn't.

Tully saw April about once a week, depending. She'd rented a place in Alliance and taken a job doing some kind of dancing. Tully didn't ask for specifics, but he could guess at its nature. He didn't see Ella. She'd once come into the bar where April danced. "She was with some farmer," April said. "It was no good, her being there. I couldn't dance at all like I like." Every night that he could Marlen went into town, where, forty pounds slimmer and in a new set of clothes, he for a time consistently drew double takes. He went to dances, he went to bars. "Call me a socializing fool," he said.

In late April the number-two and number-five alfalfa fields took a hard freeze, the block on the old Case cableless cracked, and the hydraulic on the flatbed truck began to work only sometimes. By this time Tully's father had entered a tidying phase, cleaning out the basement, his desk, the kitchen cabinets. Like Marlen, he didn't eat much, but while Marlen grew lean, Coates, Sr., just got small. He kept punching new holes in his belt—the end lolled down like the tongue of a tired dog.

April, who was driving a new Thunderbird, one night mentioned in passing that a Lebanese had married her, but strictly for immigration reasons. His name was Essa; he worked for the railroad, in management; they lived in the same house but separate rooms; and her marriage didn't mean anything needed to change between her and Tully. One day in May he saw them coming out of Gibson Discount in Alliance. Seeing her was like seeing a high school friend dressed up as an adult in the junior play. April was wearing a pantsuit. The Lebanese was in slacks and a tie, his graying hair combed straight back, smoking a cigarette and pushing a new red rotary lawn mower across the asphalt parking lot. He looked forty. "Thirty-two," April told Tully a few days later.

On the first warm day in June, Tully's father drove into town and came back with sweets. He didn't eat his supper but afterward heated Hershey's fudge sauce and put out mountainous sundaes for all three of them, Reddi-Wip, almonds, cherries, the works. He ate slowly. When he finished his, he made himself another, and when that bowl was empty, he began on the jar of maraschino cherries. He ate them one by one. Finally the cherries were gone, and his father, running his finger into the syrup at the bottom of the jar, said, "Where's the flatbed parked at?"

The next day his father rode the old mare out to work on the truck's hydraulics, rode out carrying a wooden toolbox with a wide leather strap tacked to it for a handle—like some old-fashioned country doctor, Tully imagined. When he hadn't come back by noon, Tully went out on the ATV and found him up at the river field, smashed between the frame and lift bed of the six-ton truck filled with alfalfa silage. He was unquestionably dead. The hydraulic worked when Tully tried it, but when the bed raised, all he saw was the way the scalp had moistly torn free and the way a bolt had made a neat hole in one of the broken parts of the skull. Tully lifted the body away and laid it down in the turnrow and covered the smashed-in part of it with his shirt. He stood aside then and heaved, but nothing came up. He began to hear a sound. It was the old horse, tethered to the fence by a lunge line, tail-slapping her rump for flies.

That night, after they'd taken Coates, Sr., off on a gurney, after all the telephone calls, after two of the neighbors had come with casseroles, April ended a long silence by saying, "This'll probably sound bad, but it was almost like he was already dead. This just sort of makes it official."

Tully nodded. Her words seemed right, and yet they didn't account for how sudden the final part of the process felt. "You know," he said, "all that ice cream is probably still in him."

They were out at the porch stoop, April and Marlen sitting

on it, Tully standing nearby. A mild westerly carried cotton-wood fluff, the sound of buzzing electrical wires, the smell of fermenting silage. Tully could see the relay tower if he leaned a little. He wanted to pass on some word to his father, but he had the terrible feeling that he'd lost the right to believe in that sort of thing. He leaned back and closed his eyes. His resentment of his father had slipped away—he could hardly remember what it had felt like. That didn't seem funny to him. What seemed funny was how it had been converted to taking his father as is, and that *was* funny, in two different ways: one, that the minute you took a wider view of the way your father lived was the minute you realized he was a dead man, and two, that if you'd opened up to this view sooner instead of looking askance, he might've had enough room to make a decent life in. It was all pretty disappointing.

Out of the silence Marlen said, "This is the first time in my life where I can't even begin to think right," and in that moment a feeling unlike any other Tully had ever had for Marlen welled up suddenly inside him. He reached over and laid a hand on Marlen's shoulder, began to work gently at the muscle there, felt Marlen only just slightly give himself up to it.

After another little while April stood up and said she'd like to stay longer but she had told Essa she'd be home an hour ago. Marlen stirred himself and said yeah, maybe he'd take off too. Tully went to a knoll and watched their taillights part, the Thunderbird moving west toward Highway 87 and Alliance, Marlen's big Duster heading north toward Highway 20 and Goodnight.

He walked to the tack room and took the bridle down from where his father always hung it. When he came out of the barn, somebody was there, a tall dark form, over near the cotton-wood.

"Hey," he said.

"Hey," Ella said.

Tully walked toward her, talking. "How long you been here?"

"Dunno." She ducked her head. "Not that long."

He looked around. "Where'd you park?"

"Up the way. I had a feeling she might be here."

"She married an A-rab," Tully said. "Talk about funny."

Ella nodded at the bridle. "Going somewhere?"

"For a ride, yeah." He stood staring at her. "Wanna come along?"

Ella said sure, and they were walking out toward the horse shed when she stopped. "There's one thing I have to know. I have to know if your feelings for me have gone sour."

Tully gave a low laugh and said no, he didn't think they had.

The two of them headed out for the truck. They rode bareback, the old horse rolling slowly beneath them. The moon was mostly hidden, and in the dark the rolled bales in the river field looked like sleeping sheep. "I like this," Ella said. "But how come we're doing it?"

Tully didn't answer. What he meant to do was retrace this just the way it had happened, get it straight in his mind.

When they got to the truck, Tully tied up the mare where his father had tied her. He started up the engine and tried the hydraulic. It went right up, the box tilting at forty-five degrees and holding. Tully stared at it a long time and then stepped forward to where his father had stood and, bending at the waist, leaned his head under the box. He stayed there and reached back with his left hand for the lever. It reached. It reached easy. Tully kept his hand tight around it for a second or two, thinking, and then stood up straight, stepped aside, and shot the lever back. The box slammed down fiercely, metal on metal, Tully let out a little grunt, and the truck jumped on its springs.

Tully had stood once in a circle of players up on the football field watching one of his buddies not come back to life. The silence then was like the silence now. It made loud the buzz of crickets and the blatting of a ewe. It made the world too mysterious for human beings.

Finally, Ella said, "That was horrible."

Tully kept staring at the truck. What his father had done wasn't right, he knew that, but at least it was something of his own, an act he had thought out and had completed and had taken responsibility for. His.

Ella and Tully rode back the way they came, but slower, looser-reined, the old mare with her smooth, rolling walk mostly finding her own way. When they got down along the river, Tully felt Ella behind him making some adjustment to her blouse. Then she rolled up his flannel shirt. He'd almost decided he'd misguessed her intent when he suddenly felt her bare skin against his back, and Tully was caught short at how fiercely he craved every single aspect of Ella Smalley, top to bottom, inside and out, A to Z.

Tully's firstborn was a boy. They named him Russell, after nobody. Russell Christopher Coates. When the boy was old enough, Tully would tell him bedside tales about a kid—a pistol—named R.C., who, come to think of it, looked a lot like Russell Christopher, except R.C. was left-handed, not right. This R.C. had a soapbox that took him to fairs, rodeos, and whatnot, and got its power from no one knew where; it would just keep taking him from one interesting place to another. "R.C." was a name his pals loved to call out, because it would get up in the air and carry from county to county and sometimes on cold nights from state to state, which, Tully said, would often scare the people in South Dakota. These stories would always end with R.C.'s worries melting away like peppermints, at night while he slept, an idea Tully had gotten from a Willie Nelson song. Tully himself didn't care for peppermints, but whenever he was in Scottsbluff he stocked up from Woolworths, so that last thing each night, if Russell promised not to chew it, Tully could take a peppermint from a tin and lay it on his son's tongue before saying good night.

Amy Herrick

PINOCCHIO'S NOSE

Sarah was sitting on her bed watching the moon sail high above the treetops, when a cloud, blowing suddenly out of the sky, crossed its path and threw the night into blackness.

She had been leaning on the windowsill in the oddest state of dumbness, feeling, at once, emptied and lit up, waiting maybe for some big thing. But when the moon went out, it was not at all what she was expecting. It's the end of the world, she thought, and shut her eyes tight and held her breath.

When she opened them, she saw that a little light had been switched on in the empty apartment on the top floor of the house across the way. This apartment had been sitting vacant for some months now and she had thought they didn't mean to rent it anymore. She crouched down and peered out from behind her curtains.

In a moment, a young man appeared and leaned way out of the curtainless window. Craning his neck, he searched the sky, then frowned and stepped back into the room and began to undress. He undressed hurriedly, dropping his clothes on the floor, and Sarah, who was not much used to judging and comparing the bodies of men, held her breath and watched with terrific concentration. This man was not really quite a man, but a boy, a few years older than her brother. He was of exquisite build, but rather on the small side, and when he took off his shirt he had what looked exactly like the beginnings of wings on his shoulder blades, little feathered nubs. This, she knew, ought to be the most distracting marvel, but she found that, after all, when he took off his shoes and then his pants and underpants, it was the male parts that got her. Her brother had grown modest in the last few years and she realized that it had been some time since she had viewed these things. She stared furiously. How did you reconcile their foolish, dangling appearance with the tales you heard of pursuit and wild surrender, shameless pleasure and complete disaster? As soon as he had finished undressing, the young man strode from the room and disappeared.

The moon, silver and careless, a little fingernail of a boat, slipped out from behind its cloud and sailed away across the night, while from her brother's room next door, first there came several loud bangs, followed by a series of mysterious popping sounds, and then silence.

In the morning she found that spring had arrived overnight. The dogwood tree was in full bloom and held its earnest white blossoms up to the sky like little plates. As she walked to school squirrels raced up and down fences and birds shot through the air carrying twigs and string and bits of old mattress ticking. Insects fizzed and buzzed through the yellow veils of forsythia, and the air, as it warmed up unevenly, was gold in some places and in other places blue, and, in all places, smelled complicated and delicious. She did not notice the three little boys hiding behind the privet hedge at the corner. They jumped out at her yelling and howling, and in her confusion she imagined that the ground had opened up and spit them out. She recognized them, though. They were little neighborhood boys, three or four years younger than herself, who had never paid the slightest attention to her before. They threw themselves upon her, yipping gleefully and pulled fiercely at her blouse, her skirt, her hair.

"Let go of me, you little creeps! Stop it!"

This only seemed to make them noisier and hungrier. She told herself not to panic, but they were pinching her in a peculiarly knowing way, and then one grabbed her breast and squeezed it hard between sticky little fingers, and another grabbed meanly at the inside of her thigh.

"Goose her! Goose her!" screamed the one who seemed to be the leader. He tipped his face towards her and grinned. She grabbed for one of his pointed ears which stuck out malevolently, but it slipped through her fingers. Hands tugged excitedly at the buttons of her blouse and hands scrabbled up her skirt and started determinedly to pull down her underpants. She screamed breathlessly and tried to run, but they clung to her like jellyfish, laughing horribly.

"Let go of me, you little creeps! Let go!" At this moment a girl she'd never seen before, dark-haired and about her own age, appeared down at the end of the block. This girl stood there staring for a few moments, then dropped her books and ran towards them yelling, "Hey!" She grabbed the nearest boy around the waist and pulled him off Sarah. She slapped his face once, hard, and let go of him. He scuttled back off into the privet hedge. Then she grabbed hold of the one with pointed ears and wrestled him to the ground.

Having only one to deal with now herself, Sarah was able to give him a good kick in the shins, and he went hobbling off to join the first. When Sarah turned around she saw the girl standing over the leader, waving a little pearl-handled pocketknife at him. He lay on the ground watching her in silent terror. "Just a little bit of nose for my nose collection," she said, bending toward him.

He put his hands over his nose and screamed, "No!" She

laughed and gave him a little kick and said in a raspy voice, "Get outta here." He was gone in a second.

The girl snapped the blade of her knife shut and stood staring at it fondly. Sarah stared at the girl. She was tall, almost as tall as Sarah, and had a wide and diabolical-looking mouth. She wore ballet slippers and blue jeans and her long dark hair was loose. She had a mole on her left cheek which looked distinctly fake. Sarah thought she was stunning and had a brief intimation of disaster, of how the laws of gravity and fate will suddenly grab you up and send you plummeting helplessly toward some central mystery which you want nothing to do with.

"Thank you," she said stiffly. She pulled her skirt down and buttoned her blouse. "Do you always carry a knife?" she asked in a disapproving tone.

"Certainly," the girl said. "It was a gift from my French tutor." Sarah, examining the girl sharply, saw that she was lying, and felt her own face turn red with embarrassment, as if it were she that had been caught out. The girl just laughed happily. "Which do you think is more fun, to struggle hard and receive a great reward, or have someone give you a wonderful gift you weren't expecting at all?"

Sarah, who was a hard worker and loved to ponder philosophical questions, thought for a moment and said she preferred to earn her rewards. Then, realizing this was a most peculiar conversation, and that she was certainly going to be late for school, she quickly gathered up her books, thanked the girl again, and hurried off without looking back.

Her first-period class was English, and when she had seated herself and gathered her wits, she glanced to her left and noticed that Mitchell, the small, devious redhead who sat two seats down, had grown, overnight, a pair of huge and unmanageable feet. He was trying to keep them hidden under his desk while he solemnly studied the blackboard. When she looked to her right, she was astonished to see that Hazel, who had always been a vague and unsurprising kind of girl, had, somehow, come into possession of two large and buoyant breasts. She shielded them with tender confusion inside her arms.

It's the end of the world, Sarah thought. Panicking, she checked herself over for any signs of unusual change, but wasn't able to identify anything new. At that moment, the door to the classroom opened, and the demon girl who had come to her rescue with the pearl-handled knife walked in and presented her pass and yellow card to the teacher. The teacher, Mrs. Dukofsky, an aged and dragon-faced woman, glared at these offerings as if they were the entrails of a chicken, while the class examined the new girl curiously. After a moment, she turned suddenly and raked the class with a long, defiant stare, so that the students all shuffled and murmured in their seats.

"All right, Robin," the teacher said. "Welcome. You may take the empty seat in the back, next to Sarah. Sarah will catch you up and give you the back assignments."

The girl marched down the aisle without looking right or left and slid in next to Sarah. "Call me Esmeralda," she whispered coolly, "and don't give me any back assignments."

Sarah, startled, looked directly into her eyes, which she had not meant to do. The girl gazed back at her without smiling. It was, Sarah thought, an otherworldly gaze, cruel and electrically green. Sarah determined to have nothing further to do with this girl and, in fact, decided to lie low in general for the next seven years, read books and sleep, maybe. However, when the bell rang at the end of the class, Robin leaned over and said, "God, this is some collection of boys you got here. Maybe it's something in the water."

Sarah looked around the room defensively, but realized it was true—they were not an impressive lot.

"In fact, the only decent guy I've come across since I moved into this neighborhood is my French tutor. He's quite gorgeous, but then, being French, he's not from around here."

There was something about the smug and insinuating way that she said this that infuriated her. "You should meet my brother," Sarah said.

Robin looked at her sharply. "Your brother?"

Sarah had never done such a thing before. She stood riveted to the spot, waiting for some other message from outer space to issue from her mouth, but nothing came. At last, not knowing what else to do, she said, "Yeah, he's terrifically handsome."

She knew, as soon as the words were said, that her only hope was to get out of there as quickly as possible, but before she could get her books together, the girl said, "Hey, I'm free this afternoon. How about I come over and meet your brother? You could help me with the math homework. I'm having a terrible time with the math homework."

Sarah, who had recently won a citywide math competition, said, "I'm terrible at math. You'd better ask someone else," and fled from the room.

Her brother was sitting on the front steps when she arrived home. He grabbed her ankle as she tried to pass and threw her into the grass. Then he went back to reading the newspaper and eating an apple. Next to him lay two bananas and several volumes of the encyclopedia. His plan was to know everything. She examined him from where she lay. He had a large inquisitive nose in the middle of a long mournful face, and, with his legs like a grasshopper's and his hair sticking up all over the place, he was the goofiest-looking boy she had ever seen.

"I'm doomed," she thought.

"Listen to this," he said, tapping the newspaper. "Some scientists now think that if you could compress the atmosphere enough to create a black hole, you might be able to make a new world, a junior universe that would split off from the old one like a bubble. It would exist in the same space as the first world, but in a different dimension. Theoretically you could do this in your basement."

She tried to get up on her knees and gather her books together, but he reached over with his foot and gave her another shove.

"Why is everyone bothering me?" she yelled.

He looked at her, his eyebrows raised in surprise. "What do you mean? Who else is bothering you?"

She blushed guiltily, but said nothing.

He examined her closely, then sighed. "Believe me, whatever it is, it's not a real problem. You want a real problem, look in the newspaper. Do you know how many homeless people there are in this city? Do you know this lovely green spot we're standing on, and the whole area for hundreds of miles around, will probably be a desert in twenty years if we don't do something about the ozone layer?"

Sarah managed to roll herself out of his reach and then to stand up. "Let me pass, please."

"Eh? Eh? No te comprendo." He peeled a banana and ate it down in a couple of large bites.

"LET ME PASS, PLEASE," she said loudly, in case he was going to continue to pretend he was a foreigner.

"Sarah, you know I can't let you by unless you give me some token."

"Freddy, for God's sakes, let me by. I don't have anything to give you."

He smiled at that and finished the other banana. She wanted to scream, but knew that would give him too much satisfaction.

"Okay," he said. "Just look into my eyes for a sec. That will do."

She bent over and glared into his eyes furiously. God, how she hated him.

At last he sighed and looked away.

"Well," she said sarcastically, "did you see anything?"

"Sure I did, sure. I saw that you love me with all your heart."

"What?" She stamped her foot on the ground. The still evening rang with the sound. "Be serious."

"Serious?" he said. "Serious? I am serious. Deadly serious." With that, Fred rolled over and pretended to be dead.

"Cut it out, Fred!" she screamed. But he just lay there, inert. "Okay," she said. She stepped over him and went in the house and up the stairs to her bedroom and then walked over to the window and peered out cautiously. Her brother was lying on the sidewalk in exactly the same position. He lay there looking just like a dead grasshopper.

That night, the young man across the way was wearing green pants of some soft velvety material and a white tunic. He walked to the window and stood there and looked out as if he were looking for something. Could it be me, she wondered? She held herself as still as possible and didn't breathe. He undressed slowly tonight, as if either he was very tired or he wanted to give her time to look. Because his movements were so languorous and so inviting, because she was so intent upon seeing her fill, it wasn't until he was all done and standing there stark naked, his legs slightly apart, his face tipped to the sky, that she saw his hair was on fire. He didn't seem to be bothered by this, or even to notice, and the flames appeared more playful than dangerous. Still, she was seized by an unholy desire to call out and give him warning, or maybe just to let him know she was there. Somehow, she understood this would be the worst possible thing she could do, and she grabbed the edge of the bedspread and stuffed it into her mouth. She sat like this for several minutes, resisting the urge to step out onto the soft and mud-sweetened air and walk over to him, when suddenly, there was a loud crash, and then swearing, from her brother's room. Her naked man frowned and slammed the window shut and disappeared from view.

Before English class began the next morning, Robin leaned over and asked in a husky voice if she could borrow Sarah's math homework. "I'm having trouble with a couple of the problems."

Sarah did not look at her, but answered curtly that her math homework was in her locker. At this moment Mrs. Dukofsky entered the room. Robin put a piece of gum in her mouth and heaved a sigh.

"So," said Mrs. Dukofsky, who never wasted a minute,

"where does Pandora get her name from?" They were studying Greek mythology this semester.

No one breathed. There was a general hope that before she could call on someone, a fiery pit from hell would open at her feet and she'd fall in.

Robin leaned over and placed a small note in Sarah's lap.

She didn't touch it, but it stared up at her interrogatively. "Do you think it would be better to marry young and rashly, or old and wisely?"

Sarah shoved it in her desk.

"So?" said Mrs. Dukofsky. "Who can tell me the answer? Surely someone has done the homework?"

Sarah knew she had only herself to blame for what was about to happen, but felt herself unjustly harassed and badgered from all sides.

"Sarah?" the teacher asked briskly.

Sarah blushed and looked around, but none of her classmates even glanced at her. She noted that Larry, who, as of yesterday, had always been an intelligent and unadorned person, today was wearing a metal-studded leather band on his wrist and a thunderbolt-shaped earring in his ear. Robin cautiously unwrapped another piece of chewing gum under cover of her desk, popped it in her mouth, and blinked once like a crocodile.

Sarah faced the teacher unhappily. "It means 'all gifts' because the gods each gave her some special gift when she was born."

"Good," the teacher nodded and turned away.

Sarah took the little piece of paper out and wrote on the back of it, "I shall never marry," and shoved it across to Robin without looking at her.

It was a good answer, Sarah thought, truthful and clear and to the point. She felt confident that if she kept alert, it wouldn't be hard to avoid any demon influences.

A moment later Robin passed a new note over. "I know what you mean, but I plan to marry several times. Probably three."

Sarah eyed this with distaste for several moments. When she looked up, she found that Mrs. Dukofsky, who only a second before had been standing at the front of the room, was now, somehow, planted in front of Robin's desk like an aged and hungry viper.

"Do my eyes deceive me? Are you chewing gum in my classroom?"

Robin smiled at the teacher coolly, then shrugged her shoulders.

"Now, I will tell you," said the teacher, "that when I was a girl, we weren't given a choice in such matters. However, this is a different time and place, so in this classroom I usually offer a couple of alternatives."

You are a fungus, Sarah thought.

"Either I will expect a paper tomorrow on—umm—let's say, Zeus and his taste for vengeance, or you may put that gum on your nose and wear it there for the rest of the period."

Now, no one had ever chosen the gum humiliation before, but Robin bit the inside of her cheek and seemed to consider. Then she took the gum out and, carefully rolling it into an indecent and Pinocchio-like shape, stuck it on the end of her nose. Mrs. Dukofsky stared at this coldly and then returned to her desk. The class sighed with delight.

Sarah couldn't imagine it, how anyone could embrace such an embarrassment, but Robin appeared well pleased with her bargain.

When the bell rang at the end of class, Robin took the gum off her nose and put it back in her mouth and leaned over and said, "You know what I discovered yesterday?"

Sarah, knowing that at any moment some terrible disaster was certainly going to occur, tried to gather her books together quickly. "No, I don't," she said in as discouraging a voice as she could muster.

"I discovered that my French tutor is quite rich."

"Oh," said Sarah.

Outside a persistent spring wind was rattling the windows, which Mrs. Dukofsky liked to keep tightly shut because she had a horror of pigeons getting in the room and flying around.

Sarah was having the most amazingly difficult time lifting her math book off the desk. Suddenly it seemed heavier than any earthly object ought to be.

"He's going to take me to Paris this summer."

"Why?"

"Why what?"

"Why's he taking you to Paris this summer?"

"Because Paris, my dear, is the city of love."

Sarah tried to grasp the book again, but this time it seemed to wiggle in her fingers like a cold fish, and she dropped it, startled. What had happened to the steadiness of the world? She saw, in a flash, how difficult it was going to be to be certain of anything.

At this moment, Mrs. Dukofsky sailed by them. As she went through the door, Sarah saw that someone had taped to her back a rough sketch of a fabulously proportioned naked woman. Sarah blushed deeply, but Robin merely squinted a little and smiled. "My grandfather is quite rich, actually," Sarah said.

Robin turned to her, delighted. "You're kidding! Do you think he'll leave you any money?"

Sarah tried to lift the book again, but it stayed stuck. She could not imagine what terrible thing afflicted her. "He's leaving it all to me and my brother. But it's not money exactly."

"What do you mean?"

"I mean it's diamonds and emeralds. He keeps them hidden in the house."

Robin's eyes opened wide. "Where?" she whispered.

Sarah thought for a moment. "In his salt shaker, on the kitchen table. It's one of those big ones. He keeps a little salt in it to fool people, and the rest is diamonds and emeralds. I'm the only one who knows."

"Wow," said Robin.

Now, at this moment, something or someone pushed the window open several inches and Sarah knew it was probably her grandfather who had died three years ago and left her his bird-watching binoculars. The spring wind rushed in and softened the chalky air and filled the room with the smell of the distant and central tree of the world about to break into bloom.

"What will you do with them?"

"With what?"

"All the diamonds and emeralds and stuff."

"Oh. I'll give them away. To poor people. To homeless people."

"Ah," said Robin, exhaling slowly, staring at Sarah. "You see. I knew I was right. From the moment I looked at you I knew you were a person of substance, someone who understood what was important. I'm an airhead, a cream puff. You can help me look the sorrows of the world in the eye. How about I come over after school today? We can do the math homework together and talk. You can introduce me to your brother."

Sarah could have sworn that the mole on her cheek had moved up several inches since yesterday. "My brother has basketball practice today," Sarah said, although her brother viewed all organized sports with suspicion and disdain and had never touched a basketball in his life. At this moment her math book came free of the desk. She grabbed it up and, not looking at Robin, fled from the room.

She went into her brother's room that night just to check and see if there might not have been some slight improvement which could give her cause for hope. She saw, with dismay, that he looked more preposterous than ever. Over his usual careless attire he was wearing one of their mother's flowered aprons, and, as he bent solemnly over some little jars on his windowsill, his nostrils fully and horsily dilated to sniff some scent. He was a great sniffer.

"Are you gardening?" she asked.

He eyed her broodily without answering. His room, as always, looked like a band of gypsies had just left by the window after first scattering shoes and dirty dishes, mysterious toys, and books of literature on every conceivable subject.

"What's that stuff on the windowsill?" she tried again.

"I can't tell you."

"Tell me."

"Wild strawberries couldn't drag it out of me."

She shrugged and turned to leave.

"All right, all right. I'll tell you. But you gotta cross your little tooth fairy's heart and hope to die if you ever tell a soul."

"Okay," she said, feigning immense indifference.

He rubbed his nose and considered for a moment. "Well, what it is, is I'm searching for the origins of life."

"What?"

"I'm starting from scratch, and so I got several different mediums going here. I got sand, I got seawater. I got clay, and I got my favorite—dust balls. Now you think about all the cruelty and madness and sorrow in the world. You think about all the pollution and the dolphins washing up on the beach. Think about nuclear bombs and the ozone layer and military spending, and then tell me you think it wouldn't be a good idea to start over fresh."

It's true, she said to herself. It's time I knew about these things. But no sooner had she tried to picture one of them in her mind than it got jumbled up with the next, and, furthermore, when she thought about the jars on the windowsill, she knew it was perfectly possible he was pulling her leg. She tried to step closer to the windowsill to get a better look, but he blocked her way.

"My God," he said. "What's happened to you?"

"What?" she said nervously and tried to back up, but he was much too fast for her. He reached for her arm and, pulling her closer, scrutinized her face craftily. "You look different."

"I do not."

"Yes you do." He dragged her over to his dresser mirror and pointed. "Look. You got a funny shine on you or something— like you stuck your nose in a light socket. What is it?"

"Cut it out. I look exactly the same as always," she said, but seeing the two of them together in the mirror, she was outraged to observe how clear it was that they were brother and sister. "Let go of me."

"Is it a boy?" he asked incredulously, as if a boy were something he was not, as if boys were not seen much around these parts. "It's a boy, isn't it? Oh, the rush and pickle of time. Why just yesterday you were a little girl hanging upside down on the monkey bars with your dress floating around your head."

"Let go," she said and slapped at him furiously, but hit only air.

She could think of a hundred other people she'd met in books or movies who would have made perfect siblings, but the stars had gathered them up out of the primordial slosh of creation and thrown them out of the sky shackled together. He danced at the other end of the room like a tremendous Rumplestiltskin, grinning and waving his garden trowel, and unless she could find some way to dissolve him back into the dust and mud from whence he'd come, she was doomed.

In the night she was awakened by the sound of singing. It was difficult to tell if it was coming from far away or near, as it was very dark and the singing was so unlike anything she'd ever heard before. For a while she was afraid to move, so she just lay there listening, as if maybe these were the last sounds she was going to hear. She would have thought the singing was quite sad if it didn't also seem so very unhuman as to probably not understand about sadness.

When she finally got up, she looked out the window and knew right away that the singing was coming from the dogwood tree in the back of the yard. It was hard to tell if it was just one voice or many, but she rather thought it was many, that each bud about to split itself open was singing of a terrible and true sorrow of the world. In spite of the fact that the sing-ing was mostly sad, it was the most spellbinding music she'd ever heard. She was just trying to figure out why this might be so when a light went on across the way, and the window was thrown open, and her naked man leaned out.

"Give it a rest, for God's sakes," he yelled.

For a moment, the tree, as if offended, fell silent. Then it gathered itself together and continued on. Sarah was filled with the most mysterious feeling of confidence and elation, as if it were not a done thing yet, but any minute now she was going to solve a big riddle which would give her the power she needed.

The man bent down to the floor and picked up a shoe. He leaned way out and, with all his strength, threw the shoe. It hit the tree with a soft "chonk" and dropped to the ground. This time the tree fell silent and, maintaining an injured and inno-cent air, stayed silent. The man eyed it suspiciously, but it didn't make a peep.

Sarah, knowing full well that she shouldn't, that she mustn't, her heart pounding with fear, leaned out the window and said, "Hello."

He jumped as if stuck from behind with some little sharp object and then stared at her outraged. "How dare you?" he said. "Have you no shame?"

She thought this was odd since it was he who was naked and not herself. But before she could say anything further, he leaped onto the windowsill and, gathering himself for a big jump, flew, his wingspread alarming now, up into the ailanthus tree. He seemed to sit there for a moment getting his bearings, hissing like a swan. Then he took off into the night.

In the morning she looked out the window and searched the trees for a glimpse of him. The sun shone brightly and the air was still and warm, but he was nowhere to be seen. She looked down and saw Robin sitting on the fence across the street watching her house. Spotting Sarah in the window, she waved excitedly. Any minute now, her brother would go bounding out the front door, and there it would be, the final disaster. There was nothing to do but go down and tell her the truth. She dressed more quickly than she had ever done before, grabbed her books, raced down the stairs, out the front door, and across the street. She came to an awkward halt in front of Robin and grabbed her by the arm. "Come on, I've got something to tell you, but not here."

It was the kind of morning in which anything might be true. A mockingbird, delirious with spring, sang like water sings when it is rushing over stones, and the air felt like the kind of silk Sarah would have preferred to use for her wedding pajamas if, after all, she decided to get married. Even as they walked by them, unidentifiable green shoots opened themselves up into daffodils, tulips, and hyacinths (the same tender blue as the sky). Sarah tried to keep her eyes on the tops of the trees, especially the white-blooming pears where it would be easy to camouflage a pair of wings.

At the end of the block, they spotted, huddled inside a forsythia bush, the same little thugs who had ambushed them the other day. Robin opened her knife and Sarah grabbed a big stick. They strode forward brandishing their weapons and the forsythia bush trembled and shook, and the little boys stayed right where they were.

When they were safely past them, Robin said, "Which do you think is the more powerful force—sex? or friendship?—I mean, in the long run?"

Sarah looked at her admonishingly. She might have been inexperienced, but she was not naïve. "Why sex, of course."

Robin laughed. "Well, what was it you wanted to tell me?"

Sarah cleared her throat. A robin flew so close by, she could have reached out and taken the worm from his beak. "It's about my brother . . ."

"Yes?"

"He's dead."

"What?"

"It's true. He was hit by a car on his way home from school yesterday."

"Oh my God, I'm so sorry." Robin, however, did not look at all sorry. She was studying Sarah hard, as if taking her measure for the first time. They were passing, at this moment, a bed of flame-colored tulips. Robin stopped and embraced her and said, "Let's sit down here." She pulled Sarah down into the tulips, then covered her own face with her hands. She seemed to be working herself up to something and, in a moment, she began to sob.

Sarah was distressed. "Oh, please don't cry. He wasn't a very nice person anyway. I wasn't at all fond of him."

"No, no," Robin sobbed. "It's not your brother I'm crying about, it's my French tutor."

"What's wrong with him?" Sarah asked suspiciously.

"He's gone."

Confused for a moment, Sarah turned and stared up at the trees again. "Who's gone?"

"My French tutor. I told you. I found a note this morning saying he'd been called away on a special assignment. Very hush-hush. He's a spy, I think. He could be gone for years. He could get killed."

Now Sarah gazed around at the tulips which seemed to flank them protectively, holding themselves slender and erect as young soldiers.

"I'll search for him everywhere. I'll go to the ends of the earth."

At this moment Sarah saw her brother turn the corner down at the end of the block.

"Let's go," she said to Robin urgently. But Robin didn't move. Sarah looked at her imploringly and then down at her brother heading towards them. My God, what was he wearing today? He had on the strangest hat she'd ever seen. It looked like a beanie with an antenna on top. And what was even more inexplicable was that he was bouncing a basketball down the sidewalk.

She held her breath and waited for the darkness to come and the stars to rain down on their heads. But, of course, they didn't. Her brother threw the ball into the air and it flew up through the forsythia and up through the pear blossoms as high as it could into the steady spring light and then it fell back to the sidewalk with a nice "plonk."

Robin, hearing the basketball, turned and squinted in his direction. "Oh, my God. What is that?"

Sarah wanted to sink into the sidewalk and disappear, but there was no avenue of escape that she could see, and Fred came bouncing toward them. When he drew level with them he stopped. He stopped and stared as if they were the ones from outer space and not he. Sarah closed her eyes hopelessly and waited to hear what mortifying thing he would have to say.

But Fred didn't say anything. After studying them for a minute as if he were making botanical observations, he merely said, "Morning, ladies," and tipped his hat. Then he threw the ball into the air again, caught it, and continued dribbling on his way.

Sarah, drunk with relief, watched his back as he galumphed away, tall and extremely disheveled, his shirt half in and half out, his jeans unrolling around his ankles, his hair mashed down by his absurd hat. He was, no doubt, trying to electrify his brain with moon rays.

"Do you know him?" Robin asked in a whisper.

"No," Sarah swallowed.

"I thought he acted like he knew you."

"Yeah, well, I know him a little. He lives on my block."

"My God. What's his name?"

"His name? His name is Ralph."

"Ralph?"

"Yeah."

"Is he brilliant or something?"

Sarah eyed her uneasily and realized now that Robin's mole had disappeared. "That's what *he* says."

"He's gorgeous."

Sarah stared at her. She made a face around the word as if it were a pebble that had appeared quite by magic in her mouth. "Gorgeous?" she whispered.

Whether Robin, a girl about her own age and height, from the same planet and historical epoch, was seeing Fred with completely different eyes than her own, or whether this was a stupendous act of kindness, delivered up to ease her humiliation because she knew perfectly well this was Sarah's brother, there was no way of knowing. Fred was gone.

"You'll introduce me," said Robin.

Sarah stared at her impassively. "Show me the math problems you're having trouble with," she said.

Robin took her math homework out and showed it to her. It had been done with stunning incompetence. Sarah took a deep breath and was about to begin at the beginning when a window flew open behind them.

"You girls! What are you doing in that tulip bed? Get out of there at once!"

They rose hastily, grabbing their books, and tumbled out onto the sidewalk.

"What were you looking for when I saw you standing in the window?" Robin asked.

Sarah sighed, seeing that they were going to be friends till the end of the world, and the end of the world was nowhere in sight. A little wind blew the pear trees which seemed, for one moment, full of winged men, and the next moment stood empty.

Murray Pomerance

DECOR

(1)

"Listen," Trudy Kay had Ettie Savage on the telephone and she was breathing somewhat more forcefully than normal. "About your living room. You'll remember I was talking to you the other day. I want you to know I haven't forgotten. I've been thinking. I've been turning it over in my mind. We've got to do something about that room. We absolutely have to. Do you know what it's like now? It's depressing. I get depressed when I go in there. It's cramped and tight and you can't figure out where anything is. Do you remember when we were designing it with Ed? Do you remember? The whole idea was to have *space*—" After saying *space* she paused and gave a forceful breath, as though to create space over the telephone. Then, when all Ettie could do was insert a tiny "Well," she carried on: "The furniture. We have to do something about the furniture. Because nobody in his right mind can find a place to sit down. And I'll tell you another thing, there aren't enough ashtrays, but that's something else. But you have to be able to sit *down*. I don't know how you can live there. I don't understand where you sit. It was originally intended—don't you remember what Ed originally intended?—there'd be plenty of incidental activity going on, but I don't know how you can do it. Everybody's afraid to sit. *I'm* afraid to sit. Ed didn't expect people would be burning holes in the sofa with their cigarettes or cutting holes with scissors or letting the dogs do their, you know, *business* on the chairs. You know . . . And the piano, you see what I mean? The piano. And the plants. And the pictures. It's all gone wrong, it's all gone meshugge. You know what I mean, meshugge?" Ettie coughed a little, in a genteel fashion although she knew perfectly well how to avoid gentility. "I can't believe you like it that way. Tell me. You like having everything all over the place? Because *I* couldn't tolerate it. *I* just die when I'm in that kind of situation. Robert Keneally's coming out. He comes out, you know. He's coming out anyway so I thought I'd just get hold of him and we'd go over the place with a fine-tooth comb. If you're talking decoration there isn't anybody else, I'm sure you know that. Trust me. He'll take one look at your place and it'll be pure creativity." When Ettie put the phone down and looked around the room it seemed fine, it was as it always had been, so she thought she'd better have a look with her glasses but trying under all the magazines she couldn't find them.

(2)

On a day when there was nobody in the house, and when the dogs had been boarded and the plants watered and the bird feeders on the patio filled to capacity, Trudy Kay gained access to the house. She rolled into the graveled drive in her 1971 Ford Fairmont with the clutch that stuck. She waited. A 1979 Honda Civic rolled in after her, as gray as the gray translucent sky. Robert Keneally got out. He wore maple-colored corduroy trousers, a burgundy velour shirt, a pair of slippers. They stood for long minutes in the graveled drive and she pointed and he nodded and she pointed up at the yawning oak trees and he looked away. They came into the house as though perhaps she would sell it to him—"Isn't it wonderful?" "Isn't it spacious?" —and his eyes were rolling over the hibiscus and the poinsettia and the tumbling jades, the spreading lawns of violets, the Boston ferns blocking the light like jungle growth. She gave him the long tour, so that before they arrived at the living room they passed all of the bedrooms, and the four baths, and the study, and the parlor, the kitchen, the basement, the wine cellar, the sauna, and the nook where breakfast could be taken beneath a poster of a Toulouse-Lautrec. "Ahhh," said Robert Keneally, "Yes, yes, yes, yes, yes, yes, yes."

(3)

Next to the living room, and six steps above it, was a parlor, and in the parlor were picture windows, and through the picture windows drizzled a light that was even and melancholy and blue. Robert Keneally stood there for long minutes, turning his face from the window to gaze around the high, small room. The room filled him with a sense of pleasure. Then he stepped down the stairs to the lower space, where in the corner there was a canvas by Willem de Kooning and a Steinway concert grand on the lid of which two dying pink amaryllidaceous flowers sat. He ran his hand over the surface of the piano, ebony, needing polish. "I think," he said softly, "This . . . there." And his aquiline nose and eyes as dark as coals gave onto the parlor. "Where the window is." He stepped away, and stepped back, and stepped away. "With the keyboard . . . against . . . the window." Trudy Kay was watching every move he made. It did not occur to her that there was a dancer in him. "Against the wall? You mean against the wall? All the way over there?" He lowered his voice as she waited and his answer rang out in the silence like an incantation. "The window," he moved back and forth along the keyboard, "is here, you see. Here. The keys . . . are beside . . . the window . . . in the window light . . ."

(4)

She sat herself on the sofa that would need to be recovered, that had cigarette burns and puncture wounds from scissors all over its surface, and over the top of the television listings from the *Times* she scanned the wall where he was standing. There was the de Kooning, and then a Prohaska, and then a Motherwell and a Dash and a very small thing by Lee Krasner. "You know," she said, and her voice had an insistent buzz, "I don't know why, but that wall doesn't do a lot for me. I think the paneling can go." Beneath the row of paintings, glowing in the late afternoon light, was paneling. "I think the paneling can go because, search me, it doesn't give me that satisfying feeling. Do you know what I mean, Robert?" He was moving very quietly with a folding ruler. He had the ruler folded out to six feet. He was using it vertically and horizontally on the wall in question. To no one in particular he murmured, "Bookshelves." "Brilliant!" she said. "Bookshelves would be very nice. And I think the paneling goes, wouldn't you say? It definitely doesn't speak up for itself." Keneally moved his ruler. "Why?" his voice was softer than ever, directed only at himself although he stared at her while he spoke. "Why? We're covering with bookshelves. If we're covering with bookshelves why play with the paneling?" And she thought for a moment, squinted up her wrinkled eyelids, lit herself a cigarette and puffed it zealously. "It's just me, you see. My idiosyncratic taste. But in my place when I did the walls I used rosewood, not this stuff, and my walls have stood up considerably better than these if you ask me. But rosewood does that, doesn't it, Robert—stands up? Tell me, don't you adore this ceiling?—" He was moving slowly around the room, squinting at the windows, placing the extended ruler along the fronts of the chairs and whispering to himself. "Robert, don't you think this ceiling's marvelous? Ed didn't come up with that on his own, you know. Do you know who suggested that to Ed?" He looked at her openly. "Me," she said, "It's one of the only things in this place that hasn't gone to the dogs, if you'll pardon the expression. I'll tell you, Robert," she doused the cigarette, "The more I think about it the more I'm convinced—that wall has to go. It's an eyesore. You walk in here and you look at it and immediately you want to leave." He was moving along the wall in question, skimming the air with his finger. "Bookshelves . . . here . . . I think . . . ," and his palm was clasping and unclasping itself over the surfaces of the Krasner, the Dash, the Motherwell, the Prohaska, the de Kooning. "An original de Kooning—my God!" Then Trudy Kay gave a peremptory little sigh and spoke with a wheeze that was sinister. "Robert—although I have to admit the bookshelves are brilliant, I have to say: one way to look at this is that you're solving the books problem. And the other way—is that you're creating the pictures problem. Isn't life delicious!"

(5)

"You'd think," said Trudy Kay, "she'd keep some crackers here. I'm fainting. All she has is saltines. What's saltines when you're fainting? You'd think she'd have some decent cheese biscuits. Do you suppose she has any cheese? If I have to eat saltines there might at least be some cheese. She probably hasn't bought any cheese in months. The refrigerator is probably full of exotic cheeses she bought three months ago. You see, it's that kind of a family, Robert. We're trying to get the living room right for a bunch of people who sit around eating saltines.

Do you see what I'm trying to say? See, we could do the kitchen over again, too. There'd have to be a new refrigerator and new cupboards. The oven I know she put in just last year. We'd have to take the counters apart completely. You know it doesn't take much, sometimes I think even if I had a little piece of cheddar I'd be satisfied."

(6)

He had wanted to make a map on a piece of paper that had blue lines and he had asked her for a pencil. "Pencils everywhere and none of them have a point," she said. "Isn't it perfect? Isn't it exactly what you'd expect? That's how they live here, without pencils." So she had gone out to her car to get him a pencil and in the silence he had taken himself to the windows that gave onto the patio. There was an aviary of sorts out there. The cherry trees, the wild pear, were laden heavily with feeders, and the pine was heavy with feeders, and the birds were fluttering and jousting from perch to perch in the silvery light that was shooting in shafts through the branches. He did not know how to name them, but the artist's eye in him was held unmeasuring and shuddering with joy at the manifold finches, the gold finches and purple finches; and the reckless blue jays swooping and scattering; and the cowbirds who strutted haphazardly; the grackles who poked; the crows poking with the grackles; the indigo buntings, one turned fully turquoise and one molting; the cardinals, male and female, singing from flaming beaks, "Chew, chew"; the doves swirling along the patio pave like aging waltzers at the Waldorf; woodpeckers pecking at suet and orioles with blazing wings and tawny-breasted towhees, black-capped chickadees, proud and prancing pheasants craning their ringed necks both curious and terrified, terrified and curious as they caught his eye and strode away. There were a dozen garbage pails, battered, some lettered so that he could read them: "Bird mix," "Blk sunflr sds,"

"Thistle sds," "Cracked seed," "Millet," and others in a row behind now, as a cloud moved, shining with a radiance of pure silver. "The money they must have to do this!" he whispered to himself, and he held a great sigh within his chest, and then she was back with a pencil from the car but it turned out to have no point so he was reduced to using a pen with blue ink to make lines on the paper already covered evenly with lines that were blue.

(7)

As he sketched, Robert Keneally hummed. He hummed "Top Hat" and "S'wonderful, S'marvelous That You Should Care for Me," and then "Cheek to Cheek" with a little shift of his hips. Trudy Kay took his place at the window and gawked at the birds feeding. "Isn't it something, those blue jays?" she was rather loud. "They're such criminals. He's got them all over, you know. The property is covered with them. Did you know— he's a naturalist. He's always been that way. Well, you can see by all the trees. Look at that blue jay! The blue jays are just pigs, you know, they just dive in and eat everybody else's food. I'll tell you what I think—if ever there was a bird who couldn't mind his own business, it's the blue jay. Look, look—" she was cackling, "They take from everybody!" The decorator was standing back from the scene of his imaginary creation to a moment of imaginary evaluation. His eyes screwed tight. His fingers spread out in front of him. He paused and took a slender cigarette and inserted it between his lips. "Mmmm," he said. "It's going to be lovely." And he moved, ahead, back, to the side, ahead, back, to the side, and his hands were limp at his sides, and he seemed to know where the paintings would be rebirthed and to see the wall covered with books and the furnishings reestablished. "Do you know what I have?" said Trudy Kay. "I have sparrows."

(8)

They had moved out to where the cars were parked and were conferring a last time on the gravel. "Let me tell you what I think we should do, Robert," she said. "I'm honestly not exaggerating, not that I would ever exaggerate, but I really do get a sense from the place . . . and you have to remember I know what Ed had in mind when he did the original designs, I mean, I know everything . . . that it should be . . . another place altogether. The two of them had a long conference with Ed, believe me, and I was there for all of it. Because who do you think brought Ed in in the first place? Who do you think got them Ed?" He looked into her eyes. "Right. Because we go back a long way, Ed and I. We go back to Provincetown." "My God," he said softly. "Sure—we go back to Provincetown, and you know what it was like in *those* days. So I made the connection for him. Well, I made it for all of them. And I know what they were talking about. I understand the spirit of the thing. You know what I mean by spirit, Robert. That wall, the paneling, really should go. Really. The whole damned thing, once and for all. And we'll do the bookshelves, which is your idea. It's a terrific idea, Robert. We'll do the bookshelves. And then we'll put the piano somewhere out of the way, maybe in the parlor. But, you know; we'll have to leave the parlor window free because they let the dogs in and out there. You know they have dogs—I'm sure I told you. Little dogs. Pekingese or Balinese or terriers or something. They're coming in and out all day long. A thing like that would drive me crazy. I'll tell you what else. We could think about redoing the floor, because I'm not wild about the floor she's got in there if you want to know the truth. The dogs are always, you know, crapping on it and the whole thing is just generally out of the question. And the more I think about it the more I'm convinced we should take that paneling out and maybe—we're getting pretty adventuresome here, Robert—expand the room outwards over the patio. Do you know what I mean, on the far side, where he's got that bird stuff? Because the only thing out there is the birds, you know. We can dispense with them if we have to. It's just blue jays, isn't it? They'll find somewhere else to eat. Or we could relocate the whole thing, the feeders and everything, inside the garage, a kind of bird schmooze-house. That would be charming. And it would give us double the living room. Can you imagine the view! See, Robert—do you know how long I've known Ettie? Thirty-five years. That's a hell of a long time." "It certainly is," he whispered. "That's a hell of a long time and I know the way she thinks. You have to respect the way a person thinks, that's my bottom line. I'll tell you how she thinks. She's not happy with this. She tells everybody she's happy because she doesn't want to upset—him. Because why? Because he's very sensitive. I should have told you, maybe it's not very important, but he's sensitive. She's never for a minute been happy with the kitchen and she doesn't like the piano down there. Since the piano's down there she never plays it anymore. She used to play it all the time. And the blue jays—they're driving her crazy. She wants shelves for books. That was a fabulous idea, Robert, really. But fundamentally she's not happy, she's not fulfilled, which is my bottom line. She wants space, that's what she wants. She wants freedom. I think if we could just clean the place out and start over again she'd be a lot happier." He saw what she meant. He took his piece of blue-lined paper on which he'd made a blue map and he folded it and stuffed it in his hip pocket. He gently touched the handle of the door of his car. "Do you really want to know what I think of that paneling?" she was half turning away from him, lowering her voice so that no creature hiding in the trees could overhear. "How long did I say I've known them, thirty-five years? For thirty-five years every time I go into that room I think I'm at a funeral."

(9)

Their two cars were parked beside one another on the gravel driveway, the driveway shaped like a half moon that opened doubly onto the street. Her car was facing one direction, his was facing the other. At the steering wheels, with their windows down, they could be conversing in a kind of intimacy. "Robert—you'll let me handle it with her, right? There's no need at this level for you to be getting involved. I've known her for thirty-five years." They drove away from one another and he mused as he drove along the majestic dunes that it was, in all truth, one of the most beautiful houses he'd ever seen. He put a cigarette to his lips. He thought about an interesting new design for bookshelves that would let the magnificent paneling glow through.

(10)

Ettie stood in a still posture with Doc at the window while the finches and orioles and doves quibbled for their food and the scrambling dogs yelped with joy to be home from the kennel, and while Trudy Kay, in her bathtub, dreamed of pulling out the garden Ettie had planted and replacing it with Japanese bonsai, and while Keneally made careful drawings of the grand piano by the blue window light of the parlor, guiding his hand in a meticulous silence but hearing in his thoughts Ettie sitting at the keys and playing, perhaps from memory on a sombre afternoon, Chopin.

Joyce Carol Oates

WHY DON'T YOU COME LIVE WITH ME IT'S TIME

The other day, it was a sunswept windy March morning, I saw my grandmother staring at me, those deep-socketed eyes, that translucent skin, a youngish woman with very dark hair as I hadn't quite remembered her who had died while I was in college, years ago, in 1966. Then I saw, of course it was virtually in the same instant I saw the face was my own, my own eyes in that face floating there not in a mirror but in a metallic mirrored surface, teeth bared in a startled smile and seeing my face that was not my face I laughed, I think that was the sound.

You're an insomniac, you tell yourself: there are profound truths revealed only to the insomniac by night like those phosphorescent minerals veined and glimmering in the dark but coarse and ordinary otherwise, you have to examine such minerals in the absence of light to discover their beauty: you tell yourself.

Maybe because I was having so much trouble sleeping at the time, twelve or thirteen years old, no one would have called the problem insomnia, that sounds too clinical, too adult and any-

way they'd said "You can sleep if you try" and I'd overheard
"She just wants attention—you know what she's like" and I
was hurt and angry but hopeful too wanting to ask, But what
am I like, are you the ones to tell me?

In fact, Grandmother had insomnia too—"suffered from insomnia" was the somber expression—but no one made the connection between her and me. Our family was that way: worrying that one weakness might find justification in another and
things would slip out of containment and control.

In fact, I'd had trouble sleeping since early childhood but I
had not understood that anything was wrong. Not secrecy nor
even a desire to please my parents made me pretend to sleep, I
thought it was what you do, I thought when Mother put me to
bed I had to shut my eyes so she could leave and that was the
way of releasing her though immediately afterward when I was
alone my eyes opened wide and sleepless. Sometimes it was
day, sometimes night. Often by night I could see, I could dis-
cern the murky shapes of objects, familiar objects that had lost
their names by night as by night lying motionless with no one
to observe me it seemed I had no name and my body was
shapeless and undefined. The crucial thing was to lie motionless, scarcely breathing, until at last—it might be minutes or it
might be hours, if there were noises in the house or out on the
street (we lived on a busy street for most of my childhood in
Hammond) it would be hours—a dark pool of warm water
would begin to lap gently over my feet, eventually it would
cover my legs, my chest, my face . . . what adults called
"sleep" this most elusive and strange and mysterious of experi-
ences, a cloudy transparency of ever-shifting hues and textures
surrounding tense islands of wakefulness so during the course
of a night I would sleep, and wake, and sleep, and wake, a
dozen times, as the water lapped over my face and retreated
from it, this seemed altogether natural, it was altogether desir-
able, for when I slept another kind of sleep, heavily, deeply,
plunged into a substance not water and not a transparency but
an oozy lightless muck, when I plunged down into that sleep

and managed to wake from it shivering and sweating with a pounding heart and a pounding head as if my brain trapped inside my skull (but "brain" and "skull" were not concepts I would have known, at that time) had been racing feverishly like a small machine gone berserk it was to a sense of total helplessness and an exhaustion so profound it felt like death: sheer nonexistence, oblivion: and I did not know, nor do I know now, decades later, which sleep is preferable, which sleep is normal, how is one defined by sleep, from where in fact does "sleep" arise.

When I was older, a teenager, with a room at a little distance from my parents' bedroom, I would often, those sleepless nights, simply turn on my bedside lamp and read, I'd read until dawn and day and the resumption of daytime routine in a state of complete concentration, or sometimes I'd switch on the radio close beside my bed, I was cautious of course to keep the volume low, low and secret and I'd listen fascinated to stations as far away as Pittsburgh, Toronto, Cleveland, there was a hillbilly station broadcasting out of Cleveland, country-and-western music I would never have listened to by day. One by one I got to know intimately the announcers' voices along the continuum of the glowing dial, hard to believe those strangers didn't know *me*. But sometimes my room left me short of breath, it was fresh air I craved, hurriedly I'd dress pulling on clothes over my pajamas, and even in rainy or cold weather I went outside leaving the house by the kitchen door so quietly in such stealth no one ever heard, not once did one of them hear *I will do it: because I want to do it* sleeping their heavy sleep that was like the sleep of mollusks, eyeless. And outside: in the night: the surprise of the street transformed by the lateness of the hour, the emptiness, the silence: I'd walk to the end of our driveway staring, listening, my heart beating hard. *So this is—what it is!* The ordinary sights were made strange, the sidewalks, the streetlights, the neighboring houses. Yet the fact had no consciousness of itself except through *me*.

For that has been one of the principles of my life.

And if here and there along the block a window glowed from within (another insomniac?), or if a lone car passed in the street casting its headlights before it, or a train sounded in the distance, or, high overhead, an airplane passed winking and glittering with lights, what happiness swelled my lungs, what gratitude, what conviction, I was utterly alone for the moment, and invisible, which is identical with being alone.

Come by any time dear, no need to call first my grandmother said often, *Come by after school, any time, please!* I tried not to hear the pleading in her voice, tried not to see the soft hurt in her eyes, and the hope.

Grandmother was a "widow": her husband, my step-grandfather, had died of cancer of the liver, when I was five years old.

Grandmother had beautiful eyes. Deep-set, dark, intelligent, alert. And her hair was a lovely silvery-gray, not coarse like others' hair but finespun, silky.

Mother said, "In your grandmother's eyes you can do no wrong," she spoke as if amused but I understood the accusation.

Because Grandmother loved me best of the grandchildren, yes and she loved me best of all the family, I basked in her love as in the warmth of a private sun. Grandmother loved me without qualification and without criticism which angered my parents since they understood that so fierce a love made me impervious to their more modulated love, not only impervious but indifferent to the threat of its being withdrawn . . . which is the only true power parents have over their children. Isn't it?

We visited Grandmother often, especially now she was alone. She visited us. Sundays, holidays, birthdays. And I would bicycle across the river to her house once or twice a week, or drop in after school, Grandmother encouraged me to bring my friends but I was too shy, I never stayed long, her happiness in my presence made me uneasy. Always she would prepare one of my favorite dishes, hot oatmeal with cream and brown sugar, apple cobbler, brownies, fudge, lemon custard tarts . . . and I sat and ate as she watched, and, eating, I felt hunger, the hunger was in my mouth. To remember those foods brings the hunger back now, the sudden rush of it, the pain. In my mouth.

At home Mother would ask, "Did you spoil your appetite again?"

The river that separated us was the Cassadaga, flowing from east to west, to Lake Ontario, through the small city of Hammond, New York. After I left, aged eighteen, I only returned to Hammond as a visitor. Now everyone is dead, I never go back.

The bridge that connected us was the Ferry Street bridge, the bridge we crossed hundreds of times, Grandmother lived south of the river (six blocks south, two blocks west), we lived north of the river (three blocks north, one and a half blocks east), we were about three miles apart. The Ferry Street bridge, built in 1919, was one of those long narrow spiky nightmare bridges, my childhood was filled with such bridges, this one thirty feet above the Cassadaga, with high arches, steep ramps on both sides, six concrete supports, rusted iron grillwork, and neoclassical ornamentation of the kind associated with Chicago Commercial architecture, which was the architectural style of Hammond generally.

The Ferry Street bridge. Sometimes in high winds you could feel the bridge sway, I lowered my eyes when my father drove us over, he'd joke as the plank floor rattled and beneath the rattling sound there came something deeper and more sinister, the vibrating hum of the river itself, a murmur, a secret caress against the soles of our feet, our buttocks and between our legs so it was an enormous relief when the car had passed safely over the bridge and descended the ramp to land. The Ferry Street bridge was almost too narrow for two ordinary-sized automobiles to pass but only once was my father forced to stop about a quarter of the way out, a gravel truck was bearing down upon us and the driver gave no sign of slowing down so my father braked the car, threw it hurriedly into reverse and backed up red-faced the way we'd come and after that the Ferry Street bridge was no joke to him, any more than it was to his passengers.

The other day, that sunny gusty day when I saw Grandmother's face in the mirror, I mean the metallic mirrored surface downtown, I mean the face that had seemed to be Grandmother's face but was not, I began to think of the Ferry Street bridge and since then I haven't slept well seeing the bridge in my mind's eye the way you do when you're insomniac, the images that should be in dreams are loosed and set careening through the day like lethal bubbles in the blood. I had not known how I'd memorized that bridge, and I'd forgotten why.

The time I am thinking of, I was twelve or thirteen years old, I know I was that age because the Ferry Street bridge was closed for repairs then and it was over the Ferry Street bridge I went, to see Grandmother. I don't remember if it was a conscious decision or if I'd just started walking, not knowing where I was going, or why. It was three o'clock in the morning. No one knew where I was. Beyond the barricade and the DETOUR— BRIDGE OUT signs, the moon so bright it lit my way like a manic face.

A number of times I'd watched with trepidation certain of the neighborhood boys inch their way out across the steel beams of the skeletal bridge, walking with arms extended for balance, so I knew it could be done without mishap, I knew I could do it if only I had the courage, and it seemed to me I had sufficient courage, now was the time to prove it. Below the river rushed past slightly higher than usual, it was October, there had been a good deal of rain, but tonight the sky was clear, stars like icy pinpricks, and that bright glaring moon illuminating my way for me so I thought *I will do it* already climbing up onto what would be the new floor of the bridge when at last it was completed: not planks but a more modern sort of iron-mesh, not yet laid into place. But the steel beams were about ten inches wide and there was a grid of them, four beams spanning the river and (I would count them as I crossed, I would never forget that count) fourteen narrower beams at perpendicular angles with the others, and about three feet below these beams there was a complex crisscrossing of cables you might define as a net of sorts if you wanted to think in such terms, a safety net, there was no danger really *I will do it because I want to do it, because there is no one to stop me.*

And on the other side, Grandmother's house. And even if its windows were darkened, even if I did no more than stand looking quietly at it, and then come back home, never telling anyone what I'd done, even so I would have proven something *Because there is no one to stop me* which has been one of the principles of my life. To regret the principle is to regret my entire life.

I climbed up onto one of the beams, trembling with excitement. But how cold it was!—I'd come out without my gloves.

And how loud the river below, the roaring like a kind of jeering applause; and it smelled too, of something brackish and metallic. I knew not to glance down at it, steadying myself as a quick wind picked up, teasing tears into my eyes, I was thinking *There is no turning back: never* but instructing myself too that the beam was perfectly safe if I was careful for had I not seen boys walking across without slipping? didn't the workmen walk across too, many times a day? I decided not to stand, though—I was afraid to stand—I remained squatting on my haunches, gripping the edge of the beam with both hands, inching forward in this awkward way, hunched over, right foot, and then left foot, and then right foot, and then left foot: passing the first of the perpendicular beams, and the second, and the third, and the fourth: and so in this clumsy and painful fashion forcing myself to continue until my thigh muscles ached so badly I had to stop and I made the mistake which even in that instant I knew was a mistake of glancing down:

seeing the river thirty feet below: the way it was flowing so swiftly and with such power, and seeming rage, ropy sinuous coils of churning water, foam-flecked, terrible, and its flow exactly perpendicular to the direction in which I was moving.

"Oh no. Oh no. Oh no."

A wave of sharp cold terror shot up into me as if into my very bowels, piercing me between the legs rising from the river itself, and I could not move, I squatted there on the beam unable to move, all the strength drained out of my muscles and I was paralyzed knowing *You're going to die: of course, die* even as with another part of my mind (there is always this other part of my mind) I was thinking with an almost teacherly logic that the beam *was* safe, it was wide enough, and flat enough, and not damp or icy or greasy yes certainly it *was* safe: if this were land, for instance in our backyard, if for instance my father had set down a plank flat in the grass, a plank no more than half the width of the beam couldn't I, Claire, have walked that plank without the lightest tremor of fear? boldly? even gracefully? even blindfolded? without a moment's hesitation? not the flicker of an eyelid, not the most minute leap of a pulse?—*You know you aren't going to die: don't be silly* but it must have been five minutes before I could force myself to move again, my numbed right leg easing forward, my aching foot, I forced my eyes upward too and fixed them resolutely on the opposite shore, or what I took on faith to be the opposite shore, a confusion of sawhorses and barrels and equipment now only fitfully illuminated by the moon.

But I got there, I got to where I meant to go without for a moment exactly remembering why.

Now the worst of it's done: for now.

Grandmother's house, what's called a bungalow, plain stucco, one-story, built close to the curb, seemed closer to the river than I'd expected, maybe I was running, desperate to get there, hearing the sound of the angry rushing water that was like many hundreds of murmurous voices, and the streets surprised me with their emptiness—so many vacant lots—murky transparencies of space where buildings had once stood—and a city bus passed silently, lit gaily from within, yet nearly empty too, only the driver and single (male) passenger sitting erect and motionless as mannequins, and I shrank panicked into the shadows so they would not see me: maybe I would be arrested: a girl of my age on the street at such an hour, alone, with deep-set frightened eyes, a pale face, guilty mouth, zip-up corduroy jacket and jeans over her pajamas, disheveled as a runaway. But the bus passed, turned a corner and vanished. And there was Grandmother's house, not darkened as I'd expected but lighted, and from the sidewalk staring I could see Grandmother inside, or a figure I took to be Grandmother, but why was she awake at such an hour, how remarkable that she should be awake as if awaiting me, and I remembered then—how instantaneously these thoughts came to me, eerie as tiny bubbles that, bursting, yielded riches of a sort that would require a considerable expenditure of time to relate though their duration was in fact hardly more than an instant!—I remembered having heard the family speak of Grandmother's sometimes strange behavior, worrisome behavior in a woman of her age, or of any age, the problem was her insomnia unless insomnia was not cause but consequence of a malady of the soul, so it would be reported back to my father, her son, that she'd been seen walking at night in neighborhoods unsafe for solitary women, she'd been seen at a midnight showing of a film in downtown Hammond, and even when my step-grandfather was alive (he worked on a lake freighter, he was often gone) she might spend time in local taverns, not drinking heavily, but drinking, and this was behavior that might lead to trouble, or so the family worried, though there was never any specific trouble so far as anyone knew, and Grandmother smoked too, smoked on the street which "looks cheap," my mother said, my mother too smoked but never on the street, the family liked to tell and retell the story of a cousin of my father's coming to Hammond on a Greyhound bus, arriving at the station at about six in the morning, and there in the waiting room was my grandmother in her old fox-fur coat sitting there with a book in her lap, a cigarette in one hand, just sitting there placidly and with no mind for the two or three others, distinctly odd near-derelict men, in the room with her, just sitting there reading her book (Grandmother was always reading, poetry, biographies of great men like Lincoln, Mozart, Julius Caesar, Jesus of Nazareth) and my father's cousin came in, saw her, said, "Aunt Tina, what on earth are you doing here?" and Grandmother had looked up calmly, and said, "Why not?—it's for waiting isn't it?"

Another strange thing Grandmother had done, it had nothing to do with her insomnia that I could see unless all our strangenesses, as they are judged in others' eyes, are morbidly related, was arranging for her husband's body to be cremated: not buried in a cemetery plot, but cremated: which means burnt to mere ash: which means annihilation: and though cremation had evidently been my step-grandfather's wish it had seemed to the family that Grandmother had complied with it too readily, and so immediately following her husband's death that no one had a chance to dissuade her. "What a thing," my mother said, shivering, "—to do to your own husband!"

I was thinking of this now seeing through one of the windows a man's figure, a man talking with Grandmother in her kitchen, it seemed to me that perhaps my step-grandfather had not yet died, thus was not cremated, and some of the disagreement might be resolved, but I must have already knocked at the door since Grandmother was there opening it, at first she stared at me as if scarcely recognizing me then she laughed, she said, "What are *you* doing here?" and I tried to explain but could not: the words failed to come: my teeth were chattering with cold and fright and the words failed to come but Grandmother led me inside, she was taller than I remembered, and younger, her hair dark, wavy, falling to her shoulders, and her mouth red with lipstick, she laughed leading me into the kitchen where a man, a stranger, was waiting. "Harry this is my granddaughter Claire," Grandmother said, and the man stepped forward regarding me with interest, yet speaking of me as if I were somehow not present, "She's your granddaughter?" "She is." "I didn't know you had a granddaughter." "You don't know lots of things."

And Grandmother laughed at us both, who gazed in perplexity and doubt at each other. Laughing, she threw her head back like a young girl, or a man, and bared her strong white teeth.

I was then led to sit at the kitchen table, in my usual place, Grandmother went to the stove to prepare something for me and I sat quietly, not frightened now, yet not quite at ease though I understood I was safe now, Grandmother would take care of me now and nothing could happen, I saw that the familiar kitchen had been altered, it was very brightly lit, almost blindingly lit, yet deeply shadowed in the corners, the rear wall where the sink should have been dissolved into what would have been the backyard but I had a quick flash of the backyard where there were flower and vegetable beds, Grandmother loved to work in the yard, she brought flowers and vegetables in the summer wherever she visited, the most beautiful of her flowers were peonies, big gorgeous crimson peonies, and the thought of the peonies was confused with the smell of the oatmeal Grandmother was stirring on the stove for me to eat, oatmeal was the first food of my childhood: the first food I can remember: but Grandmother made it her own way, her special way stirring in brown sugar, cream, a spoonful of dark honey so just thinking of it I felt my mouth water violently, almost it hurt, the saliva flooded so and I was embarrassed that a trickle ran down my chin and I couldn't seem to wipe it off and Grandmother's friend Harry was watching me: but finally I managed to wipe it off on my fingers: and Harry smiled.

The thought came to me, not a new thought but one I'd had for years, but now it came with unusual force, like the saliva flooding my mouth, that when my parents died I would come live with Grandmother—of course: I would come live with Grandmother: and Grandmother at the stove stirring my oatmeal in a pan must have heard my thoughts for she said, "—Claire why don't you come live with me it's time isn't it?" and I said, "Oh yes," and Grandmother didn't seem to have heard for she repeated her question, turning now to look at me, to smile, her eyes shining and her mouth so amazingly red, two delicate spots of rouge on her cheeks so my heart caught seeing how beautiful she was, as young as my mother, or younger, and she laughed saying, "—Claire why don't you come live with me it's time isn't it?" and again I said, "Oh yes Grandmother," nodding and blinking tears from my eyes, they were tears of infinite happiness, and relief, "—oh Grandmother, *yes.*"

Grandmother's friend Harry was a Navy radio operator he said, or had been, he wore no uniform and he was no age I could have guessed, with silvery-glinting hair in a crewcut, muscular shoulders and arms but maybe his voice was familiar? maybe I'd heard him over the radio? Grandmother was urging him to tell me about the universe, distinctly she said those odd words "Why don't you tell Claire about the universe," and Harry stared at me frowning and said, "Tell Claire what about the universe?" and Grandmother laughed and said, "Oh—anything!" and Harry said, shrugging, "Hell—I don't know," then raising his voice, regarding me with a look of compassion, "—the universe goes back a long way, I guess. Ten billion years? Twenty billion? Is there a difference? They say it got started with an explosion and in a second, well really a fraction of a second a tiny bit of tightness got flung out, it's flying out right now, expanding,"—he drew his hands, broad stubby hands, dramatically apart, "and most of it is emptiness I guess, whatever 'emptiness' is. It's still expanding, all the pieces flying out, there's a billion galaxies like ours, or maybe a billion billion galaxies like ours, but don't worry it goes on forever even when we die—" but at this Grandmother turned sharply, sensing my reaction, she said, "Oh dear don't tell the child *that*, don't frighten poor little Claire with *that*."

"You told me to tell her about the—"

"Oh just *stop*."

Quickly Grandmother came to hug me, settled me into my chair as if I were a much smaller child sitting there at the kitchen table, my feet not touching the floor; and there was my special bowl, the bowl Grandmother kept for me, sparkling yellow with lambs running around the rim, yes and my special spoon too, a beautiful silver spoon with the initial C engraved on it which Grandmother kept polished so I understood I was safe, nothing could harm me, Grandmother would not let anything happen to me so long as I was there. She poured my oatmeal into my dish, she was saying, "—It's true we must all die one day, darling, but not just yet, you know, not tonight, you've just come to visit haven't you dear? and maybe you'll stay? maybe you won't ever leave? *now it's time?*"

The words *it's time* rang with a faint echo.

I can hear them now: *it's time: time.*

Grandmother's arms were shapely and attractive, her skin pale and smooth and delicately translucent as a candled egg, and I saw that she was wearing several rings, the wedding band that I knew but others, sparkling with light, and there so thin were my arms beside hers, my hands that seemed so small, sparrow-sized, and my wrists so bony, and it came over me, the horror of it, that meat and bone should define my presence in the universe: the point of entry in the universe that was *me* that was *me* that was *me*: and no other: yet of a fragile materiality that any fire could consume. "Oh Grandmother—I'm so afraid!" I whimpered, seeing how I would be burnt to ash, and Grandmother comforted me, and settled me more securely into the chair, pressed my pretty little spoon between my fingers and said, "Darling don't think of such things, just *eat*. Grandmother made this for *you*."

I was eating the hot oatmeal which was a little too hot, but creamy as I loved it, I was terribly hungry eating like an infant at the breast so blindly my head bowed and eyes nearly shut rimming with tears and Grandmother asked *is it good? is it good?* she'd spooned in some dark honey too *is it good?* and I nodded mutely, I could taste grains of brown sugar that hadn't melted into the oatmeal, stark as bits of glass, and I realized they were in fact bits of glass, some of them large as grape pits, and I didn't want to hurt Grandmother's feelings but I was fearful of swallowing the glass so as I ate I managed to sift the bits through the chewed oatmeal until I could maneuver it into the side of my mouth into a little space between my lower right gum and the inside of my cheek and Grandmother was watching asking *is it good?* and I said, "Oh yes," half choking and swallowing, "—oh *yes.*"

A while later when neither Grandmother nor Harry was watching I spat out the glass fragments into my hand but I never knew absolutely, I don't know even now: if they were glass and not for instance grains of sand or fragments of eggshell or even bits of brown sugar crystalized into such a form not even boiling oatmeal could dissolve it.

I was leaving Grandmother's house, it was later, time to leave, Grandmother said, "But aren't you going to stay?" and I said, "No Grandmother I can't," and Grandmother said, "I thought you were going to stay dear," and I said, "No Grandmother I can't," and Grandmother said, "But why?" and I said, "I just can't," and Grandmother said, laughing so her laughter was edged with annoyance, "Yes but *why?*" Grandmother's friend Harry had disappeared from the kitchen, there was no one in the kitchen but Grandmother and me, but we were in the street too, and the roaring of the river was close by, so Grandmother hugged me a final time and gave me a little push saying, "Well —goodnight Claire," and I said apologetically, "Goodnight, Grandmother," wondering if I should ask her not to say anything to my parents about this visit in the middle of the night, and she was backing away, her dark somber gaze fixed upon me half in reproach, "Next time you visit Grandmother you'll stay—won't you? Forever?" and I said, "Yes Grandmother," though I was very frightened and as soon as I was out of Grandmother's sight I began to run.

At first I had a hard time finding the Ferry Street bridge. Though I could hear the river close by—I can always hear the river close by.

Eventually, I found the bridge again. I know I found the bridge, otherwise how did I get home? That night?

Mary Michael Wagner

ACTS OF KINDNESS

It's the day after payday, and all over the city people are overdosing. Our calls have all been people celebrating. After a drop at Mount Zion, we drive up to the crest of Pacific Heights, and pull over at Vallejo and Divisadero, to look at the small patch of bay with its sailboats.

We're there five minutes, when we get a Code Three about a guy down and maybe not breathing. I'm driving, so Simon picks up the handset. As he reaches across the front seat, I notice his bare wrist, where his shirt cuff raises up. He presses his lips against the small holes of the microphone, scribbling information down on the clipboard. Another heroin overdose; we both groan. Simon drains the coffee from his Styrofoam cup, and jokes with me. The way he makes me laugh, taking the edge off things, makes me grateful. We've been on 24-hour shifts, Tuesdays and Thursdays, for six months now, and we feel like next-door neighbors who talk over a backyard fence and who borrow candles from each other when the electricity goes out.

I flip on the lights and siren, and we're driving, dipping low and easy through intersections. Simon's feet in dark-colored bucks are up on the dashboard. He offers me a raisin from his bran muffin, playfully wedging it between my front teeth. There is heat from his finger tips and the smell of rubbing alcohol.

When we arrive, I'm in charge of the call. Fire is already there, the lights blinking on their truck, people from the project milling around waiting to see what might be carried out. I sling my bag with supplies over my shoulder, and Simon grabs the oxygen. It's a small apartment, the furniture is new-looking, grainy imitation wood. There's a nice stereo and TV and a black snake in a terrarium twined around a dry white branch. The firemen, all looking big like lumberjacks to me, are circled around the guy, who is laid out on the floor. One of them is already pumping O_2 into him. I watch the guy's stomach fill with it. He's young and his shirt is pulled up. His stomach is yellowy brown and so smooth that for a second I want to touch it. The fireman with the bag-valve-mask says he was barely breathing when they got there. I feel the adrenaline in my spine and then the guy becomes a body to me, a responsibility. I kneel down and check his pulse. It is far away, reedy. His arms are clammy. Heroin is easy though, an injection of Narcan can bring practically anybody back, no matter how far away they've gone. I stab the guy twice in the upper arm with two different syringes. After a minute, he juts up, yanks off the mask, and yells, "What the fuck are you people doing in my house?"

After we drop him at General, we call back in and then drive up to Bernal Heights. Simon's laugh is machine-gunny, but soft. His Kentucky accent is all over the front of the ambulance, so that I can barely drive. The way he talks makes him seem awkward and boyish. The way his trousers, the two pockets in back, dip down low, as if his pants were too big. The way I've wanted to touch him since the first day we drove together.

Things are quiet so I park. I climb into the back and lie down on the gurney; Simon lies down on the couch that runs alongside. The aisle between us is narrow and dark. The coiled nasal canulas look eerie and reptilian above us. He tells me a ghost story he heard growing up, about the woman with the golden arm. His voice is mock-ghoulish. "Give meee back my arm. Give meee back my arm." He claws at my forearms, raising the hair there. Then he is quiet. He climbs off the couch, leans over me, picks up my arm. He feels for my radial pulse. "Bounding," he reports. "Uh oh, we've lost her pulse, cardiac arrest." He leans over to give me mouth-to-mouth. His face hovers close to mine, hesitating. His breath smells of coffee and Certs. We've played this game before, but always pulled back, so that now we both seem startled when Simon puts his mouth on mine. We both forget to breathe. I pull him down onto me. I want him to get all the way on top of me, so I can feel his whole body against mine, but he says he needs to call in and check with Central about something. The heat of his body goes away. I hear him joking with the dispatcher as I fall asleep on the gurney. Outside the tinted windows it becomes night and the electric buses make sucking sounds like the noises old men, sitting on crates, make with their teeth when I walk by in running shorts. When we have a call, he nudges me awake, his fingers shy and tentative under my shoulder.

We get off work at four in the morning. It is still dark. Simon looks haggard, driving us in his truck. We go home to my apartment. I tell him I live on a musical street. Next door is an opera singer, a couple of houses up, a trumpeter, on the other side of the street, a piano player. I tell him I go sit on the stoop of the piano player. I imagine that it is a woman and that she never stops her music, for whenever I go at night to listen, she is always playing. I sit on her cement stoop and can hear her clearly behind draped windows on the second floor.

When we get to my apartment, the opera singer is practicing. For once, I'm grateful for her rudeness, her weird hours. I open the Venetian blinds. We lie down in the small square of moon on the carpet, pulling blankets from the bed over us. The woman's voice is solemn and full. She is singing Puccini.

Simon touches my face. I think about what I've seen him do with those hands, patting arms of people who are wide-eyed afraid, maybe even dying. How those hands have brought back to life a kid who drowned in a country club pool. I feel floating and happy and want to say all the clichés I know. I want Simon to say my name over and over, as if we were in some dark place and he could only find me by calling. But as he squeezes my body, the dreaminess goes away. His tongue makes me so I can't think or protect myself. I thrash against him like a tide.

When we are finished and have kicked the blankets away, Simon whispers that he's been lonely. He whispers it like it's something to be ashamed of, like it's something he's never told anyone but me.

I wake up on the floor with Simon's legs entangled with mine. I move away and sit on my bed. I put on silk undershorts and smooth oil onto my legs, lifting my knees up to my chest. I know that he is awake and watching me through the slit his arm makes over his face. I feel ashamed, so I want to overpower him in some way. Maybe I want him to fall in love with me. He pretends he's just waking up.

We have to be on shift again at four the next morning, so we spend the day together. We go see an old Fred Astaire and Ginger Rogers movie at the Castro. I don't pay attention. I think about going back to Kentucky with him. I imagine the South to be like his accent, which is lulling and outdoors-sounding. I think of us living out in the country. We'd have yellow farm equipment, yellow like my brother's Tonka trucks, machines that chew up the land. I would want a tire swing—a barn—a llama. Simon. I would want him to come to bed smelling of dogwood trees and soil and hay.

Blinking out of the movie, into the late afternoon, we laze along Castro Street. I ask him questions just to hear his accent. His voice makes me think of boys with hairless faces and paper routes, boys who play basketball in pocked driveways wearing ragged canvas hightops. I ask him to tell me about home.

He says, "You know more people die of lung cancer in Kentucky than any other state."

"Of course they do," I say, "It's all those coal mines." I think of men with their foreheads sooty like Ash Wednesday, unstrapping hats with small round lights on them.

He laughs, "No, it's the tobacco, it's the biggest crop. Everybody smokes."

I do not want to believe this. I think of Kentucky as hills and hills of impossible color, bluegrass, where people drink iced tea and sit on porch swings. I cannot see these people with cigarettes wedged between their innocent white teeth.

We make love again that night. Afterwards, before we fall asleep, Simon gets out of bed and puts on his boxer shorts and a sweatshirt. He says it's because he's cold, but under the covers it's warm. I think it is really because he feels afraid of something.

We go to work at four groggy. They tell us we won't have an ambulance until five, so I go to take a nap in the bunk beds upstairs. I can't sleep, so I put my shoes on and go back downstairs to get the book I left in the common room. The door is cracked. The light from the room is orange. I hear Simon's voice, its accent, like doorbell chimes across a yard. It makes me freeze, I don't know why. I've already walked through the slit of doorway, the conversation has already washed over me, someone else is answering him: "Jesus, in the back of the ambulance. It's probably the one I'm taking out today. You let her snail all over my gurney."

I stand there, half in the room, looking at a cigarette burning down in the ashtray. I cross my arms over my chest. I feel like these men can see inside me. I feel that Simon's the one who should feel caught. I smile, pointing at my book. "I left my book," I say.

At five we go out on our shift. I act like nothing's happened, but all morning I make mistakes. Heartbeats sound so distant I can't count them. I forget to throw away the needle from a syringe and leave it pointing dangerously on the counter. Simon picks it up and throws it away. I need to get back my rhythm of working.

We pick up someone with AIDS over on Noe. His flannel pajamas are big on him, like he is a child wearing his father's pajamas as a joke. They smell of old fruit juice and urine. I can't start the IV, the man's arm seems pale and utterly veinless. Simon takes the needle from me and rubs the man's forearm, bringing a pale blue vein to the surface of his skin. He slides the needle in easily, the glass reservoir filling with blood. The man's rattling breath makes me shiver. I want to ask him how he got it. "Did somebody you love do this to you? Was it the first and only man you ever loved? Did he do something stupid and maybe even spiteful once, in a dark, curtained-off room in a grimy bar, before coming home to you?" Simon checks the vitals. I offer to drive. It begins to rain. In the mirror, I see Simon adjust the drip.

When things quiet down early in the afternoon, we stop at Denny's. I take a raincoat out of the cabinet before climbing out of the ambulance, but just carry it over my arm into the restaurant. We both order French dips. The rain streaks the glass windows. It is too late in the season for rain like this. I remember when my mother made me and my brother walk to school in a storm. She opened the door, held out her hand, palm up: "See, there's not even a drop. Besides, a little rain's not going to hurt you." The sky was a curdled black. But I knew about rubber, how it protected you from getting struck by lightning. I walked out in a rain coat and rubber boots, holding an old inner tube over my head. In Kansas you can see lightning for miles and miles, so you can never be sure how far away it really is. In the short gaps between houses, my brother and I seemed to be the highest things around. I crouched down as I walked—crooked spears of lightning rammed into the fields around us. My mother yelled out at us, "Just stay under the rubber hood of your slicker and keep both feet on the ground and you'll be fine."

I open my eyes. Simon is saying something to me. He's swabbing French fries through a small mound of ketchup. With the other hand, one that is also sticky with ketchup, he's playing with my fingers. He's smiling at me. He asks if I'm all right. "Fine," I say, "just cold." I pick up the slicker and ease it on over my shirt, fastening all the snaps. Then I lift my sneakered feet off his side of the booth. I press both rubbery soles firmly down onto the cold tiled floor.

We sit like that eating hot fudgecake sundaes, the vanilla ice cream making my teeth hurt, not talking or looking at each other, until we get a Code Three. Then it's not like we're on a date anymore, we don't have to be mad at each other anymore, the sound of the siren outside the closed windows is familiar and gets caught in our chests.

The rain has stopped and the clouds are thinning. The house is white, but most of the parts that haven't burned are smudged black. The fire makes the air quivery. Simon and I move inside the circle of yellow police tape, our foreheads sweaty like we've been standing too long in front of a grille in an all-night diner.

The flames have just started on the second floor. I see a face appear then disappear in the unshattered panes of glass. It is ghostly. I think I hear a voice, a child's. I yell to Fire. A few of the firemen jog up to the house carrying a ladder. In their masks and helmets, they look like insects. They lean a ladder against the sill of the window. One of them climbs up, a hose strapped under his armpit. He smashes the window with a small ax, and the people in the street sigh together like a crowd at a sporting event. For a long time he stands at the window sending water into the jagged hole in the glass. My skin is itchy and uncomfortable. I tell myself there's no way I could have heard a voice, not over the crackling of the fire and the gushing water. I ask Simon if he saw anything, and he tells me not to worry, that it was probably my imagination. He says people see things in flames that aren't there, like in clouds. I lean back against the ambulance, the scissors in the holster around my waist feeling comforting, like a gun I could use if I had to.

The fireman comes out of the smoking window with a little girl held in his free arm. Simon and I run over with the gurney. The fireman sets her down. Her arms and face are blistered, but I know it's the smoke, not the burns, that might get her. The skin around her nostrils is raw and charred from inhaling the hot smoky air. Her heart's still going, but it's faint and drowned. Her throat is swollen and closed from the smoke. I hand Simon an airway, and he eases the tube down her throat. I start pumping O_2 into her with the bag-valve-mask. I call for one of the firemen to drive us to the hospital, so we can both be in back in case we start to lose her. We push her through the open door to the ambulance and climb in. Someone shuts the door behind us. Simon takes the oxygen. I put a clean sheet over her gently, because this is all we can do for her burns in the field. I check her pulse and blood pressure. Her vitals are waning. Her throat is so swollen she's not getting enough oxygen. When I look at Simon, I see his jauntiness has evaporated. He seems pale and confused. His arms stick out in front of him like a sleepwalker's. The girl's burned face looks peaceful as if she weren't trying to stay alive anymore. In her ears are little gold dots. They are the kind of earrings you get when you've just had your ears pierced for the first time.

At the burn center orderlies in white are waiting for us. They whisk her away from us as soon as we have opened the ambulance door.

Even after we have filled out all the forms, Simon and I sit drinking coffee in the cafeteria, not wanting to leave. He looks so lost that I want to take him home and feed him warm, comforting things—sweet potatoes, corn pudding, turkey. I want to tell him he will never have to sleep alone again. But we have to take the fireman back, so we crumple our cups and throw them away and go back outside where he is hanging around the emergency room dock smoking a hand-rolled cigarette.

When we get back, the house is still smoking. Fire is carrying out a body, I cannot believe how brown it is, and how small. I hear people on the street say it is the little boy who lived in the house. His arms are spread as if he had been running to hug someone. I can tell by the way they are carrying his burnt body that there is nothing left inside him. The medical examiner puts the child in a white bag that zips. I am told by a fireman, rolling a flat hose, that the boy had squirted barbeque-lighter fluid into the gas furnace. The girl was his babysitter.

Simon and I get another call and wave to the firemen close to us, like we've just met them for drinks or something. We climb into the front seat and I nudge the ambulance through the people still hanging around in front of the house.

I let myself fall into work as if I were falling off a very high place and all that exists are what my hands grab hold of, IV bags and wrists and blood-pressure cuffs. At four in the morning Simon drives us to my house in his truck. It is not yet light, but teenage boys ride bare-waisted down Haight Street on bikes. They don't hold onto the handlebars. I want to lean out the window and touch their long smooth backs. I have not forgotten what happened this morning. I sit far away from Simon. When we get to my house, I don't want to let him inside, but I do.

I don't want to get into my bed, I want to be asleep already. I don't take off my clothes. I lie down on the bed nudging the wall, probably getting it dirty from the grit on my uniform. I tell Simon I just want to sleep. He doesn't move to touch me. We are so light on the bed, I imagine us like the skin of onions wound around air or dry leaves.

I dream that Simon and I are married and that we have two daughters, who are scarecrows. Simon chases them through fields and fields of corn, flicking lit matches at them, trying to light their straw pigtails on fire. I run after him. I try to grab him around the ankles and pull him down. The dream smells of manure and sulfur and when I wake up, I am sweating, but very cold. I get up, take off my uniform, and put on sweat pants and two sweat shirts.

I call the emergency room. The nurse tells me the girl died minutes after we brought her in. I sit on the bed and watch Simon sleeping. Then I dig my toes into his shoulders. "Hey," I say. He lifts his head quickly as if he hadn't been asleep at all. "I don't want you here anymore," I say. "I want you to leave." He doesn't say anything. He gets out of bed and starts putting on his clothes. With my eyes closed, I hear his hands moving into sleeves.

I tell him to shut the front door when he leaves, that I'm going to sit and wait in the backyard until he's gone. He looks hurt, but I refuse to see it.

Outside, the night feels like summer nights in Kansas, the kind that has heat lightning. I sit on the grass and Simon comes out the back door. He looks large and intimidating. I want to shout, "I told you to get outta here," and throw rocks and sticks at him as if he were a mangy dog who might have rabies.

He sits down close enough to touch me. I draw my knees up into my sweat shirt. "That girl died," I tell him, saying it like it's his fault.

"I know, I just called the hospital."

"I wanted her to live," I say, "but I keep thinking she would have felt responsible for the boy. Still, I wanted her to live." Then I can't stop talking, even though I don't want to tell him anything else. I tell him about my dream. I tell him I don't trust him anymore, not after what he told everyone we work with.

He plucks up blades of grass, until I look at him like even that proves he's violent and dangerous. He puts his hands at his side and talks with his head tilted down: "I want to not have said those things. I want to feel like I'll never act like that again. When we were driving that girl to the hospital, I knew just by looking at your neck that you were praying. I thought I might cry. Then I hated you."

He moves towards me. I still want him to leave, but I also want him to love me. There are other things too, that I want. I want us to move to Kentucky where there aren't cities or overdoses or betrayal, where we'd fly over our farm in a biplane that droned and vibrated under our thighs and all we could see would be hills of bluegrass for miles and miles, like the sea.

Simon says in the quietest voice I've ever heard him use, "I saw her there too. I saw her in the window and I wanted to make you think it wasn't true. I just wanted to protect you. Even if only for a minute."

I want to say, who cares, it's too late for being kind. But the truth is, kindness is the only thing that matters. And the truth is that we should be curled up someplace safe, like our parents' bed during a lightning storm, like the back of the ambulance with the doors locked, me on the gurney and him on the couch, not even holding hands, just breathing the same close air that smells of astringent and gasoline.

Yolanda Barnes

RED LIPSTICK

Lettie's coming.

She's coming. On her way.

That was her calling on the telephone. Telling me she'll be here soon.

Lettie.

Jesus Lord. So much to do.

"Who is this?" I said. "Who?" My voice harsh, not like me at all. That ringing phone had pulled me from my bed, that's how early it was, and I'm up by seven every morning. It's been that way for years. "Who?"

"Albee?" she said. I didn't know her voice. Imagine that. She spoke again, this time adding a weight to her words, leveling her tone with authority, calm. "Albertine."

"Lettie."

Lettie Lettie Lettie. Her name rolls along in my mind like a prayer, a curse. Like the singsong of a children's nursery rhyme, a chant to jump rope by: Here comes Lettie. Here she comes. Lettie. Lettie. My best-best friend. Lettie. Lettie. The one I loved. *Oh, but that was a long time ago.*

On her way back to me at last. I stood in the hallway after we hung up, wearing just a nightgown, my feet bare against the hallway floor, bumps on my arms and the back of my neck, a chill I was feeling and at the same time not feeling. I was bound to get sick, I was thinking, in spite of the flu shots. Nothing would save me. Such strange thoughts. About my heart, leaping so against my chest. It would jump out, I was certain, and I crossed my arms, trying to hold it back. All these bits jumbled inside me. Until I couldn't think at all, like the times now I am driving and suddenly people honk their horns at me, an ugly, rude chorus, when I have no idea what wrong I have done, making me stop in my tracks, same as the little brown rabbit startled in the woods, black eyes bright and body stiff, stopped in the middle of the intersection and so nobody can go until I'm able to breathe again.

I have to reach for breath after Lettie calls. The weight of my crossed arms squeezed against my breasts. What a sight I would make for the woman doctor who worries about my blood pressure. Until I begin to rub my arms, my cheeks, the still rabbit coming back to life. Lettie's on her way and I have to prepare.

First move I make is to pull on my old housedress with the green and brown and yellow checkered squares, torn and stitched with safety pins beneath the right arm. Tie a kerchief around my head on the way to the front yard, the first sight that will greet Lettie. I carry the broom for sweeping the curb where dirt and slips of paper and soda cans have collected. But first the lawn. Down on hands and knees, my eyes narrowed and searching the grass for weeds, I crawl about, snatching at dandelions and crabgrass until green streaks stain my palms. When the walk catches my sight. My new walk that Mr. James in the green house on the corner just finished building without taking a penny. Mr. James with his pretty wife who nudges him to help the old widow down the street. He laid the walk just the way I asked, with bricks of different colors—pink, of course, but also coral and burgundy, yellow and green and gray. Like a crazy quilt, that's what I told him. Like Joseph's coat.

I squeeze my eyes tight and see Lettie strolling along that new walk. The way she was years ago, wearing one of her dresses, bright-colored and the skirt swinging, brushing the back of her knees. Her plump cheeks and skin the shade of black plums. Her hats—the straw one with the scarves tied around the brim, the tails drifting down her back and that man's hat tilted on her head, shadowing one eye. I see her hair dyed yellow. (How my Harald talked her down for that! "A woman with skin that black," he said, like it was some crime. "She's got no *business*.") I see tripled strands of fake pearls slapping against her breasts as she stepped, and her lips, slick and shiny red, open and stretched across laughing teeth.

"Miz Clark?" I hear, and open my eyes. Sonya from across the street stands on my lawn. "Miz Clark?" she says. They all call me that. "How you doing today, Miz Clark?" they say; "You getting along all right, Miz Clark?" No longer Albertine. Nobody remembers Albertine but me. "Miz Clark?" Sonya is saying. "You doing O.K., Miz Clark?" Her little boy and girl dressed in blue uniforms, on their way to the Christian school. They hold Sonya's hands and stare at me with dark brown eyes, the girl's hair all in braids and fastened with blue-and-white barrettes.

"You've been working hard," Sonya says. "I saw you." Her voice is weak, surprising because Sonya's a big woman. A big yellow woman. The way she fusses at me is how I imagine a daughter would. I know I should be thankful for neighbors like her. "Maybe you should rest," she says, but I just grin and pat her fleshy arm. Tell her to stop worrying. That's all I say. She wouldn't understand the rest, that I haven't felt so good in a long, long time.

Lettie never said what she wanted when she called. But I know. The same as how I know almost everything about Lettie. More, probably, than in those days we talked all the time. I know about that new house of hers and how each of her daughters turned out, about each wedding, each birth of a grandchild, each baptism, communion, graduation. I know about her boy, her baby. How his motorbike skidded on an oil-slicked road. He was nearly killed and I know that nearly killed her. There are people who tell me these things, Essie in particular, but sometimes I wonder if I need them. I feel I would know no matter what. I would just know.

"Can I come over today, Albee?" she said. "I've got something to ask you." What answer possible, except "Of course, Lettie." All this time her words swirling in my mind until, finally, while working in the yard their meaning comes to me, makes me sit back on my heels although this causes great pain in my legs. Already my palms sting, my back hurts from all the pulling and stooping but I have taken certain pleasure in all these aches, accepted any sufferings stemming from Lettie's visit as natural and expected. Now, at this moment, I don't feel a thing. "So that's what she wants," I say, then snap my mouth shut, in case Sonya's back across the street, watching.

There's a sickness eating through Lettie, Essie told me. She says it can't be fought. "They put her in the hospital time after time," Essie said. "But she always comes out." I could picture Essie on the other end of the telephone, shaking her head, black curls trembling. But I know better. Lettie is a cat. What else Essie tells me, that Lettie's alone. "Alonso's left her," she lowered her voice when she told me this, and on my end of the phone I nodded my head. My whole body nodding, my shoulders rocking back and forth, my toes in it too, tapping the floor. Ah, Alonso. Couldn't take any more. Lettie's carryings-on and her lies. Her arrogance. See there. I'm not the only one. "And the children," Essie said. "All gone too." That boy turned out no better than her. Traipsing around the country. Living with one woman after another. The twins, Claire and Carla. "They won't have nothing to do with her." Essie's tone hushed. Gleeful. "Won't even let her in their homes."

"It's payment due," I said. "Fortune's wheel turning round. All Lettie's deeds coming back to her. All the evil, all the lies, all that boozing, all her selfishness. All the suffering she's caused." I had to catch myself, listen to Essie's silence. It made me press my lips tight. Nobody wants to hear me talk that way. Alone. That's why Lettie's coming back. She needs my help.

She'll be here soon, and so I move inside to the living room. She'll only pass through here, Lettie and I were never living-room friends. Still I take my old dust rags and wipe the Beethoven bust on the piano. I grip the bench and lower myself one knee at a time to clean the instrument's feet, pushing my fingernail through the cloth to get at the dust in the carved ridges. I pour lemon oil on the coffee table and knead it into the wood. The centerpiece is an arrangement of silk-screen flowers. It would be nice to replace it with a token from Lettie, but there is nothing. A punch bowl that Harald dropped years ago. When we were children I'd give Lettie presents. Little bracelets with dangling charms and necklaces with mustard seeds captured in glass balls. I stole from my mother's jewelry box a pin shaped like a bird with rhinestones in its breast. Lettie and I believed they were diamonds. How Mama whipped me when she found out. I gave Lettie the toy circus animals my daddy bought me when I was sick with chicken pox. Tiny, tiny things. When I shut my eyes now I can see them still: a lion, a monkey, a capped bear holding a little red ball. Lettie won't remember.

In the kitchen I fill a bucket with ammonia and hot water, sink my bare hands in and swirl the rag about. My fingers look strange, puffy, bloated, plain except for the wedding band I still wear though Harald's been gone, what?, almost ten years. In the moment it takes to squeeze the rag my hands have turned a raw red. I was the fair-skinned one with the pretty hair. Lettie standing in the schoolyard behind me, playing with my ponytail, saying "This is good stuff." Combing it with her fingers, plaiting it, dressing it with ribbons. She chose me, I remind myself as I clean. "Me." Wiping down the windowsill above the sink where I keep my pot of violets, the ceramic swan with the white, curved neck, the goldfish bowl. Harald's glasses. The last pair he owned, cracked in the brown frame. Oh, Harald never liked Lettie. He saw before I did. The way his face turned mean at the sight of her children here. But I didn't mind taking care of them, I tried to tell him, since we couldn't have any of our own. "Fool," he said. He knew what Lettie was doing, how she got those fancy hats and bottles of perfume cluttering her glass-topped vanity. "Fool," he said, and I thought he meant Alonso.

I want Lettie to see those glasses. And the drawings held by magnets to the refrigerator. Sonya's children colored those and signed them with love and kisses. I want Lettie to take note of the cabinets beneath the sink; Mr. James built those, yes, the same one who did the walk. And the large bowl on the table, let her see that, too, filled with figs and oranges and lemons and tomatoes and yellow squash. My neighbors pick these from their trees and gardens and carry them over in grease-stained paper bags. All this will show Lettie. "See, I have friends. See what my friends do for me. Lettie? Do you hear? I have a good life. I keep busy. I substitute-teach and lunch twice a month with Essie. I attend all the meetings of the neighborhood block club, elected secretary two years in a row."

I shake my head. Standing in the middle of my kitchen, hands on hips, the rag dripping ammonia-water on the floor. I have no time for this, there is much more to do. A new, fresh tablecloth and the good curtains, yellow ones that match my kitchen, I need to get them down from the hall cabinet. I will fix tuna sandwiches, cut in triangles and trimmed of crusts, just how she likes, and put the rest of the coconut cake on the party platter with the red and yellow tulips decorating the border. When Lettie comes I will put on a pot of coffee. We used to sit at this very table and drink cup after cup. Lettie making me laugh. If I had more time I would get on hands and knees and scrub the floor. I would wipe down the cabinet doors, the woodwork, the walls till free of fingerprints and grime and grease. Sort through the cupboards, throw out the clutter, the excesses, and reline the shelves with fresh, new paper. I would clean this house to its bones, its soul. I would cook Lettie her favorite meal, gumbo with sausage and crab and shrimp. All that and more if I had the time. But a million years would not be enough to prepare for Lettie.

It's remarkable to me that I didn't know her voice. Of course it's been several years since we spoke on the telephone or anywhere else. But that doesn't mean I had stopped hearing Lettie. No. I've heard her voice often. Still it follows me around, sits on my shoulder and whispers in my ear, pops up at the strangest times. Once when I was slicing eggplant and something about it, its deep black purpleness, I think, like Lettie's color, made me think of her and I swear I heard her laughing. Another time I was humming some nonsense tune I made up as I leaned over the back-porch sink washing my clothes and her voice rose up over mine, singing one of those common, nasty songs she used to know. I must hear her in my sleep too, because sometimes I wake in the night answering her.

Something to ask me, that's what she said, and that is just like Lettie. Seems like she was always wanting something from me. Never the other way around. Didn't Harald say that? And Essie? Oh, I was a good friend to her, everybody knows that. But I've learned my lesson now. I'm stronger than before. "Where are my little toy animals now?" My voice bounces against the tile walls of the bathroom. I hear in it the frantic pain of the old crazy woman filthily dressed who stands at the bus stop and shouts all her business. With trembling fingers I unbutton my old plaid dress and soap a washcloth to rub against the back of my neck, my ears, beneath my arms. Fill the basin with water and bring my face down.

People wondered after I let Lettie go. Prying, nudging questions. Essie tried to find out, oh, how she tried. She was so certain it was some one, huge thing. She questioned me about Lettie and my Harald; she knew how Lettie was. But I never answered. Let Essie think whatever she wants, tell her tales. But this is how Lettie and I came to end.

The Christmas party at Essie's house and me still in my widow's black although Harald had been gone more than two years. That's how deeply I felt, Lettie should have known that. At this party I was sitting on Essie's flowered couch, a paper plate on my lap, listening to Chloe. I was eating one of those big black olives, nodding my head to whatever talk she was talking when I heard Lettie's voice coming from the kitchen (who did not hear?) saying, "No, I don't think it's time Albertine stopped wearing black. Black suits Albertine." And then she laughed. I heard her laugh.

I went home after that and took off that black dress. I sat on my bed dressed only in my slip, my arms folded against the chilled night air, and began to think about Lettie and me. I combed through our history together.

Pulling memories like loose threads. One for the time after my third miscarriage when Lettie said to me, "Obviously the Lord doesn't intend for you to have babies, Albertine. Not every woman is meant to be a mother." A thread for the time creditors were after me, when I could have lost this home Harald and I worked so hard for (and I'll let you all know I never asked for a dime) and Lettie's answer: "Every tub must stand on its own bottom." Another for those two days Harald stayed in the hospital, those terrible last days, and she never came. Every insult, every hurt, every slight since childhood. All thought forgotten or excused or forgiven. All that I had chosen not to see. I sat there in the dark with goosebumps on my bare arms, pulling them from a place deep within me, weaving these threads together. Lettie had never been my friend. She had never loved me as I loved her.

The face I wash is old and full, skin loose and drooping beneath the chin, at the neck. Never have I been one of those women to worry about vanity and I do not try to hide my age now. I pat on a little bit of powder and line my mouth with lipstick, pale pink, not red like Lettie. Once, foolishly, I asked Essie, "Does she ever mention me?" Anything would have pleased me, even spiteful words. "Does she?" And Essie waited, I could hear her thoughts weighing whether to spare me, before answering what I knew to be true. "No," she said. "Not once." I hold my brush with tight, curled fingers. My knuckles hurt. Twist my hair and pin it in two tightly wound coils.

At the closet I fumble through my hanging dresses. Which one? The black dress with the white polka dots. No. Eh heh. Nothing black today. The green one? The striped one? None of them seems right. Lettie will show up here in something red, hem swinging, slapping. She'll wear a hat with a feather sprouting out, or the brim trimmed with fur. Strutting up my walk without shame.

I could say no. That would serve her right. Laugh at Lettie when she asks for my help. Like she would do me. Leave her deserted. Yes. Exactly what I should do.

Such unChristian thoughts ruling my mind as I stand before the closet. Finally, I shake my head and get back to business. It's the striped dress I finally choose.

Getting time now. She'll be here. Here. I rush over to press my dress, scorching my arm below the wrist. A bad burn, but the hurt will come later. For now I am free. Standing next to the ironing board, it takes long minutes to button up that dress. Lettie.

Sometime past two o'clock I wrap the sandwiches in wax paper and push the plate far back in the refrigerator. Cover the cake and set it back on the counter. She should have been here two hours ago. Just like Lettie. To keep me waiting. And then I realize, such a horrible thought it makes me sink into one of the kitchen chairs. I brace my elbows against the table. She's not coming.

Has nothing changed?

I hear her first. Jump up and run to the window with loud thudding steps that shake the floor, stand behind the sheer yellow curtains. Lettie's here. That's her car. The gold Cadillac. I remember how she fussed and nagged until Alonso bought it though they barely had money enough for a house to live in. I step back from the window, clap my hands, lift my feet and turn in a circle. I have to do something with all this feeling bouncing inside me. "Lettie," I sing.

Does she ever think of the time she took me to the beach? I watched through the window that day too when she drove up in the Cadillac, new and gleaming then. "Let's go somewhere," she said, and I tugged the kerchief from my head. We drove, little Alonso not even born yet and the twins mere toddlers, fussing in the back seat, nearly two hours along the coast to a mission town. Lettie wearing her strawhat that time with a yellow scarf tied around the brim, the tail fluttering out the window. We came to a beach with the prettiest, clearest water I've ever seen, white pebbles that hurt my stockinged feet.

Lettie left us behind, her two babies and me, to climb the rocks. She found herself a place to settle, her straight black skirt pulled up, showing her thighs, and a bottle of orange pop in one hand. Her hair still colored yellow then. Harald was right: a common-looking false blond. I remember the babies crawling over my stomach, their reaching, slapping hands in my face struggling for attention, when all I wanted was to stare at Lettie sitting so bold on her rock. Not seeing us at all. And I was thinking, "We ought to take these babies. Harald and me. Away from her. Raise them right." Treacherous thoughts, not like me at all, and I tried to shrug them off, a burdensome cloak around my shoulders, heavy, anchoring me. "We could run into the ocean," I whispered to those babies, gathered in my arms. "Disappear. Drown. She'd never know." And though it was hard I waited and waited until it seemed enough time had passed so I could stand and call to her, wave her back to us, shouting, "Lettie. Lettie. Let's go home."

All the times I have remembered that day and what warning I should have taken. But I've learned. I won't be a fool again. I hurry back to the window. "It's her. Lettie." Starting up my new walk. "What will she say about that?" I whisper. "My walk of different colors? About my dress? What cruel things?" And then I see her. I see Lettie.

She's got skinny. Too skinny. Oh, that's a bad skinny.

A step closer to the window, my face pressed into the curtains. Where is her hat? She wears a wig, a cheap one, too obvious; it is brown with strands thick and straight as a horse's mane. She wears a black dress.

Black!

Lettie is dying.

Essie was right, I can see that now. This sickness has defeated her and now me too. Robbed me of my Lettie. Left me empty-handed. What business have I got against this woman here? I leave the window, don't want to see anymore. Betrayed again.

Racing all around my kitchen, the nervous little brown rabbit. All the things that should give me comfort. I reach up and take Harald's glasses from the windowsill, hold them to my lips. But from them get nothing. No power. Compared to Lettie it's worthless. Everything in my pretty yellow kitchen, worthless.

So I walk back to the window and push the curtains aside. A ghost stands on my front porch, and inside myself I feel something falling. Falling.

"Lettie." Her name leaves my mouth in a wail. It carries through the glass pane and causes her to look my way. Through the window our eyes meet. Startled eyes, wondering, watchful. And then I see, what I have been searching for all along. Her red lips. Red. Red. Nothing but red. Oh, Lettie's always worn the brightest red lipstick, ever since she was a girl and her mother couldn't slap her into stopping. *See there.*

At once I am laughing. *Lettie's here. Still. She hasn't left me. Not yet. Why, I'd bet anything, beneath that wig, she still dyes her hair blond. Scarce, nappy, yellow hairs. I'd bet my life.*

She stares at me. And then, slowly, smiles.

I let go the curtain, fall back and lean myself against the wall. Breathless.

She will ask me for this favor. I know it, and without hesitation I will answer. Yes. Always yes. Anything to keep Lettie near.

And I begin to imagine the caring of Lettie. Shopping in the market, picking out the finest okra, the best green beans. For her. Plaiting Lettie's hair, pinning it up at night so she can sleep in comfort. Peeling potatoes to simmer in a stew to feed her. Washing her soiled underclothes. Bathing her, soaping and scrubbing her pathetic, racked limbs. Sitting by her bedside, squeezing her hand when she cries out in pain.

All these visions bring me joy. My victory.

Now I stand in the middle of my kitchen, alone on the checkered tile floor, and listen to the doorbell ring. Twice more I hear it, dainty and distant, but still I have trouble moving. Finally, after what seems an instant, what feels my lifetime, I take my first step. On my way toward greeting Lettie.

David Long

BLUE SPRUCE

Laurel is up in the cool shadow on the porch roof, in dungarees and a sweatshirt, scraping off pine needles with a snow shovel. Below, an old garden hose snakes across the knobby dirt, its pinhole leak shooting up a spray that fizzes in a slash of sunlight. There's a breath of wind, a commotion in the lilacs. Down the lane, stones are finally warming in their sockets. Between branches, she can see the water tower on Buffalo Hill, the long gravel slide below the golf course, the blinding curlicues of the river.

Eva appears on the walk, church-dressed. "What's this?" she says, squinting. "You're not ready?"

"Not going," Laurel calls down. "Which I told you."

"Well, I guess I just don't believe that."

"Believe it. It's too fine a day."

"After all Mrs. Proctor did for you."

"I'm a rat," Laurel says.

Eva's car—a balky, inherited Buick—is in the shop again, so she is obliged to take Laurel's silver-flecked Prelude. She wiggles in, makes a fine show of adjusting the mirrors and the seat, angling the wheel down, as if Laurel were grotesquely outsized. The lane is just dry enough to send up a thin slipstream of gumbo dust that lazes off into the milkweed as she drives away. Go, *go*, Laurel thinks, and once Eva is safely out of sight she claps her hands on her jeans and makes for the ladder. It is a fine day. Her heart is rushing with mischief.

Routinely called the Mahugh sisters, they are, in fact, sisters-in-law. Eva was a Bean, married to Laurel's younger brother Eddie. People often take Eva for the older of the two, when, in fact, Laurel is fifty-six, and Eva, who has the raddled face of an ardent smoker, has just reached fifty. Laurel is the less familiar figure in town; before her return, three years ago, she had spent almost thirty years overseas. She was a civil-service employee with the Air Force, posted mainly in the Far East. She has a rangy, uncomplaining body, and a bantering way men have been drawn to (though not, as it's turned out, for long). But she's had a life, seen a good many things. In Manila, she once watched the head of a young man being carried on the point of a stick down a honeycomb of tiny, sweltering streets. "His eyes were wide open," she later reported to Eva. "You felt he was going to hurl words at you. Oh, and just imagine what they'd be!" Eva waves away such stories, as if they're spurious, told for the sake of shocking her. "That's just your mean streak talking," she sometimes says.

The other Mahughs—two brothers, another sister—have blown to the four winds, Eva says. By this she means: Billings, Casper, Wenatchee. Eva and Eddie stayed in town. For years, Eddie worked under his father, old Warren Mahugh, at Equity Supply, and after Eddie's mother passed away he and Eva sold their place and moved back into his parents' house to look after Warren. Laurel may have seniority, but Eva has lived under this roof with a husband, which must count for something. She was the one who nursemaided Laurel's father—he was diabetic, nearly blind, and full of staunch, gloomy ideas. Did she ever gripe in public, ever shirk, ever lose patience? Each fall, she'd catch herself thinking, Now, he can't last another winter, can he? and hate herself. Finally, one February, he did die. "Oh, I know how you must feel," she told Eddie, but that wasn't true—she didn't have any idea.

She and Eddie were alone in the house then. What *she* felt was a joy laced with dread. She thought Eddie might bloom, with Warren out of his way, but he seemed, if anything, quieter —a nearly middle-aged man with a long, sombre face roughed up each morning by a razor. She waited, she watched him. He was so familiar. He was always checking on things, giving his odd sighs, his barely audible status reports. But he didn't seem to have anything you could think of, really, as desires. "Would you want to take a little trip?" Eva asked him. He didn't think so. Summer came and passed, cool and rainy, hardly any respite at all. "What can I do for you?" she would ask. "What is it you want?" No, she never quite forced it out of him.

One morning that fall, he told her he'd be hunting over west of Swain's Creek. "Who with?" she said, surprised. He'd skipped the last few seasons, and she thought he'd lost the taste for it.

"No one," he said.

"Is that a good idea?" she asked him.

"I don't see that it matters," Eddie said. That was his valedictory. They found him barely half a mile from the truck, seated under a balsam, his gun barrel resting on the front of his jacket, and his head blown to nothing. The jacket had once been Warren's.

"Had he been acting funny?" the sheriff asked Eva.

"No, no. I can't help you," she said. "Go away."

"Mrs. Mahugh . . ." The man looked exhausted, standing in the kitchen doorway, tapping his hat against his pants leg. But he did go away after a while. It occurred to her later that maybe he wanted her to beg: *Oh, God, no—he must have fallen; he must have tripped over something. . . .* But Eddie was never clumsy, never careless.

Laurel had been posted on Guam, and by the time she could

get home, Eddie had already been buried. "She couldn't wait
one more day?" Laurel asked, incredulous at the news. "God,
that woman—"

One of her brothers took her shoulder. "Eva's awfully keyed
up," he said. "You know how she gets."

It was sleeting. Laurel had been travelling two nights, sitting
up in rancid clothes. Someone gave her a drink, a plate of cold
chicken. Eva had locked herself in her room. The next morning,
Laurel drove up to the cemetery alone, and walked through
the slop of horse-chestnut leaves. There were her parents, Warren and Grace. There was Eddie, first of the
next bunch. "What are you *doing* here?" she asked him,
furious. Eddie made no more of an answer than he would
have alive.

Laurel stood in the wind, bareheaded, stubbing her toe
against the chunks of brown sod. They'd been conspirators, she
and Eddie, born fifteen months apart, both of them long and
thin. Each had Warren's hatchet nose and faint, almost colorless
hair. As they grew up, Eddie taught her solitary tricks he'd
learned—how to hot-wire the truck, how to hypnotize a
chicken with a penlight. Later on, Laurel taught him dirty lim-
ericks (though Eddie would surely never pass them along), and
got him to undo his top shirt button and use a little after-shave,
and not act so cowed. "Cheer up, Eduardo," she told him. "You
can be sweet, girls like a sweet boy." But Eddie didn't cheer up.
The muted, flinching part of him took over. Laurel left town. In
California, she went to night school and worked days for a
shipping company. When Eddie eventually graduated, she
phoned him long-distance. "Come and see the ocean," she offered. He sounded enormously far away. "Who knows," he
said, "I might just do that." But Laurel knew he never would.
A year later, she passed her Civil Service test—she was in Oki-
nawa. Had she run out on him, abandoned him? She wrote to
him now and then, but finally gave it up—he never answered,
what was the use? Eva sometimes wrote to her—airmail letters

full of dull, dutiful goings on. Eddie moved through them like a stick man.

Laurel had just put in for retirement when the cable reached her in Guam. She was camped out in her flat, waiting for the paperwork to clear, waiting for something new—which turned out to be housekeeping, back home. She had no intention of staying on in Montana, much less with Eva. Good Lord, what an arrangement. But by the end of the second week, the rest of the family had scattered. Eva was a mess. Untranquillized, she sobbed in place. Dosed, she strayed—Laurel found her on the stairs, cheek pasted to the wallpaper, and another day out in the loft of the shed going through boxes of machine parts.

"God only knows how I'm going to manage all this," Eva said.

Laurel didn't reply. But didn't she, somehow, offer those mealy-sounding words Eva required? Didn't she handle the bank, didn't she fix the first hundred suppers and endure their consumption, didn't she find somebody to cart off Eddie's drill press and the ancient Willys he'd had up on blocks near the chicken yard, not to mention six pairs of curly-soled boots loitering in the vestibule?

The house has gray-shingled walls, and stands alone at the top of the property. Pinewoods rise in back, alfalfa stretches south to the road. A few ravaged plum and crab-apple trees cling to the lumpy hillside. Mainly, it's a big, dark place, with a cluttered, wraparound closed-in porch. The "catchall," Laurel calls this, "the outdoor closet." It reeks of lacquer dust and creosote and ancient bug killers; its windows are like the bottom of an old baking dish. The house is further obscured by six towering blue spruce trees, installed by Warren Mahugh himself in the spring of 1929—a gift to his new wife, Eva reminds people. They're historic, symbolic of love: grand, sheltering trees. However, they were planted too close together and much too close to the house—it's as if he'd never envisioned them *growing*. The lower limbs have scrubbed the color from the shingles. The roots have infiltrated the foundation, the septic line, the flagstones in the walk. The trees drip sap, the needles clog the gutters and turn the soil too acidic for grass. They suffocate, Laurel says; they bury the household in an intractable gloom.

Eva has a headache, driving home. The spring sun is vicious—suddenly the world's all glass and stainless steel. The luncheon after Mrs. Proctor's service, held in a hot, fruity-smelling room, was thinly attended, and what could be said, really, about their old teacher Mrs. Proctor, years retired, her mind in tatters? We live too long, Eva thought, that's all there is to it. She finds herself staring, wishing for a beer. Just one, cold as a spike. Her head behind the car's visor, she is nearly to the top of the lane before she sees what has happened.

The trees have been cut down.

They're fanned out from the house, colossal green hulks stretching clear across the lawn. One has snapped off a section of rail fence, the top of another is curled awkwardly against the well house. The trunks have been cut into sections, and two are already limbed. There's a rusty, high-walled truck in the drive. Laurel is standing at the porch steps talking to a man kneeling by a red gasoline can. All this Eva sees in an instant. None of it seems remotely possible.

The man she recognizes as Ethan Wilder, a widower who lives down by the big curve, among a welter of vehicles and sloping outbuildings. She knew the wife a little from church—cancer of the ovaries, Eva recalls. He's wearing plastic goggles and a stocking cap and coveralls, woodchips from head to toe. He has grown a thicket of beard—that she notices, too.

Laurel steps forward, arms spread wide. "Shoot me," she says. "I just made a decision. The day had come."

Eva is beyond speech.

Ethan, who has been about to resume the limbing, lets the chain saw hang in one hand, now perceiving what he has done.

"Oh, now," he says. For all his size—his large shoulders and sloping belly—his movements seem gentle and precise.

Laurel touches one bare, sweaty forearm. "This will all be fine," she says reassuringly. "Really. Don't you worry."

Ethan draws back and tips his goggles up onto his forehead. "Mrs. Mahugh, now I never—" he says to Eva, but she is already striding off into the house. Laurel turns in time to see her kick nastily at the brick propping the porch door open. Ethan casts another look at the carnage. "I best leave this for today," he says. Moments later he rumbles away in the truck.

"That was the most *savage*—" Eva says.

"It wasn't either savage," Laurel says. "Such melodrama. You'd never do anything if it weren't for me."

Holding a dripping colander, she steps back from the sink window. "Look at the light in here," she says. The sky has gauzed over since midday, and the room is brandy-tinged, a tough light to nurse anger in.

Eva is still in her funeral outfit, though her earrings have been plucked off and deposited by the creamer. "I don't think I can eat," she says.

"You'll thank me," Laurel says.

There had been a little modernizing after Eddie and Eva moved back in. Eddie lowered the ceiling and laid in new countertops, and now there is a freestanding dishwasher, with a chopping board on top. But the cupboards are old, with chipped glass pulls, and the deep old porcelain sink remains, with a swan's-neck faucet and squeaky taps. Things clatter in this kitchen, voices carry.

"As God is my witness," Eva says, but no threat follows, and there's nothing, really, to suggest that God is going to make her vindication His special project.

"Have a glass of beer," Laurel says.

"I saw your eyes," Eva says. "There was *glee* in them."

"That's me. Lover of life."

It's going on midnight when Laurel finally slides under the covers in the downstairs bedroom. She lies on her back, savoring the cold sheets. There's a Walkman under her pillow, playing some Charlie Parker. She has no intention of sleeping yet. The screens are on, and the night enters deliciously, molecule by molecule. The music is dazzling, druggy. Her last conscious thought is she'd bet money Eva is upstairs in her cane rocking chair, with the lights out, smoking.

And so she is. Eddie had told Eva, years ago, never to smoke in bed. "Promise me!" he insisted. As a boy, he'd seen the Saxon Hotel fire downtown—six bodies laid out on the sidewalk under sheets. So Eva promised, continues to promise. She sits in the dormer, rocking. With the storms off, the night makes noise again—it's as if her ears have popped. But there's none of that rustle, that *sh-shushing* against the roof peak.

One spring, she remembers, crows took to the spruce, nasty braying things. She had sent Eddie out to scare them off, at five-thirty in the morning. He fired his shotgun in their vicinity —even in full daylight, you couldn't see them back in the branches. The crows flapped off, six or eight of them, heading toward the Mastersons' hayfield. But they were back the following morning, racketing, voices like hacksaws. Eddie slept on—soft simple sleep—he never dreamed, so he said (and never smelled unpleasant next to her, she remembered, only a little stale and sugary). She poked him, made him go out again in his bathrobe and spray more shot up at the crows. He stood back by the well house, a gray figure in the early light. Cones and needles rained down, but no dead crows. Eddie came back to bed. She thanked him, and he said, "Now, don't *thank* me, Eva," and went straight to sleep again, as if he'd been switched off. The next morning they went through the same drill. On the fourth day of it he said in that resigned way of his, "Eva, you're going to have to just put up with it." And so she had. June and July passed, and then the crows were gone, as if they'd been a black mood she'd outlived.

*   *   *

Drizzle in the A.M.

Laurel has her coffee in peace. Eva is off at church—this churchgoing is spotty, Laurel has noticed; not a response to guilt but to the creep of chaos. And Eva had to ask Laurel for the car again. "No sweat," Laurel said. "And why don't you gas it up while you're at it." Didn't *that* frost Eva.

Ethan Wilder is supposed to return after lunch, with his boys, but Laurel imagines that's off. The sound yesterday, that was what surprised her. The ground shaking—a great *whump*—made her jump straight in the air. She stood off to the side, awaiting the next. *Whump!* She shouted at him, her heart racing, but he couldn't hear over the saw.

Laurel carries her coffee out the side door. The stumps are oozing. Cones and debris everywhere. She steps back into the grass, getting her feet wet, looking at the house. It needs paint desperately. Maybe she'll have the porch ripped off, a deck put on, some latticework. But it looks naked now—tall and wan, an embarrassing old thing. The soffits are dry-rotted, the shingles are heaped with moss, and where they're not, they're thin as scales.

Laurel was right about Ethan Wilder. Kept his distance all day Sunday, letting the dust settle. Monday, her lilac suit out of dry dock again, she is back at work. She has her pension—decent, actually—but a few months of living with Eva made her hustle a job downtown in a den of lawyers. Shirtliff, the senior partner, stops before her desk this morning, red-cheeked, unsticking filaments of sweaty white hair from his forehead. He's found the sacrament of walking, pounds out the miles swinging little nickel-plated hand weights. "And how's your liver and lights?" he asks.

Laurel has her reputation in this office: utterly proficient, immune to the ordinary tomfoolery, a gamer. "Couldn't be finer," she answers, stretching, mock-languid. Shirtliff smiles, showing teeth. Later, she can hear him humming a bit of sad, lilting melody: "The days be fast a-wasting, and all the fair maids . . . something something." But nothing engages her today. Her mind idles, slips off into the sounds of traffic, the moseying of the dusty air. She finds herself in imaginary conversation—not with Shirtliff but with Ethan Wilder. She is smelling the pitch again, breathing the blue exhaust from the chain saw. She almost calls him, then laughs at herself—*You old bird*. At five, she gets into her car, finds it still reeking of Eva's mentholated smoke. She downshifts at the railroad crossing, and is startled again at how the house sits up at the top of the fields, so *exposed*. Then, roaring up the lane, she sees that the truck has come and gone, carrying away branches. Only the trunks remain, like fallen columns.

By Tuesday night, the trunks have been cut into stove rounds and stacked against the wire fence of Eddie's chicken run. A huge amount of wood—they'll be burning it winter after winter. The grass is muddy now, tracked by chunky tires and boot heels, but there's been an attentive raking. All that's left is eight or ten small mounds of needles and sticks waiting to be picked up. Tuesday is one of Eva's nights to cook. Supper appears at six o'clock straight up (even this is a concession, Eva insists—Eddie never could wait *that* long). And here it is: skinned chicken, steamed limas, Minute Rice and pimento. Monkish portions. There's been a realignment of the kitchen table: Laurel's chair now faces the sun. She smiles; this is nothing. "They make handsome blinds these days," she says. "Little slats—*louvres*."

"Why don't you go ahead and start," Eva says from the stove, seeing that Laurel, as usual, hasn't bothered to wait. Finally Eva sits, gets up for the lemon pepper, sits again.

"Any sweets?" Laurel asks.

"You know better than to ask," Eva says.

"Still peeved, are we?"

Eva looks at her, fork raised. "You make everything . . ." she begins.

What's the word she will light on? *Petty? Squalid?* Say it, Laurel thinks. Render judgment. But Eva fills her mouth with rice. Laurel watches the muscle in her jaw pumping, pumping, raising a knob of shadow.

Wednesday the stumps are gone. Ethan had explained before he'd made the first cut that ordinarily he'd yank them with his tractor and a tow chain. But there was a good chance—old as they were, and possibly grown into the stonework—that he might have to dose them with ROT-X and let them molder. "Or you could leave them be. Some do," he said. "If it was me, I'd want them gone."

And so they are gone, like huge wisdom teeth. The holes are filled in with dark, peaty loam—so fine-grained it must have been sifted through a screen. Now it's been seeded and tamped and sprinkled.

Eva seems brighter that night. Lacks the stuff for holding a deep grudge, Laurel imagines.

By Thursday evening, Eva's car has been restored to service, and she's out in it, apparently. Laurel, home from work, scans the counter for a note, sees none. She changes, and then roams the downstairs, awash with energy. She fixes a drink and takes it to the front steps. It's not quite warm enough to sit out. Nevertheless, she sits, stretching her legs, lightly goose-bumped. The sun is shouldering down through a ledge of cloud, striking the mountains across the valley pink. The pink of candy hearts, she thinks—of undercooked pork.

Up the lane, a moment later, lumbers Ethan Wilder's truck. He descends gingerly from the cab.

"You're an artist," Laurel says, waving her hand at the neat, bare earth.

This embarrasses him—not what she had in mind at all. She touches his chest. "No, look how you've opened it all up—you have no idea the gloom we had here."

But he won't look at his handiwork. He's not in work clothes, either. He's wearing chinos, a checked shirt with a brass-tipped string tie, clean boots. The panels of cheek above his whiskers have a shine.

What's going on? Is she supposed to offer him something? A beer?

"Well," she says. "I expect you'd like to get paid."

"Eva's not here?"

"Actually not," Laurel says brightly.

But there's a moment's sag in his shoulders, a settling of his substantial weight—she catches it. "Would you give her a message?" he asks. "Say . . ." But no, it's apparently not anything he can put into words.

The hayfields brighten, the days stretch out, a frail green haze begins to obscure the topsoil along the foundation. Evenings, Ethan Wilder becomes a common sight at the Mahugh house. He listens to Laurel's notions about the renovation, stands outside with her, looking where she points, offers the occasional "Uh-huh, uh-huh, don't see why not," and gets up and measures possible openings. But Eva is nearby, wearing Bermudas and a jaunty navy-striped blouse. She's had her hair hennaed. Furthermore, she's begun to take an interest in the remodelling.

"What do you think about skylights?" she asks Ethan one night. "Wouldn't they be, oh, I don't know, kind of—"

"Stimulating," Laurel says.

Eva coils, but then says, "Yes, I guess that is what I meant."

Of course, the only place you could stick a skylight in an old frame house like theirs is Eva's room, still called—cloyingly, Laurel feels—the master bedroom.

"You don't fool a soul," she tells Eva when they're alone again.

"You can't pick a fight with me," Eva replies.

"No, really. Anybody could see what you were up to out there."

Eva stubs out her Kool and gets up. "Won't take the bait," she says.

* * *

On July Fourth it comes up rain.

"Further evidence God isn't a working stiff," Laurel says.

No rise out of Eva.

"We were wondering," Eva says, later that day—*we:* she and Ethan, there it is—"if you wanted to come down to the lake and see the fireworks with us."

"You're kind," Laurel says. "But I don't believe I'll be able to squeeze that in."

Eva waits by the door, watching the lane, fiddling with her rain hood. "Well, you were invited," she says. "So you know."

Laurel shakes her head. "Look at you," she says.

"I look fine. There's nothing wrong with me."

Lord, what have I wrought? Laurel thinks, once they're gone, but it's not a thought she can bear. The house feels clammy— no place to be. She grabs her jacket finally, and drives to the movies, and by the time they're out, the rain has all but quit. She has that flushed, stupid feeling. She sweeps her hand through the beaded water on the car's roof, splashing some down into the neck of her shirt. *What now?* She swings out onto Montana Street, thinking maybe the Dairy Queen, then doesn't stop after all. She veers down through town—*cutting the gut,* isn't that what they used to call it? The lights smear by, packs of tiny fireworks dance and spit in the limited darkness. The traffic curls around the courthouse, low-slung cars like hers, thick with kids, but when they begin to turn out and loop back she goes straight and finds herself alone on the road, fighting back a sudden weakness of heart. She turns onto McCandlish, and takes the long way, past the orchards and the horse pastures, and, for no good reason, past Ethan Wilder's. The house is flanked by a woodlot, down out of the wind. All she's ever seen of it is the spidery antenna coming off the steel roof.

She makes the big curve and crests the hill and pulls off the road there, where she can see the whole lower valley, down to the north end of the lake. The sky is low and empty—nothing but black-bottomed cloud, and an occasional minor rocket launched from a boat. Cars are streaming away from the landing—they're backed up a mile at the cutoff to town.

Laurel stands breathing the wet air. Spectacle's over, she thinks.

Next morning, everything lies under a heavy mist. The Mastersons' sheep bleat in the distance. Ethan and his two boys arrive. "Boys"—they are twenty-five and twenty-eight, with tool belts and thermoses, and long glossy muscles extending from their shirtsleeves. Laurel moves past them, looking each one in the eye. She hands Ethan a square of paper with her work number. "Look, now call me if there's *anything*—I mean it," she says. She's galled at the idea of Eva presiding.

Shirtliff is out of town, and the younger men in the office are grumpy from the long weekend. Laurel forgoes lunch downtown and guns the car home, squinting fiercely. The air is glazed with light now, as the fog tries to burn off.

And yes, the porch roof has gone. The stained, rattling old porch windows are stacked on the truck bed, and the stud walls have been bared. Ethan's two boys are crouched in the wreckage, wolfing sandwiches and swilling cartons of milk. Ethan sits with his back to the shakes, legs splayed, slicing apple and cheese. Eva is standing before them, with her hands stuffed in her sweater pocket. "Can't I get you something else?" she asks Ethan.

"Don't hover, Eva," Laurel says.

Ethan collapses his little knife and gets up. "Can't pack it away like I used to," he says pleasantly. The boys yawn and rise. The wrecking bars come out again. Eva trails after Ethan, stepping anxiously, as if the ground were mined. Just beyond the new grass, he stops by a pair of sawhorses and begins jerking nails from the salvaged wood. An easy, practiced motion, a brief wincing sound.

This can't possibly last, Laurel thinks.

In the next days, posts are sunk, cedar decking creeps around the side of the house, and a sliding glass door goes in. Huge, immaculate Thermopanes replace the stingy downstairs windows. Foam is blown into the walls, and one of the boys spends a morning on a stepladder tapping new shakes into place. Ethan is careful to ask Laurel, "How's this look to you now? This pretty much how you had it pictured?"

"Yes, it seems perfectly—" Laurel says. But what? For all the pointing and talking out loud, she hardly had it *pictured* at all. Wasn't it more a craving? Light! Air!

At last, one of the boys—Martin, the lankier, unmarried one —climbs onto the main roof and saws out a long rectangle of shingle and planking as, inside, Laurel watches Ethan cut away plaster and lath and rafters. Eva has smothered everything with sheets. The dust flies everywhere, swirling in with the fresh air. The other boy, Walt, has taken the truck down to pick up the skylight. He's the younger, more subdued one, with an oily-faced, hugely pregnant wife. Something about him reminds Laurel of Eddie: the way he turns away as he's spoken to, expecting blame.

Now he's back from Sperry Glass, empty-handed. "Sent the wrong size," he reports.

"Cripes!" Ethan says, the most violent display of temper Laurel has yet seen out of him. "How long'd they say?"

The boy shrugs, starts explaining: the manager wasn't in, there was a question about who'd actually written down the measurements, the company is clear back in *Toledo* . . .

Ethan puts a hand up. "Run and get me that roll of Vis-Queen," he says. "The black."

Walt removes himself, dodging past Laurel in the doorway. Ethan wipes his eyelids with his thumbs and takes a slow breath, looking around at the white-draped room. *This is her bedroom*, his face says. *These are her things. . . .*

Eva is down on one knee, collecting chunks of plaster in a dustpan. "Eva?" he says, hesitating, then touching her shoulder. "*Eva*. I'll get that."

* * *

This, as it turns out, is the first night Eva fails to come home. It's Saturday noon before she surfaces. Laurel is picking at leftovers in the kitchen. "I was this close to calling out the gendarmes," she announces.

Eva gives her that look, her minute tremor of disapproval. "I don't believe that for a second," she says. "You knew where I was."

Laurel scrapes her chair back and slides the rest of her lunch into the compost. "Aren't you something," she says.

Eva sets down her bag, a little green canvas thing with a strap, digs into the pie saver for a fresh pack of Kools, and rips into them. "I'm a perfectly ordinary person," she says. "With ordinary needs. I have no pretensions to the higher life."

Without meaning to, Laurel laughs.

Eva turns. "I know what you're going to try next and you can save your breath," she says.

"What? Tell me."

Eva's eyes burn. "I will not have you spoiling this," she says.

"Now, why on earth would I want—" Laurel begins, by rote. But it's true, she was already casting about for some disparagement, some sly prediction.

"You've said the last hateful thing to me," Eva says, exiting, trailing smoke, her hips switching with vindication. Out into the dining room she goes, and up the stairs, *clip, clip.*

Water runs briefly in the pipes. The house settles into a heavy stillness and the minutes pass. Laurel's legs weave among the chair rungs. It's hot, finally, wilting hot, hot down into the earth.

Is she hateful? Is that all she is, another sour, disappointed soul?

There is at least this: she has held her tongue about Eddie. She has never once gotten into it with Eva, never pinned her down: *Tell me why a happy, married man, with a wife he adores, drives his truck forty miles back in the hell-and-gone and puts his shotgun in his mouth. Explain that away, Eva.*

There is no blaming Eva; there is no story, with its simple satisfactions, to badger out of her. Eva is as baffled as she is.

Laurel stands, unsticks the blouse from her stomach, and mounts the staircase, calling lightly from the landing, "Eva? Eva?" It will be miserable up on the second floor—hotter yet, stuffy, the stale air hardly stirring.

She touches Eva's door and it gives. There's an old-fashioned lacquered suitcase open on the bed, some white things folded inside, a camisole. But—it's crazy—Eva has gone to the opening in the roof and scissored a jagged, three-sided hole in the black plastic. She's on tiptoe, looking out, framed against the sky, with her dark head of hair blowing. From the back and below, she looks as if she might begin to rise and disappear. Laurel has to wonder, just for a minute, if she will hold her down.

Harriet Doerr

WAY STATIONS

The train from the border was two hours late and, when it finally rolled into the station, no one left the sleeping car.

"They missed it in Juárez," said Richard Everton.

"Or were left behind after one of the stops," said his wife Sara. "In Palacios, or El Alamo, or Santa Luz. Maybe Steve wanted to take pictures." But her concern began to sound in her voice. "As for Kate," she went on, "Kate's lived in so many time zones that she's stopped needing clocks. She's like the people here," Sara said. "She tells time by the sun and stars."

And once more the Evertons walked the length of the train from the locomotive to the rear car, making their way through crowds of laden passengers, boarding and unboarding the day coaches.

Richard was questioning the conductor when Sara called. "There's Kate."

She waved to a reluctant, red-haired woman who clung to a furled umbrella and hesitated at the top of the train's rear steps as if the platform were thirty feet below and in flames.

Sara had time to say to Richard, "Something's wrong," before she lifted her face to Kate and asked, "Where's Steve?" For Kate had apparently come by herself to spend a week in Ibarra.

The Evertons stood with the porter below the vestibule and all three raised an arm to bring Kate to them before she could suffer a change of heart and simply travel on.

At last she spoke. "I'm alone," she said, and stepped down.

The Evertons led their guest away from the station, saying nothing to each other and only "No," to the vendors of bananas and tacos, baskets and lace. Except that Kate, approached by a ragged child crusted with dust, bought his entire stock of candy-coated gum and paid for it in dollars.

While Richard lifted Kate's suitcases into the car, she stood motionless, her umbrella planted against the ground like a divining rod.

Richard took it from her. "There won't be rain for three months. Not until June," he said.

Sara, looking in the direction of the platform, said, "Here comes Inocencia."

An old woman, wrapped in a number of shawls and bent as a gnarled branch, approached them in a patchwork of skirts that swept the dirt and stirred up discarded trash.

Ancient of days, Sara thought, and of winds and frosts and cobblestones. "Inocencia begs in Ibarra," she explained to Kate, "and here in Concepción, when she can get a ride."

On the way back to Ibarra Kate sat with Richard in front and Sara behind with Inocencia. I would like to call her Chencha as the cura does, thought Sara. It is less formal. But there was something in the old woman's blackbird eyes, something about her slippered feet set parallel on the floor that discouraged intimacy.

They turned north from the station toward the mountains and in ten minutes were on a narrow road winding around hillsides and through gullies.

"How was the train?" Sara asked. "Did the fan work? Was there ice?"

As though she had not heard, Kate made no response. She has traveled so much that details like these are immaterial to her, Sara supposed.

Neither of the Evertons asked about Steve. Once Richard pointed to three silos clustered in the corner of a field like white wigwams and once to a vineyard covered with the green mist of breaking leaves. "Revisions in the landscape since you saw it last," he said.

From the back seat Sara watched Kate nod.

After that Richard said nothing at all and Sara spoke once. Reminded when they passed the chapel of a crumbling *hacienda*, she said, "Next Wednesday is the day of the priests. We are invited to a program." This information produced no answer.

Not until they turned west at a pond where cows grazed in the muddy bottom, not until the car started to climb toward the hills did Kate utter a word. Then she said, "We are separated." Not "Steve and I." Simply "We." As if she were pronouncing separation to be a universal condition, a state in which every man and woman slept and woke. Sara looked at the back of Richard's head, as if for reassurance.

As they neared the summit of the mountain grade, Kate spoke again. "Steve decided at the border not to come. There was no way to let you know in time." She appeared to be talking to herself. "He says living with me is like serving a sentence." She might have been addressing the burro asleep on its feet in the road ahead of them.

But they blame themselves, Sara thought, in sight of each other, for the death of the child. Since the day of the accident, guilt has taken up quarters with them. And blame just outside the door, rattling the knob.

Divide the blame, Sara wanted to tell her friend, who sat mute and stiff in the seat ahead. Blame the precocious two-year-old and his suddenly longer reach. Blame the box beside the door, the latch that didn't stick. Blame your quiet street and the one car on it. Blame the mother of five who drove it and who wept at the time and is probably weeping still. Blame her.

Sara said all these things silently to Kate as they reached the top of the grade. Now the car was bumping down the stony track into Ibarra and Inocencia was edging forward from the back seat.

"She wants to get out here," Sara told Richard. "In front of the church." For these steps seemed a better source of alms than either the grocer's or the baker's door, now that a dozen black-shawled women and a few old men were gathering to celebrate noon mass.

Descending to the street with a rattle of coins, Inocencia stooped to search the ground as if she might discover a silver peso among the cobbles. Then she made her way around the car, approached Kate's window, and thrust in a hand like a parrot's claw.

Kate seemed not to recognize its purpose. Eventually Richard had to extend his long arm across her in order to drop small change into the old woman's palm.

"God will repay you," said Inocencia.

The beggar addressed this remark to everyone in the car. When, wondered the Evertons. How, wondered Kate.

For the first three days of her visit Kate came to breakfast at ten, two hours after Richard had left for the mine and Sara gone into the early shade of the garden to water and trim. With the sun already above the trees, the Evertons' guest entered the whitewashed kitchen, found coffee, fruit, and rolls, and ate in front of the dining room window. Through it she gazed at Sara tearing apart iris and dividing ferns. And gazed further to the olive trees and beyond them to the high wooden gate that opened on the road. Entering this gate every morning as Kate started to eat and advancing with deliberation toward the house came Lourdes, the cook, who arrived in midmorning to prepare lunch and dinner and to save, if she could, the Evertons' souls.

Kate's Spanish was limited to simple phrases. Those of curiosity: "What is the destination of this bus?" or "Is there a direct route to the international airport?" And those of crisis: "Please deliver an urgent message," or "A single bed, please. My husband is not with me." When Lourdes came into the dining room to talk, the visitor understood only a few words.

Kate knew the words for thin and eat, and also for when and why, but not the answers. She knew that Don Esteban was Steve. So when Lourdes said, "Will not your husband follow you by a later train?" and, "Have you had an illness to make you look so pale?" Kate, rather than let an awkward silence fall, replied indiscriminately with "*No*" or "*Si.*"

Concerned by the portent of these responses, Lourdes began to leave talismans among the guest's folded clothes. So that when Kate rummaged for a sweater or a scarf she would find bits of knotted twine or graying ribbon hidden in them. Once she discovered half a tortilla curling on her window sill.

On the third day of her visit as she lay apparently asleep in a hammock woven of maguey, she opened her eyes to ask Sara where the scraps she had found came from and what they meant.

"Lourdes wants you to be well and safe."

"I thought it might have something to do with getting into heaven."

"That, too," said Sara.

The hammock had not known such constant use since the day a month ago when Richard strung it up. Here, a few feet above the ground, Kate lay morning and afternoon, often with an arm across her eyes.

She can't sleep at night, Sara told herself, and abandoned hopes of conversation. Instead, she skirted the hammock at a distance and suppressed impulses to point out hummingbirds in the jasmine or a stray turkey on the path. Once or twice a day she was called to the gate by a visitor.

At these times Kate, roused from sleep or sorrow, would become aware of talk across the garden. *"Señora,"* she would hear a strange voice say, and then Sara's *"Dígame."*

"What does that mean?" the guest finally asked. *"Dígame."*

"It means 'tell me.'"

That night in bed, Sara said to Richard, "Do you think that hammock lends itself to grieving?" and Richard said that if so, it was a problem easily cured.

He was almost asleep when Sara said, "Do you think she should take a trip somewhere? Arrive by river boat and narrow gauge railroad at a place she doesn't know?"

Richard said, "That might work."

"She used to be obsessed by going places," and Sara reminded him of Kate's years of impulsive wanderings.

"But you're not her Saint Christopher," said Richard.

He removed the hammock before breakfast the next morning.

"The cords were fraying," Richard later lied to Kate.

That afternoon the two women walked up the dirt lane to the ruined monastery of Tepozán. Next to the chapel, the monks' roofless habitations had become wells of sunlight. Kate and Sara crossed the paved courtyard to lean on the balustrade that bordered an arroyo. The place was ringed with silence. They heard neither the ore truck climbing the mountain nor the shouts of boys carrying hot lunches to the miners. Now and then an old woman on a cane limped into the chapel and another one limped out.

"Do they still use the chapel for mass?" asked Kate.

"Only on special days." Sara turned her face up to the sun. "There's a procession once a year behind the effigy of *El Señor,* the patron of Tepozán."

"Señor who?"

"Christ," said Sara.

After a pause, Kate said, "Didn't we have a picnic under

those trees?'' surprising Sara who was convinced by now that her friend had erased permanently any memories, even the slightly happy ones, of her past.

Sara remembered the picnic under the ash trees. It had been three years ago, a wet green August day between the rainstorms of one afternoon and the next. The Evertons had brought Kate and Steve to the monastery to eat because of this greenness, of the ash trees, of the corn planted in the patio behind, of the twisted grapevine near the well, even of the cactus on this hill.

That day at Tepozán they had spread a wool *sarape* on the pink stone of the balustrade and sat along it in a row. Damp weeds made a tangled rug under their feet and the washed leaves overhead still dripped from time to time. While they ate bread and cheese and slices of papaya, a herd of goats chewed their way across the hillside behind, shaking bells and loosening small rains of stones. This picnic was so tranquil, with the sun on their backs and the stillness held in suspension, that Sara believed a charm had fallen on each one of them.

Then Steve said, "How is the experiment working out?"

At first the Evertons thought he was speaking of a medical experiment, of pills that might, in combination with others, add new dimensions to Richard's life.

"What experiment?" said Richard.

"The mine," said Steve. And again Richard and Sara were silent. For they had long ago stopped thinking of the mine operation as an experiment. The experiment had turned, almost from the beginning, into a lifelong effort.

"How much longer will you be here?" Steve asked, as if he considered the tunnels and ladders of the mine, the rough streets and leaning roofs of Ibarra, and the thousand people who lived under these roofs to be a point of interest in a travel guide, recommended for a side trip.

"Indefinitely," said Richard.

* * *

And now, three years later, standing with Kate at the monastery in hot dry March, Sara said, "That was the greenest day of the summer."

Kate said nothing. Finally she walked away, letting her words drift back over her shoulder.

"How can we live with death between us?"

That "We" again, thought Sara.

That night in bed, Sara said to Richard, "It's hopeless. She is numb to everything."

He turned to his wife. "Tell me what to do."

"You could show her the mine."

The following day Richard sent his foreman to the house in the pickup truck with instructions to bring Kate to the mine. She was gone all morning and returned at one, blown and dusty.

She found Sara on the porch looking out over Ibarra as if she had noticed it today for the first time. Kate sat on a bench beside her.

"This is what Richard has always wanted, isn't it? This place, these people, you in this house." Then she went on as if in logical sequence, "I think Steve is in love with another woman. Someone happy."

Later she said, "All that machinery, those crushers and cells and belts. They're like Richard's personal creations."

Half metal and half hope, Sara silently commented. An alloy.

An hour later Kate said, as though there had been no pause, "Then he and the foreman drove me all over the hills to look down the shafts of abandoned mines."

Earlier, from the porch, Sara had noticed the pickup traveling cross-country, winding steeply into sight around one hillside and out of sight around another. So they had visited them all. Reciting the names of mines to herself, Sara strung them together like beads.

The Mercy, the Rattlesnake, the Incarnation, La Lulu.

* * *

That night Richard reported, "She's not like you. She's not interested in mines."

"There's still the village," Sara said. "Tomorrow I'll try that."

On Tuesday the two women followed the eroded ruts that led from the house to the village. As they entered the plaza, a spiral of dust whirled from the arcade, lingered over the cobblestones to suck up straw and paper, then careened in their direction.

"It was cleaner three years ago," said Kate.

"You came in August, in the rainy season. Summer in Ibarra is a different time, in a different place."

They sat on a cement bench facing the church. The bench had been donated by Pepsi Cola, whose name was lettered on the back.

"Steve and I should have been religious," said Kate.

"Why?"

"Religious people blame God."

Out of his house next to the church appeared the cura, followed by his elderly assistant. As soon as the priests reached the street half a dozen stray dogs on the church steps stretched in their sleep, lifted their heads, and rose to trot after the older man.

The cura approached the bench and Kate was introduced. "But we met on your last visit," said the priest. "Is your husband with you?" When there was no answer, he went on, "I shall expect all four of you, then, tomorrow evening at the nuns' school." And when there was still no reply, he said, "At eight o'clock," and the two priests walked away, their habits brushing the cobbles and six gaunt hounds strung out behind.

Kate watched them disappear behind the post office. "In Ibarra even the dogs believe," she said. Then, "Do we have to go? Tomorrow night?"

"We will explain that Steve was detained," said Sara. And when Kate sat on as though the bench had become her newest refuge, Sara started across the street. "Let's go inside the church. It's been repainted."

They mounted the steps, entered the empty nave, and were wholly immersed in blue, the blue of lakes, of water hyacinths, of October noons. Sara and Kate stood on the buckling tile floor as they might at the bottom of the sea.

Encased in glass at the altar stood the Virgin, a plaster statue wearing a filigree crown and a white satin dress.

"Lourdes helps make her clothes," said Sara. "All this is new since last year, the gown, the beaded slippers, the nylon stockings, the rhinestone necklace." She regarded the serene face.

"This Virgin hasn't always been here," Sara said. "She came from a closed chapel in another village and probably, before that, from another one somewhere else." The figure's calm brown eyes rested on her. Sara added, "All the way back to Spain."

"Then, for her, Ibarra is only a way station," said Kate.

Sara turned to look at her friend. She is becoming perceptive again, Sara thought. I must tell Richard tonight.

They walked into the east transept to look at the statue of the Virgin of Sorrows and into the west transept to look at the painted stations of the cross, then left the church. Standing outside sunstruck for a moment, they made out the indistinct forms of the cura, his assistant, and six dogs coming toward them through the colonnaded shadow of the arcade. And noticed, too, Inocencia on the top step, bundled into all the garments she had ever owned, her hand outstretched.

Sara was reaching into her pocket for a coin when the cura came up behind them. "I have remembered something," he said to Kate. "On your husband's last visit he took a colored picture inside the church and promised me a copy. But I never received it." He noticed that Doña Sara's friend, this woman so fair of skin and red of hair, was like a child, easily distracted, a moment ago by the dogs and now by a hornet that, after hanging uncertain at the door, had in a single angry rush entered the nave.

The cura went on, "If your husband has the photograph with him, it would be an addition to tomorrow's observance."

Neither woman spoke. The cura continued as he might if he had been talking to himself. "Of course, it may have been lost in the mail. Especially if posted as an ordinary letter. To certify is best. Otherwise we risk a loss."

Now he is doing it, and with such authority, thought Sara. That "We" again.

The day of the priests dawned and remained overcast. At noon Sara looked up and said, "It's usually not this cloudy in March."

That evening when they started for the nuns' school, Kate came to the car with her umbrella.

"You won't need that," said Richard. "The first rain of the season isn't due until the twenty-fourth of June, the day of John the Baptist."

"Is it always on schedule?"

"About as often as the train from Juárez. But that's no reason to change the timetable."

Lourdes rode to the village with them, carrying a package wrapped in purple paper. Inside it, she told the Americans, was a table cloth she had embroidered for the cura.

"Does everyone in Ibarra bring a present?" asked Sara.

"Only those who are Catholics."

"You mean everyone except us."

"Except you and two socialists and a communist."

At the nuns' school two children led the Evertons and Kate the length of the patio between benches already filled with townspeople. Ahead of them they saw an empty platform and in front of it seven wooden chairs.

From one of these, the cura rose to introduce the Evertons' guest to his assistant, Padre Javier, and to his aunt, Paulita. Only now, with the Americans assembled, did he notice Steve's absence. Sara opened her mouth to explain and Richard also seemed about to speak. But Kate broke in before excuses could be made.

"We are parted," she said in her elementary Spanish. "*Estamos partidos.*"

Even if the cura had correctly heard her say, "*partidos,*" he might have misunderstood, for the word could imply separations of any width from a hair's breadth to the vast reaches between the poles. As it was, in the excitement of the moment, he failed to grasp Kate's meaning. Confused by his own exhilaration and her accent, the priest believed her to say, "*Estamos perdidos,*" and assumed the North Americans were actually lost. As if they were unable to see the seven chairs, he seated the Evertons and Kate one by one, and in the vacant place, without further questions, deposited his own brown overcoat.

Padre Javier, the empty chair and Richard were on the cura's left; the three women, with Kate in the farthest seat, on his right. The cura's intention had been to divide the men and women into congenial separation, with the two strangers who had difficulty with the language at some distance from himself. Now an unoccupied chair intervened on the men's side but, in any case, the cura had things to say privately to Don Ricardo, matters involving repairs at the school, restorations at the monastery, preservation of the church's mosaic dome—all excellent suggestions for the use of mine profits.

The program began with an outpouring of tributes. All those in Ibarra with close connections to religion—the president of Acción Católica, the chairman of Catholic Youth, the organist, the sexton, the mother superior of nuns—all stood to certify that, without the cura, there might be neither church nor chapel in Ibarra, nor a single Catholic to enter them.

Tributes were still being offered when a sudden gust blew in from the street, a hush descended, and rain began to fall. The Evertons looked up into the drizzle as if into the face of a betrayer and the cura reached across Richard for his overcoat. At his right, Paulita, sitting between Sara and Kate, put up her umbrella.

Now, under this precipitation, two dim lamps, and the guidance of a nun, children of the parish school presented two plays. The first one involved a ten-year-old father, a nine-year-old mother, and a doll. But in this drama there followed so many arguments and tears, so many clutchings up and tossings down of the doll that the plot remained obscure. As a finale, the father tugged a goat onto the platform, the mother said, "Praise God," and the two parents embraced the doll and bowed.

"He has given up card playing to become a farmer," Paulita explained to Sara and Kate, who had buttoned their sweaters to the neck and tucked their hands into the sleeves.

Sara turned her head to see Richard, strands of black hair limp on his forehead, engaged in conversation with the cura. She noticed his unsmiling mouth and how the old scar on his cheek shone white. The priest is asking for something, Sara told herself, but it is no use. Richard will die of pneumonia before the mine can afford the contribution. Beyond her husband and the empty chair, Padre Javier sat with his white head bowed, sleeping as soundly as he would under a roof, on a mattress with two blankets.

Paulita laid her hand, light and brittle as a fallen leaf, on Sara's arm. "It is only sprinkling," she said, "but come closer," and, shifting her umbrella, she tried to pull the two North American women under it.

The second play concerned the awakening of faith in a small, shy boy, recognized at once by Sara.

"He's one of Lourdes' grandchildren," she told Kate, who had spread a white handkerchief on top of her head as though it were a shawl, and waterproof.

They watched this child, on his steep ascent to priesthood, mature and age before their eyes. By means of a brief disappearance behind a stone column where he changed, item by item, from sandals to black shoes, denims to black pants, and added a jacket, hat, and eventually a stiff white collar. Through these various incarnations he was urged on, first by his family, then by his teachers, and finally, when he put on the collar, by his congregation, played by all the other children in the school, who now crowded onto and around the platform, each carrying a present.

Everyone applauded, the children bowed and disappeared leaving a pile of vividly wrapped packages behind.

The cura, recognizing his cue, rose from his seat and moved forward.

Kate chose this moment to lean in front of Paulita and question Sara. "Where am I to go?" she said, as though she had not noticed the child priest attain his goal step by step, but, instead, had sat here, damp and oblivious, planning an itinerary of her own.

"Stay with us longer," Sara said, and as the cura opened his mouth to speak, saw under the limp white handkerchief a negative shake of Kate's head.

The cura was explaining the hierarchy of the church. "There is a direct line," he told the audience. "It leads from you through your priests to the bishop, and from him to the cardinal, and then to the pope, and from the pope to God."

Sara imagined this line extending straight up, like a Hindu rope trick, into the sky over Ibarra, where it intersected the courses of the planets and the patterns of constellations.

"The priests of Ibarra are your spiritual parents," the cura said. "The *señor* Everton and his *señora* are your material parents."

Sara believed she saw Richard turn pale and she stood up to leave. With Kate between them, the Evertons left the nuns' school through crowds of expectant faces, already happier and more composed, already better fed.

Kate, rising early the next morning, brought her train ticket to the breakfast table.

"It's for tomorrow," said Richard in a voice grown husky overnight. "From Concepción to Juárez. We should be at the station by six in the evening." He looked up from his plate.

"But you're leaving too soon. There are things you haven't seen."

"Yes, stay on," said Sara. But in the end Kate refused their invitations to visit outlying points of interest—the hot springs, the bull ranch, the cathedral in an adjoining state.

"None of them is far from here," said Richard, and on his way out, left some maps beside Kate's plate. She was still there, alone, looking at maps, when Lourdes arrived for the day.

"How did you like the program?" she asked Kate.

"Very much," said the visitor, and added, "Your grandson is a fine actor."

Lourdes said, "Yes. And he already helps his father mold and fire clay pots."

"How many children do you have?" asked Kate.

"Six," said Lourdes. "Two dead."

Kate reached for her coffee, which had grown cold. "And how many grandchildren?"

"Fourteen. Three dead."

A moment later Kate heard, as she had all her mornings in this house, Lourdes' clear contralto filling the kitchen and the adjoining rooms with song. She sang love songs and songs about places. "*Ay, ay, ay*," sang the cook.

Before she left for the village that afternoon, Lourdes approached Kate. "*Señora*, I saw the tickets. Do you mean to leave us?" When Kate nodded, Lourdes shook her head and said, "So soon."

At noon on Friday Kate heard Sara say, "*Dígame*," and saw the visitor was Inocencia, asking again for a ride, this time to the railroad station.

"How did she know we were going?"

"As soon as Lourdes left here yesterday afternoon, all of Ibarra knew," said Sara.

That afternoon they drove off at dusk, seated in the car as they had been a week ago. On this trip neither Richard nor Inocencia had anything to say. Kate and Sara each spoke once.

"Lourdes put this in my bag," said Kate, and held up a twist of red thread.

"It is meant to bring you back," said Sara.

When they arrived at the station two trains, one facing north and one south, were already there, standing on adjacent tracks and preparing for departure.

"The southbound is six hours late," said Richard, "and the northbound half an hour early."

He hired a porter and said to Kate and Sara, "Wait here." Inocencia had already established herself beside the nearest train, reciting lists of her infirmities at the open windows of day coaches. Through the glass door of the waiting room Sara could see Richard attempting to validate Kate's ticket at a counter besieged with hands, peso bills, and protestations.

When she turned back to the platform, Kate had disappeared. Sara ran up to Inocencia. "Where is the North American *señora?*" But the old woman misunderstood and began to beg from Sara.

The southbound express, on the farther track, was now in motion, was gliding almost silently past a switch to the mainline, and when Richard emerged from the waiting room with Kate's ticket, all that could be seen of the train was the red lantern at its rear.

At this time Kate's porter, without suitcases or a client, came to the Evertons with a message. The *señora* had taken the other train. That one. And he pointed down the tracks in the direction of the Mexican states of Jalisco, Guanajuato, and Michoacán. The porter handed the Americans a note.

Using a pencil and a scrap of newspaper, Kate had written, "I've gone on."

On the way back to Ibarra, Inocencia dozed on the backseat while Sara sat in front and watched stars come out over the mesa.

"But where will Kate go?" she asked her husband.

"It depends on how much she tipped the conductor. Perhaps all the way to Mexico City."

"But if not, if she couldn't make him understand, what then?"

"Then one of the stops between. Felipe Pescador for instance." And they remembered an old town near a lake gone dry, a town of a church, a bar, and a straggle of farms.

"Or La Chona," said Sara. "It has an inn. And that plaza."

On the moonless road to Ibarra she reminded Richard of the trees in the plaza of La Chona. So ambitious was the gardener that he had clipped a pair of laurels into the crowned figures of Ferdinand and Isabella and then trimmed a tree that faced them into Christopher Columbus, presenting his report. And behind Columbus, as though he had brought them along, three leafy ships, the Niña, the Pinta, and the Santa María, sailed up the graveled path.

Perri Klass

DEDICATION

The baby is two weeks old, and Martin's wife is leaking. When the baby cries, her breasts start to leak, and her shirts all have dried milk stains, symmetrically placed, one on each side. At night, the baby sleeps in a bassinet next to their bed, and wakes up crying, and Martin in the morning finds damp patches where the milk leaked onto the sheets.

Everything is leaking. Martin watches his wife hold the baby to her shoulder after nursing, always murmuring the same ritual phrase. "Big burpee," she croons, drawing out "big" into two syllables for emphasis. And the baby burps, often leaking a little milky stuff, and automatically his wife murmurs, "good girl, what a good girl." The baby leaks out the other end too, though Martin knows his wife is conscientiously trying to spare him all exposure to diapering. It is clear to him that she doesn't think he'll be able to take it.

Martin's wife, Julia, has always been both superbly organized and extremely neat, and he has a little trouble adjusting now to all the stains, the disorder and dampness. She showers sometimes twice a day, but a few hours later she no longer smells like herself; she smells of milk and faintly even of blood.

She is still superbly organized, in her way—look how she had the baby in the second week of summer vacation, after submitting all her grades. Look how she nurses the baby; she had a special nightgown all ready, with slits in the front, and a pile of novels she had been meaning to read. He finds her in the rocking chair, the baby sucking away for dear life, and Julia reading her way through one book after another.

Of course, she knows what she's doing. She's done all this before. Maybe one reason he finds this so disconcerting is that it reminds him of something he would rather not think about in detail: Jimmy's infancy, Jimmy's early childhood. Jimmy's father.

Jimmy, who is ten, has started calling his mother The Mammal. He seems to be mildly amused and mildly disgusted by the whole baby business, and with Martin he affects a male camaraderie, which Martin is glad to reciprocate. Martin has said, once or twice to friends, since marrying Julia, that this must be the ideal way to have children. To acquire a very bright child at the age of seven, by marrying its mother. To skip all the early stuff, before it can talk. To befriend it, and form a relationship based on mutual regard. In fact, Martin is very proud of being close to Jimmy; it is just the kind of thing so many of his friends thought he would never be able to do.

The baby is only two weeks old, and Jimmy has to play in a chess tournament, so Martin takes him and Julia stays home. Martin is proud to be walking into the high school cafeteria with Jimmy, and even prouder when Jimmy wins his first game. Martin himself is not much of a chess player, and Jimmy can beat him every time. He watches with admiration how Jimmy concentrates, how Jimmy scowls down at the board while the clock is ticking, and thinks how his old friends would be surprised to see him, surprised to know he could watch hours of a game he doesn't particularly like, all because he cares about a ten-year-old.

At home, Martin imagines, Julia is curled up on the couch

holding the baby. The baby, newly awake, opens her eyes wide and reaches out with her hands, reaches out for nothing. "Froggy," Julia will say, softly, or maybe "Fishie." And kiss the baby on her cold little nose, and smooth down the tracing of dark hair on her head. The baby will look around a little more, now folding her hands in front of her, and then begin turning her head to the side, insistently, mouth open. And by then, Julia will be leaking.

The baby is the most beautiful thing Martin has ever seen.

Julia had been married before, but not Martin. His friends did not expect him to get married, not in his late forties, all of a sudden. Some of them probably assumed he was gay, which was not true and never had been, while others had met one or another of the quiet serious literary women with whom he had had quiet and ultimately insignificant love affairs. His life seemed to fall of its own accord into gentle even patterns, a good life for a writer. He was increasingly successful; he wrote short carefully dense novels about complicated unhappy people. Each one took him a long time to write, and seemed to him extremely incendiary; he felt he was always stealing plot from the lives of people around him, from his friends' marriages and divorces, their emotional convulsions, their failures and their collapses. But the critics, when they complained, complained that his novels were too much alike, too clearly reflective of his own inner landscape. Still, he was taken seriously, he was discussed. He also wrote a series of murder mysteries, intricate puzzles set in an invented college town, solved by a mild-mannered eccentric aging graduate student. In every book, the perpetual student put aside his dissertation to find the murderer, and finally came back to it, in the end, the mystery solved. These mysteries had been quite successful, and the extra money coming in had made it, as Julia had pointed out, an even more ideal time to have a baby.

She was a molecular biologist, a professor at the state university. She had been divorced five years before Martin met her from another biologist, who had moved to Washington, D.C., to work at the National Institutes of Health, and had gradually stopped paying child support. Jimmy had no clear memory of his father. No one had heard from him in years. Julia met Martin when he called her to check out a question for a mystery novel: Could you definitively identify a murderer by matching his genes to the genes in a blood stain? Martin had set up a young man to be falsely accused, then had to wonder: could this sort of thing now be tested scientifically? The biology department had referred him to Julia, since she studied genes. She couldn't really answer the question, but they had fun with it on the phone, and he ended up telling her quite a bit of his plot. It was she who invited him to meet her for coffee, but it was he, actually, who proposed, six months later. His friends might be surprised to know that; they seemed to assume that Julia willed, planned, and managed the whole romance. On the contrary, he was the one who argued her into marriage, insisting that the three of them, he and she and Jimmy, would work as a family. It was, however, she who brought up the idea of having a baby, two years later, and argued him into it.

Martin is amazed at the ferocity of the baby, less than eight pounds of pure will. I want, I want, I want. If Julia cannot immediately pick her up and feed her, her crying intensifies, her tiny face turns dark red, and she screams so hard she loses her breath, exhausts herself by forgetting to breathe in between wails. Then there is a pause in the screaming, while she gives up and takes the breath she needs, and then louder than ever, she starts again. She does not "cry herself to sleep," a phrase Martin is sure he has heard somewhere. Julia finally lifts her up from her bassinet and the baby stops screaming and roots around in the air; making her kissing-fish face, expecting a nipple in her mouth. "It's coming, it's coming," Julia tells her, laughing, moving to the rocking chair, settling down, unbuttoning her shirt. When Julia actually puts the baby up against her bare breast, the baby makes no noise at all. Her whole tiny body shivers with determination and she jerks her head more and more insistently to the side, trying to connect with the nipple. Martin finds himself thinking of the term 'heat-seeking missile.' "Relax," Julia tells the baby, guiding the breast to the proper angle. "Relax, no one's going to take it away from you." The little pink mouth suddenly lunges, clamps, pulls in on Julia's breast, and the baby's body stops trembling, all at once, as Julia's body seems to shudder gently in return. The connection is made, the rocking chair begins to creak.

Martin can hardly believe that he is partially responsible for the creation of anything so determined, so fierce. He had expected to be frightened by the baby's vulnerability, to be afraid of hurting it or doing something wrong. Instead, he frequently finds himself quailing before the furious red gnome face, apologetic because he does not have what she wants.

You didn't tell me you wanted another child, he had said, rather accusingly, to Julia. Is that why you married me, then? No, she said, I married you because I love you, and in fact I love you so much that now I want to have a baby with you.

Her voice was perfectly serious. He has at times wondered whether it is because she is a scientist that she can talk in such bald and unapologetic ways.

Don't worry, she said. I'll take care of the whole thing. I know you weren't bargaining for a child. You'll end up being glad we did it.

His friends mostly shook their heads. Poor old Martin, domesticated at last. Lots of unfunny jokes about late-night noise and dirty diapers. About what would happen to his quiet life. To his writing. His friends, Martin knows, were much too used to him. He had let them believe in him too absolutely, he had given them decades of constancy, the fastidious soft-spoken bachelor, writing his books and listening to his records. He had a domesticity all his own, with no squalor in it; friends came for dinner to drink excellent wine and eat his imaginative salads, his veal stew, his roast chicken.

Now he suspects, watching Julia with the baby, that she has been yearning for a new baby for years and years. She seems to have ready a whole range of voice tones he has never heard; all far from the good-humored manner she uses with Jimmy, who would not, of course, tolerate being kissed or hugged. In fact, in the evening, Jimmy and Martin exchange a smile and a shrug, listening to Julia, who is leaning back in the armchair, propping the baby up in a sitting position on her lap, face to face. "Let's see a little smile," Julia is crooning, "Was that a smile? Did you think of something funny? Let's have a smile for Mommy."

"Actually," says Jimmy, "I read in your book that they don't smile for weeks and weeks."

"Books don't know everything, do they, little Fishietoes?" Julia is kissing the baby's tiny toes, taking them between her lips and making smacking noises. "Let's see how *you* like being nibbled on," she murmurs.

Jimmy looks at Martin and shrugs again. "The Mammal has gone a little soft in the head," he says, not unkindly.

Jimmy wins his first chess game. The second game will not start till the afternoon, so Martin takes him for lunch, skipping the fast-food burger joint and taking him instead to a nearby steak house, with red plush seats and lots of gilding, the light fixtures, the woodwork. It isn't at all Martin's kind of place, but it's obviously fancy, and Jimmy is impressed. Martin urges him to go ahead and order the sixteen-ounce New York sizzling strip steak; he himself was planning to have only a caesar salad, but changes his mind at the last minute and orders a sirloin steak and a baked potato. Jimmy is trying hard to explain how chess ratings are calculated; he has no rating yet but a few more tournaments and he will have a number. The ratings are based on what seems to Martin complex arithmetic, and arithmetic interests him less than chess but Jimmy does not require him to respond. Martin cuts small pieces off his steak, which is actually excellent, and lets Jimmy talk, vigorous with the triumph of the morning.

Jimmy's face, over his steak plate, is unexpectedly like Julia's. Martin has not been able to see any resemblance between the baby and Julia, or the baby and himself. The baby looks like the baby. But Jimmy suddenly looks just like Julia, a smaller softer version of her square faintly freckled face, her straight dark hair, her intelligent widely spaced eyes. Julia wears contact lenses, normally, though since the baby's birth she has been wearing her big tortoiseshell-rimmed glasses. Jimmy also wears glasses, with round lenses and electric blue frames; maybe that's why Martin is so struck now by the resemblance. Jimmy's frames are intended to be funky, playful, maybe even trendy, so he won't look like a too-serious, too-bookish little nerd. Martin himself has perfect eyesight, and wonders suddenly whether the baby will grow up to need glasses. But he shies away from this thought, as he does from any thought which forces him to consider the baby grown up, a daughter, a girl, a young woman.

Jimmy's speech is now climbing toward the heights: grandmaster ratings, international grand masters, world champions. His steak is cooling, only half eaten. Martin allows himself—a much easier fantasy—to imagine Jimmy growing older, Jimmy winning a big chess tournament, exchanging a quick secret smile with Martin and Julia, as he goes up to the platform to claim his trophy.

Perhaps, Martin thinks, he will dedicate his next book to Jimmy, one of the mysteries. Jimmy is old enough to read it, old enough to appreciate the dedication. But how would the dedication run—"for my stepson"? Or just, "for Jimmy"? It would be a good thing to do, he thinks, since eventually he will want to dedicate a book, "for my daughter," and it would be terrible if that made Jimmy feel bad.

"Do you want any dessert?" Martin asks.

"No, I don't think I should. You see, I get a little nervous right before I have to play, and it's better for me not to eat too much."

"Don't worry about finishing the steak," Martin says. "Sixteen ounces is too much for anyone."

Julia tells him what the baby wants. "I think she's just very tired," Julia says, when the baby is screaming and waving her arms around wildly. "She's worn herself out and she doesn't have enough brains to go to sleep." Then she turns to the baby. "Dope," she says fondly, "little dumbhead. We're going to wrap you up and rock you till you drop." Then she puts the baby on a light cotton blanket, and wraps her tight as a sausage. This neat package of howling baby Julia puts on her shoulder, and settles once again in the rocker, back and forth, back and forth. "You don't have to sit here and listen to this," she tells Martin. "You can retreat to your study till she conks out."

But Martin stays in the armchair, watching the rocker tip forward and backward, listening without surprise as the baby calms down, gulps, hiccups, and then falls silent.

"She likes being wrapped up tight," Julia says. "It reminds her of being inside. Makes her feel secure."

Julia is such a neat person that the graduate students in her lab complain about it; they are not allowed to leave anything. Stray journal articles have to go in the filing cabinet, glassware goes back in the cabinets. Jars must be lined up, labels facing out; Julia cannot concentrate if something in the lab is out of place. The house that she and Martin bought together, soon after their marriage, has lots of closets, lots of built-in bookshelves. Julia had always kept it orderly, by force of personality.

Now almost every room in the house is strewn with baby equipment. There is the room which is going to belong to the baby, which is of course fully furnished; Julia had it done by her seventh month. But the baby hasn't been in there much. Julia keeps asking Martin if he minds having the baby in with them, so much simpler for her at night, and he keeps assuring her that actually he likes it. So in their bedroom, his and Julia's, there is the bassinet, and a diapering table, and diapers. T-shirts and sleepers, all piled up. In the living room is a baby seat, with a curved bottom, which is meant to rock the baby to sleep, but the baby doesn't like it. Also sundry baby presents brought by droppers-by or mailed by out-of-state relatives. Martin's mother, who is seventy-eight, and who had given up hope of grandchildren, has so far sent a snowsuit, two party dresses, a pair of fuzzy bunny-rabbit pajamas, and a teddy bear, twice the size of the baby, with a music box in it. Pull the string and you get "Au Clair de la Lune."

In the bathroom is a little plastic tub, sitting under the sink, also baby shampoo and baby scrub and baby lotion. And sometimes sleepers, hanging up to dry. In the kitchen, along with the blue jar of Julia's vitamins, there is now a little bottle of baby vitamin drops. And everywhere, everywhere, more diapers, more sleepers, more containers of baby wipes.

Not in Martin's study, of course. His study is sacrosanct. It's a beautiful room, too, a room Julia insisted on his taking when they moved in. He would have given it to Jimmy for a bedroom but Julia said no. Jimmy would be fine in the little room on the third floor, with its sloping roof. Martin had to take the big room with the four windows, because Martin would be writing in his study, every day. And much to his surprise, he is. This must be, again, the influence of Julia. It would be Julia's way of thinking, of course; if you want to write a book, then go every day to your study for x number of hours, and write until you have a book. And that is what Martin finds he now does; no more agonizing, no more wasting hours and hours of time brewing pots of coffee and doing the crossword puzzle.

Since his marriage, he has finished a "serious" novel, and is now working on a new mystery, the one he thinks he might dedicate to Jimmy. The "serious" novel, when it is published, will probably disappoint some of his friends; there is nothing in it, as far as Martin can tell, about his marriage, the changes in his life. And yet, at the same time, he cannot help thinking that his book is something new, something which has never existed before on earth. What he really imagines is people reading it and finding themselves shaken, maybe even in tears. What, after all, could be sadder than what happens in his book, that people of good will should misunderstand each other and hurt each other and lose each other?

His friends have asked, in ironic tones, if Martin is going to write about having a baby. This surprises him; he has never gotten such questions before. Did nothing ever happen to him that anyone thought was worth writing about? Anyway, he privately doubts he will ever write about the baby. It would be Julia's story to tell, really. He cannot imagine what she felt, having the baby inside, or feeling it coming out, or now, when that voracious little mouth latches onto her nipple.

The boy Jimmy is to play in the afternoon is older. He must be fourteen, which is the upper limit for Jimmy's division. He is as tall as Martin, and pudgy, an overgrown boy the size of a man. On his face, as badges of his adolescence, he has several bright red pimples and a faint ghost of a moustache. He looks nasty, Martin thinks with some alarm, watching Jimmy march up to him. They shouldn't let a boy Jimmy's age play someone like this, he thinks, then tells himself that size doesn't matter in chess. And after all, if Jimmy loses, he'll be able to comfort himself that he lost to someone older.

"Hi there, Junior," says Jimmy's opponent. "Ever played in a tournament before?"

"Yes," says Jimmy. "I have."

"So you know how the clock works, right, kid?"

Martin recognizes that the older boy is trying to rattle Jimmy, to psych him out, as Jimmy would put it. Martin would like to grab this big, ugly boy by the collar and warn him, "Shut up and play. No funny business."

"Feeling nervous, huh, Junior?" asks the older boy. Jimmy does indeed look nervous. He is fingering something on a chain around his neck, something which had been hidden under his T-shirt. "Is that your lucky charm?" his opponent asks.

Jimmy smiles, an open lovely smile on that face which looks so much like Julia's. "Yes," he says. "As a matter of fact, it is."

"Always wear it when you play?" The sneer is unmistakable.

"As a matter of fact, I do." Jimmy adjusts his glasses. "It's a piece of ossified whale testicle. My mother got it for me." He looks up at the clock on the wall. "Do you want to start?" he asks.

The baby is the most beautiful thing Martin has ever seen. Julia thinks so too, he knows, but she takes it for granted. Of course the baby is beautiful, of course she loves the baby. Martin finds himself holding the baby at arm's length so that her face is a couple of feet from his own. She stares at his nose, and then her eyes cross, those steely baby eyes. Will she have Julia's eyes, Jimmy's eyes, when she grows up? The baby turns her head to the side and tries to suck on Martin's hand, and he settles her against his chest and offers her a finger. Her mouth clamps on, and he can feel the suction massaging the last little joint of his finger. If there were milk in that finger, the baby would get it out. If his nail were not fastened on tight, she would have that too.

Jimmy passes through the room and sees him with the baby. "Where's The Mammal?"

"Your mother is taking a shower."

Jimmy comes over and stares into the baby's face. "She looks like you," he says, finally.

Has Martin imagined it, or is Jimmy's tone a little grudging, a little resentful? He tries, unsuccessfully, to make a joke of it. "Do *I* have a round little red face? Am I bald and tooth-less?"

"She has the same chin that you do, and the same cheek-bones," says Jimmy, unamused. He leaves the room, kicking a paper diaper out of his way.

In his mind, Martin finds himself making speeches: "Oh, come off it with this eternal-wisdom-of-women stuff. I can guess why she's crying. And stop protecting me so much. You don't have to run save me when you hear that little grinding in her stom-ach. I know what it means and I could cope." But is he making these speeches to Julia, or is he making them to some larger audience, all his old friends, maybe?

Late at night, hearing the baby's cries from the bassinet, he waits until Julia has pulled her into their bed, then rolls to face them. Julia lies on her side, her nightgown unbuttoned. The baby is a small shape in the glow of the nightlight, fastened to Julia's breast. In the quiet night, the baby's slurping noises are clear and distinct. On Julia's face, Martin catches that look of bemused, enslaved adoration which he knows is on his own whenever he holds the baby.

"I'm sorry she woke you," Julia whispers.

"I'm not." He puts up his hand and covers the baby's head.

"She's so little," Julia is still whispering, though in fact a screaming banshee would not deter the baby from the business at hand. "Look how little her head is, it fits right in your hand."

"She's perfect," says Martin.

"We'll take good care of her, won't we?"

"Of course we will," he says.

Jimmy puts his hand up to his neck at frequent intervals to touch his lucky piece. His moves take longer, on the ticking clock, than the moves he made in his morning game. To Martin, it looks like all the pieces, white and black, are clumped to-gether in the middle of the board. He cannot tell which player has the advantage. Jimmy's sneakered feet are anchored to the legs of his chair. The big boy jiggles in his seat, reaches up to finger his moustache shadow. Martin cannot believe that Jimmy can beat him, but he tries as hard as he can to will Jimmy's victory. "Make a mistake, make a mistake," he thinks over and over, staring at pimple-face.

Martin doesn't know whether there actually was a decisive mistake. But he let his mind wander, and when he comes back to concentrate on the chessboard, he senses that Jimmy is ahead. The game goes more and more slowly. Finally the big boy resigns, looking angry, and without another word to Jimmy, goes stomping off.

Jimmy stands up. He looks suddenly very small and very young, standing there in his blue glasses, his sneakers and jeans and T-shirt. Martin finds himself stepping up to the boy, enfolding him in a victory hug, though this is not something he would normally do, hug Jimmy, especially in public. Not something Jimmy would normally permit.

Jimmy grins at him. Jimmy is flying high. He whispers into Martin's ear, "He tried to psych me out, but I beat him anyway!"

There are big wet milk stains on the front of Julia's blouse, another wet place on her shoulder. And there is a suspicious dark patch on one leg of the baby's terrycloth sleeper, but she is sound asleep in Julia's arms and there is no point waking her up. Martin and Jimmy come charging into the living room, and announce Jimmy's triumph.

"You should see the big jerk he beat this afternoon," Martin says. "You should have seen Jimmy wipe the floor with him."

"I beat him, Mom, I beat this guy who must've been almost fifteen! And Martin's gonna bring me back tomorrow for the next round!"

Julia folds the baby closer to her, reaches out with her other arm to hug Jimmy, who allows a quick congratulatory kiss on the forehead, then pulls away. So instead, Julia puts her arm around Martin, pulling him down next to her on the couch, smiling at him, not with the eternal wisdom of women, but as if she is glad to see him, glad to have him home.

Daniel Meltzer

PEOPLE

What did he think of my idea, I wanted to know.

He'd be talking with his people, he said. He wanted to run it by his people. He would want to run some numbers.

I could touch base in a week or so, or one of my people.

He himself would be out of pocket for a while, but I could check in with his girl, or one of my people could check in with his girl or my girl could check in with his girl.

At some point down the road I should meet with his people directly, he said, even bring some of my people in to sit down with some of his people as we get further along in the process.

My other line beeped. I excused myself. It was my girl. It's my girl, I said.

He said he'd be meeting with his people that day, on a number of matters, my idea being one of them. It was definitely something he wanted them to look at. He thanked me for bringing him my idea and said we'd be talking further once his people had had a chance to look at it. I thanked him and went back to my girl.

She was calling from a photo studio downtown where she was posing for another underwear spread. The photographer was in the darkroom, she was on a break and she wanted to know what he said.

He's going to talk to his people, I said.

He likes it, she said.

He didn't say that, I said. It could mean he doesn't understand it, or that he doesn't like it and he doesn't want to commit himself. Plus he's out of pocket for a while and there would be no word.

She sighed and said it was a good idea and not to be negative. She was cold out of the lights, she said, and was going to get some tea. We could have dinner, she'd make some pasta and salad. I'd bring the wine and dessert, as always.

We've known each other less than a year. I hadn't really thought of her as my girl, or my woman or whatever we're supposed to call them, but we see a lot of each other when she's around. She makes good money modeling bras and panties or bathing suits sometimes and travels a lot, posing in front of the Acropolis or Buckingham Palace or the Berlin Wall or the Pyramids or with kangaroos or llamas or lions or even polar bears.

I don't have a girl of the kind he would have assumed I meant. I have Linda and she's my girl in a different way. But she's not really my girl.

Actually, I do have a girl. Her name is Fanny and she's seven and lives with her mother in Chattanooga, of all places. But she's my little girl. When she was born she was our baby. But not *my* baby. My wife Jill was my baby then. First she was my girl, then she was my baby. First Fanny was our baby and now she's my girl. My little girl.

Jill hasn't been my baby since after Fanny was born and certainly not since she discovered Country and Bill. Bill is a good old boy, but he's not Jill's boy. She calls him her man.

* * *

Bill plays acoustic guitar with the Mississippi Misfits. He was an up-and-coming when he and Jill met at Yoga at the Y. Now he and the Misfits are hot, Jill says.

Jill and Bill are in Chattanooga with Fanny and Jill is working as a disc jockey on a local station. She's helping her man, plugging his records and personal appearances and the like. Fanny's taking up fiddle.

The last time we spoke Jill was experimenting with a Southern accent. Jill likes to experiment. I never did, she said. It was what was wrong with me.

At her urging, I tried loosening up, opening up, being more open to change. I let my hair grow. I did various drugs. I got in touch with my feelings. I got an earring.

Jill was very shy when I first met her. She was inexperienced with sex. She said later that she should have had lovers before she met me, that she should have experimented before me, that she should have gotten certain things out of her system.

I had gotten it all out. I thought I had. Girls, when we used to be able to call them that. Pot, rock-and-roll. I was getting back to basics at a time when she needed to test her limits.

We had Fanny right away. I had a good job and we got day care and so on and Jill didn't have to give up her job. But she got tired of it after a while, anyway. She missed Fanny all day, she said. So she quit. I was doing all right, so I said go ahead. Then she got bored at home doing the domestic stuff. She took up painting, classes at the Arts Students' League, photography, then photo-journalism. She turned the bathroom into a darkroom. I got shaving cream on an important negative once. It could have won a prize, she said. It was an accident, but she was very upset.

Yoga relaxed her, she said. I went along, but I couldn't sit in that position because of my back.

Some people sit still to relax. I prefer to be in motion, get around. I like to travel, look out a train window or just walk the city. Or a hike in the country once in a while.

* * *

She met Bill at Yoga, had an affair with him and took off with him and Fanny in a van. I got Fanny back for a while, but she cried. I see her one weekend a month now. She comes here, sleeps in her old room, and looks more and more like me. But she talks with an accent now, says things like y'all and gree-its. She calls me her Daddy Jim.

I'm out of work. I got laid off after the crash. They gave me a good severance and the first thing I did was take a long vacation. Eight weeks. I went all over Europe and even into Russia. I met Linda in Berlin. She was standing in front of the Wall in white lace bra and panties, drinking a beer. I didn't know what to make of her. I offered her my jacket. She smiled. The photographer and her assistant came back with some sausages and thought I was molesting their model. Linda explained. I was embarrassed but I laughed along with them. I ran into them the next day at the airport. They were flying back to the States. I was on my way to Venice. I looked her up when I got back home and called her. She was very sweet, not what you would expect from someone who appears half-undressed in every newspaper in the country just about every week.

She looks deep into my eyes when I speak. You're an idea man, she said to me on our second or third date, you're out front.

Linda is from upstate. She lives in a large loft on a top floor downtown in the flower district. It's not much of a neighborhood, but the loft is enormous under its tent-like skylight, and of course it always smells like a garden. It's very sparely furnished with just a few very modern pieces, painted brick walls, high-tech lighting, and a king-sized bed.

The first time we made love I thought I was dreaming. She is even more impressive in the flesh than in the papers. Plus, she's a very romantic lover, completely uninhibited and very responsive.

After we make love, we lie awake and talk. She is very bright and a good listener. She has seen quite a bit of the world and she has learned much from her travels. She's encouraged me to be more confident and to get my ideas out. She says they have global possibilities.

Being an idea man has required a completely different way of thinking. But change is good. And knowing Linda has been good. In more ways than one, obviously. There is a great deal of commerce in ideas these days, a lot going on that most people are not aware of.

I sold short the summer before the crash. I did all right in the market, plus the severance. I told them the crash was coming, but they wouldn't sell when I knew we'd peaked. As a result, the company lost a lot. They unloaded me along with some others when the sales started to fall off. I can spot a trend before it hits, but I was low on the pole and they resented that I had taken my profits before the crash when they hadn't. With my severance and my profits I don't have to rush into anything. I'm in a good position, Linda says. Linda knows a lot about positions.

After my troubles with Jill, I thought I had lost interest in sex for good. Linda brought me back to life. She says I turn her on with my seriousness, with my ideas. None of them are earth-shattering. I just step back, get a little wider view, see things from a slightly different angle.

So I have these ideas which Linda says have global potential and I'm out there networking; poised, as Linda says, to happen. But it occurred to me that something was missing, something wasn't in place. I couldn't make it happen by myself. I didn't have any people.

That night, after the phone call, after dinner and after we had made love under the stars in her king-sized bed on the satin sheets, with the quadrophonic playing Tristan, I told her I was concerned because I don't have any people. It seems important, I said, to have people. He had indicated an expectation that I would have people.

Linda stretched her long white body and squeezed her eyes shut. Wagner was killing us with the love-death and the morning's roses downstairs were filling the room through the vents.

People, Linda said. She got serious, got up and got us some mineral water, her young skin glowing in the moonlight as she slid across the floor to the kitchen island and back.

I think my talent is that I can see just a little bit ahead of most people. But this time Linda was even ahead of me.

You don't need any people, she said as she handed me the glass of water. You're beyond that.

But he said down the road his people would want to meet with my people, I said as she slipped beside me and dropped her wet hand to my thigh. I called you my girl.

Your what? She lifted her hand.

I explained it to her. I could have said my woman, I said.

They don't talk that way, she said. And I didn't have to impress him. Do you think of me as your girl?

I don't know, I said.

Roses, she said, inhaling the delivery downstairs.

He said his people would be running the numbers on my idea.

And?

The numbers'll be fine, I said.

And you didn't need any people to know that, did you?

No, I said.

My ex talked that way, she said. He was always just in on the red-eye from the coast to log in with his people on some property, taking meetings, doing a deal. They think it makes them sound hip. It's just intimidation, exclusionary, but they can't intimidate you, baby. They need you. Travel light. You're the idea man. Word's getting around.

She was right. Just the week before, she had introduced me to someone at a party and he said he had heard of me.

The following week, Linda set me up with an attorney, and I incorporated. During our brief meeting, I wondered whether the lawyer, an athletic-looking, middle-aged man with an office across from City Hall, had ever slept with her. He probably had, I concluded, but he was very cordial and business-like. They shook hands when we left. I shook his hand too.

We went down to a stationery shop and ordered a letterhead. I made her Vice President.

This makes you my people, I said.

Your what?

My people. I can touch base with you now, run things by you, bring you into the process.

Wait a minute, she said.

You're my vice president, I said.

That's just on paper. It's your show, baby.

She had begun calling me baby.

But Linda looked worried. Her face had taken on a serious expression. Not like the face of an underwear model.

The following month in the *Times* magazine, she looked different, older. Still sexy, maybe even more so, but older. Thirty-ish.

We ordered billing forms, took a post office box.

The man called me back the following month. Not the man, actually. His girl. My machine now answers with the company name. It's Linda's voice now and she's got a sexy voice, much sexier than mine. His girl left a message. I called back.

His people thought the idea was interesting, he said, but they had a problem with the numbers. They didn't see how it could possibly be made to work, given the numbers.

I asked him to be more specific and they were obviously talking low concept.

They're right, I said, if you approach it that way. But if that is what they're thinking, if that's the way they want to go, then you should probably pass on it. We could show them very simply how it works high concept, I said, which is the only way I would want to see it approached anyway. But if they think that's out of their reach, then. . . .

I'll talk to my people, he said. I'll get back to you.

I'll be out of pocket for a few days, I said. You can set it up with my office.

That's how I avoided calling Linda my girl.

A couple of days later he called and Linda got back to him. She booked us for an hour with his people the following Monday, informing him of our fee, which was twice what she gets for posing for the underwear ads, then sent a note to confirm. She put off a shoot for the Victoria's Secret Christmas catalog to be there and bought herself a suit and a briefcase.

Give them only the bare essentials, Linda said. They want more, let 'em book another hour. We want to arouse their interest, not completely satisfy their curiosity. You give them everything, what the hell do they need you for after that? Let 'em take an option. How much should we ask for an option? First refusal? You got another prospect lined up?

I didn't, but it wasn't hard to come up with half a dozen other firms who conceivably would be interested.

We put together a proposal, threw in some graphics and looked up three recent surveys that backed up our premise. We gave them just enough to show that it would fly, but not enough for them to run with.

On Monday, we showed up at 11:00 A.M. at his office, which was about half the size of Linda's loft. White carpeting, Bauhaus, tiny track lights hitting Warhol lithos along the white walls, a pencil-thin black desk with no drawers. He ushered us through a doorway into the conference room and introduced us to his people: six men and one woman, all wearing dark suits and glasses, in chrome and leather swivel chairs around a mahogany table. Each had a lined legal pad and two sharpened pencils and a glass of water before them. Two carafes center table. They were all named Henderson or Mitchell or Davis or something like that. Linda's suit was from Chanel. Just low enough at the neck, high enough at the hem and trim enough in between. The men looked impressed. So did the woman.

We gave them an hour. I did most of the talking, since it was my idea, for about forty minutes. I talked very high concept all the way. Throughout my presentation they bobbed their heads up and down through their bifocals or little half-moons as they balanced the figures and charts on the page with the verbal picture I was giving them of the global possibilities Linda and I had worked out. When I was done, Linda went into licensing, rights, and our role in development.

There were a few questions, mostly having to do with renewals and other matters indicating a generally positive reaction, but Linda cut them off at the hour, telling them we had another appointment.

Excuse me, one of them asked Linda as she rose and smoothed her suit. Haven't I seen you before?

Linda took off her horn-rimmed glasses with the windowpane lenses and shot him with her deep blues, smiling just slightly as she snapped the gold-plated locks on her case.

I don't know, she said. Have you?

We took a cab back to the loft, made love with the sounds of trucks coming and going outside and a fresh updraft of peonies all around us, had lunch at a French restaurant, took in a movie, came back to the loft and made love again.

We lay in silence for a while afterward. The perfume from the peonies had faded. The next morning's flowers had not yet arrived.

I wanted to stay, but Linda had to be up early for the Victoria's Secret shoot. I dressed, let myself out. You were good, she called to me in the half-light as I reached the door. You too, I said.

The sun had set when I got back to my place. There was a message on the machine. It was Jill, asking if it was all right if Fanny kind of skipped next weekend, sugar, on account of her man Bill had invited them all over to Macon to meet his people.

I went for a walk.

It was warm and everyone was out; walking their dogs, licking their ice cream, shouting over the traffic, sipping wine from plastic glasses outside theaters or from paper bags in doorways, playing their music, courting, snorting, sporting their labels, dealing, stealing, feeling, ranting at their demons, seeking, fleeing, hiding, making their night.

I walked the length of the island, passed through many different neighborhoods, sections, districts, down canyons of immeasurable sleeping wealth, took a rail in my hand and pressed my face against a wall of fog.

Water lapped beneath my feet. A ferry horn sounded in the distance. I could hear voices, but could not make out what they were saying. Finding a phone, I punched the eleven-digit number.

Hullo? a husky baritone with a mouth full of food drawled. In the background, what might have been a reel was being scraped from a fiddle. Hullo? he demanded again. Hullo? Who the goddamn hell is it?

I replaced the receiver. Someone on the ferry laughed. Once more the horn. And then all was silent. Except for the lapping of the water at my feet. I breathed the mist, held it, let it go, turned and walked back uptown.

Les Myers

THE KITE

Ferguson, the groom, stands outside the chapel in a rented bell-bottom tuxedo and patent leather shoes, waiting for the ceremony to begin. He flicks away his cigarette. Then, suddenly, a bird swoops down, snatches up the cigarette butt, and takes to the air again, disappearing under the eaves of the church. Later, at the altar, Ferguson is oblivious to the promises he's making to God and to Sheila. He's thinking about that cigarette smoldering somewhere in the roof of the wooden church. Silently he rehearses the shout that will empty the building and bring the whole thing to a halt.

But the fire never gets started. In no time at all, Sheila and Ferguson have been married twenty-two years. Ferguson finds himself alone in a hotel room, thinking about marriage and passion, when he reaches under the bed for a magazine, and puts his hand on something strange. He lets out a yell. His first thought is there's an animal under the bed. Then it occurs to him how unlikely that would be, there, in a luxury hotel room, forty stories above Times Square.

He hikes up the dust ruffle and peers over the side. It is a woman's shoe he has touched, a purple suede pump with a low

"The Kite," by Les Myers, first appeared in *The Chariton Review*, copyright © 1991 by Northeast Missouri State University.

vamp and a three-inch stiletto heel. He lies on his back and holds the shoe. He tosses it gently in the air and fingers the suede. A faint crease across the instep suggests it has been worn at least once, though the sole is unacquainted with pavement. Slim feet, slender ankles . . . He tries hard to conjure up a woman to fill the shoe, and, on each of the next three nights, he falls asleep with the lights on and the spiked heel against his chest.

He finishes his business in the city and flies home with the shoe in his briefcase. He hides it in his dresser but is not surprised when it greets him at the front door the next day. The shoe sails through the air and hits him on the jaw. Sheila seems genuinely surprised by the accuracy of her throw.

"Please tell me it's an affair and not some perversion you've picked up."

"I'm having an affair."

"No, you're not."

"Okay, I'm not having an affair." He kisses her behind the ear. She stares at him through narrowed eyes, and then pats his tender jaw. Her hands are cool and moist. They smell faintly of bleach.

"Then who does the shoe belong to?"

"I don't know." He picks up a sheaf of mail from the hall table and thumbs through it. "I found it under my bed in New York."

He wants her to ask why he brought it home, even though he, himself, doesn't know. She shakes her head and walks away, no longer interested in the game. He takes the shoe to the kitchen, wraps it in a paper bag, and drops it in the garbage pail, then follows her outside. He wants to talk. He wants to talk about marriage, love, passion, spiked heel pumps—anything at all—but it occurs to him they've already said everything they will ever say to each other at least once.

She is out on the deck, cleaning flower pots she bought at a yard sale. The pots are soaking in a bucket of water and bleach. She pulls some clean pots out of the bucket, and plunges in a stack of dirty ones. Air bubbles furiously from the pores in the clay.

"Happy birthday, by the way," Sheila says. "We're going out for dinner tonight."

"Oh," he says.

He goes back in and fixes a white wine spritzer for Sheila and a scotch for himself. The phones rings. He puts down the drinks and takes the call in the kitchen.

It's a recording, randomly dialed by a computer. Ferguson starts to hang up, then realizes the voice is familiar. He is asked to touch the pound sign on his phone if he is fifty-five or older and would like more information on how to join a senior citizens' advocacy group. Ferguson, exactly fifteen years shy of qualifying, smiles and punches the button anyway, still trying to identify the voice that now promises him a free magazine, discounts at participating merchants, and cut-rate travel . . .

Travel. Of course. It's the Greyhound Man. It's the same deep, authoritative, but friendly voice that at one time echoed through bus terminals all over the country. The summer before his senior year in high school, Ferguson emptied his bank account, stole a few hundred dollars more from his parents, bought a bus pass and travelled till his money ran out, and always, no matter the city, the Greyhound Man was there ahead of him to suggest another destination.

"I didn't hear the phone ring," Sheila says, appearing in the doorway. "Who is it?"

He hands the phone to her, but the message is over by the time she gets the receiver to her ear.

She hands back the phone and shakes her head.

"Old timer's disease," she says, tapping Ferguson's skull.

"You mean Alzheimer's."

"That's what I said."

* * *

The next morning at the office he is asked—having been appointed, just recently, vice president of sales, central region—to sit for a photograph that is to be included in his company's annual report. He enters a small room on the first floor of the building and is met by two young women. One is the photographer, who wears camouflage fatigues and an olive drab pocket t-shirt. She is busy adjusting her camera and grunts to acknowledge him. The other woman, who is wearing a short denim skirt and a white blouse with several of the top buttons undone, takes his arm and introduces herself as Lisa.

"I'll be doing your makeup," Lisa says, pressing him into a chair in front of a portable gray backdrop. She turns his chin gently to the left and the right, then fastens a vinyl bib around his neck.

"What are you going to do to me?"

She smiles as she studies his face. "First, I'm going to get rid of those bags under your eyes." She places a finger on each of his temples and pulls the skin upward. "And then I'll see what I can do about these crow's-feet."

"You do this for a living?"

"I freelance for ad agencies, sometimes the tv stations."

She dabs his face with moist cotton, then applies the makeup with her fingertips. She brushes on powder and stands back to examine her work.

"The last time someone put makeup on me," Ferguson says, "I was in high school—starring in the senior play. I was the grandfather in *You Can't Take It With You*." Lisa leans over him and brushes more powder on his forehead. Her blouse opens, inches from his face. "Ever see it?" he asks.

She nods and tips his head to the side. "Moss Hart and George Kaufmann."

"Right."

She steps back again. Her partner moves in with the camera and asks him to lift his chin and sit up straight.

"I fell in love with the girl who did my makeup," Ferguson says.

Lisa nods politely as her eyes come to rest, not on Ferguson, but on the camouflaged backside of her partner. "And what ever happened to her?" asks Lisa.

He had married her of course.

Twenty-two years ago, Sheila powdered his hair and added fifty years to his face with a brown pencil. Eyes closed, stomach jittery with mild stage fright, Sheila's fingers playing over his face, he had been aware of a tautness in his chest, a tug, a sense of being pulled abruptly in an unfamiliar direction.

He had made love to Sheila after the cast party that followed the final performance of the play. His first time. Sheila, he wasn't sure about. She hadn't intended to let things go as far as they did and had turned pissy afterwards. As she pulled her clothes back on, she asked him angrily if it was as good as he thought it would be. He told her it was. But when they were both dressed and had brushed the grass off their clothes and were walking back to the car, he remembered, with a pang, something he had seen the previous summer.

He had taken the bus as far west as San Diego, where he spent several afternoons on a nude beach, smoking hashish-loaded cigarettes and watching the hang gliders float down from the cliffs above. He stood in waist-high water and watched a glider spiraling towards him. The pilot was a woman. She wore a powder-blue helmet and nothing else. For a few seconds, their eyes met, and he had the feeling that if he could hold her gaze he would be able to see the world as she was seeing it at that moment—the cliffs, the sand, the water. Then an updraft caught the glider and it disappeared in the glare of the midday sun.

Ferguson blinks his eyes. Lisa reaches in to lift his chin and boost his tie. He catches her eye and tries fitting her with a powder-blue helmet, but she, too, backs away, and dissolves behind her partner's flashing camera.

That same day he leaves the office at one o'clock. He steps into a cab and asks the driver to take him to Lambert Field. He's supposed to fly to O'Hare, have dinner that night at the home of an associate, and then attend a meeting the next morning at The Palmer House.

As the cab heads north through downtown St. Louis, they turn a corner and pass the bus station. Ferguson tells the driver to stop.

He pays the driver and carries his garment bag and briefcase into the terminal, and smiles as he is greeted, once again, by the voice of the Greyhound Man, who announces the immediate departure of a bus for Chicago. The terminal is smaller than Ferguson remembers it, and to his surprise, almost empty. He buys a ticket, then calls his secretary, and asks her to get a message to his associate in Chicago. He would be arriving late and would take a rain check on dinner and they would catch up with each other at the meeting the next morning.

He gets on the bus as the driver is about to close the door. They pull out of the terminal and the bus is suddenly surrounded by picket signs. A half-dozen cops appear. Ferguson has forgotten about the strike. The striking drivers curse and pound on the sides of the bus as it waits for a light. A rock glances off a window behind him. He turns around and notices there are only four other people besides himself on the bus, a woman and boy and an elderly couple, all sitting very low in their seats.

The woman and boy move up from the back of the bus. She's in her mid-twenties, very attractive, in an exotic way. She wears a long skirt printed with somber flowers. A gray sweater is draped over her shoulders and tied around her neck. Her complexion is dark, her hair straight and black and cut short. She sits across the aisle from Ferguson and pushes her son onto the floor between them, as far away from the windows as possible. Ferguson glances at the book she's carrying. The title is in a language he doesn't recognize.

"This demonstration," she says in accented English, her voice shaking, "what is it?"

He is taken aback by the terror in her eyes.

"It's a labor strike," he explains. "Nothing to worry about." But he remembers that a driver was shot to death by a sniper a few days earlier, somewhere in Kentucky or Tennessee.

They cross the river into East St. Louis and head north on I-55. They relax a bit when the city is behind them. The woman's name is Ileana. Her son, who is five, is named Iosif. She tells Ferguson that they left Bucharest early in December, just before the fall of Ceausescu. She is a high school language teacher. They have been staying with an uncle in Springfield, Missouri, since they arrived in America six weeks earlier, and now are on their way to Appleton, Wisconsin, where she has a cousin who has found her a job in a paper mill.

The boy speaks for the first time. He pleads with his mother. She shakes her head no. It's clear that whatever it is he wants, he's been asking for it all day, and that Ileana is about to give in. She frowns and pulls a long package from the net bag on the seat beside her. She speaks to Iosif and then translates for Ferguson.

"It is a kite, a present from his uncle. I tell him not to open it."

"Ninja Turtles," the boy explains, holding up the kite and pointing to the masked characters on the label. "Cowabunga dude!" he shouts in a deep little voice.

The driver turns around and sees the boy sitting in the aisle. Ferguson notices the beads of sweat on the driver's face, which is unsettling because it is chilly on the bus, almost uncomfortable. The driver seems about to say something like *Get the kid the hell out of the aisle*, but then changes his mind and turns his attention back to the road.

Ferguson pulls a magazine from his briefcase, but is unable to read. He looks up warily every time a car passes. Just south of Litchfield, someone in a pickup roars past, leans out the window and raises a finger.

Ferguson is nervous but he does not regret the whim that put him on a bus instead of a plane. Flying scares the hell out of him, it always has. Everything else being equal he would rather worry about rocks and the unlikely possibility of a sniper than about metal fatigue, wind shear, and pilot error. He's in no hurry. As long as he makes his meeting in the morning it doesn't matter how he gets there.

He closes his magazine and turns to Ileana. "So many changes in your country," he begins, trying to draw her into conversation again. "All for the best, I hope."

"Not so many changes," she says, closing her book. "Some names have changed, little else."

He glances at her wedding band.

"What does your husband do?"

"A university professor," she says. "He is dead now a year."

Ferguson feels his scalp prickle as he recalls the stories he has read about Romania under Ceausescu.

"They pulled him from his classroom. A week later he was found in the street, dead."

"I'm so sorry," he says.

She reaches down and touches her son's head. "His name was also Iosif." She doesn't seem to notice that Iosif has opened the kite and is trying to fit the crosspieces together. "You have a wife?" she asks.

"Yes."

"She is lovely, I imagine."

"She is."

"And children?"

"Two, both in college."

"Very nice."

The bus turns off the interstate. It moves through quiet streets lined with frame houses. The redbuds are flowering.

Jonquils and early tulips bloom by front steps. A moment later the driver turns into the depot and announces a twenty-minute rest stop.

"Are you getting off?" Ferguson asks.

"This is not Chicago?"

"No, Bloomington, Illinois. We're halfway there."

"We will stay here."

Ferguson stands up and points to his briefcase and garment bag. "Watch these for me, will you?" He gets off and lights a cigarette and walks around the parking lot to stretch his legs.

A lone picket paces on the sidewalk. The striking driver stares at him with disdain. He jabs a finger in the direction of the bus. "Fucking scabs. I've got five kids to feed at home."

Ferguson shrugs. He draws on his cigarette and tosses it away. He goes inside and buys a newspaper and two Cokes and takes them back to the bus. He hands the Cokes to Ileana.

"You are kind."

"I thought he might be thirsty."

He opens the paper. There's an article about the strike on the front page. Greyhound now says it's going to fire the drivers who walked out.

Just south of Dwight it happens. They are approaching an overpass when there is a series of popping sounds. Glass shatters and flies everywhere. The driver yells for everyone to get down. He floors the accelerator, then screams, but he continues driving until several of the tires go flat. The bus swerves onto the shoulder.

The driver's face is bloody. Ferguson sweeps away pieces of the windshield with his shoe and helps the driver stretch out on the floor. A few minutes later a state trooper coming from the other direction slows, turns on his flashing lights, and bounces across the median. An ambulance arrives, followed by three more state troopers. The driver walks to the ambulance, leaning on a paramedic, and is taken away.

The troopers question them and take down their names.

They spend several minutes examining the passports of Ileana and Iosif. Her hands shake as she takes the documents back and zips them into a pouch that had been hidden under her blouse. One of the troopers gets in his car and talks on the radio. A few minutes later he walks back to the bus.

"Well, I've got some bad news, folks. There's another bus behind you—in Springfield, I think. They told the other driver to stop and pick you all up, but when he heard what had happened, he walked off the bus and didn't come back. What they want you to do is to check into a hotel up the road. They've got to send a bus down from Chicago and they're not sure they can find a driver to get down here tonight."

"Hell, it don't matter to me." The elderly man who had been sitting at the back of the bus with his wife pulls open the luggage compartment and removes a suitcase. "I ain't getting back on no damn bus anyway. I told her we should have taken the train."

One of the troopers takes the suitcase and escorts the man and his wife down the shoulder to his patrol car.

"We will stay here," Ileana says. "And wait for the next bus. I have no money for hotels."

"You can't, ma'am," a trooper tells her. "Somebody's still running around here with a gun."

"Don't worry," Ferguson says to Ileana. "I'll take care of the hotel. The bus company will reimburse us anyway."

She turns her back a moment and stares across the median. "I have no choice," she says quietly, turning to Ferguson. There are tears in her eyes. She draws her son's face to her hip. "I must trust you."

The trooper drops them off at a small motel, just outside of Dwight. Ferguson asks for two rooms. He helps Ileana carry her suitcases up the stairs. Then he closes his door, takes off his shirt and tie, and changes into a pair of jeans. He lies down on the bed, and starts shivering, as it finally sinks in how close he, all of them, had come to being shot.

After a while he picks up the phone and calls Greyhound in Chicago. He speaks to an agent who puts him on hold for five minutes, but then comes back on and confirms what the state trooper had said. Another bus would be there at five in the morning, on the dot. Make sure everybody's ready, he says.

Ferguson does some quick calculations and decides that if things go smoothly he will still make his nine o'clock meeting with time to spare.

There's a knock. He opens the door, but no one is there. The knocking continues, and he notices there is a second door that opens directly into the adjoining room. He unlocks it and opens it to find Iosif smiling at him.

"He needs help to assemble his kite," Ileana says from inside.

Ferguson enters their room. She is sitting by the window. Her eyes are puffy and red.

"Are you okay?" he asks.

"Yes, I was not expecting such excitement. The driver, you think he is okay?"

Ferguson nods. "He had a bad cut on his forehead, but he'll be fine."

"I must call my cousin, collect. Please show me how to mark the telephone."

She gives him a scrap of paper with a number on it. He punches it in and adds his own calling card number. He hands the phone to her and listens with interest, trying to follow the story of the sniper as it is recounted in Romanian.

"He is very worried," she says, hanging up.

"Everything will be okay."

"Yes, I think so." She accepts the cigarette he offers her. "Have you called your wife?"

He hasn't, but then Sheila isn't expecting him to call anyway. He really doesn't feel like explaining why he is sitting in a rather rundown motel on the outskirts of Dwight, Illinois, with a young, attractive Romanian political refugee and her child.

Iosif drops the kite on Ferguson's lap. In his eagerness to put the thing together, the boy has torn out all four corners.

"I don't know that I can fix this." Ferguson lays the kite on the bed. "It's broken."

Iosif doesn't seem to understand.

"How about some food?" Ferguson says.

"I will give you some money."

Ileana tries to push a five-dollar bill in his hand. He waves it off. "I'll be back in a minute."

He steps outside. There is a large grassy field across the road from the motel. Some sort of factory or school, he is not sure. A tractor pulling a mower makes a last pass across it. First cutting. A warm breeze blows out of the south. The smell of cut grass fills his nostrils. The sun is setting.

He walks down the road to a quick shop and returns in a few minutes with two brown paper bags. One contains a package of buns, some lunch meat, a squeeze bottle of mustard, a quart of milk and a six-pack of Michelob; the other, a coloring book, a box of eight crayons, some scissors, and a bottle of white glue.

"Open the door," he shouts. Ileana lets him in. He empties the bags on the dresser and spreads out the food. Iosif drops the torn kite and picks up the crayons.

"You sit," she says to Ferguson. "I will do this."

He pops open a beer and offers it to her.

"No, thank you," she says. "Perhaps I'll have a sip later."

He pours milk for the boy, and watches her make the sandwiches, one slice of meat on each bun.

"Put a couple more pieces on that one for me," he says. "I don't know about you guys, but I'm starved."

"Yes, I am hungry, too."

So is Iosif, who polishes off his sandwich quickly, downs the milk in a few swallows, then picks up the crayons again. He opens the box and slides them out of their paper sleeves, one by one.

Ileana sits facing Ferguson, with her sandwich in her lap. She takes a sip from his beer.

"You have sons or daughters?" she asks.

"Two boys."

"And both at the university?"

Ferguson nods proudly, wistfully. He opens his wallet. "That's Tom, and that's Mark."

"You are married very young."

"Yes." Too young, and, of course, out of necessity. He, himself, had missed his chance to go to college. But really there was nothing to regret other than the fact that the boys in the picture seemed to have grown up when he wasn't looking. He was on the road a lot when they were young. He'd leave on Monday, come back Friday, and they would seem a year older every time.

Iosif takes the crayon wrappers to the windowsill where he lines them up in order from light to dark, then pairs them up and puts them in four ranks, and marches them to and fro like toy soldiers. Allegiances between colors form, then dissolve. There are wars, truces. Anarchy prevails briefly and all the colors are swept to the floor.

"Well, I should probably get going," Ferguson says. She looks puzzled.

"You have another engagement?"

He laughs. "No, I just didn't want to wear out my welcome."

"Oh, you must stay for a while."

"I was hoping you'd say that."

He takes the scissors and cuts the paper bags open and glues them together. He trims them into an oblong diamond shape. Iosif abandons the wrappers and comes over to watch. Ferguson borrows the black crayon, and using the torn kite as a model, he sketches the outline of Michaelangelo, the Ninja Turtle, onto the brown paper. He adds an orange mask and a monogrammed belt.

"Cowabunga!" he shouts, surprised at how well the turtle turns out.

"Aren't you clever," Ileana laughs.

Iosif fills in Michaelangelo's outline with green crayon. Ferguson creases the paper to make a sort of hem, and strings a piece of cord along the edges. He glues it all together and lays it on top of the lamp shade.

"We'll let that dry a few minutes," he says. He goes next door to his room and tears a thin pillowcase into strips. The pillowcase becomes a tail. The plastic crosspieces of the original kite are fitted to the new. Ileana applauds as he turns the finished kite over to the boy, who dashes around the room dragging it behind him on the floor.

"Hold on," Ferguson laughs. "Let's take it outside."

"Oh, but it's dark now."

He pushes back the drapes. A row of neon-lit hawthorn trees rustles on the other side of the parking lot. "Yes, but we've still got a breeze."

She protests again but throws up her hands finally and smiles. They brush against each other as they go through the doorway. She puts a hand on his arm and starts to say something, then changes her mind, and closes the door.

They walk across the road and several hundred yards into the dark field before Ferguson decides there is no more hazard of power lines.

Iosif runs. The kite waggles and rises behind him and disappears quickly in the darkness. The wind picks up suddenly, and the boy shrieks as the string starts whizzing off the spool. Ferguson grabs for the string and lets out a yell as it cuts him.

He gets the kite under control and the three of them sit on the grass. Moonlight glances off the upward curving string. Ileana seems to forget who she's with and puts her head on his shoulder. He can't see the kite, but his hand has been laid open, and the pull is real.

Ken Chowder

WITH SETH IN TANA TORAJA

There's always too much to say. Which may be why I didn't say anything—on the phone, four A.M. my time.

But Kirsten talked. She gave details. Seth had fallen down facefirst in his Danish kitchen; he wasn't conscious long, maybe five minutes. His baby was just three months. The new wife was named Dorthe. Dorthe held Seth in the kitchen. Only a little blood came out of his mouth. The new wife ran screaming into the street. A little wet snow was falling.

I knew a few things about Seth. His middle name was Benton, his age thirty-nine; his birthday was May 19th, but Seth never liked celebrating his birthday, even at fifteen. Seth's eyebrows ran together; his ears stuck out top and bottom, as if stapled down in the middle. His rimless glasses pinched twin purple spots into his nose. He was half-Jewish, from his mother's side. He had lived in Denmark sixteen years. He and I sometimes loved the same women.

I didn't tell Kirsten these facts. Of course she knew them all. Kirsten knows everything.

* * *

"I don't know why you came," Kirsten says to me. "Now, I mean. After the funeral."

Kirsten pours tea from a shining white vacuum jug. Her Godthaabsvej apartment is similarly white. The furniture is pale and unpainted, and has been in her family a hundred years.

I look past her, toward the patterns the ice has made on the windows: *isblomster*, the Danes call them. Ice flowers. "I don't know," I say. "I might write about it."

"Write about it?" she says; her tea must taste terrible.

"I think mainly I'm just trying to remember things," I say, struggling.

Kirsten shakes her head. "As if you had a choice about it."

What I remember about the first time with Kirsten is this: it was a blue day in October, sixteen years ago, and Kirsten's eyes were too big to be believed—her simplest look seemed like staring. So this was Seth's lover from the year before, when she was an exchange student in Vermont. We arranged to meet in an old bar in the center of Copenhagen, one with absurd things dangling from the ceiling—a tired boot, a wooden fish, an open book, an empty birdcage, all pat symbols from seventeenth-century Dutch emblem books. In Jan Steen's world they imply some grave sin, usually adultery, which his characters seem brilliantly pleased about. I drank a Carlsberg Elephant, a strong beer, Kirsten a Green Tuborg, the regulation model. Her English flowed remarkably, even for a Dane. She was utterly quick; she knew what I was saying at sentence's launch. Around her neck wound a scarf in yellows and russets, crocheted with elaborate use of negative space, cobwebbed trickery; she'd made this herself. Let's see. What else. A moon face, set off by very short black hair in a monkish cut. This hair was virtually impossible: deep black in Denmark, stridently short in 1974. Her eyes tilted in different directions, as with Modigliani. She blinked often, and quite beautifully.

We talked about Seth that day, of course. I said Seth had asked me to look her up; she asked why. Kirsten has a way of turning her head when she expresses dissatisfaction, demonstrating by the oblique angle that it's not her listener she's unhappy with: so she glared at an empty birdcage. Seth gave up too easily, she said—gave up just when there was something worth troubling over.

"He just doesn't believe that love conquers all," I said.

"He doesn't believe anything conquers anything," Kirsten said. "He's only interested in the difficulties."

Kirsten is bright, practical, and stubborn. Her practicality is sometimes overwhelmed by her passions. Most of this was immediately obvious.

"You're right," I said. "But isn't this what makes Seth interesting himself?"

We went out into the slanting northern sunlight so she could show me the Round Tower. You trudge up a spiralling ramp rather than stairs, because the king of that time had a wonderful dream. In his dream the king drove his team of white horses to the top of a tall stone tower; he looked out over his city, and a great peace came to him. There has been such a thing as imperial will, creating pyramids and palaces and labyrinths of flowers and great flowerings of misery; so Kirsten and I made the royal promenade, gazing out over the copper spires of Copenhagen. I think I took her arm; it's hard to remember. But I do remember thinking, as Kirsten and I stood there, hovering in the blue over Copenhagen, that I knew who it was Kirsten wanted, and I didn't doubt that she'd get him.

Kirsten passes me a cup of tea. "I thought of you as an ambassador from Seth," she says. The cup is low and round, and holds only a small amount of tea. Even that much steams. The day is so cold the old windows show only ice; the ice is elaborately patterned, like marbled endpapers, or cross-sections of snowflakes.

"Is that what I was?" I ask.

"It's not so cruel to say so," she says, reacting to what I haven't said. "You thought the same thing at the time. It wasn't till later," she says. Kirsten's English is perfect, even when her sentences don't quite end.

We came down from the Round Tower. Kirsten had to babysit for her roommate's daughter. She asked if I wanted to come along. All right. She bought some chestnuts and I got a bottle of wine, maybe Bergerac, something like that. She lived in the suburbs, a train ride away. The toy train shunted through a dark wood. Later I would come across a map of that forest on which every single tree was marked. And in supermarkets in Denmark there were cellophane-wrapped packets of autumnal leaves for sale; leaves for sale, and I come from New England.

The apartment building was like any other, a block exactly matched by five others, side by side. It was 1974, so I thought of the first hexagram in the *I Ching*, The Creative.

It furthers one to cross the great water. Seth and I had hitch-hiked across the country in 1968, a week after we graduated from high school together. I got sunstroke in Ohio, in Chicago we had a tug-of-war with two black kids over Seth's guitar, we lost the tug, we were busted for hitchhiking in North Platte, Nebraska. We carried just two books: the *Odyssey* and the *I Ching*.

Kirsten cross-hatched the chestnuts and seated them in salt, in an enameled frying pan. She boiled small potatoes for the child and peeled them. "They're asparagus potatoes," Kirsten said, as if that were an explanation. What I remember most clearly about that evening was this persistent quality—of things, or perhaps one overwhelming thing, that could not be explained.

I don't know if I spent the night there. It's odd, the things you remember, the things you forget. The selection process doesn't seem to be based on pain, the repression of it, or on feeling, the retention of it. I can see myself sitting on the sofa, alone, late, writing Seth a letter. Candles burned, making the room seem lovely and warm, glowing like a Delft *fijnschilder's* genre scene. I'd come a long way, to sit in a Danish living room, these many candles shining around me; I was finally, I thought, in Europe. This idea too warmed me. I was twenty-three, and not impervious to romance.

I wrote Seth on graph paper. Among the blue lines I wrote: *I really think Kirsten wants to get back together with you.* I wrote: *I think this is a great idea: I like Kirsten.* Then I almost added: *It's hard to tell whether her eyes are gray or green.*

Dear Seth. You were in Connecticut, working with retarded children—a job you hated, because it was all patience. I was in Denmark, sitting in Kirsten's house, writing to say that you and she should get back together. No, I didn't mail that letter right away.

Dear Seth. We were two boys who used to look at girls together. At first they were as unapproachable as death. In many ways we were like any two boys of the time: the peace marches —the U.N. in April, the Pentagon in October; the dope smoking; the car accidents. We posed for photos in paratrooper boots, daffodils in our hair. We went to college, cut off blue jeans, memorized the lyrics to "Uncle John's Band." Standard stuff. But maybe one thing was not so common. We talked about our fears. We had them; they were similar. And it's only now I know: we were right to be afraid.

This is a record cold spell. Kirsten goes to the window, stands in the attitude of someone looking out. But of course you can't look out. She makes a fist and rubs with the side of her hand, leans down and blows hot on the ice, almost kissing it. Ice flowers run together, and part of the window goes solid white.

"People don't know how to relate to the ex-wife," Kirsten says, not quite facing me. "They think divorce means you don't love each other any more. I'd like people to understand that I hurt."

"You were the person who knew him best. Everyone knows that."

She's still not facing me. "Seth still loved me," she says.

"I know he did," I say.

"He still did," she says. Her voice sounds broken. The tea is steaming, Kirsten is rubbing furiously on the window, the ice is dripping and running down into her sleeve. I want to tell her that she's wrong: that Seth was finally content with his relationship with her, and yet content with Dorthe; that, at the end, Seth was happy. That's the kind of thing you say when someone dies, after all. Even Kirsten had said something similar on the phone: "Seth was so excited about being a father," she said. "You can't believe how happy he was."

But the fact is that I don't know what Seth thought then, or what he was happy about; I wasn't around at the end, and I never did see Seth very happy.

"Tea's getting cold," is all I can say.

The second time I saw Kirsten she came out to Roskilde, where I was staying, for a party. She shrugged off a big black coat; underneath were white Can't Bust 'Em overalls. She looked thin and large-eyed, like some nocturnal marsupial in New Zealand. We sat and ate herring, then roast pork and pickled red cabbage, we drank beer and *akvavit*, and by midnight we'd cleared the turquoise end-tables and were dancing on them, blind-drunk go-go stumblers. We played "Papa was a Rolling Stone"; we played "Say It Loud, I'm Black and I'm Proud." Kirsten got up on a table for Junior Walker's "Monkey Jump." Lookit that monkey jump. She came down when "Cleo's Mood" was on; we kissed then. Someone was hitting something, maybe bongos; someone else was reeling around a turquoise table in a blue terrycloth dress; Kirsten and I were kissing on the bamboo floor mats—no, I can't remember how we got down to the floor. Then a strange fact scaled the high walls of my drunkenness and sexual heat: Kirsten was crying. Kissing, and crying.

"What's this now?" I said.

She cried without much in the way of facial contortions; she seemed to simply accept the stream of tears. She said, "After all this empty time, that it should be you. Seth's good friend."

I was moved, though I couldn't say why. Maybe I was just glad that someone could feel something in my arms, for whatever reason; just glad that love could mean something to someone.

We slept together that night. I woke up in the middle of the night and spent a long lame time trying to figure out where I was. A wallhanging, thick strands of knotted yarn and string, slumped on the wall above me like a twisted body. I switched on a light, and a more literal reality rushed back to me.

The next morning Kirsten left early. I took out the letter I'd written to Seth. It struck me as being true: yes, it would be a good thing if Seth and Kirsten could get together. I mailed it.

I don't make too many claims for myself in all this. Seth is dead, and he'll always be dead. But I did mail that letter.

It took me three weeks to get to Denmark. I missed Seth's funeral; I always miss funerals. When I finally got to the cemetery, Holmens Kierkegaard, it was raining assiduously. Nobody had told me where Seth's plot was, so I just wandered crookedly in the rain. Here was a woman in a trenchcoat, bending over a granite marker, carefully setting down a pink nosegay. She straightened quickly, snapped open a pastel-striped umbrella, and was lightly away, heels clicking on flagstone. The whole procedure seemed much rehearsed. I checked her flowers—they were carnations, which seemed strange. But of course each culture has its own idea of decorum with death. The people of Tana Toraja, Sulawesi, put their bodies in holes in limestone cliffs; they wrap the corpses in cloth, then rewrap them each year—till the time comes when no one knows who that was. My father's ashes sit in a tin urn in my brother's basement, between a warped guitar that Joe Spencer's been storing there for years and a scale model of the Cutty Sark that my brother still claims he'll someday finish. But in my family nothing is ever finished; we just put the ashes on the shelf.

I came to a gravesite overladen with flowers, new enough so there was no marker, old enough so the flowers were sodden, wilted. I remembered a tiny cemetery in a black hamlet in lowland South Carolina, where I'd been amazed that the flowers were all plastic. Now I understood why that was: so they, at least, would never die.

There were sodden lilies, irises, roses, many chrysanthemums. I stood before all these dying flowers, thinking of how Seth had wept for the death for my father, though the two of them never got along. I began to wonder how that old city, Heaven, could be constructed so all the decent people who disliked each other on earth could be situated out of each other's way.

This is the spot where I cried. But I couldn't even do that without an uneasiness creeping into my mind. Maybe this wasn't Seth's grave; maybe I was spending sorrow on some dead stranger. For a minute I tried to hang onto the drops, save them for the right place. But I suppose I knew that this was a right place. It was worth weeping over: someone was dead here. People die.

The rain came harder. That was a week ago; the cold hadn't set in yet, freezing this little country fast in its tracks.

I slept with Kirsten, then mailed the letter to Seth. He wrote her, she wrote him back, she kept sleeping with me. The month was November, the darkness swooping down on Denmark. The first snow came, a heavy fall. Over mint tea Kirsten said, "Gabe. I've been thinking." I knew what that meant. We put our boots on. In a small crowd of black snow-lined trees—each of them marked, I knew, on some map—we agreed that her relationship with Seth was the essential one. We didn't sleep together again.

I went to France. The pain was there, but it was remarkably short-lived. When I came back to Denmark for Christmas, Seth had already arrived. There were already plans.

The wedding was for the sake of Immigration, theoretically. Seth and Kirsten would move to New York, get an apartment on the upper West Side. And it was an unseasonably sunny day in January when Seth and I walked, arms around each other, to the Lyngby town hall, singing that song by the Dixie Cups: *Goin to the chapel / And we're / Gonna get married*—a song in the first-person plural.

It seems so important to Kirsten to look out this window. She runs hot water onto a green washcloth, keeps rubbing in circles. Ice melts in layers.

"You know what?" I say. "I'm actually sitting here feeling bad about an incident at your wedding dinner, sixteen years ago. Seth was kidding around, saying that, with all the wine, he knew he'd get a good night's sleep—'If Kirsten's snoring doesn't keep me up,' he said. I said, 'Kirsten doesn't snore.' Seth asked me how I could know that. 'She just doesn't seem the type,' I said.

"You've told me that story before," Kirsten says. "Anyway, you were wrong. Sometimes I do snore. When I drink too much red wine and fall asleep on my back. Seth knew that."

I think I know why I lied to Seth. It was a wedding, after all. Kirsten wanted to wait to tell him, wait till things were going well. Telling him then would've been putting up more hurdles; with Seth there were always hurdles enough. Yes. That's why.

Kirsten stops rubbing the window. "Come look at this," she says. I come closer. She's in black leather pants, not unusual for Denmark this year, and a bright red sweater; I notice the mascara only now. She gestures toward the hole she's made in the ice. Godthaabsvej is a main street; but no one's out there. Just one man on the street—wrapped up like a burglar, only his eyes naked—hurriedly pulling a small dog from a hydrant.

"I am living in a necropolis," Kirsten says.

"It's just the cold," I say. "Just weather."

"Seth was so happy about the baby," she says. "He was . . . elated." It's as if she's talking about the man yanking the dog on the street: her gaze is fixed there. She says, "You know what Dorthe thinks? The new wife? She thinks he died because his heart couldn't stand the stress."

"What stress?" I ask.

"The stress of being happy," Kirsten says.

I can see the tips of her eyelashes coming together in rapid blinks. "Isn't it pretty to think so," I say.

"No," Kirsten says. "It's not."

"I want to kill you, you know," was the first thing Seth said. It was summer, 1974. The three of us were renting a cottage in Connecticut. I was running an A. B. Dick press, Kirsten working retail in a basket shop, Seth driving No-Nonsense pantyhose around Connecticut in a No-Nonsense pantyhose van.

"Why is that?" I said. Seth was standing over my bed; I had been sleeping, apparently. This old wallpaper was graying, with pink tea roses in rows; this was, let's see, a Sunday; Sunday, and Seth wanted to kill me.

"Because of Kirsten," Seth said. I just waited. "She told me about you two. Last fall."

"So. Finally."

"Yes, damn it," Seth said. He sat heavily on the end of the bed; his sigh sounded like a catalogue of human failures. "Yes. Finally," Seth said.

Kirsten is in some pain. She keeps going over memories as if she could rewrite them. She wants to know why she left Seth, five years ago now. Ever since what she calls "this situation with Seth," which means his death, she hasn't been able to sleep. Sometimes the situation overcomes her, she feels brutalized, forgets politeness. "What the hell can you write about it?" she says. "That you had a friend who died, so you feel bad?"

I want to use the word *consolation;* but it's a tiny word, a throw rug for a vast floor. I draw the slicer across the cheese, lay the slices on the thin square of dark bread. No, there's no consolation. I can't shape pain into patterns, place it on the palm and blow it away like dandelion puffs. But here we are, all the same: drinking tea, eating cheese, alive, as if by reflex.

She turns to me. We're close. Her eyes are vastly open; she looks so fierce, and so helpless.

I've drunk most of the tea in the world. The ice flowers have begun to grow back over the melted spot. The darkness is beginning again, outside. "Guess I'll go now," I say, standing up.

"You don't have to go."

"Well. I have to go sometime. So." I kneel and pull off the house slippers, hold them out to her. She looks down at the slippers with a trace of incomprehension, then up at me. I see something in the way she looks; and only then do I think I know. She comes to me and we begin to kiss.

We haven't kissed in sixteen years. When we stop, we look at each other a while. I say, "I thought I was the only one who wanted to do that."

"No," she says.

"I hope I'm not the only one who wants to do it again."

"No."

We go to bed. It feels fragile there, and new. Neither of us can recall what it was like to sleep together. The exact motions, the movements of love, are lost. "I remember I used to like you doing that," Kirsten says at one point. "I think. I don't know."

No, we don't know. We've changed, we've forgotten, everything is different; we're not doing this because we used to, sixteen years ago. The question comes to me, like a fog rolling in: "Why *are* we doing this, you think?"

Kirsten shrugs. "We have this situation together," she says.

I almost ask, Does that mean love, or grief? But sometimes the two are indistinguishable, so I just lie there, holding her. It feels as if we're rocking; the thin skin of the earth wobbling, making waves. We could dive off this bed, swim to the planet's center; the ocean would open up, accept us, tell us all its secrets. The mysteries are common knowledge, for the moment.

"You could begin here," Kirsten says.

"If I write about it, you mean?"

She nods. I keep looking to the patterns in ice on the windows: flowers are being carved out of cold, elaborate systems are being constructed from the randomness of things.

"Or we could end here," I say.

"Oh yes. That could also be," she says, and Kirsten gives me the unlikely grace of her smile.

I leave early. As I step outside I'm splattered with cold. Overladen with clothing, I totter toward the bus stop through the dissipating smoke of my own breath. The few naked patches of my face stiffen in the anesthetic air, numbed, ready for the knife. But I can just feel it: something is writing itself there, carving out some crucial indecipherable message; ice flowers are forming, pushing cold roots down into human skin. All the same, I hurry on to where I'm going, heedless, because some kind of door will be waiting for my knock.

Alice Adams

THE LAST LOVELY CITY

Old and famous, an acknowledged success both in this country and in his native Mexico, though now a sadhearted widower, Dr. Benito Zamora slowly and unskillfully navigates the high, sharp curves on the road to Stinson Beach, California—his destination. From time to time, barely moving his heavy, whitemaned head, he glances at the unfamiliar young woman near him on the seat—the streaky-haired, underweight woman in a very short skirt and green sandals (her name is Carla) who has somewhat inexplicably invited him to come along to this party. What old hands, Benito thinks, of his own, on the wheel, an old beggar's hands. What can this girl want of me? he wonders. Some new heaviness around the doctor's neck and chin makes him look both strong and fierce, and his deep-set black eyes are powerful, still, and unrelenting in their judgmental gaze, beneath thick, uneven, white brows.

"We're almost there," he tells the girl, this Carla.

"I don't care; I love the drive," she says, and moves her head closer to the window, so her long hair fans out across her shoulders. "Do you go back to Mexico very often?" she turns now to ask him.

"Fairly. My very old mother still lives there. Near Oaxaca."

"Oh, I've been to Oaxaca. So beautiful." She beams. "The hotel—"

"My mother's not in the Presidente."

She grins, showing small, white, even teeth. "Well, you're right. I did stay there. But it is a very nice hotel."

"Very nice," he agrees, not looking at her.

His mother is not the doctor's only reason for going to Oaxaca. His interests are actually in almost adjacent Chiapas, where he oversees and has largely funded two large, free clinics— hence his fame, and his nickname, Dr. Do-Good (to Benito, an epithet replete with irony, and one that he much dislikes).

They have now emerged from the dark, tall, covering woods, the groves of redwood, eucalyptus, occasional laurel, and they are circling down the western slope, as the two-lane road forms wide arcs. Ahead of them is the sea, the white curve of beach, and strung-out Stinson, the strange, small coastal town of rich retirees; weekenders, also rich; and a core population of former hippies, now just plain poor, middle-aged people with too many children. In his palmier days, his early, successful years, Dr. Zamora often came to Stinson from San Francisco on Sundays for lunch parties, first as a semi-sought-after bachelor ("But would you want your daughter actually to marry . . . ?" Benito thought he felt this question), and later, less often, with his bride, the fairest of them all, his wife, his lovely blonde. His white soul. Elizabeth.

After Elizabeth died, now some five months ago, in April, friends and colleagues were predictably kind—many invitations, too many solicitous phone calls. And then, just as predictably (he had seen this happen with relatives of patients), all the attention fell off, and he was often alone. And at a time impossible for trips to Mexico: rains made most of the roads in Chiapas impassable, and he feared that he was now too old for the summer heat. Besides, these days the clinics actually ran quite well without him; he imagined that all they really needed was the money that came regularly from his banks. (Had that always been the case? he wondered. Were all those trips to Chiapas unnecessary, ultimately self-serving?) And his mother, in her tiny stucco villa, near Oaxaca, hardly recognized her oldest living son.

Too much time alone, then, and although he had always known that would happen, was even in a sense prepared, the doctor is sometimes angry: Why must they leave him now, when he is so vulnerable? Is no one able to imagine the daily lack, the loss with which he lives?

And then this girl, this Carla, whom the doctor had met at a dinner a month or so before, called and asked him to the lunch, at Stinson Beach. "I hope you don't mind a sort of last-minute invitation," she said, "but I really loved our talk, and I'd wanted to see you again, and this seemed a good excuse." He gratefully accepted, although he remembered very little of her, really, except for her hair, which was very long and silky-looking, streaked all shades of brown, with yellow. He remembered her hair, and that she seemed nice, a little shy; she was quiet, and so he had talked too much. ("Not too unusual, my darling," Elizabeth might have said.) He thinks she said she worked for a newspaper; it now seems too late to ask. He believes she is intelligent, and serious. Curious about his clinics.

But in the short interval between her call and this drive a host of fantasies has crowded old Benito's imagination. She looked about thirty, this girl did, but these days most women look young; she could be forty-two. Still a long way from his own age, but such things did happen. One read of them.

Or was it possible that Carla meant to write about him for her paper? The doctor had refused most interviews for years; had refused until he noticed that no one had asked, not for years.

"What did you say the name of our hostess was?" he thinks to ask her as they round the last curve and approach the first buildings of the town.

"Posey Pendergast. You've never met her?"

"I don't think so, but the name—something goes off in my head."

"Everyone knows Posey; I really thought you would. She's quite marvellous."

"Quite marvellous" is a phrase that Benito (Elizabeth used to agree) finds cautionary; those marvellous people are almost as bad as "characters." All those groups he is sure not to like, how they do proliferate, thinks old Benito sourly, aware of the cruel absence of Elizabeth, with her light laugh, agreeing.

"I'm sure you'll know some of her friends," adds Carla.

Posey Pendergast is a skinny old wreck of a woman, in a tattered straw sun hat and a red, Persian-looking outfit. She breathes heavily. Emphysema and some problems with her heart, the doctor thinks, automatically noting the pink-white skin, faintly bluish mouth, and arthritic hands—hugely blue-veined, rings buried in finger flesh. "I've been hearing of you for years," she tells Benito, in her raspy, classy voice. Is she English? No, more like Boston, or somewhere back there, the doctor decides. She goes on. "I can't believe we've never met. I'm *so* glad Carla brought you."

"This is some house," he says solemnly (using what Elizabeth called his innocent-Indian pose, which is one of his tricks).

It is some house, and the doctor now remembers walking past it, with Elizabeth, marvelling at its size and opulence. It was right out there on the beach, not farther along, in Seadrift, with the other big, expensive houses, but out in public—a huge house built up on pilings, all enormous beams, and steel and glass, and diagonal boards.

"My son designed it for me," Posey Pendergast is saying. "Carla's friend," she adds, just as some remote flash is going off in the doctor's mind: he used to hear a lot about this Posey, he recalls, something odd and somewhat scandalous, but from whom? Not Elizabeth, he is sure of that, although she was fond of gossip and used to lament his refusal to talk about patients. Did he hear of Posey from some patient? Some old friend?

This large room facing the sea is now fairly full of people. Women in short, silk, flowered dresses or pastel pants, men in linen or cashmere coats. Rich old gringos is Benito's instant assessment. He notes what seems an unusual number of hearing aids.

He and Carla are introduced around by Posey, although Carla seems already to know a number of the guests. People extend their hands; they all say how nice it is to meet the doctor; several people say that they have heard so much about him. And then, from that roster of Anglo-Saxon names, all sounding somewhat alike, from those voices, nasal Eastern to neutral Californian, Benito hears a familiar sound: "Oh." (It is the drawn-out "Oh" that he recognizes.) "Oh, but I've known Dr. Zamora *very* well, for a *very* long time."

He is confronted by an immense (she must weigh two hundred pounds), short woman, with a huge puff of orange hair, green eyeshadow, and the pinkish spots that skin cancer leaves marking her pale, lined forehead. It is Dolores. Originally Dolores Gutierrez—then Osborne, then Graham, and then he lost track. But here she is before him, her doughy face tightened into a mask, behind which he can indistinctly see the beauty that she was.

"Benito Zamora. Benny Zamora. What an absolutely awful name, my darling. So *spic*," said Dolores, almost fifty years ago.

"How about Dolores Gutierrez?"

"I can marry out of it, and I certainly plan to. Why else would I even think of Boy Osborne, or for that matter Whitey Satterfield? But you, you simply have to change *yours*. How about Benjamin Orland? That keeps some of the sound, you see? I really don't like names to begin with 'Z.' "

"This is an extremely ugly room," he told her.

She laughed. "I know, but poor dear Norman thinks it's the cat's pajamas, and it's costing him a fortune."

"When you laugh I feel ice on my back." He shivered.

"Pull the sheet up. There. My, you are a gorgeous young man. You really are. Too bad about your name. You don't look so terribly spic."

They were in the pink-and-gold suite of a lesser Nob Hill hotel, definitely not the Mark or the Fairmont, but still no doubt costing poor Norman a lot. Heavy, gold-threaded, rose-colored draperies, barely parted, yielded a narrow, blue view of the San Francisco Bay, the Bay Bridge, a white slice of Oakland. The bedspread, a darker rose, also gold-threaded, lay in a heavy, crumpled mass on the floor. The sheets were pink, and the shallow buttocks of Dolores Gutierrez were ivory—cool and smooth. Her hair, even then, was false gold.

"You know what I'd really like you to do? Do you want to know?" Her voice was like scented oil, the young doctor thought, light and insidious and finally dirty, making stains.

"I do want to know," he told her.

"Well, this is really perverse. *Really.* It may be a little too much for you." She was suddenly almost breathless with wanting to tell him what she really wanted, what was so terrifically exciting.

"Tell me." His breath caught, too, although in a rational way he believed that they had surely done everything. He stroked her smooth, cool bottom.

"I want you to pay me," she said. "I know you don't have much money, so that will make it all the more exciting. I want you to pay me a lot. And I might give it back to you, but then again I might not."

After several minutes, during which he took back his hand, Benito told her, "I don't want to do that. I don't think it would be fun."

And now this new Dolores, whose laugh is deeper, tells him, "This is a classic situation, isn't it, my angel? Famous man runs into an old lady friend, who's run to fat?" She laughs, and, as before, Benito shivers. "But wherever did you meet my darling old Posey?"

"Just now, actually. I never saw her before."

"The love of my life," Dolores declaims, as the doctor reflects that this could well be true, for he has just remembered a few more lines from their past. "I really don't like men at all," Dolores confided back then. "I only need them, although I'm terrified of them. And now I've fallen in love with this beautiful girl, who is very rich, of course. Even thinner than I am. With the most delicious name. Posey Pendergast. You must meet her one day. She would like you, too."

Wishing no more of this, and wishing no more of Dolores, ever, Benito turns in search of Carla, who seems to have vanished or hidden herself in the crowd that now populates this oversized room, milling around the long bar table and spilling out onto the broad deck that faces the sea. As he catches sight of the deck, the doctor instinctively moves toward it, even as Dolores is saying, "You must come back and tell me how you made all that money, Dr. Do-Good."

"Excuse me," he mutters, stiffly, making for the door. He is not at all graceful in the usual way of Latins; Elizabeth said that from time to time.

From the deck San Francisco is still invisible; it lurks there behind the great cliffs of land, across the surging, dark-streaked sea. The tall, pale city, lovely and unreal. Benito thinks of his amazement at that city, years back, when he roamed its streets as an almost indigent medical student—at Stanford, in those days a city medical school, at Clay and Webster Streets, in Pacific Heights. How lonely he used to feel as he walked across those hills and stared at massive apartment houses, at enormous family houses—how isolated and full of greed. He *wanted* the city, both to possess and to immerse himself in. It is hardly surprising, he now thinks—with a small, wry, private smile—that he ended in bed with Dolores Gutierrez, and that a few years later he found himself the owner of many sleazy blocks of hotels in the Tenderloin.

But that is not how he ended up, the doctor tells himself, in a fierce interior whisper. He ended up with Elizabeth, who was both beautiful and good, a serious woman, with whom he lived harmoniously, if sometimes sadly (they had no children, and Elizabeth was given to depression), near St. Francis Woods, in a house with a view of everything—the city and the sea, the Farallon Islands.

Nor is that life with Elizabeth how he ended up, actually. The actual is now, of course, and he has ended up alone. Childless and without Elizabeth.

The doctor takes deep breaths, inhaling the cool, fresh wind, and exhaling, he hopes and believes, the germs of self-pity that sometimes enter and threaten to invade his system. He looks back to the great Marin headlands, those steep, sweeping hills of green. Far out at sea he sees two small, hopeful white boats, sails bobbing against the dark horizon.

Looking back inside the house, he sees Carla in intimate-seeming conversation with withered old Posey. Fresh from the intimations of Dolores, he shudders: Posey must be even older than he is, and quite unwell. But before he has time for specula-tion along those lines, he is jolted by a face, suddenly glimpsed behind the glass doors: bright-eyed and buck-toothed, thinner and grayer but otherwise not much aged, in a starched white embroidered shirt (Why on earth? Does he want to look Mexi-can?), that lawyer, Herman Tolliver.

"Well, of course they should be condemned; half this town should be condemned, are you crazy?" Tolliver grinned side-ways, hiding his teeth. "The point is, they're not going to be condemned. Somebody's going to make a bundle off them. And from where I'm sitting it looks like you could be the guy. Along with me." Another grin, which was then extinguished as Tolliver tended to the lighting of a new cigar.

In that long-ago time (about forty years back) the doctor had just opened his own office and begun his cardiology practice. And had just met a young woman with straw-blond hair, clear, dark-blue eyes, and a sexy overbite—Carole Lombard with a Gene Tierney mouth. A young woman of class and style, none of which he could ever afford. Elizabeth Montague: her very name was defeating. Whoever would exchange Montague for Zamora?

None of which excused Benito's acquiescence in Tolliver's scheme. (Certain details as to the precise use of Tolliver's "hotels" Benito arranged not quite to know, but he had, of course, his suspicions.) It ended in making the doctor and his wife, Elizabeth Montague Zamora, very rich. And in funding the clinics for the indigent of Chiapas.

After that first encounter with Herman Tolliver, the doctor almost managed never to see him again. They talked on the phone, or, in the later days of success and busyness, through secretaries. Benito was aware of Tolliver, aware that they were both making a great deal of money, but otherwise he was fairly successful in dismissing the man from his mind.

One morning, not long before Elizabeth died, she looked up from the paper at breakfast (Benito only scanned the New York *Times*, did not read local news at all) and said, "Didn't you used to know this scandalous lawyer, this Tolliver?"

"We've met." But how did Elizabeth know that? Benito, shaken, wondered, and then remembered: some time back there had been phone calls, a secretary saying that Mr. Tolliver wanted to get in touch (fortunately, nothing urgent). Just enough to fix the name in Elizabeth's mind. "Is he scandalous?" Benito then asked his wife, very lightly.

"Well, some business with tax evasion. Goodness, do all lawyers do things like that these days?"

Aware of his own relief (he certainly did not want public scandals connected with Tolliver), Benito told her, "I very much doubt it, my darling."

And that was the end of that, it seemed.

*   *   *

Carla is now talking to both old Posey and Herman Tolliver, but the doctor can see from her posture that she doesn't really like him much, does not really want to talk to Tolliver. She is barely giving him the time of day, holding her glass out in front of her like a shield, or a weapon. She keeps glancing about, not smiling, as Tolliver goes on talking.

Is she looking for him? the doctor wonders. Does she ask herself what has happened to old Benito? He smiles to himself at this notion—and then, almost at the same moment, is chilled with longing for Elizabeth.

A problem with death, the doctor has more than once thought, is its removal of all the merciful dross of memory: he no longer remembers any petty annoyance, ever, or even moments of boredom, irritation, or sad, failed acts of love. All that is erased, and he only recalls, with the most cruel, searing accuracy, the golden peaks of their time together. Beautiful days, long nights of love. He sees Elizabeth at their dining table, on a rare warm summer night. Her shoulders bare and white, a thin gold necklace that he brought her from Oaxaca shines in the candlelight; she is bending toward their guest, old Dr. McPherson, from med-school days. Benito sees, too, McPherson's wife, and other colleague guests with their wives—all attractive, pale, and well dressed. But none so attractive as his own wife, his pale Elizabeth.

"Oh, there you are," Carla says, coming up to him suddenly.

"You couldn't see me out here? I could see you quite clearly," he tells her, in his sober, mechanical voice.

"I was busy fending off that creep, Tolliver. Mr. Slime." She tosses her hair, now gleaming in the sunlight. "I can't imagine what Posey sees in him. Do you know him?"

"We've met," the doctor admits. "But how do you know him?"

"I'm a reporter, remember? I meet everyone."

"And Posey Pendergast? You know her because—"

But that question and its possible answer are interrupted, cut off by the enormous, puffing arrival of Dolores. "Oh, here's where you've got to," she tells Benito and Carla, as though she had not seen them from afar and headed directly to where they stand, leaning together against the balcony's railing. "Carla, I'm absolutely in love with your hair," says Dolores.

Carla giggles—out of character for her, the doctor thinks—and then, another surprise, she takes his arm for a moment and laughs as she asks him, "Why don't you ever say such flattering things to me?"

Is she flirting with him, seriously flirting? Well, she could be. Such things do happen, the doctor reminds himself. And she seems a very honest young woman, and kind. She could brighten my life, he thinks, and lighten my home, all those rooms with their splendid views that seem to have darkened.

"Don't you want some lunch?" she is asking. "Can't I get you something?"

Before he can answer (and he had very much liked the idea of her bringing him food), Dolores, again interrupting, has stated, "He never eats. Can't you tell? Dr. Abstemious, I used to call him."

"Well, I'm really hungry, I'll see you two later." And with an uncertain smile (from shyness? annoyance? and if annoyance, at which of them?) Carla has left. She is pushing back into the room, through the crowds; she has vanished behind the glass.

Looking at Dolores then, the old doctor is seized with rage; he stares at that puffy, self-adoring face, those dark and infinitely self-pitying eyes. How he longs to push her against the railing, down into the sand! How he despises her!

"My darling, I believe you're really hungry after all" is what Dolores says, but she may have felt some of his anger, for she deftly steps sideways, on her high, thin, dangerous heels, just out of his reach.

"Not in the least," says Benito rigidly. "In fact, I think I'll go for a walk on the beach."

Down on the sand, though, as he walks along the dark,

packed strip that is nearest to the sea, Benito's confusion increases. He feels the presence of those people in that rather vulgar, glassed-in house behind him—of Dolores Gutierrez and Herman Tolliver, and God knows who else, what other ghosts from his past whom he simply failed to see. As though they were giants, he feels their looming presences, and feels their connection to some past year or years of his own life. He no longer knows where he is. What place is this, what country? What rolling gray-green ocean does he walk beside? What year is this, and what is his own true age?

Clearly, some derangement has taken hold of him, or nearly, and Benito is forced to fight back with certain heavy and irrefutable facts: this is September, 1990, the last year of a decade, and the year in which Elizabeth died. He is in Stinson Beach, and if he continues walking far enough along the coast—he is heading south, toward the Golden Gate—he will be in sight of beautiful, mythical San Francisco, the city and the center of all his early dreams, the city where everything, finally, happened: Dolores Gutierrez and his medical degree; Herman Tolliver and those hotels. His (at last) successful medical practice. Elizabeth, and all that money, and his house with its fabulous views. His fame as Dr. Do-Good.

His whole San Francisco history seems to rise up then and to break his heart. The city itself is still pale and distant and invisible, and he stands absolutely still, a tall figure on the sand, next to an intricate, crumbling sandcastle that some children have recently abandoned.

Hearing running feet behind him, at that moment the doctor turns in fright (expecting what? some dangerous stranger?)—but it is Carla, out of breath, her hair streaming backward in the wind. His savior.

"Ah, you," he says to her. "You ran."

"And these aren't the greatest running shoes." She laughs, pointing down to her sandals, now sand-streaked and damp.

"You came after me—"

She looks down, and away. "Well. It was partly an excuse to get out of there. It was getting a little claustrophobic, and almost everyone I talked to was hard of hearing."

"Oh, right."

"Well, shall we walk for a while?"

"*Yes.*"

Walking along with Carla, the doctor finds that those giants from his dark and tangled past have quite suddenly receded: Dolores and Tolliver have shrunk down to human size, the size of people accidentally encountered at a party. Such meetings can happen to anyone, easily, especially at a certain age.

Benito even finds that he can talk about them. "To tell you the truth"—an ominous beginning, he knows, but it is what he intends to do—"I did some business with Herman Tolliver a long time ago, maybe forty years. It came out very well, financially, but I'm still a little ashamed of it. It seems to me now that I was pretending to myself not to know certain things that I really did know."

"You mean about his hotels?"

"Well, yes. Hotels. But how do you— Does everyone know all that?"

"I'm a reporter, remember? Investigative." She laughs, then sniffles a little in the hard, cold ocean wind. "He had an idea a few years back about running for supervisor, but I'm sure he was really thinking mayor, ultimately. But we dug up some stuff."

"Here, take my handkerchief—"

"Thanks. Anyway, he was persuaded to forget it. There were really ugly things about pre-teen-age Asian girls. We made a bargain: the papers would print only the stuff about his 'tax problems' if he'd bow out." She sighs, a little ruefully. "I don't know. It might have been better to let him get into politics; he might have done less harm that way."

This walk, and the conversation, are serving both to calm and to excite the doctor. Simultaneously. Most peculiar. He feels a calm, and at the same time a strange, warm, quiet excitement. "How do you mean?" he asks Carla.

"Oh, he got in deeper and deeper. Getting richer and richer."

"I got richer and richer, too, back then. Sometimes I felt like I owned the whole goddam city." Benito is paying very little attention to what he is saying; it is now all he can do to prevent himself from speaking his heart, from saying, "When will you marry me? How soon can that be?"

"But that's great that you made so much money," Carla says. "That way you could start those clinics, and do so much good."

Barely listening, Benito murmurs, "I suppose . . ."

She could redecorate the house any way she would like to, he thinks. Throw things out, repaint, reupholster, add mirrors. His imagination sees, all completed, a brilliant house, with Carla its brilliant, shining center.

"How did you happen to know Dolores?" Carla is asking.

By now they have reached the end of the beach: a high mass of rocks left there by mammoth storms the year before. Impassable. Beyond lie more beach, more cliffs, more headlands, all along the way to the sight of the distant city.

"Actually, Dolores was an old girlfriend, you might say." Since he cares so much for this girl, Benito will never lie to her, he thinks. "You might not believe this, but she was quite a beauty in her day."

"Oh, I believe you. She's still so vain. That hair."

Benito laughs, feeling pleased, and wondering, Can this adorable girl be, even slightly, jealous? "You're right there," he tells Carla. "Very vain, always was. Of course, she's a few years older than I am."

"I guess we have to turn around now," says Carla.

"And now Dolores tells me that she and that Posey Pendergast were at one time, uh, lovers," Benito continues, in his honest mode.

"I guess they could have been," Carla muses. "On the other hand, it's my impression that Dolores lies a lot. And Posey I'm just not sure about. Nor any of that group, for that matter.

Tolliver, all those people. It's worrying." She laughs. "I guess I sort of hoped you might know something about them. Sort of explain them to me."

Not having listened carefully to much of this, Benito rephrases the question he does not remember having begun to ask before, which Dolores interrupted: "How do you know Posey?" he asks Carla.

"It's mostly her son I know. Patrick. He's my fiancé, I guess you could say. We keep planning to make it legal, and I guess we will. Any day now." And she goes on. "Actually, Patrick was supposed to come today, and then he couldn't, and then I thought—I thought of you."

The sun has sunk into the ocean, and Benito's heart has sunk with it, drowned. He shudders, despising himself. How could he possibly have imagined, how not have guessed?

"How nice," Benito remarks, without meaning, and then he babbles on, "You know, the whole city seems so corrupt these days. It's all real estate, and deals."

"Get real," she chides him, in her harsh young voice. "That's what it's like all over."

"Well, I'll be awfully glad to get back to Mexico. At least I more or less understand the corruption there."

"Are you going back for long?"

The wind is really cold now. Benito sniffs, wishing he had his handkerchief back, and unable to ask for it. "Oh, permanently," he tells Carla. "A permanent move. I want to be near my clinics. See how they're doing. Maybe help."

The doctor had no plan to say (much less to do) any of this before he spoke, but he knows that he is now committed to this action. This permanent move. He will buy a house in San Cristóbal de las Casas, and will bring his mother there, from Oaxaca, to live in that house for as long as she lasts. And he, for as long as he lasts, will work in his clinics, with his own poor.

"Well, that's great. Maybe we could work out a little interview before you go."

"Well, maybe."

"I wonder if we couldn't just bypass the party for now," says Carla. "I'm just not up to going in again, going through all that, with those people."

"Nor I," the doctor tells her. "Good idea."

"I'll call Posey as soon as we get back. Did she tell you the house was up for sale? She may have sold it today—all those people . . ."

Half hearing her, the doctor is wrestling with the idea of a return to the city, which is suddenly unaccountably terrible to him; he dreads the first pale, romantic view of it from the bridge, and then the drive across town to his empty house, after dropping Carla off on Telegraph Hill. His house with its night views of city hills and lights. But he braces himself with the thought that he won't be in San Francisco long this time. That as soon as he can arrange things he will be back in Chiapas, in Mexico. For the rest of his life.

And thus he manages to walk on, following Carla past the big, fancy house, for sale—and all those people, the house's rich and crazily corrupt population. He manages to walk across the sand toward his car, and the long, circuitous, and risky drive to the city.

Frances Sherwood

DEMIURGES

If it is suppertime, Rosie McGrath is listening to her favorite song, Prince's "Little Red Corvette." She is eating quesadillas at her kitchen table, pickles, green olives with pimentos, drinking Evian Spring Water, and reading Ann Rice's *Interview with a Vampire.* She is toying with the idea of writing a romance novel, has sent for the formula. She is thinking of doing something along the lines of a mature romance, or maybe it would be an immature romance. Everything above the neck. The power of suggestion.

Rosie has never been married, has no kids. She can't remember what she was doing when everybody else was getting married. In the Midwest where husbands dutifully mow their lawns every summer Saturday morning and potluck reigns supreme and people are coupled unto death, she feels she has been kicked out of the ark. Perhaps in New York City or even Seattle, she might feel more attuned, more like a postmodern woman living in late capitalism and that androgyny was the wave of the future and that at least she was on the beach, but in South Bend, Indiana, she imagines herself looming up over the landscape of broken cornstalks like a sore thumb or a King

Kong caught in a tower, a bebearded Rumpuzel, roaring out his misery.

Rosie met Jamshid at Dances for Peace. Sponsored by the Pagan Group of the Unitarian Church, they were held every other Tuesday. At these occasions people linked hands, danced in lines and circles as if world powers would be swayed from collective madness and the celestial influences could be made to infinite pity by a tap, tap, tap and a clap, clap, clap. That kind of quixotic gesture was really Rosie's style.

She had read somewhere that the Australian aborigines believed that the world, in dreamtime, was sung up by the ancestors, that the ancestors had gone on walkabout and that lizard and ant jumped out of their mouth, man too. All the world was their song. Something about that account appealed to her, deeply. In her way, she wanted to do much the same thing, that is, create her own world through wishful thinking and story telling. She worked at it, counted on it. For instance:

On the weekends she walked about South Bend conjuring creatures and comfort, and during dreamtime called on ancestral figures to do her bidding. Each night, her blond hair arrayed on her pillow like thatched straw and her eyes tightshut in intense concentration, she summoned up from the cave of her sleep a roan stallion. Rounding the estuary, he would kneel before her and in

a deep human voice, head bowed, intone:

Your wish is my command.

Make him, Rosie prayed, make Jamshid love me.

Jamshid was beautiful, its own excuse, and according to the poet Rilke, "the start of a terror we could only just barely endure." He had the face of a Byzantine boy-emperor, and the manner of a Russian anarchist about to go before the firing squad. Long live anarchy she could imagine him crying the moment before the shots rang out and were enfolded forever in the glacial white of Siberia. He would lie crumpled, a ribbon of blood snaking its way out of his left nostril. Oh Jamshid, Jamshid. She would run forth to cradle his poor dead body, tears staining her babushka. Jamshid, my dear heart.

Eros and Thanatos was what Rosie and Jamshid talked about on their rambles through South Bend, and somehow he connected those subjects intimately. He had asked her what autoerotic affixation was, and she had answered coming and going at the same time. He liked that. Of course, he liked that. Another piece of evidence. He was foreign and she had to explain things to him. She felt like a decadent American, somebody whose tongue and hands could be cut off where he came from. Once she had cried in frustration. Don't you understand, she had moaned, don't you understand anything? He had gotten terribly disconcerted, ignored her and then said her tears were contrived. Everything is contrived she had answered testily. Often these discussions took place on Saturday afternoons in dark, dusty bars, six martinis gone, and scribbling notes on damp cocktail napkins. It was all talk, only talk.

At the airport though he had put his tongue politely in her mouth. That was the most thing they did. They had dropped some acid that time and driven out to see the shuttles come in from Chicago and Cincinnati. The lights on the runway ran like watercolors smearing streamers of pink and yellow. She brushed her breast against his arm and he had groaned. Apparently he was carried away. She had to proceed carefully, she knew, not rush things.

Her conversations with Jamshid then were like carefully composed love letters in code and when not with him she daydreamed and had a running dialogue in her head. But the best times were dreamtime, which felt like working night shift on cold, snowy nights, in a factory puffing its own smoke. Inside was warm and cozy, pillowed in images and set in corner stones. They manufactured cutout dolls, horses, caves, estuaries, you name it.

Daytime, Rosie masqueraded as a Latin teacher in a girls' school, doing imperatives and conjugations, amo, ama, amas.

It was not a bad place, Sacred Heart. On the outskirts was a row of boxy hedges. There were columns at the front entrance. The lunchroom was bright and airy, the girls angelic, the pace brisk, efficient. Nuns darted here and there like magpies on God's important errands. Although she was a teacher, Rosie carried a red lunch box with a flower-painted thermos. Her students asked if she was hippie once, if she was a flower child, and rolling her eyes meaningfully, Rosie would answer:

Never you mind.

If it was anything it was her hair which gave her away. Long, stick straight, always in her eyes, so she had to whip her head around. And sometimes, Fridays, seventh period, she put a dollop of vodka, Absolut in with her V8. Then at the height of her powers, all's right with the world, the room would begin to glow with aphorisms and faintly in the back of her mind, she would hear the Roman legions tramping along the Via something or other.

Oh Miss McGrath, you look so pretty.

Women, women, calm down. They loved being called women at Sacred Heart High.

Which is where Rosie met Paul by the way. He was a substitute, and loomed over the horizon of giddy girls like an ostrich with a peaked fluff of hair, a startled look on his face, long neck, Adam's apple. He also painted houses in the summer. His truck had a Colorado license plate, green with snowcapped mountains. And his favorite food was Macademia nuts.

I like your lunch box, Paul said meaningfully in the lunchroom that first day.

I like your license plate.

Later alligator.

Paul was thirty-five, Jamshid twenty-eight, and Rosie, truth be known, was a good forty-five. She looked, she hoped, younger, but often felt she was falling through the cracks, and would be found years later on some archaeological dig, a rusted hint of twentieth century technology, smattering of pottery, politics. Extremities in Distress, the label in the Museum of Ancient Art would say.

I'm my own duenna, she told Jamshid.

What's that?

An older woman serving as chaperon to a young lady. Except I'm not very good at it.

She also felt like a demimonde, that is, a fallen woman. But the pits were curiously platonic.

She hoped Paul would kind of tide her over, make it possible for her to go on.

The evening with Paul started at his apartment, moved to a white gay bar with a mirror stretched in front of the dance floor, where she got completely bummed out. Somewhere in that schedule they made love once in front of a mirror, his idea, and secondly in the women's bathroom of the bar, her idea. The first was not a success. The second was almost interrupted by a transvestite or transsexual, she couldn't tell which, except, he/she put his/her hand to heart, uttered a fluttery: Excuse *me*.

She usually described her life to Jamshid in the most exciting terms, actually hoping to make him jealous in several different ways.

It was important to make the setting exotic, and she phrased these little stories like a travelogue. But there were many things she didn't tell him. Like:

Passing the Farmer's Market, the city cemetery, and several fix-it shops with broken TVs in the window on the way to school a scenario would flash before her, complete with litany and ritual flourishes. It went:

Jamshid, Fix me up. Turn me on. Tune me in. The screens of the three broken TVs would be a blue blur at first, and then focusing in triplicate would be something British and classy— he, eager and intense, she angular and aristocratic, a poet*ess* with almond eyes. The story would have to do with the obstacles to their romance, and much of the action would be longing looks across the arid landscape of crowded cocktail parties. Close up, merely rubbing shoulders, Jamshid would hiss wetly: You slut.

All quite make believe.

The bona fide seduction scene with Paul started out with wine. She sloshed it around her mouth, bathed her gums, and then he kissed her emptying his wine, diluted with sticky saliva, in her mouth. She felt slightly sick, pulled away.

He hopped up, put on a record, "Music from the Morning of the World," gamelan music from Bali, went into the kitchen for some snacks. Things were rolling along. He had a really spiffy apartment all done in Simple Good Taste.

In the record, "Music from the Morning of the World," which sounded like bells and xylophones, eerie and rainy, Rosie assumed the musicians to be naked brown men with purple penises. They wore flowers in their hair so laden with scent that one sniff and you would swoon with the pain of desire. Limp lilies jangled over their ears. When it rained, and it went on for days, the leaves of incandescently green foliage turned inside out, indecently disgorged their stamen and pistils. The men sat in their open, stilted, palm-thatched huts smoking big bamboo pipes of pure hash, their eyes glazed over remembering other lives outside the tropical rain forest.

While she was thinking this Paul was inching his bare foot up her leg. She supposed he might possibly like her.

She knew, too, that she could close her eyes and pretend that Paul's long, bony foot belonged to Jamshid. However, she was not drunk enough for that. Jam's feet were narrow and delicate as a closed flower, each toe a petal folded in on itself, pink and secret.

She had seen Jamshid's bare feet the day he bathed her, and

she was more moved by them than he had been by the sight of her entire body. Coke the night before had made her feel like going through the roof. During the session her lips had been glued to her teeth and then she got the jitters and shakes, needed to borrow Jamshid's sweater.

It had started out kind of wonderfully though, her white car following his white car up the hill, hot on his tail, two white bunnies, snow on the ground crusty like day-old frosting, a Winter Wonderland. Snow on the glass plate, chop, chop, chop with a razor blade into little ridges. At one point she thought of all the young men in South Bend masturbating in unison shooting out sparks of hot white over the Holiday Inn building. She imagined herself out with a stick sorting through the gobs of come, finding Jam's, fishing it up in a jar, bringing it home to put in a blender, swirling it around to look like Encyclopedia Britannica pictures of the Milky Way. Jammy, Jammy, Jammy. They were on his carpet of brown leaves doing coke, his two chairs like seated parents watching them. Mom and Dad. He put his finger on her chin, drew it round, touched her nose. You are a very pretty woman, he said, an extraordinarily pretty woman.

Then she came down, very fast, very hard.

I need a Ritual Bath, she told him over the phone the next day, her teeth still chattering. Would you come over, do it for me? I can't sleep.

Jam arrived post haste, took off his shoes and socks, rolled up his sleeves and the legs of his jeans, and very gently set to work. He ran the bath. She had an old-fashioned tub with lion legs and an ornate faucet, rust-stained lines around the drips. He tested the water, poured in lilac bubble bath. She stood by barely able to stand thinking God help me. Then Jamshid took off her nightgown, and she was there naked before him, neat, small, her flesh tight and goosebumped.

You have the body of a child, he said.

Thanks, I guess, though she fancied herself womanly. Her

pink nipples were twitching like rabbit noses. She would have given anything, but she eased herself into the warm water like a good girl. He took the wash rag went between her toes, up her legs, between her legs. He soaped her belly and under her breasts, had her turn over, lift her arms. She remembered being high once, and sweating and thinking, saying something about sweat coming out in paisley, little toot-toots of paisley scrolling, snailing out from under her arms.

Jamshid soaped her everywhere. He rinsed her. Wrapped her in the towel. Dried her. Got her a clean nightgown. He was reverent, serious, attentive. But not the least aroused. Then he tucked her in, kissed her forehead.

Jamshid, do you like me a little.

Rosie, I *love* you, he said in his drawn out, slightly mocking way.

You mean as a friend.

As a *very* good friend, a *very* good friend.

Paul smiled at Rosie, held out a cracker in the palm of his hand like a peace offering. It was a sign, she knew, a preview of coming attractions. He would be sweet, start at the neck, nuzzle her ears, tongue between her toes. The possibilities grew toasty warm. She had been living in the realm of pure idea a good while. This was The Real Thing. She started to get happy.

Want to have sex? Paul said abruptly and giving her a beady stare which meant business no doubt about it.

It seemed a little grubby and grabby, a little fast. She was hoping for more of a prelude.

Sure, she replied. Maybe Paul *would* break the spell.

I haven't had a woman in a long time, he added.

Fat chance, she thought, of breaking the spell with an approach like a moose on the loose, but oh well, and she wondered what long time meant in his social calendar.

And without further ado he darted into the bathroom, where apparently, he kept what looked to be a year's supply of condoms.

I'm kind of pornographic, Paul explained, coming back armored and ready for battle, but taking the time to arrange the mirror just so.

The mirror did not behave, had a life of its own, wanted to make a statement about the nature of reality. Sad, not sexy it was, showing a kaleidoscope of parts less than their sum, strange and slivered juxtaposition, triangles of light and dark, frightened animals caught in the insect eyes of a headlight.

What's the Big Deal, he said, look at the mirror, it's just sex.

I *am* having sex, she thought, but still didn't look, would rather have been just talking with Jamshid, remembering at the moment of critical mass how once upon a time she had been on hallowed ground, a time that her own feelings were enough. It had happened when helping Jam plant tomatoes around his house. While securing the little leaves on stakes with strips of cotton torn from the edge of a pillow case, she had looked over at him and wondered: Is this it?

Jam, she said, we are making love now, right now.

It had visited her, this love, an incredible sense of happiness unasked for, like an angel from on high. It had pierced her heart and for a second she could not get her breath. Then the sun glanced off a car mirror, somebody passing and the second was gone.

Want to go out to a bar, listen to some music, Paul suggested, hiking up his pants. We can come back; it's never that great the first time. Tomorrow is Saturday, then Sunday. Let's see how it goes, huh?

It is Sunday morning, Jamshid liked to say in bars. It was the thing to say and sometimes bands broke out into gospel music, songs learned when they were twelve years old in church.

When she and Jamshid went to bars together, they did not go home together. Instead he walked home by himself, moving slowly, weaving slowly, weaving carefully through the flat, deserted streets of South Bend. They called them walkabouts after the Australian aborigine myths. When one went on walkabout one called up the world, it appeared in the perceiving, was heard in song. Jamshid called up block by grey block Polish neighborhoods on the west side, ghettos, caused the bridge spanning the St. Joe River to be, and finally getting home, telephoning her at eight a.m., he'd announce: I'm home, like a regular husband.

We all court desolation in one form or another, she reasoned, trying to live with it somehow, that he didn't want to go home with her. Paul wanted to go dancing and the only decent dance floor in town was Eden, a gay bar, and when they got there, the striptease was going on.

It was not as elaborate as a female striptease. The men got their few clothes off quickly. And there they were, in bikinis and tans, big white smiles on their faces like boys at the beach, Adams in a real Eden.

Rosie was reminded of the record they had heard at Paul's apartment. Eden did seem like the morning of the world, a time even before Eve when the temptation was not knowledge, but fantasy, a dreamtime, a wish. It was Woman she speculated, although she, Rosie, was not an example, who brought in the getting of wisdom. She believed the women in small Balinese villages wore sarongs. Did they bring tea to the gamelan men? Their breasts would sway to and fro like limp penises. Australian women painted cosmic maps on their breasts during festival time. Diagrams of waterholes and kangaroo tracks, boomerangs, small clouds. Did they guide the ancestors back to the original sites?

Eden was full of cut glass. A mirror spanned one wall of the dance floor so that one could dance with oneself, see oneself in the act, and on the ceiling was a glass ball made of little squares of glass which slowly revolved. The tables were glass and the bar top was glass and of course, there were stacks and stacks of glasses in pyramids and rows. Narcissus, of course, who else. Personally she avoided mirrors. She looked about, and then focusing on a group of beautiful boys, she saw him, saw Jam-

shid reflected a hundred times. Jamshid. He was holding
hands, ear-tonguing a man with a small Hitler mustache sitting
on his chair backwards like a cowboy come to town.

What's wrong, Rosie? Paul asked.

I'm so damned dumb.

What?

It was as if a heavy wind had struck, sweeping clean the
garden. The beasts and the birds were hushed, the trees stilled,
the hour of judgment at hand. Only the clink of glass from the
bar reminded her back to herself, told her that all was not shut
down.

Let's go to the bathroom, she said to Paul.

It was rather posh, not too grungy, not like in the Joe Orton
diaries, the sleazy johns of the London tube, where graffiti de-
clared: Fuck the State.

And for a short moment, her head banging against the gold-
speckled wall, she thought maybe what she had seen in the bar,
Jamshid and the other man, that they, he, had been a figment of
her imagination. But when they went out again, back to the
dance floor, she realized that the other Jamshid, the one of her
dreams and days, that one was the figment. The real Jamshid
actually greeted her, introduced her to Andy, thought nothing
of it.

And this is Paul, she said, all very civilized, boyfriend to
boyfriend. There was No screaming, No crying, No carrying
on. But Rosie's heart had shriveled to the size and texture of a
prune, her legs walked on their own, and when she kissed Paul
good night, her lips were frozen dry. His tongue was like a
great, fat slug.

Want to come in for Round Three?

What a charming way to put it.

You are a very funny girl.

Delusions of grandeur.

What?

I'll call you, Paul. Would she? I'll call *you?*

*   *   *

When she was home alone, she looked in the mirror at herself, and said to herself:

I am pretty, very pretty.

Then she said:

She left under a cloud of smoke.

Then she said:

Is this my life, is that what I have come to?

She wished she could just die, or at the very least, drop out of the game, yet she knew also that it was the only game in town, and maybe the only game in the non-politicized, western, developed world, one of the few hedges against life, and a reply to auto-erotic affixation. Other adventures belong to other times. Love was hers. She was not an artist, she was not a genius or an entrepreneur or even much of a professional. She had no family to speak of, and so what the hell was she supposed to do. Just a poor choice, that's all it was, and given the field, understandable. You had to make the best of it. What else was new or old, and who cared. In the most imperfect of all possible worlds, could one live without hope? So:

Yes, she answered herself, this is my life, this is what I have come to. Yes, yes, yes.

When the acid finally hit, spiders skittered across the floor boards, orange coffins came out of her mouth. She went to bed, pulled the covers over her head, summoned the animal forth:

Your wish is my command, he said in a deep and very human voice.

Later on Jamshid visited her like an angel, leaning down to kiss her gently on the forehead.

Sweet dreams, he said.

Antonya Nelson

THE CONTROL GROUP

TV Mitchell fell in love with his fourth-grade teacher. An odd and uncomfortable prospect, his love was a secret he confessed to nobody, not that there was anybody he could have confessed to, and not that he quite understood his feelings as, in fact, ones of love. He knew simply an unbearable ache like illness, the knot in his gut Mrs. Dugas could tie and twist with such torque he thought he might, quite literally, die.

And TV, alone among his nine-year-old peers at Hamilton Elementary, *did* comprehend death. Unlike his baffling love for his fifty-two-year-old teacher, he spoke freely about that which he understood. His mother had murdered her father, TV's grandfather. TV's tale did not differ substantially from the other gruesome stories heard over lunch from the boys' corner of the playground, but his had the unbeatable edge of truth. The others might escalate their stakes, recount baby-sitters finding dripping blood in the bath or vampires under the bed, phone calls from hatchet-bearing mental escapees, timely electrical blackouts, hairy hands sprouting from the seeming innocence of wing chairs or garden spigots.

But they couldn't outdo TV's penetrating simplicity. "She

pounded him with a hammer," he told the boys. They stood scuffing dirt, hands balled in front pockets. "She stuffed a handkerchief in his mouth," TV went on, "to keep him quiet." He carried the handkerchief with him for further drama, its pure whiteness and ancient embroidered monogram somehow proof enough. TVM, his grandfather's and his own initials, the navy threads worn nearly away under TV's worrying finger-tips. A single blow to the forehead, a round blue contusion meant to resemble a bruise from an accidental fall.

Mrs. Dugas's classroom was a portable annex set off from the rest of the school. Her students studied, primarily, animals. There were tanks of fish and gerbils and mice and miniature frogs and little chicks, who'd been hatched from plain eggs under a heat lamp. Those eggs that did not result in chicks were buried outside the annex, cracked open and poured into a hole deep enough to discourage roaming dogs. Embryonic beaks and feet could be identified floating in the bloody yolk. A snapping turtle had once escaped from Mrs. Dugas's room and now lived beneath the annex. When the class read, they read about the migration of loons, or about panda bears whose ba-bies were so small they could get lost in their own mother's fur. History was the study of those animals who were now extinct. Mrs. Dugas taught evolution, made all the children remove their shoes and contemplate their fifth, finlike, useless little toes, which would someday disappear. Her favorite subject was science. The same day TV had stepped into her classroom, Mrs. Dugas introduced two rats who would help the students understand the dangers of Coke and potato chips and candy.

They wrote in their experiment diaries. One rat would be given vegetables and cheese and milk; the other would eat Bu-gles and Fruit Loops and Orange Crush. TV was grateful for the rats, as they held the attention that otherwise would surely have been directed toward him. The children named the control rat Batman and the junk-food rat Joker. On Friday afternoons the animals were packed off to different homes, each child promising to maintain the experiment.

The changes came quickly, Joker's white coat turning slightly gray, his tail losing its pink, his eyes their shine. TV had thought neither of the rats especially handsome but eventually, by comparison, Joker became ugly. Batman continued to look the way he had. Bigger, better. They sat in their two cages, next to each other, one eating an apple wedge, one a Frito. Both rats spent most of their time standing on their hind legs reaching for the screens that kept them caged. TV had noted that, though Joker *looked* worse, he didn't seem to *feel* worse. Moreover, it was Batman, the rat named as control, who ate the more exotic diet. TV couldn't remember when he himself had last eaten a raw vegetable. But, of course, that was Mrs. Dugas's point. When TV's turn came to take home a rat, he was happy to get Joker. He cheated, poking into the cage little cubes of cheddar cheese and a nutritious piece of wheat toast. Joker obliged by eating whatever was shoved his way. TV had worried Mrs. Dugas would not give him an opportunity with a rat. It seemed natural to him that she might have reservations concerning his character. But though he looked for fretfulness in her face the Friday he departed the annex with Joker in his traveling cage she did not reveal any.

That weekend the temperature dropped into the negative. TV, believing Joker needed more space to move, turned him loose in a large cardboard box that had once held a microwave oven. He reinforced the top flaps with three volumes of the encyclopedia to make sure he wouldn't escape. In the morning he found the rat frozen, curled in what he assumed was a death position. He immediately thought of fleeing; he could not face Mrs. Dugas. Screaming his foster mother's name, he ran to her bedroom. He made note of the fact that he could see his breath.

"He can't have frozen," his foster mother told him, groggily following to the box. The rat lay where he'd been, scraggly and dead. His foster mother squatted, laying her forefinger warily on the animal's chest.

"Hibernation," she diagnosed after a moment. She carried the box to the floor heat register in the hallway and set it down. "He'll thaw," she reassured TV, then giggled. "I'd like to call the landlord and tell him even the rats are freezing."

But TV found nothing about the situation comical. He watched Joker slowly come to. When he fed him later, he made sure the food was bad, a lidful of red wine, a few chocolate chips.

In the end no gesture would have made any impression whatsoever. At the conclusion of the experiment, week ten, a man from a lab came and took both rats away. TV was shocked. He had assumed the next step would be to rehabilitate Joker, record in their diaries the bringing back of his shiny eyes and coat. The class asked if they couldn't take the rats home to keep as pets. Mrs. Dugas explained that experimental animals had to be destroyed. Joker and Batman went together. As consolation, Joker's leftover box of Cracker Jack was passed around the room for the kids to eat.

TV's new foster mother said, "I wonder which lesson will stick? You Are What You Eat? or, Life Sucks?"

But TV began loving Mrs. Dugas then, trusting her to judge him without sentimentality. She did not, it was clear, feel sorry for anyone.

TV had moved in with his new foster mother just three months ago. He was, actually, unsure he would stay with her. The last foster arrangement had not worked out; the committee deciding his future had tried an opposite approach this time, placing him not with a large family, as he had been last time, but with a single woman. This was intended to replicate his natural situation, though in his real life he had also lived with his grandfather. Joanne Link, his new parent, had another month left on trial time. She could turn him back, he understood that. He was trying to behave. She was preferable, mostly, by default. TV felt Joanne sometimes watching him. They had discussed his mother a few times, approaching the subject delicately, Joanne only too eager to back off. She did not ask him questions point-blank, pretending she wasn't interested in the details. For instance, TV had heard his mother and her boyfriend Wade planning to kill TV's grandfather. The old man had been sick for a long time, peeing his bed and screaming at people. In more lucid moments, he would apologize, saying, "I forget myself." Wade wanted to inject him with an air bubble. Apparently, air could kill you.

TV had stood on the landing in his old house listening to his grandfather wheeze in an upstairs room, his mother and Wade talking in a downstairs one. He had no idea what to do. His stealth in returning unheard to bed gave him a headache, which he nursed through the night into genuine illness. The next day, however, he did not want to remain at home with his grandfather, afraid he would be included in the conspiracy, participant or victim.

But his grandfather lived for months following TV's eavesdropping. TV had convinced himself it was a nightmare, had been on the verge of confessing this to his mother when he came home from school to find his whole life turned inside out; that is, what he'd held close and fought in himself suddenly was free, open to anyone's inspection.

Though Joanne sympathized with him, he could tell he made her nervous. She embarrassed easily and, when driven to exclamation, would not say *Shit!* but *Sugar!* She was likeable, that way. But alien. She provided TV with a generous allowance, and on weekends, let him loose and seemed happy not to know what he did. They shared a small apartment in a dirty neighborhood miles and miles from Hamilton Elementary, which was by reputation one of the best schools in Wichita. TV rode the bus.

* * *

Mrs. Dugas made it standard policy to invite the children once to her home during the year. She lived near a drainage canal and after the twenty-two fourth graders had consumed Dixie cups of orange juice and a sesame rice cake each, a rabbit-watching expedition embarked. Three mothers—the drivers—opted to stay in Mrs. Dugas's living room with a tag-along toddler. Mrs. Dugas herself changed shoes and tied a peach chiffon scarf over her hair so that she could join the search.

"Do we frighten the rabbits?" she asked the group before opening the gate between her tidy yard and the wild canal. It was late spring in Kansas, but the sky looked as if it could still threaten snow. Houses precisely like Mrs. Dugas's lined both sides of the cement-walled canal, and TV imagined them sliding in, crumpling, all of them except Mrs. Dugas's. The dank odor of stagnant water drifted in the air. "Do we frighten rabbits?"

"No," the girls in the class answered.

"Do we jab sticks in their homes or throw rocks at their tails?"

Again, the girls chimed, "No."

"Do we take nature as we find it, not as we wish to manipulate it?"

A few girls, shivering, eager to get on with the hunt, having sensed the general direction of this line of questioning, answered once more in the negative. Mrs. Dugas raised her eyebrows. TV's heart lurched; he could make out the little quiver her lip made toward smiling. It was her eyebrows, still black despite her silver hair, that most intrigued him. She knew something he wished to learn.

"Yes, yes," the girls amended.

Mrs. Dugas opened her gate. She had shared with them her secret method of watching the rabbits, the way she had discovered them years ago by coming to the canal to think—about what? TV wondered desperately—sitting down among the broken pieces of concrete and holding perfectly still until she became part of the picture, the life already there soon forgetting her presence and getting on with business. "They see the world differently," she told her class. "They rely on movement, on instinct." She could wiggle her nose, a gesture that meant disapproval. She could hear, from one end of her fourth-grade annex to the other, the illicit whisper of notes being passed, of secrets on the verge of leaving lips. Hostile looks, cast between enemies, reflected unerringly from the satellite of her sharp eyes. TV would watch her eyebrows, the lift that signaled unspoken intercession.

He followed her down the canal. Some days it mattered to him what the boys thought but other days he couldn't remember to care. They had been a group since kindergarten, neighbors and Cub Scouts together, summer camp initiates. TV's acceptance into their midst was based on his mother's celebrity, his own frankness concerning her crime and incarceration. Around Mrs. Dugas he felt a twinge taking advantage of his mother's notoriety, so around her he pretended the boys had not accepted him. He pretended he had higher matters on his mind, the same matters, coincidentally, that Mrs. Dugas seemed to have on hers—rabbits, today, perhaps a pheasant.

True to her anecdotes in the classroom, Mrs. Dugas soon settled on a broken piece of concrete and proceeded to stop moving. She had changed her clear lenses for sunglasses. The last motion she made was to secure her chiffon scarf's knot under her chin. TV kneeled a few yards from her. While she waited for rabbits, he stared at her.

On Tuesdays, after school, TV took his regular bus home, then boarded a city line to his psychologist's office in a medical complex that resembled a strip mall. For a while, the psychologist had discussed adopting him. Then his wife had gotten pregnant and the idea had been dropped. They talked about Joanne a lot, the psychologist making sure she was better than the last family, assuaging his own guilt. They'd made jokes about General Patton, the name they gave the father at the first home. TV's own name was not short for any thing less ridiculous, simply TV. It was his mother's little joke on her father, whose name had been Terrence Valley Mitchell.

TV's psychologist liked the fact that Joanne was studying to be a psychiatric nurse, though he worried openly about her weak financial setup. "It's true you can't buy happiness," he told TV, "but you *can* buy better odds."

After their sessions, TV walked across the street to a Russell Stover candy shop and bought a chocolate turtle. Waiting for his bus home, he rewarded himself for another week safely passed.

During the time TV squatted in the dried weeds growing from the upended chunks of canal concrete at Mrs. Dugas's, he devised a plan. He would invite Mrs. Dugas to lunch next Saturday. He would take his saved allowance and meet her somewhere he could reach by bus. Soon it would be summer, he would leave her classroom forever. His love for her frightened him; he did not want to kiss her or see her naked. He did not know exactly what he wanted but he felt a hunger, a physical depth of daily need for her that was going to be denied him.

On the ride back to school, in the cramped quarters of a foreign station wagon, a few kids claimed to have seen rabbits. The boys, in fear, in respect, out of anger, asked TV if he'd seen any.

He shook his head, though in truth, he had. Mrs. Dugas, without turning around, had lifted her arm slowly so as not to seem out of keeping with the rest of the animal's picture, knowing TV was behind her, knowing he would follow the point. A small brown rabbit sat terrified between the rocks.

He phoned her while Joanne was still at the hospital, hanging up on her husband the first time, feeling ashamed when she answered—as if she knew—the second.

Before inviting her he thanked her for the orange juice. She
told him, formally, perhaps with irritation, he was most welcome. He would have hung up if he had not heard her turn the
receiver away and cough, once, a moist sound that carried
through the line and gave TV a window of vulnerability, a shot.

"Can you go to lunch with me?" he asked. "At the . . ." he
blinked hard at the phone book page he'd found, the penciled
line he'd drawn beneath the ideal establishment now invisible.
"Depot!" he cried. "The Depot, on this Saturday, at twelve
noon?"

Her pause sent sweat streaming down his ribs. He imagined
a most amorphous Mr. Dugas turning a newspaper, receiving
his wife's curious raised eyebrows with a smile. He heard the
rustle of wild rabbits in the dry grass. TV sat on the floor heat
register, the only square of warmth in the whole apartment, sat
there in Joanne's director's chair asking his teacher for a date.
The lead of the pencil in his hand snapped, the page tore, his
rubber-soled hightop shoes melted onto the metal register and
lifted the cover when he raised his feet. He panicked, thinking
immediately of fire, of having to roll in the frayed and under-
sized Oriental carpet runner in the hall. The cover banged
down in place just as Mrs. Dugas spoke.

"What?" TV nearly shouted. "I—"

She repeated, "I would be pleased."

He made a dry run on Friday after school. The day had been
difficult, the subject of murder having come up during a lesson
on buffaloes in the wild West. But it came up everywhere, and
it always would. Later, at the tornado drill, TV had abstained
from attempting to peek up Mrs. Dugas's skirt with the other
children, girls as well as boys, while she canvased the halls,
checking for exposed necks or proximity to windows. In his
anxiety, he had not looked her in the eye all day, not wanting
to give her the opportunity to cancel.

After school, he leapt from the school bus and ran hard for

the city stop, taking the first downtown bus that came. Not until it was too late did he realize he'd chosen an east-west line instead of a north-south. He wound up at the transit station, a mile from his destination, near tears. This dry run would predict tomorrow's outcome, he felt. He did not want to fail. After calming himself and then consulting the elaborate city map on the wall, he took off running once more, ducking in and out of the rush-hour traffic, taking shortcuts through alleys. TV had grown up in his grandfather's old house on the east side. Wichita's downtown, though not large by any real measure, still was daunting. TV crossed a set of railroad tracks without realizing a train, moving slowly, had been approaching, the red lights of the crossing flashing, the bells ringing. A flagman, free hand on his hip, shouted out, wanted to know if TV was trying to kill himself. He ran on.

The Depot, true to its name, was located near the tracks. But it didn't appear to have existed for very long; it had never been a real depot, the only concession to authenticity a blue-and-white sign announcing its name. TV had counted on atmosphere, a romantic setting of shoeshine stands and antiquated arrival and departure charts. Its awnings, maroon, full of water, were torn. A Christmas scene, months or possibly years out of date, had been soaped onto the front windows and never washed off. TV entered, setting an alarm buzzing which ceased when the door slid shut.

"We are not opened," a voice shouted from the kitchen. "Our door is, but we aren't." TV took stock of the restaurant where he would, tomorrow, meet Mrs. Dugas. They could sit in the farthest corner, the small table under the one clean window. TV saw that the window was clean because it had been replaced in the recent past, dried caulking still left on its edges, hundreds of white fingerprints framing the glass, suggesting a frantic coded message. Nevertheless, he and Mrs. Dugas would sit here, she facing the window, TV the restaurant. It seemed to be a totally functional establishment, not one part charming.

"We're closed," a woman said from behind an opening in the cheap paneling between the dining room and kitchen. Over her head were the words Pick Up; on the other side, over a second opening, Order. New problems confronted TV.

"I know," TV said. "I'm just looking."

She leaned out and made an angry swipe at the iced tea dispenser before disappearing into the back once more. TV stood in the empty fluorescent-lighted restaurant ready to cry.

He did not sleep well. Joanne came to his room more than once in the night, frumpy and sour-smelling, sitting next to him on the bed, sleepily trying to make him feel better, misunderstanding his fear. She reminded him that he would be able to see his mother soon, that she, Joanne, would never prevent his seeing his mother. Yawning, she informed him that his grandfather had lived a full life, a prosperous life, that he had loved TV very much.

TV counted while she spoke. First he simply counted, and then he counted by twos, threes, sevens. His mother had struck his grandfather just once, killed him for his money. TV counted the number of strokes Joanne idly made on his back, the way her thoughtless hand fell just between his shoulder blades and ran in a perfunctory line to his waist, over and over. She was thirty-seven years old, unmarried, studying to become a psychiatric nurse. TV wanted to stay with her because he knew he could be placed in a worse situation. His first foster home resembled a halfway house, a full family of orphaned or delinquent children, an ex-Marine running the show like the military. Names were stenciled on towels and bedsheets and clothes. Joanne was not a bad sponsor; she tried to do the right thing. It just always turned out like this back rub, without any more than superficial thought of how he might feel receiving it.

Then he began counting rabbits, imagined himself standing above a field of them as they darted, barely visible, through the blowing grass.

*   *   *

Joanne asked him in the morning if he was part of the 69ers, a young gang in the neighborhood. Their Friday-night graffiti was the apartment building's topic of conversation each Saturday morning.

"I'm not," he told her, though he had run with them just last weekend. They, too, stood in awe of TV's past. For some reason, TV could not keep the information to himself. He tried, it wasn't that he didn't try, but it spilled, always. The 69ers had become famous for drawing the sexy yin-yang symbol of their name, a lined, naked circle, man and woman.

Joanne said, blushing, "I don't object to nudity, myself, but some people, the older ones in the building, find it offensive. I would rather you didn't hang out with them, okay?"

"I won't," TV told her.

"You get enough sleep?" she asked.

"I'm fine."

"Let's do something together," Joanne said suddenly, brightly. "Want to?"

TV looked at the clock over the stove, calculating rapidly. What could she have in mind? Why today? And how long till it was satisfied?

Now Joanne scrutinized him, crossing her arms over her scrappy bathrobe. "Are you in that gang?" she demanded.

"No!" TV croaked.

She sat back and a full minute ticked by. Then she said, more confidently, "The only thing we have going for us is honesty."

"I swear to God I'm not!"

The phone rang. For a second, when Joanne didn't move, TV believed his lunch with Mrs. Dugas was not the only thing hanging in the balance. Then, after the third ring, Joanne pushed herself away from the table and scuffed to the telephone.

TV grabbed his skateboard as a prop, held it over his chest to show her his intentions, this Saturday, were wholesome. He waited for her to nod, hoping she would not note his pocketful of fives and singles, saved allowance.

She met his eyes as he threw the front door locks, then looked away, talking to one of her parents, who made her defensive. TV slipped out.

He made the same mistake he had the day before, boarding the wrong bus. He rode along hitting his thigh with his fist to prevent tears. He yanked his grandfather's handkerchief from his pocket and wiped mud off of his hightops. At the transit station a cool rain began falling. He ran, his skateboard banging at his hip.

Mrs. Dugas had not arrived when he entered The Depot. He took the opportunity to claim the corner table, rolling his skateboard under it. He used the bathroom, shaking his head like a dog to dry his hair, over and over until he was dizzy. The mirrors were not glass but aluminum, like at a roadside rest stop, as if someone might want to break them. His image was wavy and blanched, unhealthy looking. He slapped his cheeks for color.

Mrs. Dugas wore green slacks and carried an umbrella which had a map of the world on it, half a globe. She stopped at the doorway and, backing in, shook the umbrella before releasing its spring. She touched her silver hair.

"Good afternoon, TV," she said. She stood at the table until he rose, then nestled into the plastic chair across from him.

"Hello," he said. He wanted her to like him so badly he felt sure she could read it in his eyes, like a dog's. Knowing she would have other students, he other teachers, pained TV the way irreversible facts always did. "What do you want to eat?" he asked.

Mrs. Dugas squinted at the signs over the Order window. "A Monte Cristo," she told him.

TV stood and pulled his shirt down. He went to the Order window and waited, hearing the clanging of pans in the back. He cleared his throat and said, "Excuse me." He tapped the counter with his fingers. Mrs. Dugas, her back to him, appeared to be watching the rain, which gushed through a hole in the awning like a small waterfall.

"Put forth," the woman from yesterday said, motioning with her hand for him to speak.

TV ordered a Monte Cristo, French fries, two waters and catsup. She did not write any of it down. He started to reach for his pocket to pay but she told him he paid when he picked up. He returned to the table with a playing card, the seven of hearts, which he was to insert in the napkin holder.

"But we're the only ones here," Mrs. Dugas laughed.

He laughed with her, eager to find this funny. "Did you drive?" he asked.

"My husband dropped me off. He's lunching at the Shriner's Club, around the corner."

"What kind of car?"

She rolled her lip and said, "A moderate-sized blue one."

"I rode the bus."

"Did you?"

"I only got wet because the stop is a ways from here."

She nodded, raising her black eyebrows.

"I liked those rats," TV told her quickly. "That was a good experiment."

"Have you been eating better?"

TV flushed, horrified at what his lunch of French fries would reveal.

Mrs. Dugas lowered her chin and looked up at him in what was supposed to be a teacherly manner. Yet, her lip twitched, and TV knew she did not really find fault. "Never mind," she said. "Someday it will register. You know, I don't believe I've ever had a lunch invitation from one of my students before. I've had hundreds of students—it's not my habit to exaggerate—and not a single lunch. I once went to a birthday party and another time I attended a funeral."

TV nodded, hoping she'd keep talking. If only she would just keep talking, he thought he might catch up, he might find his bearings in her voice.

"The birthday I enjoyed but the funeral, well, it was predictably depressing. The pallbearers were your age, so solemn in their suits. One of my students died, a few years ago. Actually, more than a few. Of all those hundreds, she's the only one dead." Then she added, "That I know of."

TV thought of the cemetery his grandfather had gone to. It did not allow vertical headstones and so resembled a golf course, marked every few feet by flat bouquets of plastic flowers. Only the American flag could be upright at Resthaven.

Mrs. Dugas said, "She wasn't wearing a seat belt, though that is another lesson my classes generally learn. Along with food."

The woman behind the counter shouted, "Seven of hearts?"

TV jumped up. "I'll get it," he told Mrs. Dugas, though she'd made no move to help.

On the way to the Pick Up window TV realized his money was gone. He reached for the pocket and could feel the bulk missing. His handkerchief was gone, too, probably worked loose during his dash to the restaurant. All he felt was his warm leg beneath the wet corduroy of his pants. Still, he continued to the counter, hoping something would occur to him, hoping he'd trip over a solution on the sticky linoleum floor.

"Four-seventy-three, with tax," the waitress said. She was without heart, TV saw.

He took hold of the tray on which his and Mrs. Dugas's lunch rested. "I lost my money," he said quietly, looking into the woman's hard face. He could not bear what was happening to him. "Please let me pay you tomorrow."

"You lost your money," she said skeptically, loudly. TV turned to meet Mrs. Dugas's eyes. She had heard, her eyebrows perked.

TV looked back at the waitress. "I lost it on the bus. Or running. I lost my grandfather's handkerchief, too."

"Big whoop," she said, twirling her finger in the air.

He said, more softly, "He's dead."

She stared, unfazed.

"My mother killed him," he was whispering. "With a hammer. The handkerchief was stuffed in his mouth."

The woman cocked her head, finger still in the air. "You're saying you're that kid?"

He nodded.

"No way. Really? And her boyfriend helped, right?"

He nodded again, already sorry. Mrs. Dugas had turned back to the window. TV did not know whether or not she'd heard him. Then he saw her shoulders rise, a shrug accompanying a sigh. She had heard, once again.

"Please, I promise to pay you back. I'll leave my skateboard here for collateral."

"Get some money from Grandma."

"What?"

She nudged her head toward Mrs. Dugas.

TV pleaded, "I came here yesterday." She seemed to understand that he meant he would come back tomorrow and finally released her side of the tray. "You're lying," she said. TV blinked. If only he *was* lying. But maybe she meant about the money.

TV set the tray on the table. Mrs. Dugas picked up her sandwich and briefly smiled at him. But it was her bad smile, the one she used when she'd been disappointed. Last week she had smiled that way before bodily seating John Coffey and stretching masking tape to bind him to his desk.

To TV, between bites, she quoted, " 'What you suffer does not defile you; what you do does.' "

TV ate his French fries without tasting them, working not to choke on their greasy mass, imagining his psychologist's office and the only *file* he knew anything about, the manila one with his name on the tab, crammed full of his bad life.

* * *

He found his handkerchief on the way home. It lay like a hamburger wrapper in a muddy puddle. TV made a strangling noise when he saw it there, wrung it out and pushed it in his pocket. The money was gone but he didn't care. Mrs. Dugas had refused his offer to walk her over to the Shriner's Club to meet her husband. She opened her purse at the end of the meal and TV had started to tell her not to pay when she pulled out an envelope and then a stamp, leaving them on the table like a tip. She'd had no intention of producing money.

"I'll see you bright and early Monday," she told TV. Forty-eight hours, he thought. He'd waited until she was gone before taking his skateboard to the waitress.

"This ain't no pawn shop," she told him. She pointed at his and Mrs. Dugas's table. "Gimme that envelope." When he had obeyed, she penciled an address on it and handed it back to him. "Don't forget," she warned, then laughed for the first time. She rolled her eyes, leaned through her Pick Up hole and spoke out the corner of her mouth melodramatically, "Just send me the fin, kid."

When he arrived home Joanne was sleeping, curled under a man's coat on the living room couch. Watching her breathe, it was not hard to imagine the ease with which a person could be killed. TV stood for a moment contemplating her, wondering if he would ever love her. Then he went in the kitchen and quietly shut the door. He washed his grandfather's handkerchief in the sink, using plenty of dish soap and scrubbing it between his knuckles until they stung. He rinsed it, running his fingers across the navy monogram, then dried it over the heat register, standing with his feet spread so as not to melt his soles. His lips parched and his eyes burned. Afterward, he folded the wrinkled cloth to fit the envelope.

Millicent Dillon

LOST IN L.A.

Down Fairfax Avenue Mollie ran, she knew the way, her little feet remorseless. A fierce wind was shoving her back. She bent her head and barreled forward, butted it, pushed through it, making her own, her single path.

Now, suddenly, the wind relented. Or had she gotten through it? There was a smell like snow in the air. She looked up to a sky clear as glass, blue at the edges, piercing. The sun—in it, on it—was more a promise than a threat.

Forward, she went forward, a ball of string unrolling, a cart pulled by a donkey. She passed the Nail Place, she passed the Chinese Health Food Store, she passed the schoolyard, she passed the gleaming new Savings Bank, her bank. Her right hand came up to her breast, felt through the coat, through the sweater, through the dress, touched the bankbook pinned inside her brassiere. In the bright clear air—Where had all the dreck gone?—everything seemed safe. But who knew how sun and air could trick you?

At Third Street she crossed Fairfax just as the light turned. She slowed her pace, she kept her eyes to the ground. She knew their eyes were on her, the drivers', with their cars ready to race, held up now by her, made to wait. She let their curses bounce off her skin, growing thicker than fur. What it would be to be an animal hidden, a bear in a dark cave, sleeping, safe . . . She shuddered at the thought that there would be time enough for that later, all the time in the world.

Up she hopped, upon the curb. Before her was the Farmer's Market, shining out of all the dreck around it like a village from heaven. She circled behind Dupar's Restaurant and entered the narrow alley that led to the stalls. Here, inside, was everything: the largest strawberries, the sweetest oranges, pineapples, meat, potatoes, dates, nuts, everything you could want. And here was her booth, her place, her pal, the girl in white behind the counter.

"Cold today," came the words sent out into the air to fasten on her. "And windy, after the rain."

She held the words close, then let others fly back. "You call this cold? You people don't know what cold is. But I know. Where I come from—that's a cold country."

"With snow and ice?"

"With snow and ice," Mollie nodded with satisfaction.

"I was never in snow. In my country—"

Who cared about jungles, mountains, other countries? What mattered was ice and snow, keeping yourself warm—and safe. She took some coins out of her purse and cut the woman's words off with her own. "The usual."

"How about something different today? Want to try a sweet roll? The baker just brought them in."

"A sweet roll? Pfui! They're too sweet for me. I said, I'll have the usual."

"A corn muffin and coffee?"

"And coffee."

"And cream?"

"And cream."

Mollie put the coins on the counter. "Just right," said the woman in white.

"You think I don't know how to count?" Mollie flared up as she took her cup and her muffin and went to her table.

Someone was sitting in her place. Two men, in their running suits, drinking coffee, talking, sitting in her place. She stood looking at them, her eyes on a level with their eyes. She watched the one man pick up his cup and swallow, put the cup down. She heard him say, ". . . script . . ." She heard the other one say, ". . . proposal . . ."

"I've already . . . ," said the one, layering over the other's words. ". . . gorgeous young attorney . . . success, money . . . she has it all . . . wants more . . . she doesn't know what . . ."

". . . fed up with the rat race . . . wants to get away . . ."

". . . to the simple life . . ."

"Goes to an island . . ."

"What island?"

"We'll find an island . . ."

". . . takes a lover . . ."

". . . doesn't know he's a revolutionary . . ."

"I saw where Columbia . . ." said the one, pointing at his newspaper on the table.

". . . package . . ." said the other.

They went on and on, sometimes taking turns, sometimes at the same time, the words tumbling out faster and faster. All the time she watched them, she saw how their gullets moved when they drank, swallowing, she felt the coffee warm and bitter going down their throats—the throats out of which the words jumped, ran, streamed—and she knew they had taken her place. The one turned his head toward her, did not see her, would not see her, his mouth opened with the words flying out. He stood up. She looked down at his running shoes. She watched as the one pair of shoes and then the other started to leave, not running, shuffling. She saw two shoes turn. One man was looking back at her. She looked at him looking. What do you see? she would have yelled if the words would have agreed to come out. He was coming back to the table. She prepared herself for his words as for a blow but when he came up to her he leaned across the table and picked up his paper and left.

Mollie pushed the cups aside and sank into her own chair. It was a reprieve. A vengeance not taken, almost taken. Still, there was a threat in the air. It came with or without the cold. It came when it would come, whether you were ready or not. That was the unfairness of it all. No mattered how you prepared, there was no protection. Still, you had no choice, you had to prepare. You had to be sure not to leave anything lying around that would give you away to anyone who might be watching.

She saw the crumbs from her corn muffin on the white metal table. She gathered them together with the edge of her hand, then scooped them into a napkin, which she tied up like a kerchief and put in her purse. She pushed back her chair.

"Going so soon?"

"It's not so soon." What did this woman in white know about all the things that had to be done? She was living off the fat of the land, safe in that booth on her fat tuckus, handing out a cup of coffee and a corn muffin now and then.

"You think there is time to waste?" she hurled at her and ran out of the Farmer's Market, behind Dupar's, through the parking lot, across the street, in and out of the way of the cars honking their horns. No wind was blowing to help her or hinder her. She was not shoved now, not pulled. She had to force each step of the way, put one foot carefully in front of the other. I am the one pulling, she thought, I am the donkey drowning in mud, in shit, in the mess I have made of my own life.

Passing the Nail Place, she saw in the glass a tiny woman, white-haired, bent over. Behind her, full of color, was the huge face of a young woman, red-lipped, smiling, every hair in place. A place for nothing but nails, to keep them shining, blood red, polished and sharp. Once (What was once? When was once?) she had gone to the beauty parlor to have her hair hennaed and her nails done. Now she did not, would not go. She would not pretend to look nice, to feel nice. Let them see her the way she was. If they didn't like it, they didn't have to look. She laughed savagely at the thought that her own looks could be a revenge upon others. She held up her hands to the image behind the image in the glass. Go ahead and look, she said. Dirt under the nails. So what? What'll you do to me?

There came to her suddenly the smell of earth, black, rich, as when the snow thawed in spring, after a winter so cold no shovel could dent the ground. And lying on the earth, littered, still frozen, the bodies, waiting to be buried, Mother, Father, Sister, Brother . . .

This was what remembering was, a thought and another thought and another thought, all forcing their way inside her head to her eyes . . .

Back she ran the way she'd come, past the Chinese Health Food Store, past the schoolyard, where the children were now playing, watched by a man teacher in a sweat shirt. He was talking to a child who was crying. He was holding her hand, he was comforting her, he was giving her a tissue. Why couldn't I have waited? What was my rush? Why did I have to leave then? She wrung her hands. She must get back, fly over years and over land to where she could decide this time to stay, no matter what she would have to see.

She crossed the street, dodging through the traffic and burst into the Farmer's Market from the side entrance that led into the bird store. A large woman in a red dress leaned toward a cage. Inside the cage was a large bird, green, blue, purple, red, sitting, standing on a stick.

"Pretty birdie," said the stupid woman in a coaxing voice.

It—the bird—that pisher, that shitter—did not answer.

"Pretty birdie," the woman said again. One eye opened, one eye closed, the bird looked at Mollie. "Pretty birdie," it said and winked.

Safe on her own couch in her own apartment, she sat and patted her own head. "Pretty, your hair is so pretty," she said, "the only one in the family with red hair." She stretched out to doze a little—she knew where it could take her. Soon, now, in a minute, it would come, that feeling—that it was no longer her own hand doing the patting: it was her mother's, it was her father's, it was as many different ones as she would want, she would be able to feel it so clearly, their being here. Yes, now, she could almost feel it, not her own hand on her head but the others'.

Now they were with her. Now came words, easy words, easily falling out of her mouth, out of their mouths. Pretty this and pretty that, good this and good that, I'll give you this and give you that, whatever you want, pretty this, pretty that. Over and over, the good words, the nice words, but they would not stop there. On their own they made—let—other words in.

"But who'll take care of you . . ."

"They're only neighbors not relatives . . ."

"They said I could come . . ."

"You can't expect them to take care of you . . ."

"It'll be a strange place . . ."

"You won't know anybody . . ."

"I'll take care of myself . . ."

"You're just a girl . . ."

"They said I could come, I could take Sonya's place, she doesn't want to go . . . You could come . . ."

"Why should we go now? Things will be better . . . You should wait . . ."

"I'm going . . ."

"Who'll take care of you?"

"I'll take care of myself."

She shut off the words, putting walls of sleep between her and them.

When she awoke, she said aloud, "No one ever gave me a penny. I earned every cent myself." It was her own voice saying, her own hand coming up to touch the bankbook pinned inside her brassiere.

The book was not there.

She jumped up and ran to the window. How late it must be! She raised the shade, turned on the light, all the lights. She looked on the table, on the bed, on the chair, on the rug, on the sink, in the sink, on the back of the toilet, in the tub. Where did she put it down? Did she put it down? She must find the book where it was hiding, where it was hidden. A lamp fell to the floor and broke. She must not stop looking. She opened every drawer of the dresser, the top, the middle, the bottom, she went through all the things. There was underwear, stockings, scarves. There was no hard, flat, black thing. She got down on her hands and knees and crawled along the floor. She looked under chairs, under tables, under the couch. Her hand came out with a ball of fluff. No book. No black book with gold lettering. Wasn't that what it looked like? She was not sure. Was that what it looked like? She opened the oven. Cold, greasy, black, but not the right black. She opened the refrigerator. Bundles of napkins folded like kerchiefs. She emptied each one out with all its crumbs upon the floor. No book.

She leaned on the black trunk, moaning with terror. It must be found now. Her time was almost up. Her fingers ran over the brass nails at the corners of the trunk. Her fingers plucked at the lock. Her fingers shoved the lid back. Inside, ready to leap out, were ribbons and veils, feathers and felt, everything to make, to decorate a hat. Her fingers, curled, curling, snatched them out, a handful at a time. She rubbed them between her hands, then let them fall to the ground. No book, no book. She kept snatching and rubbing, snatching and rubbing and dropping. On the floor the pile of bright colors was growing, as the trunk, emptying, grew blacker and blacker.

They had no coffins, came the words.

I don't want to hear, she cried out, I have no time. Her hands, clawing to get to the bottom, touched a hardness that slipped upon another hardness. She saw a brown paper bag folded up. Inside was the bankbook.

But hardly had relief come when it turned into warning. Someone had taken the book. Someone must have come in—

through a door, through a window, through the walls, through the air, when she was asleep. He had come in and he had taken. She should run to the neighbors, she should tell them what happened. But they would say, Who? Who takes? And she could not answer. All she knew was that he takes.

Down Fairfax she ran, passed by the cars, squeezing by the store windows. She saw, didn't they see? Vengeance was about to be taken. She ran into the Farmer's Market, she ran to her booth, to her table. The talking men were not there. The woman behind the counter called out to her but she would not answer. Surely a pal become an enemy was much worse than any plain enemy to begin with. Even an enemy who took your story and told it, the way these men had. Soon everyone would know this terrible thing, this shame, that she had not taken care of herself enough, had not done what she had said she would. They would all see her, they would know, they would point her out —point at her for what she had not done.

It was crowded now, the aisles were filled, all the tables were filled. She pushed and shoved, looking for the talking men. Her head bent, she looked at the feet going by. But there were too many feet like their feet, too many of those running shoes all alike. She looked up at faces. She saw wrinkled chins, hairy nostrils, hanging lips, mouths moving, but not the right mouths.

She reached the last booth, next to the side exit. It was the end, the very end, there was no more protection. Through the opening to the parking lot she could see the unpainted wood skeletons of many apartments being put up, and right next to them an enormous crane, high up in the sky, its x's marking the spot. So the cup of coffee she would get from this last booth would be her last.

In silence she paid the stranger behind the counter. In silence she climbed the stairs to the balcony. She picked out a table near the window. She lifted the cup, she drank, she felt the hot liquid, warming her teeth, the cage of her tongue. She looked out the window. She waited for vengeance to approach in a cloud. But there was no cloud in the sky, only blue and more blue to see. In the distance, looking north, so clear, she would never have believed it, so clear, they took her breath away, were hills to see, hills rising behind other hills, the furthest ones with snow on the top. Were those hills always there? And did she just not know it because of the dreck in the air?

Now, if vengeance would come, she would be ready. Up above, over the ceiling, over the roof, was the sky that had let go with its blanket of the softest snow. How she would run in it, how she would tumble in its drifts, how she would look up into the blue, protected by walls of white. My life is a wheel, she knew, that starts out and goes around and comes back to the same place.

She felt the hot liquid running through her. It was the coffee demanding to be let out. She ran into the bathroom, she sat on the toilet. She sighed with relief as the water came. She smelled the smells all around her. Why was the smell of others' shit so terrible, when the smell of her own was sweet?

Now, if she met those talking men in their running clothes, she would stop them, she would not be afraid, she would be ready to tell them a single story, not one life back there and another life here, but both the same. The words would not catch in her throat. They, the talking men, would not turn away. Perhaps this very moment, while she was sitting here, wasting time, they had gone to find her, would be waiting for her in her apartment, ready to listen, but they would have come and she would not be there.

Down Fairfax she ran, the sun a great weight pressing upon her, but the harder it pressed, the faster she ran. She came to her street, she came to her steps, she stumbled up the steps. She turned the key in the lock. She went in. The men were not there.

They'll come, they'll come, she told herself. They have to come now, to hear. I'll wait. Once I didn't wait. Now I'll wait.

She saw the things on the floor, piled high next to the empty trunk, the trunk waiting to receive them. One by one, she picked up the veils, the ribbons, the feathers, the pieces of felt. She straightened them out, she smoothed them down. First, at the bottom of the trunk, she put the bankbook. A hope chest, to begin again. First the book, then the ribbons, then the veils and feathers, then the felt, each layer covering over the one below, making it warm, each layer underneath holding up the one on top. No needle was needed. Things had only to be put in place to fill the hole up.

Down Fairfax Avenue she ran on her tiny feet. The wind was pushing her hard. There up ahead was the Farmer's Market. She saw—how had she never seen it before?—that it was like a great castle, circled around with walls. The others could stream in and out through the openings, but she could not go through. She stood there as they went past her, jostling her with their elbows.

She ran to the side entrance. He was there, inside, the bird, guarding. He would let her in if she said the right words to him. She opened her mouth.

"I," she said, "I—"

She saw his one eye opened, one eye closed.

"They," she said, "They—"

Kent Nelson

THE MINE FROM NICARAGUA

Barkley Ravenel did not usually pay attention to anything washed up on the beach in front of his house unless, for instance, it was a right whale or a dead sea turtle—something natural. Lately he considered the beach a thin landscape without motion or energy, a canvas devoid of any evidence of sealife. The birds, except for gulls and terns, had diminished markedly, and the shells that had formerly been profuse were now only a rim of shards at the line of high tide.

That evening he was walking with Kate Pickering, a friend of his wife's, from Richmond, Virginia, who had been their houseguest for a week. Barkley claimed Kate had been on tour ever since, eight months ago, she had lost her husband to intestinal cancer. She had been traveling from one friend to another in the Carolinas, drinking their gin and talking about how much Creighton had suffered in the end.

"I'm going to say something terrible to her," Barkley had told Muriel in private while he changed to shorts for the beach. "If she mentions that nematode Creighton again, I'll let her have it right between the eyes."

"You will do no such thing."

"I swear I will. For once I'm going to lose my patience. It might behoove you to come with us and protect her."

"Kate's a sweet soul," Muriel said. "And I do have this headache." She lay down on the apricot bedspread and lay her forearm over her eyes. "Anyway, you take your walk every evening. What difference does it make whether Kate goes with you?"

"Because I'll have to be pleasant."

"Well," Muriel said, "Kate understands."

Kate might have understood, but Barkley didn't. Moving south had changed Muriel, and she confused him. He liked breakfast at seven, dinner at eight, just as they'd enjoyed it in Philadelphia for years, but she refused to cooperate. "What's the rush to get up?" she'd ask. "Are you going somewhere?" Or, more often, "I won't be here, Barkley. I have to play tennis when it isn't too hot."

And her manners had disintegrated. Muriel's going with them that evening was the merest act of politeness Kate might have expected. And, of course, it would have freed him for his solitary vigil over the demise of the sea.

But he didn't argue with her. He stood over the bed for a moment and looked at her frizzy blond hair buried under her arm. How long had she been dying her hair, he wondered? Where had she bought that blue scarf around her neck or the gold bracelet on her wrist?

"We'll be back for supper," was all he said.

It was a balmy evening. The beach stretched before them a good mile or more until it feathered away finally, beyond the pier, into a haze of gray and brown condominiums. This particular reach of sand on the south end of the island was more private than the northern part. A few live oaks and pines had been preserved here and there amidst the huge houses, and several rows of accreted dunes protected the houses from the water. Still it was overbuilt. Houses opposed the sea on every lot, and the relics of *Homo horribilis* were inescapable: beer bottles, plastic milk containers, waterlogged boards. Barkley liked to imagine the day when a hurricane would sweep across the island from front to back and wash the evidence of man's arrogance—houses and all—to the headland.

Two older men in skimpy black briefs jogged along in front of the burnished calm of the outgoing tide. Nearby, a churlish woman packing her things stopped to admonish her child to bring to her the implements with which he was laying waste the sand sculptures of already departed children. A few people waded pensively in the shallow surf, staring blankly, Barkley thought, at their own destinies. One dreamer—hadn't he heard the news?—had rolled up his pantlegs to his knees and was casting a piece of bait into the murky waves.

Barkley had always thought of Kate as a woman contented with her time and place. She and Creighton had loved Richmond, the last undiscovered southern city, they said. When their children were grown, they had done the rounds of cocktail parties, oyster roasts, and fox hunts. She had been more retiring then, he remembered, in the tradition of Southern women, and thinner, too, before she started consuming so much gin. She had dressed elegantly and simply, as if she aspired to the page of a magazine.

On this visit, however, she seemed more physical, more intimidating. The weight she'd gained was part of it, of course, but she dressed more garishly in reds and bright greens. She was more outspoken, too. Sometimes, to his astonishment, she flat-out disagreed with Muriel. She debated the merits of onion in quiche, pine-scent spray for the bathrooms, or whether the new dishwasher Muriel had bought was as good as a Hotpoint.

Once Kate had even started in on him, and had he not been raised by parents who had served thirty-five years in the diplomatic service, he would have told her to go to hell. "Barkley," she'd said, "I don't like that shirt on you. You're too slender for stripes."

"I am?"

"You have a few good years left. You could still be an attractive man if you take heed in what you wear."

"I'll remember your advice," he said, "and I'll speak to my buyer."

That was as close as he got to rudeness.

He knew they would not be gone long that evening because the cocktail glass Kate had brought with her was nearly empty by the time they reached the first bend in the island. He was about to suggest a retreat to their porch, when Buck Walsh appeared in front of them with his chocolate lab, Westmoreland, on a leash. Barkley waved as a matter of habit because Buck never stopped to chat.

But that evening he did.

"See that thing down the beach?" he asked.

"Not yet," Barkley said.

"I'm going to get a wrench."

"What on earth for?" Kate asked. "What is it?"

"We don't know," Buck said. And off he went running.

"Who was that?" Kate asked, when Buck had disappeared out of earshot over the dunes. "He's a hunk."

Barkley didn't see anything hunky about Buck Walsh, but if Kate found him so, maybe she would drink some of his gin. Buck did a daily grind with Westmoreland to the pier and back, lumbering along as if he had four legs, the two in front too short to reach the ground. "Buck Walsh," Barkley said. "Retired military. Divorced."

"Where is the thing he was talking about?" Kate asked. "I don't see it." She held a bejeweled hand up to shade her eyes.

Just past the inward turn in the island they spotted a small knot of three or four people gathered around something in the sand. Barkley thought he recognized Alice Osborne, the cellist from Boston who spent the spring flower season there on the island, and Ned Menotti, the developer who owned an immense, three-story house behind the dunes. People said Alice was crazy, a euphemism which meant little to Barkley. If craziness produced the music Alice played, then insanity was a blessing. He had heard her in recital once in Philadelphia, and she had performed Beethoven and Haydn so perfectly that he still remembered, years later, how the air in the hall had seemed alive.

He angled away from the group, though, out toward the tidal pools left exposed by the receding sea. Even if Kate thought Buck Walsh was Tarzan, Barkley wanted to avoid those people. He didn't like Menotti's gladhanding or the importunities of the man in the yellow trousers whom he strongly suspected was Marshall Cartwright. Marshall had been a college golf star and was always challenging Barkley to play for money.

But Kate called to him. "Don't you want to see what it is?"

"If it requires a wrench, it can't be too intriguing."

"Oh, come on. Don't be such a stump."

She started off decisively toward the group, as if she were going to demand surrender of someone. Her stride across the sand, her clenched fists, her red-and-white cotton dress flouncing on her hips: he could only follow her, as was his proper duty under the circumstances.

Barkley had retired at fifty from his own management consulting firm in Philadelphia so he and Muriel could move south. "A little winter is good," Muriel had said, "but not too much, don't you think? Don't you want to relax in your old age?"

"I haven't reached my old age."

"But you'll want to explore."

He had not wanted to explore, although he hadn't minded the idea of warmer weather or golf. Pennsylvania's climate was little better than disease, and he had tired of gray days, acid rain, and the lack of a vista. And they had enough money. That part had been simple.

What had surprised him, moving south, was how lonely he felt. Muriel was gone all day playing tennis or bridge, or sometimes golf, though never with him. And she was stronger spiritually. Once, when he'd asked her to play golf, she'd simply said no. "You're too good," she said. "It's no fun to be beaten all the time."

"We'll handicap," he said.

"Don't patronize me!" she said.

Or she would shop. She'd dress up in a print blouse and slacks and go to lunch with one of her friends from the club, and afterwards they'd tour the malls. Once when he heard her jangling her car keys and she was tucking her pocketbook under her arm, he'd asked her, "Where to today?"

"Belk's, Parisian's, Macy's," she said. "Laverve wants to try the new mall across town, so I'll be late."

"Do you mind if I come along?"

"Oh, Barkley, you wouldn't enjoy it."

"I might."

"But what would you do? You're such a nickety-pick. You'd say this color wasn't right, or that design wasn't perfect. You're such a diddy-fuddy that way. Don't you trust me?"

"What does trust have to do with it?"

"And I don't spend that much."

"It isn't the money," he said.

"Then what?" She had paused almost defiantly in the white doorway to the garage.

"What do you get from it?" he asked.

She stared at him a moment and then gave a half smile. "What did you get from all those years making chemicals?"

Kate reached the group first, though Barkley had raced to catch her in order to discuss the matter. It was Ned Menotti and, alas, Marshall Cartwright who were standing around a rather odd-looking object in the sand. One of the women was Alice Osborne. She was taller and older than Barkley had remembered her from the night of the recital. She had seemed then small and vulnerable to the music, *camouflaged*, he had thought, by her instrument. Now, though, she wore a dramatic turquoise scarf over her gray hair.

Ned put out a beefy hand as soon as Barkley and Kate

walked up. "Barkley? Ned Menotti. We met once at the marina."

"I remember," Barkley said. He shook hands. "This is my wife's friend, Kate Pickering, from Richmond."

"I'm your friend, too," Kate said quickly.

Introductions went around, and Kate shook hands with both men and women.

Barkeley nodded to Alice Osborne. "I've heard you perform," he said, when Alice was presented.

"Oh, where?"

"Philadelphia. Several years ago."

"Beethoven and Haydn," she said. "My former student, Lee Rodgers, is playing one of the Beethoven concertos at Tanglewood this summer."

Alice motioned toward the other woman, who was younger, auburn-haired. She was dressed in pale blue slacks and wore a man's shirt untucked at the waist. She looked about forty, Barkley thought, and she was hardly tanned at all, which meant either she had just arrived or she stayed indoors all day, except when, as now, the sun slanted from the headland and was not strong enough to harm the skin. She had blue eyes—rather eager, he noted—and a bow mouth lightly pinked.

"So what is it?" Kate said, pointing to the object in the sand.

"We don't know," Marshall said. "Fascinating, isn't it?"

Barkley shuddered. It must be utterly fascinating, he thought, to interest such a dimwitted dolt as Marshall. But he had to agree it looked odd. It was black, cylindrical, made of— it was hard to tell what. From end to end it was about five feet long, and its diameter was perhaps two feet, maybe less, approximately that of the husk of a palm tree washed up nearby on the beach. At the ends of the cylinder were two brass fixtures, patinaed green, and attached to a sturdy-looking plate.

"Buck went to get a wrench," Alice said. "The men are going to open it for us."

"Do you think it opens?" Kate said.

"It will if we want it to," Ned Menotti said.

"I'd like the brass fittings for my flagpole," Marshall said, pointing toward the empty pole in front of a massive blue house beyond the dunes.

The houses there were monstrosities with wraparound porches and decks, gabled like Ned Menotti's or topped like Marshall Cartwright's with a crow's nest high up for a panoramic view of the ocean. Alice Osborne lived in one of them, too, but Barkley couldn't remember which one, having never been there himself.

"Alice thinks it's filled with cocaine," Ned said.

"Marijuana, at least," said Alice. "It's got to be a smuggler's container."

"I think it's the bumper from a boat," Marshall said. "You know, one of those things they hang over the rail to keep the yacht from hitting the dock—a fender."

"Out of leather?" Kate asked.

"Is it leather?" Barkley leaned over to touch the surface. It felt like hard leather or maybe rubber.

"The thing couldn't float, could it?" Kate asked.

"How would it get here," Barkley asked, "if it couldn't float?"

"Someone could have dumped it," Ned said. "Maybe a hospital getting rid of an iron lung."

"You'd be surprised what can float," Marshall said. "Bonds, loans, all sorts of things. They make boats these days out of steel and concrete."

"So," Lee said, turning suddenly to Barkley, "what do you think it is?"

Barkley felt heat rise immediately to his face. His mind went blank. It was the kind of moment he most detested—feeling he had to justify himself to others, to be knowledgeable about what he had no idea about, or witty, which was worse.

"Guess," Ned said. "I thought it was a wheel off a whale's roller skate. Buck claimed it's a roller for golf greens."

"I've got a tee time Saturday," Marshall said. "Want to duke it out?"

Barkley circled the object again, tried to lift one end. It was very heavy, and he could barely move it. A drop of perspiration fell from his forehead. "I think it's a mine from Nicaragua," he said, pronouncing the name of the country in rapid Spanish.

Ned slapped him on the back. "That's very good. A mine. Ha, ha. Very clever, Barkley. We'll all explode." Ned pinched Barkley's shoulder in the palm of his hand.

Just then Buck Walsh came trotting back up the beach like King Kong, carrying in one hand a socket wrench set and in the other a stack of plastic cups and a thermos. Westmoreland padded alongside. "I brought the wrench," he said, out of breath from running. "And I mixed some martinis."

"Be careful," Ned said. "Barkley thinks it's a mine."

Buck handed Ned the thermos.

Barkley knew Kate liked this turn of events, and he considered going on up the beach alone. He wasn't in the mood for Buck's martinis or Ned's histrionics or Marshall's vapid observations. Besides, he sensed that Lee didn't like him, or at least wanted to put him on the spot. Lee was probably short for Leafy or Leeward.

But the beach was still splotched with groups of people loading up their umbrellas and radios and coolers, and he had certainly spent enough hours wandering that wasteland. So he stood at the periphery as Ned poured the martinis.

Kate was served first, then Alice. Lee passed her cup to Barkley. "I'm not a taker," she said. "I'm a giver."

Barkley gazed into the cup. "What?" he asked. "No olive?"

He looked into Lee's eyes. They were too blue, and he didn't like the way they measured him so carefully. He didn't like, either, the way she had fastened her hair over on one side of her head with a barrette.

"Have you been in Nicaragua?" she asked. She pronounced the name the way he had, though more gently.

"My parents were in the embassy there for ten years," Barkley said. "I went to school for a while in Managua."

"It's a brilliant country," Lee said.

"This was before Somoza," Barkley said. "When the country was still civilized."

"You think it's not civilized now?"

"There are desperadoes on both sides," Barkley said. "I still watch it, of course, but more in the sense of following the Phillies or the Red Sox."

"What a terrible thing to say!" Lee said. "It's hard to get much information here," Barkley said. "The newspapers . . ."

But Lee had moved away. What he'd said wasn't exactly what he meant. He'd wanted to be impartial and he felt he had in some way offended her. He actually had wonderful memories of Managua—the gardens, the myriads of birds, the flowers, the wistful people. But it had been long ago, and he'd been so young. He remembered his mother rising early in the hazy heat and walking as if on smoke down the long hallway of the villa where they lived. His father always seemed remarkably calm, like a swimmer who, having just emerged from the pool, knew exactly where to extend his hand for a waiting towel. Meals were served punctually, and the house was of glistening clean tile.

The Sandinistas had, for awhile, taken the higher ground, but the United States policy had kept them on the run for years. It *was* hard to get reliable information. Each side revised history to suit itself. He hadn't meant to disagree.

"I'll tell Muriel," Kate whispered to him.

Barkley broke from his reverie, surprised at the intrusion of Kate's voice. "Tell her what?"

"You're staring at that woman."

"I was minding my own business," Barkley said. He took a sip of the drink Lee had given him. "Look, why don't we get along home? It's almost time for dinner."

"And miss the fun? Who is this Ned Menotti? I like the way he pours a martini."

Buck Walsh had squatted down at one end of the cylinder and had started fiddling with the various sizes of sockets, trying to see which one would fit the bolts. He found the right one, then paused to let Ned make a toast.

"To the mine from Nicaragua," Ned said, raising his cup.

They all gestured, even Barkley, and Buck turned the first bolt with some effort.

"I hope it's cocaine," Alice said. "Then we'll have a real party."

"I hope it's money," said Marshall.

"You can't snort money," Ned said.

Barkley almost wanted it to be cocaine. He knew cocaine was an evil drug used primarily by professional athletes and rock musicians, but at that moment he would have tried some himself. He would have liked to escape the dreary present with something more potent than a martini.

"Is he in the Mafia?" Kate asked.

"Who?"

"Ned Menotti."

"He's a developer," Barkley said. "It's the same thing. He built Whispering Shores up the island—leveled everything and put in condos and ninety holes of golf. He's done shopping malls, too, including the Georges Pompidou Annex in town." Barkley paused, seeing that Kate was barely listening to him. "I'll tell Creighton."

Kate stared at him in astonishment.

"I'm sorry," Barkley said. "Really."

"You bastard," she said. Then her expression transformed from shock to an eerie delight. Her whole face brightened. "Go ahead," she said. "Tell Creighton. I wish you *could* tell him."

"I didn't mean . . ."

Kate looked away toward the ocean. "You know what? Creighton was a first-magnitude bore. He was one of those holier-than-thou Jimmy Carter types. He didn't drink. He didn't smoke. He didn't tell a joke. In all the time we were married, I never knew what Creighton thought was funny. Don't you think that's sad?"

"Muriel doesn't think anything's funny."

"Creighton probably got intestinal cancer from a broom up his rear end," Kate said. "I shouldn't have said that, but God, Barkley, if you knew."

"Hey, Barkley," Ned called, "do you know what a mine looks like? Come over here."

Kate took Barkley's arm.

"The CIA does," Barkley said.

Buck had loosened all the bolts and was twisting and pulling at the plate.

"I assume a mine wouldn't sink," Barkley said. "A ship would have to run aground to strike it. But wouldn't it have to be beneath the surface. Maybe the rings were used to tether it down."

A bird flew up from behind the dunes and landed near them on the sand. It scurried a few yards, then stopped and gave a loud *whit*, as if in alert.

"It's a killdeer," Barkley said.

"Wilson's plover," Lee Rodgers said. "One breast band. They nest here in the dunes."

Barkley had never heard of a Wilson's plover. This bird, now that he looked, was a little smaller than a killdeer. Westmoreland lunged at it, and the bird flew.

Buck whacked at the eye-ring of the mine with the wrench, but the plate didn't budge. A mine couldn't be too sensitive either, Barkley thought. It couldn't blow up with the movement of the tides. He wondered what sort of trigger it would have, whether Buck's hammering could detonate it. He imagined a flash of light and an instantaneous noise. Shrapnel screamed outward into arms, eyes, cheeks, into Lee Rodgers' auburn hair.

"Here, let me try," Ned said. He took the wrench from Buck and straddled the cylinder to get a better angle to beat the thing into oblivion. But instead he threaded the wrench through the eye-ring and, using the handle as a lever, tried to break the seal. But even Ned couldn't do it.

"It must be screwed on from the inside," Buck said. "We'll have to cut it open somehow."

"I have a sharp knife at my house," Alice said. "Why don't we take it there? It's the closest place. We women will go ahead and fix food and drink."

Barkley shook his head. "Why don't we leave it until tomorrow? It's nearly time for dinner."

But the other men agreed with Alice and started to roll the cylinder toward the dunes.

"There's always one uncurious soul," Lee Rodgers said. "Kate, you can stay, can't you?"

Kate moved from Barkley's arm to Lee's, and the two women turned toward the row of big houses.

Barkley stepped backward toward the water. He was free of them, and the beach was empty now except for a few joggers heading back up toward the pier. The scene reminded him of a lovely old photograph, a tintype still and serene and fixed unalterably in the past.

Then he heard the Wilson's plover call again from somewhere at the edge of the dunes. He scanned the grasses and the sea oats around whose stems the wind had created tiny scallops. *Whit.* The bird ran out across the flats where the receding tide had left patterns of darker, heavier sand sculpted in wavelets. It was a robin-sized bird, brown and white, with a single black breast band. It stood erect for a moment, then folded its head under its wing.

Light was fading now behind the houses, but in the darkening, a glow seemed to spread like mist over the dunes and sea oats and out over the rising sea. Barkley felt a sudden pang of loneliness, and he made his way back across the barren sand toward Ned and Marshall and Buck, who were pushing the mine up and over the first tier of dunes.

Transporting the mine was a harder job than Barkley thought it would be with four grown men. It was heavy and, in the finer dry sand of the dunes, hard to turn over. It took them twenty minutes to wrestle it through three separate rows of dunes, and then they had to carry it through a thicket of freshwater reeds and wax myrtles.

When they got near the lawn, the women called to them and waved. They were bringing out trays of food and glasses to a table set with a white tablecloth and flowers.

The men brought the mine up onto the lawn. Marshall Cartwright sat down on it and wiped his forehead with a pink handkerchief. "You sure you don't want to play golf Saturday, Barkley? I'll give you ten dollars a hole, and I'll give you half a stroke."

"You're on," Barkley said.

Kate steadied herself with a hand on the table. She had been busy on a new batch of martinis, Barkley could tell, and she gave Ned a beatific smile. "So, did you boys hit it off?" she asked.

"Mission accomplished," Ned said, as if they had stormed the beach. "Are you one of the island girls?"

"I could show you around," Kate said.

"Help yourself to whatever you see," said Alice, gesturing toward the *hors d'oeuvres*. "And there are more martinis."

They all set upon the food as if they hadn't eaten in days. There was paté, Saga blue cheese, carrot strips, cauliflower stalks, and a half dozen kinds of chips and dips. And two giant silver pitchers of martinis.

After the first rush, Kate took Barkley aside. "Well?" she asked.

"Well what?" He felt the martinis breaking in his head like tiny crystals.

"Did you talk about me?"

Barkley didn't understand why they would have.

"I've been helping *you*," Kate said. "She went to Juilliard, studied with Alice. She's here for a few weeks to practice. Alice says she's a real talent."

Barkley looked over at Lee, who was talking to Marshall Cartwright about his flagpole next door.

"Don't look," Kate said. She tugged on Barkley's arm. "She likes you, don't you see?"

Barkley didn't move. He couldn't bend a finger. His first thought was that he'd been unjustly accused of initiating a crime he'd never even thought of, at least not until that very moment. It wasn't proper. And his second thought was to telephone Muriel. *Whatever Kate might say to you is untrue,* he would tell her. *I'm here at Alice Osborne's. Come and get me.*

But he realized he would never have called Muriel.

"Did he say anything?" Kate wanted to know.

"You mean Buck-the-hunk or Ned-the-Sicilian?"

"Ned is cuter," Kate said. She stared past Barkley's shoulder. "It's all right for a woman to look. She has to say yes or no."

Muriel would already have started dinner. She'd have opened a bottle of white wine from which she sipped as she cooked, and she'd riffle through the catalogues from Land's End or L. L. Bean while the roast was in the oven. At seven she'd flip on *Wheel of Fortune,* a curious program for her to watch, through she rarely missed an evening of the shrieks and groans. That was when he walked on the beach.

"What do you think, Barkley?" Ned said. "Should we tackle the mine? I think we've done our stretching exercises."

"I think so," Barkley said. The crystals were popping in his brain.

"The sharpest knife in the house is there on the table," Alice said. "Do we need more *hors d'oeuvres?*"

"We need a flashlight," Buck said.

"I have a penlight," said Marshall. He pulled a small light from his pocket.

"Let's do it," said Ned. "Those were Gary Gilmore's last words."

"Do we have enough martinis?" Kate asked. "This could take a while."

Lee picked up one of the pitchers and poured Kate's glass full. She offered the rest to Barkley, who held out his glass.

"You know birds?" he asked.

"I'm a musician," Lee said. She emptied the pitcher into his glass. "Every musician knows a little about birds." She lifted her eyes to his.

"I used to know the birds of Nicaragua," he said. "I remember all the songs and sitting in the garden. They were lovely birds."

"When it was civilized?" Lee asked.

"I was ten or eleven then."

"And now what do you do with your time?"

"Retired," he said.

"I mean, what else?"

He had understood her perfectly. The words rushed at him from nowhere. And yet he might have been mistaken. He gazed past her to where the others were still grappling with the mine. Marshall was on his knees holding the penknife for Ned, who wielded the dirk. He had wedged the blade into the leather at an angle and was jiggling it furiously, as if he were slitting the throat of a wiry animal. Buck and Alice and Kate leaned toward the small light.

Barkley felt dizzy. There was nothing in the cylinder. It was all a game played with a piece of refuse thrown up by the sea. But he couldn't think how to answer Lee, how to tell her what he felt. In the absence of words, he turned his gaze to the burgeoning dusk. The highest clouds still caught a faint glimmer of sun, and far up he thought he heard a nighthawk's buzzy call. He had not heard a nighthawk since he was a boy.

"I can almost see inside," Marshall said. "A little farther."

"It's got to be cocaine," Alice said.

"We're going to be blown to smithereens," Buck said. "Just wait."

Lee started across the lawn carrying the silver pitcher in her hand. She paused at the steps and looked back. The nighthawk called again from somewhere in the dark air.

The beach was empty now. The dunes and sea oats had lost their color, and out on the sea the lights of shrimp boats shimmered over the gray waves. It was too soon to go into the house. He would be seen. Yet he wanted to go.

Then he heard the cello. Lee had come out onto the deck above the striped awning of the porch, and her music drifted out over the lawn, mingled with the voices and laughter of the others gathered around the mine. To escape the voices, Barkley moved off into the dunes. He reeled down into a swale, climbed a hill above the wide empty strand. Lights had come on in other houses—surely in his own not far down the beach, where Muriel would be waiting. But there was no hurry now to go home. Kate was a guest, after all, and had to be entertained.

Barkley smiled to himself. He had never felt so eager or so careless. Lee's music eddied out to where he stood. Caught on the breeze, the notes lilting or solemn, fading finally into the obscuring air. He imagined the notes as the songs of birds heard long ago in the garden in Managua, notes which even now reached him and gave him pause. He imagined, too, the sea's churning up its harvest of shells, while all around him in the dunes ornamented with sea oats were hundreds of sleeping plovers.

Ann Packer

BABIES

Several women in my office are pregnant. Jennifer, my creative director, a contradiction in terms if ever there was one, is pregnant. So is Samantha, another copywriter and my one real friend here. And the receptionist, Linda, is pregnant, too. Samantha's is due first: March 25th. Then Jennifer's on April 2nd, then Linda's on May 6th. There has been talk of a betting pool. Which of them will deliver closest to her due date? My money will be on Linda: she is just twenty-two, too young to realize the possibilities for drama inherent in being early or late.

They are flushed and slightly awkward, these women, and I wish them all good fortune. To each of them I wish a big, bouncing baby with a fine set of lungs, to each of them the kind of birth that makes the doctor and nurses beam with goodwill and self-congratulation. Now there is a profession that must give incredible pleasure. Who else gets to witness the most private joys of life?

I am a copywriter at Fitch Brown Llewellen, an advertising agency. Ours is the Sears, Roebuck of advertising agencies. Not that we are so large; not at all. But we are definitely derivative. Remember those big shirts everyone was wearing a couple of years ago? With long, wrinkled shirttails hanging out and small awkward collars? They were worn over tight black pants or narrow midcalf skirts. Well, look around, then go to Sears, and you'll find that that's where those shirts are now. You won't have to look hard; they'll be hanging under a huge sign that says BIGSHIRTS.

Sears, Roebuck gets its ideas about style from the greater fashion world and then appropriates not only the idea but also, as in that huge sign, the credit for the idea. So it goes with Fitch Brown Llewellen. The big one right now is our religious adherence to a type of ad first used, brilliantly I might add, for Molson beer and the American Express card, not a few years ago. Upstairs, in the executive offices of FBL, this adherence is referred to as "buying into a principle." Down here, where the rest of us sit under buzzing fluorescent lights, we call it imitation.

I worry sometimes about those fluorescent lights. What is the effect on an unborn baby? Does an expectant mother have the right to ask such questions of 1) her doctor? 2) her boss? 3) her mother?

It is nine-thirty in the morning and Samantha is late for work. The apartment she shares with her husband, Josh, is only twenty blocks away, but she rarely arrives on time. She has taken to walking very slowly. She wears heavy, rubber-soled boots, rain or shine. She is thirty-eight, and has had two miscarriages.

My phone buzzes and I put down the newspaper and pick up the receiver.

"You'll never believe what I ate for dinner last night." It's Sam. Her office is two down from mine, but we do most of our talking on the phone.

"A hot fudge sundae with dill pickles," I say.

"What a cliché," she says. "I'm disappointed in you, Virginia."

"What did you have?" I picture her transformed, a wonderful mommy cook making herself hot cereal while Josh looks on, askance, from behind his reheated pizza.

"It's disgusting," she says.

"Well?"

"Saltines spread with mayonnaise, and I mean *numerous* saltines, twenty or more."

"That is disgusting, Sam," I say, but I feel a rush of warmth for her. I want to tell her that I read somewhere that you can't do better for your baby than to eat as many saltines as possible, every day.

"I know," she says, laughing. *"Oy gevalt."*

Since they got pregnant, Josh has been teaching her bits of his grandparents' Yiddish, a word or two a day, so the baby can start to feel a little Jewish.

I am working on a dog food campaign. Getting this assignment was the realization of my worst nightmare about advertising. My brother, the perennial student, warned me. He said, "You think it will be handsome couples drinking champagne or giving each other important diamonds. But Virginia, it may well be dog food."

The joke was on me. Kanine Krunch, it's called. At least it's the dry kind of dog food, the kind that comes in gigantic paper bags. At least it's not the wet canned kind. That is some consolation.

On my lunch hour I have begun to look for baby presents. It's too early to buy, but I want to know what's out there. There's a wonderful mobile at Babes in Arms, a little store around the corner. It's got little pastel animals hanging off curved strips of wood. Pink kittens. Blue puppies. Purple giraffes. I don't know if Sam and Josh are going to go for the bright, primary color decorating schemes plugged by the baby magazines these days, or whether they'll choose soft and cuddly in stead. But I'd like to think of them standing at the edge of the crib and touching the little animals so that they sway gently over the baby's head. I've got a few more weeks to decide.

For Linda, it will have to be something more practical, I think. She and her husband, Donald, got married just a month ago, and on his postal clerk's salary they'll be struggling once Linda stops working. A little terry cloth sleeper, maybe. A soft little sweater with a matching cap. A year's supply of Pampers.

I don't know what I'll get Jennifer.

Kanine Krunch has one distinction: only one. It is very cheap. It is the dog food you would buy if your boyfriend arrived at your house with two large black Labradors and asked you to "watch" them for a week or two while he went to Florida to see about buying a boat.

My assignment is to think of—no, to make up—another distinction. And then to "pop it" into an ad in which two extraordinarily attractive yet wonderfully mellow people have a desultory, nonaggressive (this is not a hard-sell) conversation about their pooches. The idea, of course, is that if you, the consumer, would only switch to Kanine Krunch, you would become extraordinarily attractive yet wonderfully mellow, too. What you're not supposed to notice is that this image of the good life comes straight from those Molson beer and American Express card ads. Therefore, in an attempt to claim originality, I will be asked to attach to this ad a line similar to "For the easy times in your life." Similar to, but different. That's the line Samantha used for the flip-top canned puddings.

Three months ago Jennifer called me into her office, all seriousness, to announce her pregnancy. She told me first, alone, because I was the one who would be handling her work while she was gone. She trusted me, she said, to keep the place calm while she was off having the baby.

"Six weeks, Virginia," she said. "Two before and four after. That means you'll have to go to Indiana."

"Right," I said. Indiana is where the client's main offices are. I've met the client once, here in town, but Jennifer was talking about the big meeting where we would show storyboards and chew our fingernails. The client, of course, isn't a single person at all, but a group of nearly indistinguishable men of about forty who wear suits of a slightly too-light shade of gray.

"Actually," said Jennifer, "it'll be a great opportunity for you."

Up the ladder.

"It'll give upper management a chance to see how dedicated you are." She stood up, a signal that our talk was over. "In fact," she said, "you should thank me for getting pregnant."

I smiled, but resisted her suggestion. It didn't seem like a requirement of office protocol. I stood up and headed for the door.

"Virginia," she said.

I turned.

"Aren't you going to congratulate me?"

Her real face came through and for a moment she looked softer, almost vulnerable. I felt like going around to where she was standing behind her big teak desk and hugging her, but I didn't know how she'd take it. "Congratulations," I said. "It's wonderful."

"I'm really happy," said Jennifer. And then, as if she'd just remembered that business, after all, was business, she laughed and added, "John and I decided it was time to test market a new aspect of our relationship."

I pass by Linda's desk countless times a day, on my way to the bathroom, the supply closet, the elevators. Her job as receptionist allows her quite a bit of free time, and she has taken to knitting. She holds the baby-soft yarn low in her lap, ready to drop it into the open shopping bag between her feet. The executives wouldn't like it, if they knew. They would say it was unprofessional, and of course it is. It is an entirely domestic act, a miraculous thing, really. A pair of smooth sticks, mysterious turns of the wrist, and a little garment begins to appear.

She is making a christening gown.

"Sam," I moan into the phone, "I want to be pregnant." I am kidding, half. I am thirty-four and I am not married, nor, I suspect, was meant to be. Could I ever have a baby alone? Would I?

"No, you don't," says Sam. "Your face would turn fat and your ankles would swell and you'd have heartburn on a daily basis. Believe me."

"But I want a baby," I say. "A little bundle of joy."

"Virginia, you live in one room."

"I could partition."

She laughs. "Oh, Virginia," she says.

"Do you feel like a different person now?" I ask.

She's silent for a moment. "It's not really like that," she says. "I feel like something new is starting, like I'm going to be different, but I'm not yet."

"It's so incredible, when you think about it."

"I know," she says. "At the beginning, when all I felt was nauseated, it hardly seemed like what I was going through had anything to do with having an actual baby."

"But now it does?"

"Now it does," she says.

A kind of hollow feeling comes over me. "Oh, God," I say.

Sam doesn't speak, but I can hear her breathing, slow and soft. "Listen," she finally says, "think of your freedom. What about men, what about relationships?"

"What about them?"

"Virginia," she says, teasing, "you're the queen of relationships. You couldn't stand not having at least five intrigues a year."

I am not the queen of relationships. I am more like the court jester. I'm the one who can comment, wittily, on them all. On the guys who, sliding a hand up your sweater, insist that they just want to be friends. On the men, the young and serious ones, who ask if it will make you feel claustrophobic if they leave a toothbrush in your bathroom (it will). On the fellows who sweep you off your feet for three weeks, then inform you sheepishly that the wife and kids will return from the Caribbean on Sunday afternoon. On the one-night-standers whose failure to call leaves you slightly insulted and vastly relieved. On the lovers from your past who telephone in the middle of the night and, after forty minutes of idle conversation, ask if they can come over.

I want to have a baby, but I can't think of having a husband.

Jennifer is standing in my doorway. She wants to see what I've done so far, on Kanine Krunch. The problem is, my notes would make no sense to her. I've figured out the people, but not the setting. There will be a semi-glamorous young woman with a little terrier on a leash, and a regular guy with a golden retriever running around in the background. And the guy will have an angelic little toddler sitting on his shoulders. I'm not sure what they'll say, though.

"Can you show me an outline?" Jennifer asks.

"I would," I say, "but I don't really work in outlines."

"There isn't much time left, Virginia."

In fact, there are five weeks. But Jennifer's leave starts soon and she's getting nervous. "I'll have something to show you next Monday," I say. "First thing in the morning."

She groans, and just as I am about to say okay, Friday, she comes over to my desk, leans against it, takes my hand, and puts it on her stomach. "It's kicking," she says.

This is awkward, looking up at her huge round belly, so I stand up, leaving my hand where she's placed it.

"Wait," she whispers.

At first there is nothing, then I feel her take a quick, deep breath. "See?" she says.

"That was it?" I was expecting a real kick, aimed outward, fierce, sudden.

"That was it."

It was like a wave rolling across her stomach. It had a wonderful, mysterious feel, as if it were a tiny manifestation of some grand, universal movement. Her face is flushed, and I realize that this is due only partly to exertion. The rest is pride.

I smile at her. "I'll have the outline for you on Friday," I say.

I have a blind date tonight. My brother called me from Charlottesville, the location of his current school, and told me that a friend of his from the microbiology lab was coming to New York for a conference. He said the guy, whose name was Hank, didn't know a soul here, that it would be great if I could take him out, show him the town. That's how my brother talks, "Show him the town." It's as if he only arrived in this country a few years ago, and his studies have prevented him from learning the language.

Dating, I often think, is like applying for a job. You go all out in the interview, proving your intelligence, your reliability, your suitability for this particular position, and then when—if —you are offered the job, you realize that the actual work would be tedious beyond measure. It's a real catch-22.

Promptly at eight, the buzzer rings. The intercom is broken, but I go ahead and hit the button that releases the door downstairs. Up here on the fifth floor, I figure no one will bother with the climb unless his purpose is legitimate.

I wait a minute or two, then start listening for his footsteps. Nothing. I unlock my locks, poke my head out the door, and listen. No one is on the stairs, I can tell. The buzzer rings again, and again I push the button for the downstairs door. I stick my head out my open door and listen. Nothing.

After a few minutes, the buzzer rings again, and now I realize that what I've always feared has happened. The wiring that enables me to open the downstairs door from inside my apartment has worn out, or whatever happens to wiring.

I fly down the stairs, composing apologies in my head. When I reach the door, there is Hank; it can only be Hank. He has a distinctly microbiology look about him: tall and thin, with overly large hands and a quizzical expression on his face.

"I'm sorry," I say, out of breath. "The thing must be broken, you know, the door opening thing. What happened, there was no little sound, or did the door just not open when you pushed it?"

"Virginia?" he says.

I am standing here, holding the door open with my foot, panting. Who does he think I am?

"Yes," I say. "I'm Virginia and you're Hank, right?"

He offers me a large hand, which I shake. "Nice to meet you," he says.

"You too," I say. "Sorry about the door."

"Huh?"

"The door," I say. "When you buzzed, and the door didn't work. Was there a little sound at all? Or did it just not open when you pushed it?"

He looks confused for a moment. Then he says, "I heard a noise, but I wasn't sure what it was, so I just waited for you."

Oh.

"Did I do something wrong?" he says.

"No, not at all," I say. I take a step backward. "Come on in."

He steps through the doorway, smiling shyly, and of course he didn't do anything wrong, anything at all. He's probably a perfectly nice guy. But I already know how this is going to end up: a series of small advances and retreats—his advances, my retreats—over cocktails, over dinner, over one last drink in a small, dark bar, until we are back here, at this very spot, negotiating an awkward goodnight kiss. Sometimes I don't even feel like going through with the interview.

* * *

Sam and I are having lunch. The place is full of people, most of them eating in groups of two or three. It is very noisy. The tables are quite close together, and with the extra room Sam needs the waitresses can barely squeeze between her chair and that of the person behind her. It makes me very uneasy, watching the waitresses, huge trays of food over their heads, edging behind Sam.

"Are you ladies ready?"

Our waitress is here, order pad out, already impatient.

"Let's see," says Sam. "I'll have a bowl of the cream of celery soup, and a house salad, and the breast of chicken with the milanese sauce, and an order of hot french bread. And a glass of milk."

The waitress scribbles on her pad. "Anything else?" she says, not quite sarcastically.

"That's it," says Sam.

She turns to me.

"I'll have the same," I say. "Except the milk."

Since the pregnancies, I have been giving myself small indulgences: extra time with the newspaper in the morning, full square meals at lunch, bed a little earlier than usual. Sam says that not even Josh has had such a sympathetic reaction.

When the waitress has left, I lean toward Sam. "Have you decided about the breastfeeding yet?" I ask. She wants to, but she's worried about what will happen when she comes back to work. They have those pumps now, so you can extract your milk and leave it in a bottle with the babysitter, but Sam thinks that would defeat at least half the purpose of breastfeeding, which is having the baby actually feed from your breast.

She shakes her head. "I'm still not sure," she says.

"You will," I say.

She nods and looks away, and a kind of distant smile comes over her face for a moment. Then she turns back to me. "I'm not ready to throw away my huge 32-B bras yet," she says. "I'd better breastfeed for as long as I can."

* * *

The ad is coming along. I've decided on a setting: a park. The guy is taking his adorable little girl and his golden retriever for a walk. He's throwing a stick for the dog, whose name is Sunny. The dog's name may not actually figure in the ad, but it helps me to visualize the thing. The little girl's name is Lizzie. She's about two, with big blue eyes and soft blond curls. She's wearing a dotted Swiss dress, yellow with white dots, and little white sandals.

She is sitting on her daddy's shoulders, and suddenly she puts her hands over his eyes. Moments later the dog comes back with the stick, and the daddy can't see to take it from her mouth and throw it again. The dog is jumping around, the stick in her mouth, nuzzling the guy's leg, being cute and frisky.

Enter the semi-glamorous woman with the terrier. Sunny drops the stick and begins sniffing at the terrier. The woman is immediately drawn to Lizzie, and starts talking to her. They have a cute few seconds of conversation, which the daddy enters with a mixture of friendliness and irony, because his eyes are still covered.

Finally Lizzie takes her hands away and the grown-ups start in on the dogs.

That's as far as I've gotten; now I just need to figure out how to bring in the product. The woman: "She's a happy-looking dog." Lizzie: "That's 'cause her name is Sunny." The daddy (laughing): "It's because she knows she's going home to eat soon." The woman: "Mealtimes aren't any fun at our house, are they Fido?" (I haven't thought of the terrier's name yet.) The daddy: "You must not be using Kanine Krunch." Etc., etc.

Well, it's a start.

Babes in Arms just got in a new line of stuffed animals. They're just the right size: smaller, as we used to say when playing Twenty Questions, than a breadbox, but larger than a shoe. There's a wonderful, soft gray rhino; a plush brown bear with heartbreaking button eyes; an adorable, jaunty little penguin.

"They're sure to be very popular," says the saleswoman, chattily, arranging the animals on a shelf. She's gotten to know me a little.

I pick up a rhino; who could resist? But the bear is great, too. And I'm not even ready to buy.

"We're putting them on special this week," the saleswoman says. "Half off. It's a special promotion to introduce them. They're from Sweden."

Half off is a good deal. Stuffed animals, I have discovered, are not cheap. I put down the rhino and pick up a bear. I hold him to my face. He even smells good: fresh and clean and, somehow, good for you.

"I'm going to take a bear," I say. I'll give him to Sam; the mobile is a little too expensive, anyway.

The saleswoman smiles and moves to the cash register. She's probably afraid I'll change my mind, I'm in here so often. She takes my credit card, runs it through the little gadget, and hands me the slip to sign. She wraps the bear in tissue paper printed with little baby bottles and rattles and diaper pins. She carefully puts it in a shopping bag and hands it to me. "Enjoy," she says.

It's ten-thirty when the phone rings, jolting me out of sleep so fast that I have the receiver in my hands before I can possibly speak.

"Virginia?" It's a hollow little sound, a vaguely familiar voice coming to me from far away.

"Hello?" I say.

"Virginia?" It's my brother. "Did I wake you up or something?"

"No, no," I say. "I was reading." I always feel guilty when the phone awakens me, as if I should apologize for being asleep when someone wants to talk.

"So, how are you?"

"Fine," I say, and then it occurs to me that he simply wants to chat, that it's still my turn. "How are you?"

"Okay," he says. "I'm at the lab."

"It's almost ten-thirty at night, what, do you live there?" It's actually easier to picture him on a cot next to the Bunsen burners than in his own apartment. I haven't been to Charlottesville, but when I visited him in Cambridge, when he was getting an M.A. in philosophy, he lived in a three-room apartment in which there was nothing but a bed, a table, and two chairs. What bothered me most was that he didn't have a bureau. Where did he keep his socks and underwear? On hangers?

"I've got some cells in a petri dish that need looking at every three hours," he says. "So, you know."

"Yeah," I say. I picture the cells getting restless, saying, Look at me, look at me. It's a mystery to me, what my brother does.

"So, how'd you like Hank?"

This is why he called.

"He seemed very nice," I say, evenly.

"He liked you, too."

Not this, please. "Yeah, well," I say.

"He said you seemed a little depressed."

"Depressed?"

"You know, a little down."

"Oh, no," I say. "Not at all."

"He said you were kind of quiet, so I figured, something must be wrong, Virginia isn't the quiet type."

I wonder what type he thinks I am. What type am I? "Well," I say, "I'm in a quiet phase, nothing to worry about, but thanks for calling."

"Oh," he says. "Someone's there, right? God, I'm sorry."

"No," I say. "No one's here. No one but me."

Jennifer wants me in her office, to talk, I know, about the ad. She's had my outline for four days now, and she hasn't said a word about it.

"Sit down," she says when I get there.

I sit.

She is wearing my favorite of all her maternity dresses. It's a soft teal-colored wool with a white lace collar and white cuffs. When she first started wearing it, she was hardly showing at all, and the dress flowed in an elegant line from neck to hem. But it has accommodated her belly beautifully, filling out as she's filled out. I know it was expensive, but it does not seem to me in the least extravagant.

"Virginia," she says.

I smile at her. In three weeks, or, who knows, maybe less, she'll have a baby. I've narrowed it down to something from Tiffany. Probably a spoon. It's the kind of thing she and John would appreciate.

"Kanine Krunch, Virginia."

"Yes?"

"This," she says, picking up my outline on her desk, "won't do."

"It won't do," I repeat, stupidly.

"No."

I suppose I should have anticipated this. The people aren't mellow enough, the ad does not adequately capture the spirit of understated coolness required by the executives.

"First of all," she says, "when you have a father and a little girl meeting a glamorous young woman, you invite speculation on whether the father is going to commit adultery with the young woman. Right?"

I feel my face color a little; I should have thought of that. But if I take the woman out, who will the father discuss the product with? "Right," I say.

"And," Jennifer says, "more to the point, why a little girl?" She stands up and begins to pace, her hands on her lower back as if to give herself a push. "This is supposed to be a dog food ad," she says. She looks at me, pointedly, then returns to her desk and ruffles through my outline. "Lizzie," she says. "What's with Lizzie, Virginia? You don't put adorable little children in dog food ads, you put adorable little dogs. Okay?" She gathers the outline together and hands it to me.

I am halfway to the door when she says, "Virginia?"

I turn and look at her.

"Dog food," she says. "Think dog food."

The women's magazines are full of advice on every subject you can think of. How to get a man, how to get rid of a man, how to say no to your boss, how to put the sex back in sex, how to look great in work clothes, how to look great in no clothes, how to throw a fabulous dinner party without even trying. What I like best is the advice on how to treat yourself when you are feeling down. There are, contrary to what most people think, workable remedies. Setting aside an hour, a full hour, of time when you will not think about your children or your husband or your job. You will just sit in your favorite chair (they always assume you have such a thing) and sip a steaming cup of herbal tea.

Or, if you prefer, what about buying a brand-new bar of scented soap and having a nice, long soak in the tub? Make the water as hot as you can stand it. Light a candle and turn off that bright overhead bathroom light. Put your favorite concerto on the record player (of course you have a favorite concerto). Relax.

This is, of course, laughable advice. If you are depressed, you're supposed to feel *better* after sitting there for an hour with nothing but Lemon Mist tea for company? You're supposed to feel like a new person after a long, hot bath during which you stare, through the water, at the distorted shape of your hips and thighs?

Still, here I am, in the tub. The light is on; there is no music. My drain doesn't work right, or, rather, it works too well, and as I lie here the water level gradually lowers until bits of my body begin to appear, small and then larger islands in a porcelain sea. If I were pregnant, my stomach would appear first. Pale and huge, yes, but I would love it.

The trip to Indiana is in less than a month, and I have begun to dread it. The client will meet us at the airport, me and two of the executives. We'll be taken to our hotel and offered half an hour to freshen up, then it will be out to dinner. We'll go to a steakhouse. The lights will be low and we'll be shown to a big round booth. The waitress will be there to take our drink orders before we've had a chance to think about what we want. The client will have whiskey sours. The executives will ask for Glenfiddich, settle for Dewars. And I will be unable to think of anything suitable. Aside from wine, the only thing I really like to drink is Campari and soda, and it will be months too early for that since it's a summer drink.

I will be seated between two of the men in the light gray suits. They'll ask me questions about life in New York, about the cost of living, the impossibility of parking your car, the poor public schools. They'll ask, challengingly, what I will do when I want to have children. Move to the suburbs? Send them to private school?

To change the subject, I will ask about their children, and out will come the wallets containing the studio photographs, smiling families in front of fake fireplaces. They are of my generation, these men, only five or six years older than I am, and they will show pictures of children in the fourth or fifth grade, of children, perhaps, in junior high. They will point to little blond heads, saying, this is Kerry, he's pitcher on his Little League team; this is Heather, isn't she pretty?

The client is probably a good father.

I've reached an impasse on the ad. I am keeping the guy, who, I think, will be out for a run; I am keeping the semi-glamorous young woman; I am keeping their two dogs. I am trying to think dog food. But somehow it's hard to go on, without Lizzie.

I decide that what I need is a fresh pad of paper. I head for the supply closet but stop, as usual, at Linda's desk, for a look at her knitting.

"I just have the sleeves left," she says, holding up the rest. "Donald's mother is going to do the crochet work around the neck."

"It's so pretty," I say, fingering the soft gown.

She puts it in her shopping bag and goes to the closet for her coat. It is only four-thirty, but she's allowed to leave early these days, to ensure herself a seat on the subway. She lives way out in Brooklyn, twenty-three stops away.

She buttons up, then comes over to the desk to get her things. Suddenly she starts laughing, her hand over her mouth.

I turn, and there is Samantha, walking toward us in that funny pregnant goose step of hers. She is bundled up in her wool cape, ready for the walk home, and when she sees us, sees Linda in her big blue coat, she, too, starts to laugh.

"What's so funny?" I say.

"The two of us," says Sam. "We're so . . . pregnant."

Linda giggles.

"When I see other pregnant women on the street," Sam says, "we always exchange this little smile, like we have a secret the whole world can't guess."

"You do that, too?" Linda asks, laughing.

"Of course," Sam says. She smiles at me, the trace of an apology in her expression, then turns back to Linda. "I'm leaving too," she says. "I'll walk you to the subway."

We say goodbye, and they head for the elevators. I watch them for a moment. They are so entirely unalike—Sam is tall and auburn-haired, with an elegant, angular face, while Linda is hardly more than a child herself: short and small-boned, her blond hair pulled away from her face and held by bright pink plastic barrettes. Yet what I see first and most clearly is the fact that they are both huge—huge with child, as they say. Grand with child.

The red "down" arrow appears over the door to one of the elevators. They turn and wave to me, then they are gone.

The woman ahead of me in line is pregnant. Six months, I would guess. She keeps turning around and scanning the sidewalk behind me. She is waiting for someone, and she seems impatient. Every few minutes she glances at her watch. I wonder why she's so anxious; the movie doesn't start for nearly twenty minutes.

I look away and catch sight of a billboard bearing a Fitch Brown Llewellen ad. It's for a fragrance. A woman with carefully disheveled hair stands on the beach at sunset. One strap of her sequined gown has fallen from her shoulder; her high-heeled sandals dangle carelessly from her hand. She looks into the distance. The copy line reads, "You can't forget his touch. . . ."

I look back at the woman and find that she is looking at me. I start to smile at her; I can already feel the small, intimate smile we will exchange. But she looks away, and again ranges her vision over the sidewalk behind me. She is about to turn around when her expression changes to pleasure.

A man comes up from behind me and bends to kiss her. "Sorry," he says. He is tall and has curly brown hair and little wire-rim glasses. He is wearing faded Levis that fit him wonderfully, a brown suede baseball jacket, and a blue-and-white striped dress shirt. From the shirt I deduce that he has a real job somewhere, but he's not so stuffy that he would wear his suit to the movies. When they're at home together, he's probably very sensitive to whether she feels like talking or whether she'd rather be left alone. He's sure enough of her, of them, that he's perfectly content to spend entire evenings in silence. But he's wonderful to talk to, when they do talk: he really knows her, and their conversations have a rich subtext of shared knowledge and experience. When he kisses her, it means something.

It's somehow worse to actually see men like this, to know they exist. It's as if he has been sent to remind me that the only men I might consider marrying are those who are already husbands.

He puts his hand on her rounded belly. "How's the baby?" he says.

*   *   *

Jennifer approved my new outline, her last act before starting her leave. She has been gone for a week now, and so far she has called in every day. I fill her in as quickly as possible, assuming she'll want to get back to hanging curtains in the nursery or whatever, but she lingers on the phone, asking about this meeting or that report. When I mention Sam—she's due "any day now"—Jennifer sounds impatient. I think she resents Sam for working all the way through her ninth month. It is somewhat surprising that Jennifer started her leave so early. Sam thinks she was afraid her water would break at work, which would not look businesslike at all.

It is seven o'clock at night, and the office is empty except for me and Max, my art director. He is working up storyboards, I am scripting. We sent out for Chinese.

To my surprise, my original tag line made the final cut. The last image of the ad will be the guy in his running clothes throwing the stick for Sunny, then turning to wave at the semi-glamorous woman as he heads out of the park. He stumbles, rights himself, looks sheepishly back at her, and she stands there, an amused smile on her face, and waves. Voice-over, tag line: *Kanine Krunch—food for the dogs that people like you love.*

I dip my chopsticks into a carton of Hot and Spicy Shrimp, pull out a water chestnut, and put it into my mouth. The phone buzzes and I pick it up, thinking it must be Max, who is sitting across the hall eating Beef with Broccoli.

"Szechuan Kitchen," I say. "What's your pleasure?"

"Virginia?"

"Oh, hi," I say. It's Sam. "I thought you were Max. We ordered in Chinese."

"It's starting," she says. "My water broke, I think, and I've had two contractions."

"Oh, my God."

"Just wanted to keep you posted."

"Oh, my God," I say. "Oh, my God." I've got this huge smile on my face, I must look ridiculous.

"Josh is making me get off the phone," she says. "He wants us to practice our breathing again."

"You've practiced a million times," I say.

"I know," she says, laughing. "Wish me luck."

It's a girl. I got the call at work late this afternoon. She was in labor for seventeen hours. Seventeen! Visiting hours go until eight-thirty, so I finished what I was doing before racing to the hospital.

I am hurrying down the corridor, looking for Sam's room, when ahead of me I see a pair of swinging doors and a large sign that says NURSERY. There is nothing to stop me, no sign saying STAFF ONLY or even PARENTS ONLY. I push through the doors and into a darkened hallway.

No one else is here. A huge glass wall separates me from the babies, reminding me of those one-way mirrors psychologists study people through.

The nursery is brightly lit, and there are, unbelievably, row upon row of babies. They are in cribs about two feet apart, their tiny red heads all pointed in the same direction. The cribs are numbered, 01 through 56. Only seven cribs are empty. What happens when there are more babies than cribs? The whole thing suddenly seems comical to me; ludicrous, even. I imagine baby after baby being born and brought to this room, an assembly-line gone mad. Babies making way for more babies, hospital cribs filling and emptying, filling and emptying, all over New York, all over the world.

All this time, going through Sam's pregnancy with her, it has seemed to me magical somehow. But it's just what happens: women have babies.

I push back through the swinging doors. The hospital corridor is brightly lit: clinical and matter-of-fact. I find Sam's room, knock on the open door, and go in.

"Virginia," Sam says. She is lying in bed, looking very pale and tired and happy. Josh is sitting on the edge of the bed, all wrinkled and unshaven. He is, I realize, still in yesterday's suit. There is a look of bliss on his face. Or maybe it's exhaustion.

I lean down to kiss Sam. Her face feels damp and warm. "Virginia," she says, "you would have been proud. I made it all the way through without the Demerol."

"Great," I say. That was one of the things we always talked about—would she be able to stand the pain? It was as if I was pregnant, too, I was so interested.

"I could have killed her," Josh says. "I was hoping they'd give me a little."

"He was wonderful," Sam says, smiling at him.

"You were wonderful," says Josh, touching her shoulder.

There is a moment of silence. There are things I should be saying, but what are they?

"So, Virginia," Sam says, "what do you think of Isabel?"

Josh laughs. "Can you believe we changed our minds again?"

For the longest time it was going to be James or Sarah, there was no wavering, no doubt. But the past few weeks, Sam was coming in to work with new possibilities every day. Amelia, Susan, Laura. Henry, Timothy, Jacob.

"I like Isabel," I say. In a few days, they'll take her home, and a new baby will appear in whatever crib she's in now. Maybe it'll even be Jennifer's baby, although I don't even know which hospital Jennifer is going to deliver at.

"Oh, look," Sam says. "Your timing was perfect."

I turn around and there, standing in the doorway, is a nurse, a little bundle in her arms.

Sam is radiant. "Her first feeding," she says.

The nurse comes over to the bed. "Are you ready to see Mom?" she says to the bundle. "Are you ready to say hello to Mom?"

I look at Sam, but she doesn't seem at all amused by the nurse's little show. She holds her arms out, and the nurse gently gives her the bundle. Sam looks up at Josh and smiles. She turns to me. "See?" she says.

I lean in close, and there, in the midst of an elaborate system of soft white wrapping, is a tiny pink face. "She's very cute," I say. I look up at Josh, but his attention is fixed on the bundle. He touches the little nose, then puts his arm around Sam and buries his face in her hair.

"I should go," I say.

They look at me in surprise, almost as if they've forgotten that I'm there.

"Stay a minute," Sam says. "Would you like to hold her?"

She seems to want me to, so I sit on the bed and carefully take the bundle from her.

I look down at the tiny face. She's so little, but somehow she is remarkably heavy, substantial. There's a real body inside this blanket. A real baby. I touch her cheek; it's so incredibly soft and pink and warm. I can't believe how warm she is, how I can feel the warmth of her body, all the way through the blanket and through my clothes, all the way to my breast. Which one was she, in the nursery? How could I not have wondered? I can't help it; there are tears rolling down my face. In a moment this crying will find a voice, and I am afraid to hear it.

Someone, the nurse, takes the baby from me. I don't want to look at Sam, I'm so ashamed. But I do look at her, and when I see the way she's biting her lip, when I see the squint of understanding in her eyes, I let out a single, hoarse cry. Her arms come up around me and she pulls me close and holds me. She runs her hand down the back of my head, and I can imagine how it would feel to really let myself go, to sink against her.

But I don't. I pull away and stand up. I grab a Kleenex from the box on her table and dab at my eyes. "I've got to go," I say.

"No," she says, "Virginia—"

"I'm sorry," I say. "I'll call you."

Without looking at Josh or the nurse—or at Isabel—I hurry out of the room and past the nurses' station to the main hall. I hit the button and wait for the elevator to come and take me down.

I went back to Babes in Arms and bought the mobile for Isabel; I have decided to keep the bear for myself. He sits on my couch, a mute and pleasant companion. Lately I have been spending a lot of time on my couch, too. I read there, of course, and I nap there, but that's also where I eat, my knees bent, a plate of cheese and crackers in the flat, empty hollow of my lap. I just can't be bothered to set the table.

Kate Braverman

TALL TALES FROM THE
MEKONG DELTA

It was in the fifth month of her sobriety. It was after the hospital. It was after her divorce. It was autumn. She had even stopped smoking. She was wearing pink aerobic pants, a pink T-shirt with KAUAI written in lilac across the chest, and tennis shoes. She had just come from the gym. She was walking across a parking lot bordering a city park in West Hollywood. She was carrying cookies for the AA meeting. She was in charge of bringing the food for the meeting. He fell into step with her. He was short, fat, pale. He had bad teeth. His hair was dirty. Later, she would freeze this frame in her mind and study it. She would say he seemed frightened and defeated and trapped, "cagey" was the word she used to describe his eyes, how he measured and evaluated something in the air between them. The way he squinted through hazel eyes, it had nothing to do with the sunlight.

"I'm Lenny," he said, extending his hand. "What's your name?"

She told him. She was holding a bag with packages of cookies in it. After the meeting, she had an appointment with her psychiatrist, then a manicure. She kept walking.

"You a teacher? You look like a teacher," he said.

"I'm a writer," she told him. "I teach creative writing."

"You look like a teacher," Lenny said.

"I'm not just a teacher," she told him. She was annoyed.

"Okay. You're a writer. And you're bad. You're one of those bad girls from Beverly Hills. I've had my eye on you," Lenny said.

She didn't say anything. He was wearing blue jeans, a black leather jacket zipped to his throat, a long red wool scarf around his neck, and a Dodgers baseball cap. It was too hot a day for the leather jacket and scarf. She didn't find that detail significant. It caught her attention, she touched it briefly and then let it go. She looked but did not see. They were standing on a curb. The meeting was in a community room across the boulevard. She wasn't afraid yet.

"You do drugs? What do you do? Drink too much?" he asked.

"I'm a cocaine addict," she told him.

"Me too. Let's see your tracks. Show me your tracks." Lenny reached out for her arm.

"I don't have any now." She glanced at her arm. She extended her arm into the yellow air between them. The air was already becoming charged and disturbed. "They're gone."

"I see them," Lenny told her, inspecting her arm, turning it over, holding it in the sunlight. He touched the part of her arm behind her elbow where the vein rose. "They're beautiful."

"But there's nothing there," she said.

"Yeah, there is. There always is if you know how to look," Lenny told her. "How many people by the door? How many steps?"

He was talking about the door across the boulevard. His back was turned. She didn't know.

"Four steps," Lenny said. "Nine people. Four women. One old man. I look. I see."

She was counting the people on the steps in front of the meeting. She didn't say anything.

"Let's get a coffee later. That's what you do, right? You can't get a drink? You go out for coffee?" Lenny was studying her face.

"I don't think so," she said.

"You don't think so? Come on. I'll buy you coffee. You can explain AA to me. You like that Italian shit? That French shit? The little cups?" Lenny was staring at her.

"No, thank you. I'm sorry," she said. He was short and fat and sweating. He looked like he was laughing at her with his eyes.

"You're sorry. I'll show you sorry. Listen. I know what you want. You're one of those smart-ass teachers from Beverly Hills," Lenny said.

"Right," she said. She didn't know why she bothered talking to him.

"You want to get in over your head. You want to see what's on the other side. I'll show you. I'll take you there. It'll be the ride of your life," Lenny said.

"Good-bye," she answered.

Lenny was at her noon meeting the next day. She saw him immediately as she walked through the door. She wondered how he knew that she would be there. As she approached her usual chair, she saw a bouquet of long-stemmed pink roses.

"You look beautiful," Lenny said. "You knew I'd be here. That's why you put that crap on your face. You didn't have that paint on yesterday. Don't do that. You don't need that. Those whores from Beverly Hills need it. Not you. You're a teacher. I like that. Sit down." He picked the roses up. "Sit next to me. You glad to see me?"

"I don't think so." She sat down. Lenny handed the roses to her. She put them on the floor.

"Yeah. You're glad to see me. You were hoping I'd be here. And here I am. You want me to chase you? I'll chase you. Then I'll catch you. Then I'll show you what being in over your head means." Lenny was smiling.

She turned away. When the meeting was over, she stood up quickly and began moving, even before the prayer was finished. "I have to go," she said, softly, over her shoulder. She felt she had to apologize. She felt she had to be careful.

"You don't have to go," Lenny said. He caught up with her on the steps. "Yeah. Don't look surprised. Lenny's fast, real fast. And you're lying. Don't ever lie to me. You think I'm stupid? Yeah, you think Lenny's stupid. You think you can get away from me? You can't get away. You got an hour. You don't pick that kid up for the dance school until four. Come on. I'll buy you coffee."

"What are you talking about?" She stopped. Her breath felt sharp and fierce. It was a warm November. The air felt like glass.

"I know all about you. I know your routine. I been watching you for two weeks. Ever since I got to town. I saw you my first day. You think I'd ask you out on a date and not know your routine?" Lenny stared at her.

She felt her eyes widen. She started to say something but she changed her mind.

"You live at the top of the hill, off of Doheny. You pick up that kid, what's her name, Annie something? You pick her up and take her to dance school. You get coffee next door. Table by the window. You read the paper. Then you go home. Just the two of you. And that Mex cleaning lady. Maria. That her name? Maria? They're all called Maria. And the gardener Friday afternoons. That's it." Lenny lit a cigarette.

"You've been following me?" She was stunned. Her mouth opened.

"Recon," Lenny said.

"I beg your pardon?"

"In Nam. We called it recon. Fly over, get a lay of the land.

Or stand behind some trees. Count the personnel. People look but they don't see. I'll tell you about it. Get coffee. You got an hour. Want to hear about Vietnam? I got stories. Choppers? I like choppers. You can take your time, aim. You can hit anything, even dogs. Some days we'd go out just aiming at dogs. Or the black market? Want to hear about that? Profiteering in smack? You're a writer, right? You like stories. I got some tall tales from the Mekong Delta for you, sweetheart. Knock your socks off. Come on." He reached out and touched her arm. "Later you can have your own war stories. I can be one of your tall tales. I can be the tallest."

The sun was strong. The world was washed with white. The day seemed somehow clarified. He was wearing a leather jacket and shaking. It occurred to her that he was sick.

"Excuse me. I must go," she said. "If you follow me, I shall have someone call the police."

"Okay. Okay. Calm down," Lenny was saying behind her. "I'll save you a seat tomorrow, okay?"

She didn't reply. She sat in her car. It was strange how blue the sky seemed, etched with the blue of radium or narcotics. Or China blue, perhaps. Was that a color? The blue of the China Sea? The blue of Vietnam. When he talked about Asia, she could imagine that blue, luminescent with ancient fever, with promises and bridges broken, with the harvest lost in blue flame. Always there were barbarians, shooting the children and dogs.

She locked her car and began driving. It occurred to her, suddenly, that the Chinese took poets as concubines. Their poets slept with warlords. They wrote with gold ink. They ate orchids and smoked opium. They were consecrated by nuance, by birds and silk and the ritual birthdays of gods and nothing changed for a thousand years. And afternoon was absinthe yellow and almond, burnt orange and chrysanthemum. And in the abstract sky, a litany of kites.

* * *

She felt herself look for him as she walked into the meeting the next day at noon. The meeting was in the basement of a church. Lenny was standing near the coffeepot with his back to the wall. He was holding two cups of coffee as if he was expecting her. He handed one to her.

"I got seats," he said. He motioned for her to follow. She followed. He pointed to a chair. She sat in it. An older woman was standing at the podium, telling the story of her life. Lenny was wearing a white warm-up suit with a green neon stripe down the sides of the pants and the arms of the jacket. He was wearing a baseball cap. His face seemed younger and tanner than she had remembered.

"Like how I look? I look like a lawyer on his way to tennis, right? I even got a tan. Fit right in. Chameleon Lenny. The best, too." He lit a cigarette. He held the pack out to her.

She shook her head, no. She was staring at the cigarette in his mouth, in his fingers. She could lean her head closer, part her lips, take just one puff.

"I got something to show you," Lenny said.

The meeting was over. They were walking up the stairs from the basement of the church. The sun was strong. She blinked in the light. It was the yellow of a hot autumn, a yellow that seemed amplified and redeemed. She glanced at her watch.

"Don't do that," Lenny said. He was touching the small of her back with his hand. He was helping her walk.

"What?"

"Looking at that fucking watch all the time. Take it off," Lenny said.

"My watch?" She was looking at her wrist as if she had never seen it before.

"Give it here, come on," Lenny put his hand out. He motioned with his fingers. She placed her watch in the palm of his hand.

"That's a good girl," Lenny was saying. "You don't need it. You don't have to know what time it is. You're with me. Don't you get it? You're hungry, I feed you. You're tired, I find a hotel. You're in a structured environment now. You're protected. I protect you. It doesn't matter what time it is." He put her watch in his pocket. "Forget it. I'll buy you a new one. A better one. That was junk. I was embarrassed for you to wear junk like that. Want a Rolex?"

"You can't afford a Rolex," she said. She felt intelligent. She looked into his face.

"I got a drawerful," Lenny told her. "I got all the colors. Red. Black. Gold."

"Where?" She studied his face. They were walking on a side street in Hollywood. The air was a pale blue, bleeding into the horizon, taking the sky.

"In the bank," Lenny said. "In the safety deposit with everything else. All the cash that isn't buried." Lenny smiled.

"What else?" She put her hands on her hips.

"Let's go for a ride," Lenny said.

They were standing at the curb. They were two blocks from the church. A motorcycle was parked there. Lenny took out a key.

"Get on," he said.

"I don't want to get on a motorcycle." She was afraid.

"Yes, you do," Lenny told her. "Sit down on it. Wrap your arms around me. Just lean into me. Nothing else. You'll like it. You'll be surprised. It's a beautiful day. It looks like Hong Kong today. Want to go to the beach? Want lunch? I know a place in Malibu. You like seafood? Crab? Scampi? Watch the waves?" Lenny was doing something to the motorcycle. He looked at her face.

"No," she said.

"How about Italian? I got a place near the Marina. Owner owes for ten kilos. We'll get a good table. You like linguini?" Lenny sat down on the motorcycle.

She shook her head, no.

"Okay. You're not hungry. You're skinny. You should eat.

Come on. We'll go around the block. Get on. Once around the block and I'll bring you back to the church." Lenny reached out his hand through the warm white air.

She looked at his hand and how the air seemed blue near his fingers. It's simply a blue glaze, she was thinking. In Malibu, in Hilo, in the China Sea, forms of blue, confusion and remorse, a dancing dress, a daughter with a mouth precisely your own and it's done, all of it.

Somewhere it was carnival night in the blue wash of a village on the China Sea. On the river, boats passed with low-slung antique masts sliding silently to the blue of the ocean, to the inverted delta where the horizon concluded itself in a rapture of orchid and pewter. That's what she was thinking when she took his hand.

She did not see him for a week. She changed her meeting schedule. She went to women's meetings in the Pacific Palisades and the Valley. She went to meetings she had never been to before. She trembled when she thought about him.

She stopped her car at a red light. It occurred to her that it was an early afternoon in autumn in her thirty-eighth year. Then she found herself driving to the community center. The meeting was over. There was no one left on the street. Just one man, sitting alone on the front steps, smoking. Lenny looked up at her and smiled.

"I was expecting you," Lenny said. "I told you. You can't get away from me."

She could feel his eyes on her face, the way when she lived with a painter, she had learned to feel lamplight on her skin. When she had learned to perceive light as an entity. She began to cry.

"Don't cry," Lenny said, his voice soft. "I can't stand you crying. Let's make up. I'll buy you dinner."

"I can't." She didn't look at him.

"Yeah. You can. I'll take you someplace good. Spago? You

like those little pizzas with the duck and shit? Lobster? You want the Palm? The Rangoon Racket Club? Yeah. Don't look so surprised. I know the places. I made deals in all those places. What did you think?" He was lighting a cigarette and she could feel his eyes on her skin.

She didn't say anything. They were walking across a parking lot. The autumn made everything ache. Later, it would be worse. At dusk, with the subtle irritation of lamps.

"Yeah. I know what you think. You think Lenny looks like he just crawled out from a rock. This is a disguise. Blue jeans, sneakers. I fit right in. I got a gang of angry Colombians on my ass. Forget it." Lenny stared at her. "You got a boyfriend?"

"What's it to you?"

"What's it to me? That's sharp. I want to date you. I probably want to marry you. You got a boyfriend, I got to hurt him." Lenny smiled.

"I can't believe you said that." She put her hands on her hips.

"You got a boyfriend? I'm going to cut off his arm and beat him with it. Here. Look at this." He was bending over and removing something from his sock. He held it in the palm of his hand.

"Know what this is?" Lenny asked.

She shook her head, no.

"It's a knife, sweetheart," Lenny said.

She could see that now, even before he opened it. A push-button knife. Lenny was reaching behind to his back. He was pulling out something from behind his belt, under his shirt. It was another knife.

"Want to see the guns?"

She felt dizzy. They were standing near her car. It was early in December. The Santa Anas had been blowing. She felt that it had been exceptionally warm for months.

"Don't get in the car," Lenny said. "I can't take it when you leave. Stay near me. Just let me breathe the same air as you. I love you."

"You don't even know me," she said.

"But you know me. You been dreaming me. I'm your ticket to the other side, remember?" Lenny had put his knives away. "Want to hear some more Nam stories? How we ran smack into Honolulu? You'll like this. You like the dope stories. You want to get loaded?"

She shook her head, no.

"You kidding me? You don't want to get high?" Lenny smiled.

"I like being sober," she said.

"Sure," Lenny said. "Let me know when that changes. One phone call. I got the best dope in the world."

They were standing in front of her car. The street beyond the parking lot seemed estranged, the air was tarnished. She hadn't thought about drugs in months. Lenny was handing her something, thin circles of metal. She looked down at her hand. Two dimes seemed to glare in her palm.

"For when you change your mind," Lenny said. He was still smiling.

They were sitting on the grass of a public park after a meeting. Lenny was wearing Bermuda shorts and a green T-shirt that said CANCÚN. They were sitting in a corner of the park with a stucco wall behind them.

"It's our anniversary," Lenny told her. "We been in love four weeks."

"I've lost track of time," she said. She didn't have a watch anymore. The air felt humid, green, stalled. It was December in West Hollywood. She was thinking that the palms were livid with green death. They could be the palms of Vietnam.

"I want to fuck you," Lenny said. "Let's go to your house."

She shook her head, no. She turned away from him. She began to stand up.

"Okay. Okay. You got the kid. I understand that. Let's go to a hotel. You want the Beverly Wilshire? I can't go to the Beverly

Hills Hotel. I got a problem there. What about the Four Seasons? You want to fuck in the Four Seasons?"

"You need to get an AIDS test," she said.

"Why?" Lenny looked amused.

"Because you're a heroin addict. Because you've been in jail," she began.

"Who told you that?" Lenny sat up.

"You told me," she said. "Terminal Island. Chino. Folsom? Is it true?"

"Uh-huh," Lenny said. He lit a cigarette. "Five years in Folsom. Consecutive. Sixty months. I topped out."

She stared at him. She thought how easy it would be, to reach out and take a cigarette. Just one, once.

"Means I finished my whole sentence. No time off for good behavior. Lenny did the whole sixty." He smiled. "I don't need an AIDS test."

"You're a heroin addict. You shoot cocaine. You're crazy. Who knows what you do or who you do it with?" She was beginning to be afraid.

"You think I'd give you a disease?" Lenny looked hurt.

Silence. She was looking at Lenny's legs, how white the exposed skin was. She was thinking that he brought his sick body to her, that he was bloated enormous with pathology and bad history, with jails and demented resentments.

"Listen. You got nothing to worry about. I don't need a fucking AIDS test. Listen to me. Are you hearing me? You get that disease, I take care of you. I take you to Bangkok. I keep a place there, on the river. Best smack in the world. Fifty cents. I keep you loaded. You'll never suffer. You start hurting, I'll take you out. I'll kill you myself. With my own hands. I promise," Lenny said.

Silence. She was thinking that he must be drawn to her vast emptiness, could he sense that she was aching and hot and always listening? There is always a garish carnival across the boulevard. We are born, we eat and sleep, conspire and mourn, a birth, a betrayal, an excursion to the harbor, and it's done. All of it, done.

"Come here." Lenny extended his arm. "Come here. You're like a child. Don't be afraid. I want to give you something."

She moved her body closer to his. There are blue enormities, she was thinking, horizons and boulevards. Somewhere, there are blue rocks and they burn.

"Close your eyes," Lenny said. "Open your mouth."

She closed her eyes. She opened her mouth. There was something pressing against her lip. Perhaps it was a flower.

"Close your mouth and breathe," Lenny said.

It was a cigarette. She felt the smoke in her lungs. It had been six months since she smoked. Her hand began to tremble.

"There," Lenny was saying. "You need to smoke. I can tell. It's okay. You can't give up everything at once. Here. Share it. Give me a hit."

They smoked quietly. They passed the cigarette back and forth. She was thinking that she was like a sacked capital. Nothing worked in her plazas. The palm trees were on fire. The air was smoky and blue. No one seemed to notice.

"Sit on my lap. Come on. Sit down. Closer. On my lap," Lenny was saying. "Good. Yeah. Good. I'm not going to bite you. I love you. Want to get married? Want to have a baby? Closer. Let me kiss you. You don't do anything. Let me do it. Now your arms. Yeah. Around my neck. Tighter. Tighter. You worried? You got nothing to worry about. You get sick, I keep you whacked on smack. Then I kill you. So what are you worried? Closer. Yeah. Want to hear about R and R in Bangkok? Want to hear about what you get for a hundred bucks on the river? You'll like this. Lean right up against me. Yeah. Close your eyes."

"Look. It's hot. You want to swim. You like that? Swimming? You know how to swim?" Lenny looked at her. "Yeah? Let's go. I got a place in Bel Air."

"You have a place in Bel Air?" she asked. It was after the meeting. It was the week before Christmas. It was early afternoon.

"Guy I used to know. I did a little work for him. I introduced him to his wife. He owes me some money. He gave me the keys." Lenny reached in his pocket. He was wearing a white-and-yellow warm-up suit. He produced a key ring. It hung in the hot air between them. "It's got everything there. Food. Booze. Dope. Pool. Tennis court. Computer games. You like that? Pac Man?"

She didn't say anything. She felt she couldn't move. She lit a cigarette. She was buying two packages at a time again. She would be buying cartons soon.

"Look. We'll go for a drive. I'll tell you some more war stories. Come on. I got a nice car today. I got a brand-new red Ferrari. Want to see it? Just take a look. One look. It's at the curb. Give me your hand." Lenny reached out for her hand.

She could remember being a child. It was a child's game in a child's afternoon, before time or distance were factors. When you were told you couldn't move or couldn't see. And for those moments you are paralyzed or blind. You freeze in place. You don't move. You feel that you have been there for years. It does not occur to you that you can move. It does not occur to you that you can break the rules. The world is a collection of absolutes and spells. You know words have a power. You are entranced. The world is a soft blue.

"There. See. I'm not crazy. A red Ferrari. A hundred forty grand. Get in. We'll go around the block. Sit down. Nice interior, huh? Nice stereo. But I got no fucking tapes. Go to the record store with me? You pick out the tapes, okay? Then we'll go to Bel Air. Swim a little. Watch the sunset. Listen to some music. Want to dance? I love to dance. You can't get a disease doing that, right?" Lenny was holding the car door open for her.

She sat down. The ground seemed enormous. It seemed to leap up at her face.

"Yeah. I'm a good driver. Lean back. Relax. I used to drive for a living," Lenny told her.

"What did you drive? A bus?" She smiled.

"A bus? That's sharp. You're sharp. You're one of those sharp little Jewish girls from Beverly Hills with a cocaine problem. Yeah. I know what you're about. All of you. I drove some cars on a few jobs. Couple of jewelry stores, a few banks. Now I fly," Lenny said.

Lenny turned the car onto Sunset Boulevard. In the gardens of the houses behind the gates, everything was in bloom. Patches of color slid past so fast she thought they might be hallucinations. Azaleas and camellias and hibiscus. The green seemed sullen and half-asleep. Or perhaps it was opiated, dazed, exhausted from pleasure.

"You fly?" she repeated.

"Planes. You like planes? I'll take you up. I got a plane. Company plane," Lenny told her. "It's in Arizona."

"You're a pilot?" She put out her cigarette and immediately lit another.

"I fly planes for money. Want to fly? I'm going next week. Every second Tuesday. Want to come?" Lenny looked at her.

"Maybe," she said. They had turned on a street north of Sunset. They were winding up a hill. The street was narrow. The bougainvillaea was a kind of net near her face. The air smelled of petals and heat.

"Yeah. You'll come with me. I'll show you what I do. I fly over a stretch of desert looks like the moon. There's a small manufacturing business down there.

"Camouflaged. You'd never see it. I drop some boxes off. I pick some boxes up. Three hour's work. Fifteen grand," Lenny said. "Know what I'm talking about?"

"No."

"Yeah. You don't want to know anything about this. Distribution," Lenny said. "That's federal."

"You do that twice a month?" she asked. They were above Sunset Boulevard. The bougainvillaea was a magenta web.

There were the sounds of birds and insects. They were winding through pine trees. "That's thirty thousand dollars a month."

"That's nothing. The real money's the Bogotá run," Lenny said. "Mountains leap up out of the ground, out of nowhere. The Bogotá run drove me crazy. Took me a month to come down. Then the Colombians got mad. You know what I'm talking about?"

"No."

"That's good. You don't want to know anything about the Colombians," Lenny said again.

She was thinking about the Colombians and Bogotá and the town where Lenny said he had a house, Medellín. She was thinking they would have called her *gitana*, with her long black hair and bare feet. She could have fanned herself with handfuls of hundred-dollar bills like a green river. She could have borne sons for men crossing borders, searching for the definitive run, the one you don't return from. She would dance in bars in the permanently hot nights. They would say she was intoxicated with grief and dead husbands. Sadness made her dance. When she thought about this, she laughed.

The driveway seemed sudden and steep. They were approaching a walled villa. Lenny pushed numbers on a console. The gate opened.

He parked the red Ferrari. He opened the car door for her. She followed him up a flight of stone steps. The house looked like a Spanish fortress.

A large Christmas wreath with pine cones and a red ribbon hung on the door. The door was unlocked. The floor was tile. They were walking on an Oriental silk carpet, past a piano, a fireplace, a bar. There were ceiling-high glass cabinets in which Chinese artifacts were displayed, vases and bowls and carvings. They were walking through a library, then a room with a huge television, stereo equipment, a pool table. She followed him out a side door.

The pool was built on the edge of the hill. The city below

seemed like a sketch for a village, something not quite formed beneath the greenery. Pink and yellow roses had been planted around two sides of the pool. There were beds of azaleas with ferns between them and red camellias, yellow lilies, white daisies, and birds of paradise.

"Time to swim," Lenny said.

She was standing near the pool, motionless. "We don't have suits," she said.

"Don't tell nobody, okay?" Lenny was pulling his shirt over his head. He stared at her, a cigarette in his mouth. "It's private. It's walled. Just a cliff out here. And Bernie and Phyllis aren't coming back. Come on. Take off your clothes. What are you? Scared? You're like a child. Come here. I'll help you. Daddy'll help you. Just stand near me. Here. See? Over your head. Over baby's head. Did that hurt? What's that? One of those goddamn French jobs with the hooks in front? You do it. What are you looking at? I put on a few pounds. Okay? I'm a little out of shape. I need some weights. I got to buy some weights. What are you? Skinny? You're so skinny. You one of those vomiters? I'm not going to bite. Come here. Reach down. Take off my necklace. Unlock the chain. Yeah. Good. Now we swim."

The water felt strange and icy. It was nothing like she expected. There were shadows on the far side of the pool. The shadows were hideous. There was nothing ambiguous about them. The water beneath the shadows looked remote and troubled and green. It looked contaminated. The more she swam, the more the infected blue particles clustered on her skin. There would be no way to remove them.

"I have to leave," she said.

The sun was going down. It was an unusual sunset for Los Angeles, red and protracted. Clouds formed islands in the red sky. The sprinklers came on. The air smelled damp and green like a forest. There were pine trees beyond the rose garden. She thought of the smell of camp at nightfall, when she was a child.

"What are you? Crazy? You kidding me? I want to take you

out," Lenny said. He got out of the pool. He wrapped a towel around his waist. Then he wrapped a towel around her shoulders. "Don't just stand there. Dry off. Come on. You'll get sick. Dry yourself."

He lit a cigarette for her. "You want to get dressed up, right? I know you skinny broads from Beverly Hills. You want to get dressed up. Look. Let me show you something. You'll like it. I know. Come on." He put out his hand for her. She took it.

They were walking up a marble stairway to the bedroom. The bedroom windows opened onto a tile balcony. There were sunken tubs in the bathroom. Everything was black marble. The faucets were gold. There were gold chandeliers hanging above them. Every wall had mirrors bordered by bulbs and gold. Lenny was standing in front of a closet.

"Pick something out. Go on. Walk in. Pink. You like pink? No. You like it darker. Yeah. Keep walking. Closet big as a tennis court. They got no taste, right? Looks like Vegas, right? You like red? No. Black. That's you. Here. Black silk." Lenny came out of the closet. He was holding an evening gown. "This your size? All you skinny broads wear the same size."

Lenny handed the dress to her. He stretched out on the bed. "Yeah. Let go of the towel. That's right. Only slower."

He was watching her. He lit a cigarette. His towel had come apart. He was holding something near his lap. It was a jewelry box.

"After you put that crap on your face, the paint, the lipstick, we'll pick out a little something nice for you. Phyllis won't need it. She's not coming back. Yeah." Lenny laughed. "Bernie and Phyllis are entertaining the Colombians by now. Give those boys from the jungle something to chew on. Don't look like that. You like diamonds? I know you like diamonds."

Lenny was stretched out on the bed. The bed belonged to Bernie and Phyllis but they weren't coming back. Lenny was holding a diamond necklace out to her. She wanted it more than she could remember wanting anything.

"I'll put it on you. Come here. Sit down. I won't touch you. Not unless you ask me. I can see you're all dressed up. Just sit near me. I'll do the clasp for you," Lenny offered.

She sat down. She could feel the stones around her throat, cool, individual, like the essence of something that lives in the night. Or something more ancient, part of the fabric of the night itself.

"Now you kiss me. Come on. You want to. I can tell. Kiss me. Know what this costs?" Lenny touched the necklace at her throat with his fingertips. He studied the stones. He left his fingers on her throat. "Sixty, seventy grand maybe. You can kiss me now."

She turned her face toward him. She opened her lips. Outside, the Santa Ana winds were startling, howling as if from a mouth. The air smelled of scorched lemons and oranges, of something delirious and intoxicated. When she closed her eyes, everything was blue.

She didn't see him at her noon meeting the next day or the day after. She thought, Well, that's it. She wasn't sorry. She got a manicure. She went to her psychiatrist. She began taking a steam bath after her aerobics class at the gym. She went Christmas shopping. She bought her daughter a white rabbit coat trimmed with blue fox. She was spending too much money. She didn't care.

It was Christmas Eve when the doorbell rang. There were carols on the radio. She was wearing a silk robe and smoking. She told Maria that she would answer the door.

"You promised never to come here." She was angry. "You promised to respect my life. To recognize my discrete borders."

"Discrete borders?" Lenny repeated. "I'm in serious trouble. Look at me. Can't you see there's something wrong? You look but you don't see."

There was nothing unusual about him. He was wearing blue jeans and a black leather jacket. He was carrying an overnight bag. She could see the motorcycle near the curb. Maybe the Colombians had the red Ferrari. Maybe they were chewing on that now. She didn't ask him in.

"This is it," Lenny was saying. He brushed past her and walked into the living room. He was talking quickly. He was telling her what had happened in the desert, what the Colombians had done. She felt like she was being electrocuted, that her hair was standing on end. It occurred to her that it was a sensation so singular that she might come to enjoy it. There were small blue wounded sounds in the room now. She wondered if they were coming from her.

"I disappear in about five minutes." Lenny looked at her. "You coming?"

She thought about it. "I can't come, no," she said finally. "I have a child."

"We take her," Lenny offered.

She shook her head, no. The room was going dark at the edges, she noticed. Like a field of blue asters, perhaps. Or ice when the sun strikes it. And how curious the blue becomes when clouds cross the sun, when the blue becomes broken, tawdry.

"I had plans for you. I was going to introduce you to some people. I should of met you fifteen years ago. I could have retired. Get me some ice," Lenny said. "Let's have a drink."

"We're in AA. Are you crazy?" She was annoyed.

"I need a drink. I need a fix. I need an automatic weapon. I need a plane," he said. He looked past her to the den. Maria was watching television and wrapping Christmas presents.

"You need a drink, too," Lenny said. "Don't even think about it. The phone. You're an accessory after the fact. You can go to jail. What about your kid then?"

They were standing in her living room. There was a noble pine tree near the fireplace. There were wrapped boxes beneath the branches. Maria asked in Spanish if she needed anything. She said not at the moment. Two glasses with ice, that was all.

"Have a drink," Lenny said. "You can always go back to the

meetings. They take you back. They don't mind. I do it all the time. All over the world. I been doing it for ten years."

"I didn't know that," she said. It was almost impossible to talk. It occurred to her that her sanity was becoming intermittent, like a sudden stretch of intact road in an abandoned region. Or radio music, blatant after months of static.

"Give me the bottle. I'll pour you one. Don't look like that. You look like you're going down for the count. Here." Lenny handed the glass to her. She could smell the vodka. "Open your mouth, goddamn it."

She opened her mouth. She took a sip. Then she lit a cigarette.

"Wash the glass when I leave," Lenny said. "They can't prove shit. You don't know me. You were never anywhere. Nothing happened. You listening? You don't look like you're listening. You look like you're on tilt. Come on, baby. Listen to Daddy. That's good. Take another sip."

She took another sip. Lenny was standing near the door. "You're getting off easy, you know that? I ran out of time. I had plans for you," he was saying.

He was opening the door. "Some ride, huh? Did Daddy do like he said? Get you to the other side? You catch a glimpse? See what's there? I think you're starting to see. Can't say Lenny lied to you, right?"

She took another sip. "Right," she agreed. When this glass was finished she would pour another. When the bottle was empty, she would buy another.

Lenny closed the door. The night stayed outside. She was surprised. She opened her mouth but no sound came out. Instead, blue things flew in, pieces of glass or tin, or necklaces of blue diamonds, perhaps. The air was the blue of a pool when there are shadows, when clouds cross the turquoise surface, when you suspect something contagious is leaking, something camouflaged and disrupted. There is only this infected blue enormity elongating defiantly. The blue that knows you and where you live and it's never going to forget.

BIOGRAPHIES
and Some Comments by the Authors

Alice Adams is the author of six novels and four collections of stories, most recently *After You've Gone*. She has been frequently included in *Prize Stories: The O. Henry Awards* and in 1982 she received the Special Award for Continuing Achievement.

" 'The Last Lovely City' is quite puzzling to me, in that I do not understand just where much of it came from. I do know that one Sunday I went to a lunch party at Stinson Beach, at which I saw a number of people whom I had known or heard of many years back; the party did in a sense seem haunted for me. But where on earth did I find the doctor from Chiapas? I suppose the fact that I had been writing a book about Mexico had something to do with his genesis—but he seemed to have appeared in my mind all at once, a whole person (I hope). The young woman with her streaky hair looked like a woman I once saw on a plane, but I am not sure why she entered this particular story. All of which is to say that it seems to me that stories arrive in our minds from what we might call nowhere, from a curious blend of quite disparate elements—images and observations, hurts and wishes."

Yolanda Barnes: "I live in Los Angeles where I write novellas and short stories. Also I teach in adult schools. I received my MFA in creative writing from the University of Virginia and before that I worked for five years as a reporter in Hartford, Connecticut. My short stories and a novella have been published in *TriQuarterly* and *Plough-shares*.

"The genesis of 'Red Lipstick' was an acquaintance I made with an older woman when I lived in New England. She was a pleasantly mannered woman, very smiling and calm, but a few times in conversation she revealed extreme passion and venom within her, glimpses of a wound caused by what she considered a betrayal of an old friend. I never knew what that betrayal was; she never offered details and I never asked. When it came time for me to write the story I took it back home, so to speak, bringing in my imagination and placing it in the sphere of my familiarity with people and language I recognized from my growing-up years."

Kate Braverman: "I am the author of four books of poetry, the novels *Lithium for Medea* and *Palm Latitudes,* and the short story collection *Squandering the Blue* in which 'Tall Tales from the Mekong Delta' appears.

" 'Tall Tales' is about crossing boundaries. It is an experiment in form. It began as a poem, then the characters started talking and I realized it had become something larger. 'Tall Tales' is the sort of spontaneous mutation that occurs when you recognize that the borders between a conventional poem and a conventional story are not immutable but are instead fluid.

"There was a certain cadence to the character's speech that fascinated me. I let the story sweep me off my feet with all its wild juxtapositions and lethal poses. Ultimately, 'Tall Tales' is about a world of fraudulence where the only two things that prove to be real are love and evil."

Ken Chowder: "I was born in Manhattan and raised in New England. I decided to become a writer as soon as it became clear that I would never hit a curveball; my first short story, unhampered by the death of all its main characters, ended happily; I wrote a novel in high school (unpublished, and justifiably so) called *The Great American Novelette.*

"I wrote novels until Ann Harris at Harper & Row gave my book *Blackbird Days* the Harper-Saxton Prize and then published it. Harper & Row later published two other novels, *Delicate Geometry* and *Jadis.*

"I wrote 'With Seth in Tana Toraja' during the coldest winter ever in Denmark. The inspiration for the story came, unfortunately, from having lived through it: this piece was drawn directly and exactly from life. Using personal experience for fiction has, of course, both benefits and drawbacks; I don't always choose real over imagined events. But in this case the real ones were powerful to me, and feeling something strongly is always one good way to begin to think about writing."

Millicent Dillon is a writer of fiction and nonfiction. Among her books are *A Little Original Sin: The Life and Work of Jane Bowles* and *After Egypt: Isadora Duncan and Mary Cassatt*. Her novel *The Dance of the Mothers* was recently published.

"For the past twenty years I have been caught up in the telling of women's lives, in biography and fiction. In the biographies my subjects were women regarded by the world as extraordinary. In the fiction my characters were often women whose lives appear to be 'ordinary.' Many of them are unable to feel the substance or weight of their own experience and their search is to redeem that experience, often in ways judged strange by the society surrounding them.

"With 'Lost in L.A.' I came to another kind of telling. This is the story of a woman whose life story is already being erased in her mind. Further, her existence in the minds of others is to her so tenuous it can vanish at any moment.

"Perhaps part of what drives me to tell women's lives in the way I do comes out of my own background as a writer. I did not begin to write until I was almost forty. Then there already lay behind me many years in which I had never tried to give form to my experience. It is through language, both simple and disjunctive, that I have tried to find the weight, the timbre, and the color of my own experience as well as that of others."

Harriet Doerr: " 'Way Stations' was originally intended to be part of *Stones for Ibarra*, but quickly proved not to fit. I believe this was the fault of a newly introduced character, the Evertons' houseguest, Kate. It is clear now that Richard and Sara were North American enough for the townspeople of Ibarra.

"So Kate has her separate story, set on the same fragment of map, with its church, its dry arroyo and infertile fields, and its dozen hills tunneled with mines named for coyotes, rattlesnakes, saints, and beautiful women.

"Now I'm finishing another book, this one set on the shore of a shallow lake I drove by once, a few hundred miles and two Mexican states south of the place I named Ibarra."

Amy Herrick: "I grew up in New York City and after graduating from the Iowa Writers' Workshop returned to New York to teach elementary school and write. I live now in Brooklyn with my husband, who is a tenants' rights lawyer, and my two sons. I'm a past winner of a G.E. Younger Writers' Award and have had stories published in *Tri-Quarterly, The Kenyon Review, Yale Review, Indiana Review* and *Fiction.* 'Pinocchio's Nose' eventually became the starting point for my first novel, *At the Sign of the Naked Waiter,* which is due to be published this spring.

"I first wrote a draft of 'Pinocchio's Nose' a long time ago. I wrote it because I wanted to write about that period of a young person's life when one seems to, quite suddenly, wake up. However, when I was done with it, I saw I wasn't sure what its *story* was, so I let it go. It wasn't until several years later that I reread it and saw, in a single flash, that it was about two girls who are confused by the sudden appearance of love (the fellow who shoots the arrows), and find themselves involved in a fabulous duel of lies. For me, this phenomenon, where I am suddenly *presented* with a revelation about where my work has been trying to take me all along, appears to be a kind of semi-friendly reminder that there are, indeed, large and magical forces of creation at work in the universe, but that I'm going to be given only the most uncertain control over them. This news is always discouraging and extremely exciting, at the same time."

Lucy Honig: "My short fiction has appeared in *Best American Short Stories 1988, The Georgia Review, The Agni Review* and many other journals. My first novel, *Picking Up,* was published in 1986 by Dog Ear Press (now Tilbury House). My collection of stories and novellas is currently in search of a publisher.

"After many years living in Maine, I moved to Brooklyn, where I first began teaching English to adult immigrants, and after many years in Brooklyn I recently moved to a quieter spot in upstate New York. Here I teach ESL, direct a local human rights commission, and, in between, try to finish a second novel. Now that what I do to make a living finally reconciles with and feeds into my writing, I have precious little time to write.

" 'English as a Second Language' grew out of one of my first part-time teaching jobs, when I had all my classes back-to-back one day a week in a free adult ed program. My students had come from all over the third world. In New York they were struggling to live, struggling to be understood, and grasping for insider tips on how to fit in in America. (So was I.) They were not yet saturated with American media hype, and in their very pared-down verbal renderings of their observations, of their lives, they could usually tell the difference between real feeling and baloney. Over the course of the day I'd see things more and more through my students' eyes and finally I'd emerge from the gentle intimacy of this classroom into the tumult of the streets of lower Manhattan where, for a few moments once each week, everything was brand new and totally befuddling."

Perri Klass is a pediatrician in Boston. This is her fourth appearance in *Prize Stories: The O. Henry Awards*. She has published two novels, *Other Women's Children* and *Recombinations*, a collection of short stories, *I Am Having an Adventure*, and a collection of essays about medical school, *A Not Entirely Benign Procedure*, which will be followed this year by *Baby Doctor*, a book about pediatric residency training.

" 'Dedication' was written in part out of the respect I feel for newborns, both as a parent and as a pediatrician. Little helpless beasts, weighing less than a respectable sack of potatoes, they turn adult lives upside down, turn established living arrangements inside out. And they do it by a mixture of irresistible visitor-from-outer-space cuteness and sheer biological will. When I wrote the story, I was at the beck and call of a baby daughter, living in a state of milk-stained exhaustion. Like the woman in the story, I was constantly leaking, and so I made up a first sentence in my mind, about leaking, as if that would give my soggy routine some extra literary resonance."

David Long: "I was raised in New England, went to Albion College, came West in 1972 to study writing at the University of Montana, and never left—I live in the Flathead Valley with my wife and two boys. My first collection, *Home Fires*, was published in 1982, followed by *The Flood of '64* in 1987. 'Blue Spruce' is from a third collection, almost finished.

"It began as a fragment of an abandoned story. This involved a woman whose husband has left to find work on the coast (she and her son stay behind to finish out the school year). I had her walking up the lane to give her landladies, two middle-aged sisters, the last month's rent; approaching, she sees one of the women up on the porch roof, shoveling off pine needles. The story wobbled along for a few pages, then petered out. Another one dead on the vine, I thought.

"When I reread that scene, maybe two years later, I found what I loved was the older woman on the roof, sprinkled with sun—she seemed feisty, worth knowing. I tossed out all that other, made the women sisters-in-law, and had them start nettling each other while I figured out what was really going on.

"The pine needles meant the house was surrounded by trees. I remembered the two giant spruces my neighbors had buzzsawed out of their front yard—and how violently pro or con you could feel about that. The story took a number of months to work out, but I remember the pleasure I had in describing the house—the dry-rotted soffits, the squeaky taps, the ancient bugkillers stored on the porch."

Tom McNeal's fiction has appeared in *The Atlantic, Carolina Quarterly, Epoch, Playboy, Quarterly West, Redbook* and several anthologies. He has taught English at Hay Springs High School in northwestern Nebraska and creative writing at Stanford University. He presently works as a partner in a construction firm in California and lives near Lake Arrowhead with his dogs, Dougal and Willie.

"It's hard to say how this story evolved. It began with an annoyance. This was with a student in one of my creative writing classes, a serene, blandly handsome fellow whose belief in himself was imperturbable and who in his fiction wrote repeatedly about the difficulties of letting women down easy. I'm afraid I rooted so much for his comeuppance that I began to write one for him. What occurred of course was something altogether else. About the time I began presenting this Tully character with a darkly revised version of his past, I received some serious jolts in my own life. A happy byproduct of these events

—perhaps the *only* happy byproduct, I think now, looking back—was that a sympathy for Tully took hold in me and grew until finally my yearning to restore at least some part of his happiness became, in the end, ungovernable."

Daniel Meltzer is a short story writer and playwright, and a columnist for several New York and Connecticut newspapers. He teaches in the Journalism Department at New York University and at "The Writer's Voice" at Manhattan's West Side YMCA.

"The impulse for 'People' came from a personal reaction to the way I hear the word used today, and the hollow feeling it evokes. The narrator in the story is, I think, ironically both ahead of and behind his times, an alienated outsider caught in the cogs of a world defined by commerce and devoid of emotional gratification, a world in which success is inevitable, but where love is impossible."

Les Myers: "I'm writing these notes in a motel just off Interstate 80 in Coralville, Iowa. Like Ferguson, the hero of my story, I make my living by traveling this part of the world. In addition to exotic places like Omaha and Des Moines, I have managed to travel recently—under the pretext of bird-watching—to India, South Africa, throughout Central America and several times to Ecuador and Peru. The last is the setting for a novel I'm working on.

"I graduated from the University of Illinois in 1977, taught at a Berlitz school in Barcelona for a year, coached cross country and track at Illinois Wesleyan University for another, and then put in five years as a special-education teacher, before going into sales.

"Like most of my stories, this one had its origins in images that had been tucked away in journals years ago. Laid side by side, these images somehow seemed to belong together. The bird flying off with the lit cigarette is a behavior that has been recorded many times, particularly with corvids. The nude hang-glider pilot has been floating through my memory since I first saw her above Black's Beach, north of San Diego, in 1971. My partner in business really did find a woman's shoe under his bed in a New York hotel room a few years ago. I remember the wonder in his eyes as he showed it to me, both of us astounded at how redolent this object was with unattainable essences. I've never made or flown a kite in the manner described, but I intend to do so. If I can find a place far enough away from power lines, I'll take my boys out one night and give it a try.

"I live in Ladue, Missouri, a suburb of St. Louis, with my wife and two sons. My work has appeared in *Crazyhorse, Ascent, West Branch, Quarterly West,* and *The Chariton Review,* and has been cited in *Best American Short Stories.*"

Antonya Nelson's first collection of stories, *The Expendables,* was winner of the Flannery O'Connor Award for Short Fiction (Avon). Her second collection, *In the Land of Men,* in which "The Control Group" appears, was published in January 1992. She lives in Las Cruces, New Mexico with her husband, writer Robert Boswell.

" 'The Control Group' is set in Wichita, Kansas, where I grew up. It's only recently that I've begun using Wichita as a setting for the majority of my work. I don't think it's any coincidence that these newest stories always have children as their narrators and primary characters; because I left Wichita when I was eighteen, I don't know the city as a grown-up, only as a child. "The Control Group" became a story when a few elements in my life combined in lucky chemistry. First, I have a brother who is a psychologist, and he once had a client who was this bright young boy sent from home to home, trying to live with the accident of his unfortunate and violent family life. Second, I had two different grade-school teachers who stood out in my elementary academic career. One was a kind but firm woman who really did love animals and believe they could teach better than any book, and the other an unkind and bitter woman who brought in two rats on whom our fifth-grade class performed precisely the same experiment TV's class does in this story, with precisely the same results: both rats were killed in the end. It's a lesson that has not stopped haunting me."

Kent Nelson lives in Exeter, New Hampshire with his wife and four children. He is the author of *Language in the Blood,* a novel, and *The Middle of Nowhere,* a collection of stories, both published in 1991.

"Though I grew up in Colorado and use the Western landscape for many of my stories, I've long resisted the idea of being categorized as a Western writer. It pleases me, therefore, that the piece selected for this volume is set in the South, where I also lived for some time. Nothing in this story happened, except it all did. One day on the beach I found an odd object. I dragged it home, took it apart, and made it into a story."

Joyce Carol Oates's most recent collection of short stories, *Heat and Other Stories*, was published in 1991. She has three times received the Special Award for Continuing Achievement in this series.

"Sometimes, out of a mirror, a face not quite my own rises to me—I see my grandmother's face, as it is captured in certain snapshots, and, less consistently, in my memory. This phenomenon—and the fact that I loved my grandmother, my father's mother, very much, and have never been able to write about her—underlies the composition of 'Why Don't You Come Live With Me It's Time.'

"Hammond, New York, the fictitious setting of my story, is also the setting of my novel *Because It Is Bitter, and Because It Is My Heart*. It bears a dreamlike resemblance to Lockport, New York, where I was born, and where my Grandmother Woodside lived.

"As a young girl, I was fascinated by questions I did not know were archetypal philosophical questions—clichés of the intellect, one might call them. The night sky greatly interested me; the 'Universe'; vast concepts of space, time; the mystery of human personality. Such questions, which even cosmologists falter in addressing, are most intense in us in early adolescence; afterward, we are supposed to grow up and forget them. Perhaps the writer—this writer, at least—is simply one who, so long as a question remains unanswered, cannot forget it, thus cannot repudiate the romance of adolescence.

"As a child, living close to water (the Tonawanda Creek flows at the edge of my parents' property in Millersport; the Erie Canal runs through Lockport, dividing the city dramatically in two), I was forced to contemplate bridges a good deal. Especially those old, single-lane, rattling bridges that are the bridges of nightmare—yet, somehow, we *do* cross them. Again and again.

"When I am in a realist phase—in which most of my novels are written—how I yearn for the freedom, the mythopoetics, of the *sur*real! —the kind of art that is not really to be categorized as 'fantasy'—'dark fantasy'—'horror'—'the Gothic'—yet assuredly is not *realistic*. 'Why Don't You Come Live With Me It's Time' is so close to my heart, and memory, it becomes, finally, impossible to define it as anything other than itself: an extended riddle, perhaps, in the form of a story."

Cynthia Ozick was born in New York's Yorkville neighborhood, where her parents owned a pharmacy. When she was one-and-a-half years old, the family moved to Pelham Bay, then a semirural area of the Northeast Bronx. Ozick, who was educated at New York University and Ohio State University, now lives five miles down the road from where she grew up. She is the author of four novels, three collections of short stories, two collections of essays, a forthcoming volume of (early) poems, and is currently attempting a play.

"Puttermesser Paired" is the third of Cynthia Ozick's stories to receive First Prize in the O. Henry series. Of this story she writes: "When it was first conceived, [it] was intended to be a real love story," and she adds enigmatically, "Alas."

Ann Packer's stories have appeared in *The New Yorker, The Gettysburg Review, Indiana Review,* and *Boulevard,* among others. A graduate of Yale University and the Iowa Writers' Workshop, she lives in Eugene, Oregon, with her husband.

" 'Babies' began coming to me on a dimly lit late-night bus ride from the Newark airport to lower Manhattan, and by the time I had access to a pen and paper and some light the story had become so insistent that I pretty much had to sit down and write out what I had —six pages' worth, as it turned out. The rest I wrote almost as quickly, in four or five days once I'd returned to Iowa City, and while I've never quite bought anyone's claim that a story 'wrote itself,' this one has for me that kind of magical quality—of a near-gift from the writing gods, recognizable by the speed of its arrival and by its reluctance to change.

"As for its roots, I did once work in an office with a lot of pregnant women, and I had recently been thinking about childlessness—not just my own, but that of all of my friends as we approached thirty. Everything else in the story is invention, with the exception of Virginia's one-room fifth-floor walk-up in New York. I lived in that apartment for four years, but no more, thank God, no more."

Murray Pomerance was born in 1946. He trained at length in classical piano and briefly in medicine before studying social psychology at the

University of Michigan. His fiction has appeared in *The Boston Review, Chelsea, Confrontation, The Kenyon Review, New Directions,* and *The Paris Review*. He teaches in Toronto where he lives with his wife and son.

"For me a story is a narrative space framed by formal intervals. In the case of 'Decor' I am principally interested in a rather loose triangle composed through the relations of a pressing, needful, musical, unrelenting speech and two silences: that of assured capability fallen into a kind of entropic chaos, and that of the explosive insight of creative vision. My stories are not accountings of the world I know because in composing I am intensely selective and arbitrary. I make use of the world I know in order to write stories about something else, which is not actual object or experience but abstract figuration (one might say hypothesis) that, to me, is beautiful. I didn't write 'Decor' because I know somebody who decorates houses, or someone who owns a house that got decorated, although I know people for whom these were possibilities. There are many other stories with these characters; and I've also written about events set hundreds of years ago in places I couldn't possibly have been: the court of Henry VIII; or Thirty-fourth Street and Fifth Avenue one year before I was born. I suppose in all of it I try to build experience to make it true."

Frances Sherwood: " 'Demiurges' is the second story that I have had included in *Prize Stories: the O. Henry Awards*. The first, 'History,' appeared in the 1989 edition. Also in 1989, my short story collection, *Everything You've Heard is True* came out. All of the stories had previously been published in small magazines. In 1990–91, I received an NEA grant and was cited in *Best American Short Stories*. I was a Stegner Fellow in Fiction at Stanford University and a teaching fellow in the Johns Hopkins Writing Seminars, and am associate professor of English at Indiana University at South Bend. My stories continue to appear in literary magazines and I have just completed a novel, *Vindication* based on the life of Mary Wollstonecraft."

Mary Michael Wagner was born in Louisville, Kentucky. She received her B.A. from the University of Notre Dame in South Bend, Indiana. She currently lives and works in San Francisco, where she is getting a masters in Creative Writing. "Acts of Kindness" was her first published short story.

" 'Acts of Kindness' was conceived in the back of an ambulance when I was studying to become a certified Emergency Medical Technician, which was a requirement for a job I wanted. I think my writing is about how things are never as they appear; things are never what they are on the surface. It was my first paramedic ride along and as we pulled out of the parking lot I was very nervous, envisioning all of the blood and trauma I would be seeing for the next ten hours. The first thing we did was ride to a white sale at Macy's and park the ambulance up on the curb. Since I didn't need any sheets or pillowcases I stayed in the back of the ambulance writing this story.

"I wanted to write about how an intense job is still just a job, but then someone or something gets to you and you are never again the same. I wanted to show how difficult it is for people in relationships to simply trust each other, because beneath the pleasantness, there are so many denied and inconsistent emotions.

"We live in a culture of surfaces, under which runs a current of unspoken secrets and feelings. I write because what is unnamed works itself to the surface like pieces of glass that have entered the body through a wound."

Magazines Consulted

The Agni Review, P.O. Box 229, Cambridge, Mass. 02238

Alaska Quarterly Review, Department of English, 3221 Providence Drive, Anchorage, Alaska 99508

Ambergris, P.O. Box 29919, Cincinnati, Ohio 45229

Antaeus, Ecco Press, 26 West 17th Street, New York, N.Y. 10011

Antietam Review, 82 West Washington Street, Hagerstown, Maryland 21740

The Antioch Review, P.O. Box 148, Yellow Springs, Ohio 45387

The Apalachee Quarterly, P.O. Box 20106, Tallahassee, Fla. 32304

Arizona Quarterly, University of Arizona, Tucson, Ariz. 85721

Arts Alive: A Literary Review, 17530 South 65th Avenue, Tinely Park, Ill. 60477

Ascent, P.O. Box 967, Urbana, Ill. 61801

Asimov's Science Fiction Magazine, Davis Publications, 380 Lexington Avenue, New York, N.Y. 10017

The Atlantic Monthly, 745 Boylston Street, Boston, Mass. 02116

Bamboo Ridge, The Hawaii Writers' Quarterly, Bamboo Ridge Press, Eric Chuck, Darrell Lum, P.O. Box 61781, Honolulu, Hawaii 96822-8781

Boulevard, 2400 Chestnut Street, Philadelphia, Pa. 19103

Brooklyn Free Press, 268 14th Street, Brooklyn, N.Y. 11215

California Quarterly, 100 Sproul Hall, University of California, Davis, Calif. 95616

Canadian Fiction Magazine, P.O. Box 46422, Station G, Vancouver, B.C., Canada V6R 4G7

Capital Region Magazine, 4 Central Avenue, Albany, N.Y. 12210

The Caribbean Writer, Caribbean Research Institute, University of the Virgin Islands, RR 02 Box 10,000 Kingshill, St. Croix, Virgin Islands 00850

The Chariton Review, The Division of Language and Literature, Northeast Missouri State University, Kirksville, Mo. 63501

The Chattahoochee Review, DeKalb Community College, North Campus, 2101 Womack Road, Dunwoody, Ga. 30338-4497

Chicago Review, 5801 S. Kenwood, Chicago, Ill. 60637

Chicago Tribune, Nelson Algren Award, 435 North Michigan Avenue, Chicago, Ill. 60611-4041

Christopher Street, 28 West 25th Street, New York, N.Y. 10010

Chronicles, 934 North Main Street, Rockford, Ill. 61103

Cimarron Review, 205 Morrill Hall, Oklahoma State University, Stillwater, Okla. 74078-0135

Clockwatch Review, James Plath, Department of English, Illinois Wesleyan University, Bloomington, Ill. 61702

Colorado Review, 360 Eddy Building, Colorado State University, Fort Collins, Colorado 80523

Commentary, 165 East 56th Street, New York, N.Y. 10022

Concho River Review, c/o English Department, Angelo State University, San Angelo, Tex. 76909

Confrontation, Department of English, C.W. Post College of Long Island University, Brookville, N.Y. 11548

Cosmopolitan, 224 West 57th Street, New York, N.Y. 10019

Crazyhorse, Department of English, University of Arkansas at Little Rock, 2801 S. University, Little Rock, Ark. 72204

Crescent Review, P.O. Box 15065, Winston-Salem, N.C. 27113

Crosscurrents, 2200 Glastonbury Rd., Westlake Village, Calif. 91361

Denver Quarterly, Department of English, University of Denver, Denver, Colo. 80210

Epoch, 251 Goldwin Smith Hall, Cornell University, Ithaca, N.Y. 14853-3201

Esquire, 1790 Broadway, New York, N.Y. 10019

Farmer's Market, P.O. Box 1272, Galesburg, Ill. 61402

Fiction, Department of English, The City College of New York, N.Y. 10031

Fiction International, Department of English, St. Lawrence University, Canton, N.Y. 13617

The Fiddlehead, UNB, P.O. Box 4400, Fredericton, New Brunswick, Canada, E3B 5A3

The Florida Review, Department of English, University of Central Florida, Orlando, Fla. 32816

Four Quarters, La Salle College, Philadelphia, Pa. 19141

Frisko, Suite 414, The Flood Building, 870 Market Street, San Francisco, Calif. 94102

Gargoyle, P.O. Box 30906, Bethesda, Md. 20814

Gentleman's Quarterly, 350 Madison Avenue, New York, N.Y. 10017

The Georgia Review, University of Georgia, Athens, Ga. 30602

The Gettysburg Review, Gettysburg College, Gettysburg, Penn. 17325-1491

Glamour, 350 Madison Avenue, New York, N.Y. 10017

Grain, Box 1154, Regina, Saskatchewan, Canada S4P 3B4

Grand Street, 135 Central Park West, New York, N.Y. 10023

Granta, 13 White Street, New York, N.Y. 10013

The Greensboro Review, Department of English, University of North Carolina, Greensboro, N.C. 27412

Hadassah, 50 West 58th Street, New York, N.Y. 10019

Harper's Magazine, 2 Park Avenue, New York, N.Y. 10016

Hawaii Review, Department of English, University of Hawaii, 1733 Donaghho Road, Honolulu, Hawaii 96822

The Hudson Review, 684 Park Avenue, New York, N.Y. 10021

Indiana Review, 316 Jordan, Bloomington, Ind. 47405

Interim, Department of English, University of Nevada, Las Vegas, Nev. 89154

Iowa Review, 308 EPB, University of Iowa, Iowa City, Iowa 52242

Kalliope, a Journal of Women's Art, Florida Community College at Jacksonville, 3939 Roosevelt Boulevard, Jacksonville, Fla. 32205-8989

Kansas Quarterly, Department of English, Denison Hall, Kansas State University, Manhattan, Kansas 66506-0703

The Kenyon Review, Kenyon College, Gambier, Ohio 43022

Key West Review, 9 Avenue G, Key West, Fla. 33040

Ladies' Home Journal, 100 Park Avenue, New York, N.Y. 10017

The Literary Review, Fairleigh Dickinson University, Teaneck, N.J. 07666

Mademoiselle, 350 Madison Avenue, New York, N.Y. 10017

The Massachusetts Review, Memorial Hall, University of Massachusetts, Amherst, Mass. 01002

Matrix, c.p. 100 Ste-Anne-de-Bellevue, Quebec, Canada H9X 3L4

McCall's, 110 Fifth Avenue, New York, N.Y. 10011

Michigan Quarterly Review, 3032 Rackham Building, University of Michigan, Ann Arbor, Mich. 48109

Mid-American Review, 106 Hanna Hall, Bowling Green State University, Bowling Green, Ohio 43403

Midstream, 110 East 59th Street, 4th Floor, New York, N.Y. 10022

Minnesota Monthly, 15 South 9th Street, Suite 320, Minneapolis, Minn. 55402

The Missouri Review, 1507 Hillcrest Hall, University of Missouri, Columbia, Mo. 65211

Mother Jones, 1663 Mission Street, San Francisco, Calif. 94103

MSS, Box 530, Department of English, SUNY-Binghamton, Binghamton, N.Y. 13901

Nassau Review, Department of English, Nassau Community College, Garden City, N.Y. 11530-6793

Nebraska Review, Writer's Workshop, ASH 210, University of Nebraska at Omaha, Omaha, Nebr. 68182-0324

New Directions, 80 Eighth Avenue, New York, N.Y. 10011

New England Review, Middlebury College, Middlebury, Vt. 05753

New Letters, University of Missouri-Kansas City, 5100 Rockhill Road, Kansas City, Mo. 64110

New Mexico Humanities Review, The Editors, Box A, New Mexico Tech., Socorro, N.M. 57801

The New Yorker, 20 West 43rd Street, New York, N.Y. 10036

The North American Review, University of Northern Iowa, 1227 West 27th Street, Cedar Falls, Iowa 50613

North Atlantic Review, 15 Arbutus Lane, Stony Brook, N.Y. 11790-1408

North Dakota Quarterly, University of North Dakota, Box 8237, Grand Forks, N.D. 58202

The Ohio Review, Ellis Hall, Ohio University, Athens, Ohio 45701

OMNI, 1965 Broadway, New York, N.Y. 10067

The Ontario Review, 9 Honey Brook Drive, Princeton, N.J. 08540

Other Voices, 820 Ridge Road, Highland Park, Ill. 60035

The Paris Review, 541 East 72nd Street, New York, N.Y. 10021

The Partisan Review, 128 Bay State Road, Boston, Mass. 02215/552 Fifth Avenue, New York, N.Y. 10036

Phylon, 223 Chestnut Street, S.W., Atlanta, Ga. 30314

Playboy, 680 North Lake Shore Drive, Chicago, Ill. 60611

Playgirl, 801 Second Avenue, New York, N.Y. 10017

Ploughshares, Emerson College, 100 Beacon Street, Boston, Mass. 02116

Prairie Schooner, Andrews Hall, University of Nebraska, Lincoln, Neb. 68588

Puerto del Sol, College of Arts & Sciences, Box 3E, New Mexico State University, Las Cruces, N.M. 88003

The Quarterly, 201 East 50th Street, New York, N.Y. 10022

Raritan, 31 Mine Street, New Brunswick, N.J. 08903

Redbook, 224 West 57th Street, New York, N.Y. 10019

Romancing The Past, c/o Michelle Regan, 17239 S. Oak Park Avenue, Suite 207, Tinley Park, Ill. 60477

Sailing, 125 E. Main Street, P.O. Box 248, Port Washington, Wisc. 53074

Salamagundi, Skidmore College, Saratoga Springs, N.Y. 12866

Sandhills/St. Andrews Review, Sandhills Community College, 2200 Airport Road, Pinehurst, N.C. 28374

The San Francisco Bay Guardian, Fiction Contests, 2700 19th Street, San Francisco, Calif. 94110-2189

Santa Monica Review, Center for the Humanities at Santa Monica College, 1900 Pico Boulevard, Santa Monica, Calif. 90405

Self, 350 Madison Avenue, New York, N.Y. 10017

Sequoia, Storke Student Publications Building, Stanford, Calif. 94305

Seventeen, 850 Third Avenue, New York, N.Y. 10022

The Sewanee Review, University of the South, Sewanee, Tenn. 37375

The Short Story Review, P.O. Box 882108, San Francisco, Calif. 94188

Snake Nation Review, 2920 North Oak Street, Valdosta, Ga. 31602

Sonora Review, Department of English, University of Arizona, Tucson, Ariz. 85721

South Carolina Review, Department of English, Clemson University, Clemson, S.C. 29634-1503

South Dakota Review, Box 111, University Exchange, Vermillion, S.D. 57069

Southern Humanities Review, 9088 Haley Center, Auburn University, Auburn, Ala. 36830

The Southern Review, Drawer D, University Station, Baton Rouge, La. 70803

Southwest Review, Southern Methodist University, Dallas, Tex. 75275

Special Report, c/o Whittle Communications L.P., 505 Market Street, Knoxville, Tenn. 37902

The Spirit That Moves Us, P.O. Box 820, Jackson Heights, N.Y. 11372

Stories, 14 Beacon Street, Boston, Mass. 02108

Story, 1507 Dana Avenue, Cincinnati, Ohio 45207

St. Anthony Messenger, 1615 Republic Street, Cincinnati, Ohio 45210-1298

The Sun, 107 North Robertson Street, Chapel Hill, N.C. 27516

Tampa Review, Box 19F, University of Tampa, 401 West Kennedy Boulevard, Tampa, Fla. 33606-1490

The Threepenny Review, P.O. Box 9131, Berkeley, Calif. 94709

Tikkun, Institute of Labor and Mental Health, 5100 Leona Street, Oakland, Calif. 94619

TriQuarterly, 2020 Ridge Avenue, Evanston, Ill. 60208

The Village Voice Literary Supplement, 842 Broadway, New York, N.Y. 10003

The Vincent Brothers Review, 1459 Sanzon Drive, Fairborn, Ohio 45324

The Virginia Quarterly Review, University of Virginia, 1 West Range, Charlottesville, Va. 22903

Vogue, 350 Madison Avenue, New York, N.Y. 10017

Washington Review, Box 50132, Washington, D.C. 20004

Webster Review, Webster College, Webster Groves, Mo. 63119

West Coast Review, Simon Fraser University, Burnaby, British Columbia, Canada V5A 1S6

Western Humanities Review, University of Utah, Salt Lake City, Utah 84112

Wind, RFD Route 1, Box 809K, Pikeville, Ky. 41501

Witness, 31000 Northwestern Highway, Suite 200, Farmington Hills, Mi. 48018

Woman's Day, 1515 Broadway, New York, N.Y. 10036

Yale Review, 1902A Yale Station, New Haven, Conn. 06520

Yankee, Main Street, Dublin, N.H. 03444

Yellow Silk, P.O. Box 6374, Albany, Calif. 94706

Zyzzyva, 41 Sutter Street, Suite 1400, San Francisco, Calif. 94104